"Ronie Kendig embodies the very heart of speculative fiction, taking important human issues and exploring them against a backdrop of the most extraordinary circumstances. Kendig's talent as a writer shines not only in her worldbuilding skills, but also in her ability to craft characters I can connect with on a deep level."

— LANI FORBES, award-winning author of
the Age of the Seventh Sun series

"An adventure that will have readers flying through stars, unraveling conspiracies, and cheering for a diverse cast of characters."

— SHANNON DITTEMORE, author of *Winter, White and Wicked*

"Absolutely extraordinary! Kendig has once again proven herself a victor in the realm of the space opera—brilliantly returning readers to a galaxy as captivating as her characters."

— LAUREN H. BRANDENBURG, author of *The Death of Mungo Blackwell*
and *The Marriage of Innis Wilkinson*

LADY OF BASILIKAS

Books by Ronie Kendig

ABIASSA'S FIRE

Embers

Accelerant

Fierian

THE BOOK OF THE WARS

Storm Rising

Kings Falling

Soul Raging

THE TOX FILES

The Warrior's Seal (Free Novella)

Conspiracy of Silence

Crown of Souls

Thirst of Steel

DISCARDED HEROES

Nightshade

Digitalis

Wolfsbane

Firethorn

Lygos (Novella)

A BREED APART

Trinity

Talon

Beowulf

A BREED APART: LEGACY

Havoc

Chaos

Riot

THE QUIET PROFESSIONALS

Raptor 6

Hawk

Falcon

Titanis (Novella)

THE METCALFES

Stone

Willow

Range

Brooke

THE DROSERAN SAGA

Brand of Light

Dawn of Vengeance

Shadow of Honor

War of Torment

Lady of Basilikas

STANDALONE NOVELS

Operation Zulu Redemption

Dead Reckoning

LADY OF BASILIKAS

A DROSERAN SAGA NOVEL

RONIE KENDIG

TO MY AMAZING AND VERY LOYAL READERS
who have journeyed with me, with Marco, and the rest of the epic cast of the
Droseran Saga through all the joys and heartaches, the darkness overcome
by light. Evil conquered by good. What an incredible adventure we've had,
and it was been a dream com true to see you love these characters as much
as I do. Thank you for your enthusiasm (and your tears), which not only
the Droseran Saga a success but made it possible for this story possible as a
standalone novel extension of this beloved series.

THANK YOU!!

AUTHOR'S NOTE

If you've read the paperbacks of *Brand of Light* and *Dawn of Vengeance*, you've had a brief, albeit broken-up look into this story already. You'll probably want to forget you read that. Haha!

What follows is a story that quickly took on a life of its own. Intended to be a short 50,000 word story, *Lady of Basilikas*, battled its way to nearly 90,000 words. There were snippets in the paperbacks that were out of order, and some that—after I'd written two full-length novels in the universe after those snippets were drafted—ended up being wrong for the storyworld.

It grieved me to shift course, but in keeping with the full storyworld and lore surrounding the infamous Ladies of Basilikas (the Faa'Cris), I had to change them. Yet for this author, who is not known for writing short stories—there was not enough word count to do all the things I'd hoped to reveal for King Vaanvorn Thundred and his Lady of Basilikas, Valiriana. But in the end, I think we did a smashing job of delivering the heart of their story, and it's my earnest wish you will love it!

PROLOGUE

Oaths were meant to be upheld and hold a man secure within the embrace of honor. But it was another kind of embrace that challenged his ability to stay within strict boundaries—that of a woman. Yet those littering his past paled against the one he had fallen for.

Was that why guilt tormented him? It needled and nagged, digging beneath his heart's armor. Somehow reached that center of his being where honor and integrity took shelter from his more nefarious behaviors. Prince Vaanvorn Thundred had to make this right. The thought had struck him before with others, but in every case he'd dismissed it as easily as a gnat buzzing about his head. This time, however . . . Yirene, however . . .

Yirene of Iaison was different. Better.

He must make her his own. He would make it official at dinner tonight.

Vorn closed the door to find the house already starting to awaken. He tussled his hair, wishing he could shake the nerves plying at his well-rested mind. Rounding the corner to the main corridor, he fought the urge to slow at the arrival of a contingent forming outside the guest chambers where Yirene slumbered.

He kept moving but then slowed. Glanced back. "Furymark," he called, using his Commander of Armies voice. "What do you here at this hour?"

"Prince Vaanvorn." Captain Harlen Crow gave a sharp nod. "We are sent by the king to deliver an invitation to Lady Yirene."

Now they had his full attention. "The lady . . ." He frowned. "An invitation to what?"

The captain faltered. "To sit at the king's table for the festivities."

Another festive dinner—the very one at which Vorn had intended to set petition for her. An invitation from the king was more a summons and no small favor. What purpose did Tamuro have for directing his attention toward . . .

Vorn's gut tied in a knot. "Quite an honor," he muttered, hoping his pointed words elicited the right response. "One usually reserved for royals and other family."

"The king intends to make her his queen."

"*What*?" His accursed brother had hit hard this time. Not waiting for a response, Vorn pivoted on his heels and stalked toward the royal apartments. In no way would he allow his brother to take this happiness from him. He should have known that the long look Tamuro gave him at the garden party yestereve as he walked with Yirene down by the boxwoods meant trouble.

Boots thudded, his Four—four captains assigned as his personal guards— no doubt catching up. "My prince," Tarac said in a placating voice. "Please, think—"

"I always think," Vorn bit out. "It is my brother who does not." He hiked the stairs two at a time. Pitched himself up the last three in a leap.

"He could have your head for intruding," Azyant hissed from his left. "No woman is worth losing you."

If it had not meant a delay, he would have physically countered his man. "Wrong."

The four sentries guarding the royal residence came to life at his swift approach, shifting into position before the door. "The king is not—"

"Stand aside!" Vorn demanded.

"I cannot," the tallest of the kingsguard said.

Vorn strode straight to the man, who stiffened, and cuffed him by the throat. Pinned him against the door. "Try me." With a glower, he released him and gripped the handle. Thrust it open.

Tamuro stood in the center of the chambers, arms outstretched as his steward dressed him. He started and scowled. "Great seas, Vorn. How dare you enter my private chambers uninv—"

"You knew I intended to set petition for Yirene."

His brother's surprise at being intruded upon washed away. Morphed into salty arrogance that said he was king and Vorn was not. He gave Vorn his back as he said to his chamberlain, "Black-and-grays."

Black-and-grays. The official attire.

"Tam," Vorn said, his heart beating hard, "do not do this. It is true that Iaison is an integral sovereignty, but—"

"Iaison has agreed to send carnaraks and foot soldiers to add to our number."

Waves of providence. "Cows? You—" Vorn bit back the oath. Tamuro had already negotiated the petition with the Prime Minister of Iaison—and earned a pittance of benefit for Jherako. "Tell me you are not this stupid."

Tam's expression darkened. "You dare speak to your king—"

"I speak to my brother, who even now is taking the only woman I've loved to effect a political move that will have catastrophic—"

"You don't know of what you speak!" Tamuro barked, then lifted his jaw. "As well, it is sad you have set your affection on a woman not interested in you, Vorn."

"In that, you have it backward."

Tamuro sniffed as he shrugged into his undervest. "A woman does not agree to a petition without interest in me."

Vorn stilled. "You . . . jest."

His brother smirked. "That has ever been your failing, brother. Not mine."

Vorn's anger plummeted, taking the pit of his stomach with it. He struggled to breathe. "Yirene agreed?" His mind wandered back to the woman he had left hours ago.

"Aye, over dinner last eve, after you and your rabble departed."

Shock rooted Vorn to the hand-knotted rug. So that's where Yirene had been coming from when he found her in the passage. Why had she said naught as they shared berries and cream, fermented cordi, and passion?

She used me. The hypocrisy of that thought scalded him, but the rising anger in his churning gut focused on the impudent king before him. On one of the greatest betrayals yet perpetrated by a spiteful brother.

"You always knew how to pick them, Brother," Tamuro said, ambling over to the sideboard, where he lifted up a snifter of liquor. "She is quite easy on the eyes and should produce attractive heirs." He shot Vorn a cocky grin. "Would you not agree?"

Only as he heard crystal shatter did Vorn realize he'd crashed into his brother, knocking the snifter from his hand. Red liquor bathed the wall as he hauled Tamuro up and jammed his forearm into his throat. "You had no right!"

"I had every right," Tamuro sneered. "I am *king*!"

"You are a waste and know nothing of the woman you steal from me. Your own kingsguard do not even intervene to save your pathetic life!"

The door cracked inward, and the Furymark hauled Vorn backward.

Only then able to regain his composure, Tamuro straightened his shirt and undervest. Ran a hand over his long, thin hair. "You were saying?"

"You are a disgrace to the Thundred name," Vorn shouted as they dragged him from the solar. "I swear you will pay for this! You do not deserve her!"

Tarac and Lathain deflected the kingsguard, holding calming hands to them even as they led Vorn from the royal residence.

"Get me out of here before I do something I regret," Vorn growled, his anger and humiliation acute. "She knew . . ." Grief and rage choked him as he stalked away.

"You are but a waste of breath and blood, given to passions of pleasure and violence," Tamuro yelled after him. "The better man is king. And the better man will take Yirene to wife."

Trials were going perfectly. Just a couple more and she would advance to triarii level. Lined up with the other hastati for the race through the city to the Nest within the coliseum, Valiriana had no concern about advancing. But she was focused, intent on being among the first, if not *the* first, to reach the top. Valiriana gave a devious grin to her friend, Relissa, formed up next to her.

"You have two minutes to reach the Nest—no wings! Readyyy." Decurion Cybele snapped a hand down. "Go!"

Valiriana sprinted from the training yards with the other hastati, surging down the hewn passages to the coliseum. She deferentially avoided Faa'Cris warriors walking the ancient streets of Sacrum Lapis—more commonly known as Deversoria, the vast underground city that rivaled the greatest of Droseran capitals—and beat a hard path toward the coliseum. At the stone steps leading into the great coliseum, she was a fraction ahead of her friend and scaled the stairs two at a time until her thighs burned beneath the lightweight, intuitive armor that molded to her form.

Laughing, Relissa slipped ahead.

No! Valiriana lunged forward, refusing to be outdone. They should be more serious, yet merriment filled the passage spiraling upward, upward . . . They jostled and jockeyed for lead position, giggling and rebounding off the ever-curving stone wall.

"You're slower than a Licitus learning the sword," Relissa taunted.

With a growl, Valiriana threw herself up several steps. Ahead—the door. She pitched herself at it. Exultant, shoulder to shoulder with Relissa, she burst through the opening. Stumbled onto the wide-open path that ran the circumference of the upper level of the amphitheater. She skidded to a stop, panting hard. Gripped her knees, grinning and breathing a laugh at Relissa, who slumped against a wall, laughing.

A scent whipped out.

Sensing something different—off, odd—Valiriana darted to the side, putting her back to the wall. In the blink, the other hastati gained the upper reaches of the chamber and did the same. All apparently sensing that strange tremor in the air as she had. She sought protection and scanned beyond the wrought iron rail that protected them from the drop into the cavernous coliseum with its pale gray plaster and the carved images of the Resplendent. What had she detected?

The upper level swung around, a twelve-foot-wide ledge encircling the empty amphitheater, where sparring matches, operas, and theater productions took place in the sandy pit below. But the scent came from the right, the dingy, darker—

Her breath backed into her throat at what her eyes finally relayed to her brain. To her right stood six sentries. "Licitus," she breathed around a curled lip.

Males. *In* the coliseum with Faa'Cris. As if they had the right to share the same space. Their training ground was elsewhere—the brutal passions of men had no place in the pure calling of the Faa'Cris warriors. Stomach roiling, she glanced over the thin iron rail to the coliseum floor a hundred feet below, where more Licitus were gathered.

Her skin itched. *What is this?* Men did not belong here, especially not during training hours. She was not even sure why they must endure their presence in the city at all.

"What are they doing here?"

Sharing a look of disapproval with Relissa, Valiriana moved to the far end of the ledge and took a knee, awaiting Decurion Cybele's instruction.

"Ferox is here," Relissa whispered as she knelt beside her.

Though Valiriana should not look—one more demerit due to distraction and she would not advance to triarii—she found herself staring into the gold eyes of a Licitus captain. Ferox. Brown hair. Well sculpted by the Ancient's hand.

Handsome? *Yes.*

Penitent? *Amazingly, yes.*

Annoying? *Blood and boil, yes!*

"He favors you."

"Of course he does," Valiriana bit out. "He is Licitus."

"We must appreciate the Allowed," Relissa taunted. "Even Revered—"

"I appreciate all Allowed, just as I do the cats crawling the cities of this planet, keeping the alleys clear of vermin." Why Decurion Cybele *allowed* men within the sacred walls was beyond her, but she would trust the Resplendent's decision. The hastati were here to test their combat skills against height, new landscape, danger, and— "Distraction."

The only thing Licitus did well. That is why the Licitus were here—to provide distraction during the final trial.

"When innocent blood," boomed Decurion Cybele as she emerged from the main gate, flanked by her triarii captains, "drenches the parched deserts around Deversoria, the rocks will cry out."

"So spake Vaqar," Valiriana and the other hastati replied, reciting *Poenitentiam*, one of the training tenets. Her gaze again struck Ferox, who remained silent. Licitus dared not speak the sacred words.

A smile flashed into his eyes. Rank admiration soiled his Signature.

Valiriana huffed and refocused.

"War will come, and the Ladies will emerge," continued Decurion Cybele.

"So spake Magna Domine." As Eleftheria's title left her lips, Valiriana felt the ripple in her clypeus, her wing ridge, as anticipation of battle skittered beneath her armor.

"What say you, hastati?" demanded Cybele, hovering midair, her glorious double span fanning the air with challenge.

"Laborare pugnare parati sumus!"

To work, to fight, we are ready.

And by the Lady, was she ever! Valiriana's spine twitched, wings itching for freedom.

Around the coliseum, Licitus hit buttons that dropped the wrought iron rail into the stone, removing the safety barrier. A thing so small yet symbolic of the danger the men presented.

"Incipere!" Decurion Cybele ordered.

As she rushed the edge, Valiriana stole an imperious glance at the Licitus captain. Pleased to find his attention wholly fixed on her, she lunged off the upper level and rotated her shoulders, freeing her span. Fine, supple feathers exhaled greedily and caught air. Inwardly, she embraced *Crepidine*—the settling of her heart and will deep within the cradle of the Ancient's. She spiraled upward for higher vantage. Wings teasing the air to stay aloft, she sighted enemy targets zipping toward her.

As a top-tier hastati, she was often targeted in these exercises—and welcomed it. Deftly, she sideswept the triariis' attack. Whirled to meet them. Struck one. Struggled with another, angling to hit center. She spiraled into the other Faa'Cris—Maristikior—and they rolled in the air. Then Valiriana hiked her legs and flipped Maristikior toward the far wall. Valiriana shot toward the stone, nailed it with her boot, then used it to launch back toward the fray. Sighted Haruwerian just at the brink of the ledge and—

A foreign efflux shot from the side.

Angling without thinking toward the one who'd spewed the scent, Valiriana immediately realized her mistake as, at the same time, she registered an attack from behind. No time to correct course. No time to turn and defend herself. An impact rattled down her spine and sent her headfirst into the coliseum wall.

VAANVORN
FORGELIGHT, JHERAKO
PRESENT DAY

"Clear the road! Make way for the queen!"

With a shared look at his First, Vorn dismounted, wary of the crowds the royal carriage had already attracted. His nerves jounced beneath some odd sense that things were not right. Something was off. He noted even daylight struggled to exist amid buildings and canopies. No stranger to the vagaries of the deep city center and market, he scanned the gawkers, hand on his hilt.

After one more probe of the streets, buildings, windows, and stoops, Vorn pivoted and strode toward the carriage, signaling to the footman, who opened the door and set down the step. Vorn stood with the emerging queen to his right and the crowds before him.

"You are *overly* perturbed this rise, Prince Vaanvorn," Queen Yirene said quietly as she adjusted her gray gloves.

"I am not, Your Majesty. You insisted on shopping in the market, so here we are." When her eyes rose to him, he refused her gaze, instead remaining vigilant on the thrum of wrongness. Odd—he had been here countless times in his life, but never had he felt . . . whatever this was.

"Will you always hate me, Vorn?" she whispered, a subtle touch on his arm.

The words yanked his gaze to hers before he could steel himself. He gritted his teeth.

Each brother should strive to live honestly and to set a good example to others in everything, in such a way that those who see him cannot find anything to reproach in his behavior, not in his riding, nor in his walking, nor in his drinking, nor in his eating, nor in his look, nor in any of his actions and work.

The Creed of the Ierean Brotherhood echoed in his head, calming him. Focusing him. "To hate you would be to possess fear and anger, neither of which infect my person." He held her gaze evenly, grateful for the asceticism that had anchored him in truth these last several months. "We should hurry, Highness. Darkness brings the diabolus to the Bottom."

Posture stiff at the remonstration, she huffed and turned toward the market.

First he paced her to the fruit vendor, then a small gypsy wagon bearing brightly colored scarves with jangly tassels. A few people ventured nearer the queen but knew better than to tempt the blade of Vorn and his Furymark. As she visited a stand with many wares, he shifted back, strategically placing himself with the broadest line of sight on the market. Hated they were in the middle, with routes to safety equally distant on the far ends. He traced the growing crowds and noted a pair of violet eyes. Unusual for this region. But he focused back on his task.

The queen moved at a snail's pace until the sunlight eventually sparred with the canopies for the people below. What was so fascinating about glass bottles and baubles that she lingered here, apparently oblivious of the tumult around her?

"It's the queen," a girl of ten or twelve gasped from the side where she feigned interest in ceramic wares at a stand. "Whoa, she is beautiful. Are all Iaisonians so pretty?"

"Who cares," a girl a few years older sniffed with a giggle she shot to her two friends. "Look at the prince regent."

Great seas. Vorn stalked to the other side of the small gypsy wagon so he could not hear them and nodded to the captain. "Eyes out."

Waves, what was taking Yirene so long? He glanced in her direction. Started when he realized she was not there. His gaze darted over the people in the tent. Still no Yirene. His heart skipped a beat as he moved in, signaling Tarac to tighten up on him.

Vorn scouted the racks of colorful gypsy dresses. Further in, partially in shadow, he found the queen holding up a striped scarf. Horrid thing compared to the yards of silk and satin she wore. He held a hand to Tarac, staying him.

Someone bumped Vorn. And considering his position, he knew it was no accident. His hand snapped out even as his gaze lit on a woman's face. Violet—no, brown—eyes, pinched by wrinkles. He snatched his hand back just in time.

"Hello, Prince," she crooned.

Hone honesty. Develop discipline. Seize sacrifice. Hone honesty. Develop discipline. Seize sacrifice. "Move along," he croaked, forcing himself to shift away from her. Mouth dry, confused—had not her eyes been purple one second, then brown the next? He stretched his neck. Rolled his shoulders. Heard the seams of his jerkin pop. He met Tarac's fierce gaze and knew he had seen the encounter. That discerning man never missed a thing. Oh, to be half the man Tarac was.

But wait . . .

Something's wrong.

Again, Vorn slid his hand to his hilt, drew the sword even as he turned a circle. Noticed quiet falling over the market. Tension rising. "On your queen!" he ordered, a shrill scream drowning his last word.

A blur came from the left.

Instinct drove his right leg back. Fighting stance. He let his sword sing as it arced through the air. Felt the collision of steel and flesh. The sickening slurp of his sword as he cut down the dark, frenzied, feral attacker.

Amid cries and shouts from the crowd, another creature careened at him.

Right elbow up, Vorn readied himself. Angled his arms up and drove his sword into the creature's chest. There was a luminescent quality to the blood spilling over his blade. A blue, glowing hue. The same pale whorls writhed like glowing tattoos across the face and neck of the now-dead man. "What in the dark seas . . .?"

Realization dawned. "Raiders!" He let out a ferocious whistle, calling the carriage for the queen. Why were the Irukandji here, attacking? "Protect your queen!"

Another scream came from the left. Then the right. A dozen or more. Tarac and Ba'moori were there, swords in action, raiders dying at a rate that should have made the encounter brief, save that a contingent of rabble-rousers joined the fray. Ever were the discontent plentiful these days. Vorn brought one to ground. Saw a blade angle up from the villager beneath him, and with a few quick moves, disabled the man and left him unconscious.

"She's missing! The queen is missing!"

Alarmed, Vorn whipped toward Tarac's cry. Forged his way toward the tent where he'd last guarded her. "Lock—"

A howling fury barreled into him. His boots slid on the rocks and dirt, but Vorn managed to stay upright. Foul breath seared his nostrils as the raider pinned Vorn's dominant sword arm. Vorn, however, had trained with both. He snatched his dagger and drove it into the raider's neck. The scream died with the savage, who crumpled against him. Pawed at him, caught his sleeve and slumped to the ground, taking the fabric with him.

Vorn stepped back, pulse pounding, anger rising. *The queen.* Where was she? Had the brigands taken her? "Find the queen!"

Even as the words left his lips, he caught a glimpse of that horrid striped scarf. The queen had donned it, wrapped around her head as if in disguise. He spied hands at the back of the shop exchanging something—a small glass vial. "Your Majesty!" He gestured Tarac closer.

She emerged, face flushed. "Yes, I see. Trouble. I—I took shelter," she said in a breathy voice.

Vorn would not be deterred. "What did he give you?"

She blinked, then lifted her chin. "Nobody *gave* me anything. I *purchased* perfume." She held out a small blue bottle. But hadn't the vial been clear?

He stared her down, knowing he could not—should not—challenge her publicly. But her entire demeanor spoke of deceit. "What do—"

The thunder of hooves and the groaning carriage careening into the market sent people running and shouting. Furymark encircled the coach, Vorn, and the queen even as the bell tower began pealing the alarm to take shelter. A little late but it would serve his purpose.

Vorn pivoted, caught Yirene by the arm, and hurried her toward the carriage. He bumped more than one person, forcing them aside. He thrust the queen up into the luxury box.

"For mercy's sake," she balked as she scrambled inside. "You do not have to be—"

He slammed the door. Secured it. Pounded the hull. "To the castle. Stop for no one!"

The carriage lurched away, and Furymark mounted and rode alongside, the market strangely empty and quiet, save sniffles, sobs, and nervous chatter.

Burly Azyant trudged toward him, face and jerkin bloodied. "A handful escaped into the streets, but we ran them down."

"Good," Vorn growled. "Where did they come from? *How?*"

"Unknown. It was unprecedented," Tarac said.

"Agreed," Vorn said as they moved toward their destriers. "Ba'moori and Lathain, see that the injured are tended. Discover if anyone can answer where these savages came from. I had not thought Irukandji coordinated like this. I will await your report."

"Yes, my prince."

Vorn appreciated the way Azyant and Tarac stayed with him as they left the now-chaotic market. They galloped down the street, which would dump them onto the main road back to the castle. Yet, the thought of returning to it galled. He did not want to hear his brother accusing him once more of failing in his duties. The same king who in months had not left the castle or his bottle. Nor managed to sire an heir.

"I am impressed," Tarac called, hooves clopping loudly against the cobbles. "You handled well a certain reminder by your sovereign of a shared past, did not hesitate to go to ground against the savages. You should be impressed, too."

"*Depressed* is more like."

"He speaks true, sire," Azyant said. "You are much changed since Tarac dragged you out of The Iron eleven months ago."

He smirked at the man more prone to revelry than any other of the Four. But the truth was that night had been the bottom of the pit for Vorn, lost in his anger and ale. That night Tarac suggested Vorn adopt the stringent lifestyle that had kept Tarac grounded—the way of the *Muqqadas Ritsar*, the most holy knights of the Jherakan Order, devout in their commitment to the Ancient.

Azyant gave a grunt and swiped a hand over his mouth and beard. "Speaking of The Iron . . ." He pointed to the tavern just visible down the side street. "We could slake our thirst after such a grand victory. Surely one drink will not hurt."

From his mount, Vorn eyed the place where he had once spent much time and even more coin on ale and chatelaines. He swallowed against the lure of that place, grateful there was a stronger, more powerful pull northward. "I will meet you back at the castle." And with that, he guided his destrier down another road, knowing his First would pace him.

Dusk and its scant, dying light doused the people making their way home from mills and factories. Carefully, he picked his way around them and up the hill, lured onward by the somber amber light behind stained glass windows, barely visible ahead.

"Please, my lord." A boy darted out, spooking the horse, which shifted aside and neighed. "Coin for food. My ma'ma is sick, and we have six mou'vs to feed. Please, sir!"

Hand sliding to the small pouch he kept for such instances, Vorn then noticed a swarm of urchins appear at the edges of the street. An ambush, was it?

A cluster of light-colored patches hugged the corners of a stoop, snagging his attention. After passing a coin to the boy, who then darted off, Vorn felt his heart and courage fall from their high perch. Three more children—two girls and a boy, none older than ten—huddled there, coughing. Sniffling.

What is this . . .?

He diverted around the stoop, but he knew he could not pass them. Ignore their plight. Not with the new Creed he abided. With a sigh, Vorn drew back the reins and dismounted. *This is a bad idea . . .* Traveling with but one guard in a not-so-reputable area . . . Still, he turned to the children. When they cowered, he pushed a smile into his face and crouched. "Hello. What are your names?"

The younger two shrank away, whimpering and the oldest girl regarded him warily. "Werza," she said, "but we ain't s'posed to talk to strangers."

"A good rule in general. I am Vorn."

Her eyes widened. "Are you the prince?"

Maybe here his title could buy goodwill. "I am. Can you tell me where your parents are?"

"Dead," she said morosely. "Blue fever it was. Happened last holiday."

"Sire," Tarac said quietly, "we should—"

"And what of your grandparents, aunts? Uncles?"

"We ain't got none." Rank odor wafted from the family of children. How long had they been here? "Please don't call the magistrate. They'll put us in the dungeon, and what with Sili's sickness, we'll die there."

Sickness? Was he putting himself at risk? The parents had died of blue fever . . . "I won't let that happen," Vorn said firmly, heart tugging at the wide eyes and smudged faces. "What of the foundling home?"

"They told us to go away, that they were full."

He could not leave them here. "I am going to the Sanctuary. Will you come with me? I can ensure you will receive a warm meal and place to sleep tonight."

"Sili can't walk. She's too sick."

"She can ride my Black. You can, too. Would that be okay?" With her agreement, Vorn lifted the little ones onto his horse. He walked the horse up the last of the hill and into the courtyard of the church. He tied off his Black and lowered the children to the path, then carried the littlest to the small, arched side door.

Two older women in habits and head coverings straightened, then quickly curtseyed. "Your Highness."

"These children are in need of benevolence, Sisters. See to it." He was not one to order religious devotees, but he knew his title carried weight, and he did not want an argument about the care of these three. "Clothe them and find a place at the foundling home for them."

"Oh," the rounder of the two said, eyebrows lifting. "They been overrun for months, sir. There are no beds to be had."

"Overrun?" He frowned, confused. "Since when? There are over a hundred beds—"

"Since"—the woman seemed to restrain herself—"the last two years."

Vorn scowled. That was when his brother had come to the throne. "Then buy a cot and keep them here—in my quarters, if you must. Send the tab to the castle. It will be paid." He would brook no further argument. With that, he strode in through the interior door and down a long, narrow passage. He let himself through a heavy, machi-wood door. Candlelight flickered and danced down the rows of pews and drew him to the dais. There, he inclined his head. Knelt. Closed his eyes. And paid penance for the taking of lives.

VAANVORN
FORGELIGHT, JHERAKO

The next evening, after what must have been an hour on his knees again, he heard the approach of boots. Tentative steps, but he knew that stride. He pushed to his feet and stared at the crafted-glass image of the sun, now lit by candlelight, not its fading kin outside.

For his First to interrupt this time of ritual—one Tarac himself had taught him—told Vorn this must be significant. He pivoted and started out of the small chapel. "What is it?"

"I think you should come to The Iron."

Scowling, Vorn eyed him. "What—"

"*Not* to imbibe. But to listen. Ba'moori has returned from scouting."

"The savages."

Tarac nodded.

Ten minutes delivered them to the stoop of the tavern.

"My prince," a reveler proclaimed. "It has been too long since you joined us."

In spite of himself, Vorn smiled at the greeting. Soon, though, other voices came to his ears.

"Who wants him here anyway? His own brother is breaking our backs!"

"Aye, they live in luxury while we struggle to put food on the table."

And yet, you *spend* your *coin in a tavern.* Expression tight, Vorn navigated the crowds to the rear where Azyant, Ba'moori, and Lathain were already seated. There was something primal about Vorn's presence, something that drew out the chattel and the rabble. He had not even made it halfway through the common room when he sensed the voluptuous form of Tarielye sauntering his way. And oh, she looked good.

Not trusting himself to speak, Vorn shook his head and finally reached the table. "What did you find?"

Ba'moori shared a grave look with Lathain, who gulped from a tankard.

"We found little about the Irukandji here, except that there have been sightings and skirmishes for the last few weeks. It will take scouting patrols along the border to find where they are coming from."

And this was why Tarac pulled him from his time of penitence? He glanced at his First.

"Tell him about the people," Tarac said.

Ba'moori gave him a long look. "There is unrest."

"There's always unrest. One group or another always feels sligh—"

"It's more than that. Tamuro implemented another tax while we were here, escorting the queen."

Vorn bit back an oath.

"The people are crushed and growing angry, desperate," Lathain said.

"Though none spoke it directly, I believe there may be some sort of . . . collusion between some party in Forgelight and the Irukandji." Dark eyes sparked with ferocity as Tarac lowered his voice. "It was no coincidence the savages attacked the market today."

"You suggest someone in our court colludes with Hirakys?" Anger roiled through Vorn. "That is treason."

"It is the only possibility," Tarac amended. "But perhaps not with Hirakys itself. That remains unproven. It could be the raiders are acting independently of the Hirakyn court—though they've never before shown that sort of coordinated initiative. On the other hand, you have taught us coincidence is the traitor's excuse."

"Regardless, we must increase patrols in the city," Lathain said. "Stay on top—"

"That is merely treating the symptoms," Vorn said quietly. "Between the market and the chapel, I found a dozen children in the streets, hungry and sick. I've never seen it this bad."

"Aye, the tenements are overflowing and disease rates are soaring."

"Can you suggest the king—"

"If I suggest anything," Vorn hissed, "I will be thrown out of the palace on my ear, perhaps even removed from the line completely. Then what good would I be to anyone? I must maintain my position so we can try to stay on top of things. Tamuro knew I would not be there to stop him today." He balled his fist and sighed. Had Yirene known the role she played? He shook off the thought. "But . . . agreed—increase patrols. Offer rewards for information about the raiders. I want to hear every whisper of a raider or attack."

He may have no control over what the Crown did or said, but he would not let another Thundred smother the people. Spending time among them for so many years in his rebellious youth—they were more family to him than his own brother.

"Shouldn't you be back in that palace of yours, finding ways to help your people rather than finding more taxes to break us?"

Azyant and Ba'moori came to their feet. "Beg off—"

"What," the man taunted, "is the prince afraid of the truth? He can't handle—"

Vorn rose and stayed his men. "Your words and resentment are heard, good sir."

The man barked a laugh. "Oh, are they?" The way he slurred his *r* warned of his inebriated state. "By a drunken prince who spends more time with chatelaines than—"

"Enough," Tarac barked. "You speak to—"

"Leave it," Vorn instructed. "It's not worth it—"

"I'm not worth it, eh?" The man lunged at him.

Vorn deflected the incoming punch, a clumsy effort by a man who'd had too much drink. He caught the man's arm and twisted him around, pinning him to the wall. "I think, good sir, it is time for you to go home."

"What home? That Tamuro taxed it right out from under me."

Vorn released him and stepped back. Looked to the tavernkeeper. "Get him into a room. I'll pay for the night." As the tension of the moment faded, the man all but carried to a room abovestairs, Vorn resumed his seat.

"You should have been firstborn," a gravelly voice spoke.

Was there no peace to be had? Vorn lifted his gaze to the well-dressed man, irritated when he realized who wore the expensive undervest and boots. "You mistake my mood, Gi."

"How is it possible that both king and heir could be so inept—"

Vorn came up. It was one thing to receive insult from a drunkard, but from a politician who was paid by the Crown . . .

Again, chatter died, tension rifling the thick air as Furymark flanked Vorn.

"Oh, be not offended, my prince," Haarzen Gi said with smooth deference. "We both know I speak truth. Anyone has but to look around to see the state of the realm." He inclined a head that brought to mind the Giessen domes—shiny atop with a rim of russet around the lower edges. Being commissioner to the throne meant he owed his livelihood to Tamuro, who had appointed him. But it also meant he had his finger on the pulse of the realm. Which made his next words as shocking as they were believable. "Clearly, the better man for the throne sits here."

Vorn lifted the drink before him. Only when Tarac cleared his throat did he realize he had grabbed Azyant's tankard of ale without thinking. He slammed it down, not out of anger, but to let the commissioner know he was not here to entertain politicians. "I neither deserve nor want your flattery." From his right, a tankard filled with the fruity concoction of chilled cordi slid into his hand. He gulped it.

"You are not the same prince who so often frequented this tavern before the coronation of Queen Yirene."

"And you know this because . . . your spies have reported it?" Vorn leaned forward. "Because in all the years I *did* offer my patronage to The Iron, I never saw you here."

Gi ignored the suggestion and kept talking. "The change is good—and the people are talking about you after the way you protected not only the queen, but the people, and then the children."

Vorn did not like this. The man *was* spying on him.

Gi waved to the crowded tavern. "Look around you, my prince. Your people rally and enjoy that you sit among them. It is a very shrewd tactic to gain their approval."

Vorn barked a laugh. "You mean the lowest of Jherako know I am a reveler and drunkard?"

"A reveler, perhaps," Haarzen Gi said with a shrug. "However, in these many months since Tamuro gained the throne, never have you left The Iron in your cups. And I have watched the barkeep fill your tankard this eve, not with ale but cordi—*un*fermented cordi."

Unsettled, Vorn said nothing, suddenly too aware of the way the tavern had fallen quiet, all attention drawn to them, to the dangerous ideas growing in the yeast of discontent. "Move along, Gi. I would be with friends this eve, and your careless words could land you—"

"I am not alone in my thoughts that *you* belong on the throne."

"You edge dangerously close to treason," Vorn hissed in a lowered voice. "Think you I want a throne whose supports are weakened by the pecking of greedy politicians and rampant treachery? It is a responsibility not my own."

"So you would perpetuate the complacency and corruption of the Crown?"

Vorn balled his fists at the accusation.

"My prince," Lathain whispered, voice tight. "An augur." He nodded to a swell of movement in the dark reaches of the tavern.

"Have you enjoyed the pleasures of the chatelaines this eve, Prince Vaanvorn?" A haggard woman shuffled toward them, her hunched frame seeming to struggle to bear the weight of the dingy clothes she wore.

"No," he bit out, not sure what she was doing or why she intruded on their conversation.

"You speak true. In fact you have not in some time," she wheezed. "It is good, for one day soon you will enjoy the pleasure of a Lady—"

"You are mistaken."

"A real Lady, my prince. A consort." Somehow she appeared to brighten the closer she came. It was the gray hair—scraggly and wild as the foamy wakes of the sea—rustling beneath an unfelt breeze.

Inside a tavern?

"'Eschew the woman immersed in the ways of the Fallen and debased,'" Tarac said quietly as he lifted his mug.

Hearing the Code in regard to this augur reminded Vorn of the new path his boots had been set upon. To rely on the Codes and a life committed to the Ancient, not on . . . others. "You are gravely mistaken in that, crone." To have a consort, he would need to be king, and thank the seas he was not under that burden.

Rheumy brown eyes rose to his as she stabbed a gnarled finger at him. "I speak true. Before this night is out, you *will* feel that anchor, Prince Vaanvorn Thundred." As she looked up at him, those eyes grew clear and almost . . . violet. "To your shoulders not only will come the weight of rule but the burden of saving an entire realm on the brink of drowning."

Vorn's mind flashed to that day in the market—purple-then-brown eyes distracting him before the attack. Unnerved, he blinked, and the eerie moment passed. He stood, ready to leave this godforsaken place.

"Fail to protect Jherako," the crone continued, "and you will undoubtedly pay the consequences."

Gi stood beside the augur now, no doubt pleased that his words had, of a sort, been repeated by the crone. The two seemed one and the same. But what was that?

His four captains arcing behind him, Vorn ignored the crone—she was no threat—but focused on the one who posed a risk, considering the position he held. "Is that a threat, Commissioner?"

"Call it a . . . diagnosis," Gi said as he smiled down at the augur, "just as a pharmakeia would diagnose the weeping wound of a soldier and predict its outcome based on the rank odor of infection wafting from it."

The tavern door slammed open, ushering in a contingent of Furymark.

No, not merely Furymark. Kingsguard. The small unit negotiated the crowded tavern, led by a uniformed officer. At the silver waves on the man's shoulders that indicated he was Sword of the King, Vorn fought back a wash of dread. Knew then that each step the officer took tolled the last minutes of Vorn's freedom.

Stricken, Vorn avoided the augur's exultant eyes. How? How had the crone known?

The officer broke from the main contingent and threaded his way to Vorn.

Glad he was already on his feet, Vorn exhaled heavily. "Commander Cuirsso."

The Sword tucked his chin sharply and went to a knee. "My king."

Amid the muttered oaths of his Four and others in The Iron, Vorn cursed, his chest tight with realization. Fool Tamuro. "How did my brother die?"

VALIRIANA
DEVERSORIA

"You know better. That was *not* the skill or excellence of a Faa'Cris hastati."

The Revered Mother's remonstration was well deserved. Shame coated Valiriana as thick as djell—the viscous, miraculous, healing water that filled the *sanitatem* she had emerged from an hour past, healed of the head wound and broken arm inflicted by her idiocy. Bruises, however, remained as clear reminders. "It was a mistake! If that Licitus had not—"

"Yes, a foolish mistake that is wholly yours!" the Revered Mother snapped as they wound away from the coliseum. "You are in the final days of your trials, Valiriana, and you failed miserably. Never have I seen a Daughter so easily taken down. That was the inexperience of a first-year!"

Valiriana swallowed her argument as they entered the market where Faa'Cris and those accursed Licitus mingled casually—at least until the fourth bell when the men were sent from the city back to their settlements within Sacrum Lapis.

"Well? What have you to say?"

She shouldn't resort to blaming the Licitus. They were pitiable creatures. But neither would she bear the blame for his interference. "It was his *smell*," she said, her lip curling—catching wind of a similar scent as another Licitus inclined his head to the Revered Mother, his admiration nauseating. Mercies, men reeked! "It broke my concentration."

"No." Gleaming in her white-and-lavender gown, the Revered Mother stopped and faced her. "*You* broke your concentration. Own your guilt and learn from it."

"It was not . . . I had not . . ." Fists balled, Valiriana deflated. Knew they were excuses. She must do better. Rise above the mistakes, the . . . men!

"Ferox favors you, and for that reason I instructed Cybele to invite him and the other men into the coliseum."

"You?" She gaped, barely remembering to keep herself in check. "You *invited* him? How is that fair? He was—"

"You would not be so irritated had your feelings for him been neutral."

"*Feelings*?" she balked.

"Do you deny that you find him attractive?"

"That would be a lie, but it does not mean—"

"*Acta non verba.*"

Deeds not words. Nearly rolling her eyes in frustration, Valiriana felt keenly the truth in the mantra. Anger churned and writhed against the unfairness of the situation. If she had resented Licitus before . . . well, that feeling was amplified now. Licitus were trouble, irritating and foul. Dare she say she *hated* Ferox for what he'd cost her?

"You are Faa'Cris." The Revered Mother's voice cracked like a whip in remonstration against those dark thoughts, but then her violet eyes softened. "*Hate* is a term we only direct at evil. Not those whom we dislike or disagree with. Never use it casually. It is a powerful thing, and its roots dig deep and spawn bitterness." She exhaled heavily, shaking her head. "Mayhap this will help you remember how easily men can derail our purpose when you go through hastati training again."

"Has—*what*?" Panic lit through Valiriana's chest. "No! Please." She spun in front of the Revered Mother. "It was *one* mistake. I learned. It is—" But she saw the resolve in the firm lift of the Resplendent's jaw. "Please. Ma'ma. It was not my fault. To be forced to repeat training is harsh. You are being unduly hard on me simply because I am your daughter. This punishment is unfair. The challenge was stacked against me."

"Many Fallen have spoken those very words."

Shock and indignation yanked her straight. "I am not Fallen!" Her pitched voice echoed around the great underground city and seemed to bounce off the stone ceilings and walls. "Another year—I can't!" She could not endure the humiliation—especially not for a Licitus she didn't even find that attractive. "My entire life destroyed because of a man! Why do we suffer them? They bring only breaking and destruction."

"If this breaks you, then thank the Ancient for a breaking that will make you stronger and that it happens now, within the safety of this sacred city," the Revered Mother said as she entered the academic hall. "You are young— earned your span faster than most. It is better to be prepared for what may come than to be struck down because you failed to face your weaknesses head-on." She lifted an imperious eyebrow. "Agreed?"

Later mayhap Valiriana would agree, but not yet. It was so insufferably unfair. All her friends would advance without her. A year! She would be behind an entire year. Because of a *Licitus*! A stinking, Fallen—

"Guard your thoughts, Daughter." The Revered Mother straightened. "You are strong—so very strong—and I know in time you will understand. For now, trust our ways."

Did she have a choice?

"You always have a choice."

Valiriana breathed a snort, refusing to answer her mother's voice in her mind.

The Revered Mother's faint smile fell away as she spotted someone across the temple courtyard. "I must go." As if summoned, she strode over the cobbled stones, straight toward Resplendent Kaliondre. "It is too much to be believed." Her words sailed on the cool air, evidence that the two had begun their conversation via the *vox saeculorum*.

Intrigued, Valiriana trailed them.

"I thought he was a *second* prince." Kaliondre's voice and expression were stern, disgusted.

"Yes, exactly," Ma'ma growled. "Why would his name rise on the Flames?"

"Clearly," Kaliondre said, "we have missed much. He will soon be crowned."

"Crowned?"

"Word on the street in Jherako is that King Tamuro fell to his death in a drunken stupor."

The Revered Mother slowed as they approached the great hall. "Surely . . . No, that is not . . ."

"It does not resonate, does it?"

"Not at all."

When her mother glanced around, Valiriana realized she had followed too closely. She ducked behind a vendor's stall.

"You cannot think they will approve a Sending?" Ma'ma balked. "It has not been done in many years, and for this one, this . . . lineage?"

Kaliondre sniffed. "Unlikely, but since the name rose, a Sending must be discussed."

Ma'ma sighed. "Aye, and they are unlikely to dismiss his name, yet we have found little to defend *celeres*."

Celeres . . . aboveground . . . the surface world. Where they carried out their missions to protect and defend the Ancient's children. Too, it was true that they kept a watchful eye for strong alliances, though one had not been found in quite some time.

"Agreed," Kaliondre said definitively as they resumed their path into the Temple. "No Sending."

Valiriana stilled on the Temple steps as the Resplendent passed out of sight. The very thought of a Sending . . . It sent a shudder through her, especially after what had happened to her with Ferox. Despite the words those two spoke, she knew if a man had come to the attention of the Faa'Cris, then a Sending was almost a given. And that meant deploying a trained Daughter into the world to be joined with a man, to bestow their gifts on that lineage in exchange for a Daughter.

It was revolting.

Where was Relissa? She must tell her friend what she had overheard. Hurrying up the steps, she shoved away the idea of a Lady having to yield her body and glory to a Licitus, no matter that he was a king. The thought of it made her want to scrub down in searing djell to cleanse her mind. She skipped a few steps away from the Temple. Men did not deserve what Faa'Cris suffered to assist them. No Lady should have to endure their touch!

Ugh! She pitied the Daughter chosen to go out to this king. Forced to leave the safety and security of Deversoria, all the friendships and familiarity of this beautiful, sacred city. All so she could *subjugate* herself to a Licitus.

As she rounded the corner to the baker's—a jelly-filled pastry seemed especially necessary at the moment—Valiriana was possessed of a traitorous thought. A realization—if *she* went out, then she'd avoid the humiliation of being hastati for a *second* year. But that would not work since only triarii-ranked Faa'Cris were eligible.

Was it worth it? Ha. As if! Being with a man was repugnant. She recalled how Ferox had pitched that putrid scent at her, distracting her, making her fail the trial, disgracing her . . .

No. No man was worth assuming that existence.

VAANVORN
FORGELIGHT, JHERAKO

The seven-day mourning period ended with the last gong from the clocktower an hour past.

"Majesty," Tarac said quietly, "she has boarded the ship. Plank is drawn up."

Still finding it strange to bear that title, Vorn turned and strode to the receiving hall where Vizier Balerik, the councilors, and the remainder of Vorn's Four all waited. "The mourning period is concluded," he said as he entered. "It is now time to make some decisions."

A general disquiet hung in the room.

"This is unpleasant business, so let us not waste time with empty words." Vorn stood by the hearth. "The pharmakeia has confirmed the presence of a poison in the late king's body. It is the same poison found to have stained Lady Yirene's hands, the same poison I witnessed her purchasing from a merchant in the market."

Vorn continued. "As well, the pharmakeia examined the queen and determined she does not carry a Thundred heir." He exhaled heavily, biting back the anger over the senseless murder of his brother. "After a careful inquiry conducted by myself and an official, I handed down my judgment. Lady Yirene was stripped of her crown, title, income, and banned from Jherakan lands. She just this hour set sail for—"

"What?" Vizier Balerik railed. "She *murdered* our king! How can you—"

"Perhaps you have forgotten, Vizier," Vorn said almost lazily, "that *I* am now your king. Do you challenge me?"

"But . . . sire—she—"

"My judgment stands. Considering the state of our realm, I feel it best we move on. Look to our own districts and—"

"You robbed us of a chance to hear the queen—"

"Remove the vizier from the hall," Vorn said evenly, waiting as kingsguard formed up on the man and delivered him into the foyer. Realizing the dark note on which his rule had begun, he gritted his teeth. "I know my determination was . . . unconventional, but in light of what I learned in the investigation, I believe it right." He sighed. "I want this realm, this throne, and Crown, to be known for justice and honor. It starts here, now." He gave a nod.

Tarac moved to the middle of the room. "Thank you all for coming. You may go."

Needing salty air to allay the knots in his shoulders, Vorn strode to his solar and went directly to the balcony.

The door to the solar opened, then closed. Steps drew nearer. "It was the right decision."

Vorn watched as the Iaisonian contingent left Jherakan waters under armed escort by the royal navy.

"I had no choice," he said around a sigh. "Why did I not see it?"

"That question will only torment. Nobody anticipated her actions."

The truth of what happened would forever separate Jherako and Iaison. Voice and heart devoid of emotion, he shoved back the familiar rage that had ripped through him when he learned what happened to Tamuro. He tightened his hand around a bloodied piece of paper. Gritted his teeth.

"The Furymark are nervous," Tarac said quietly.

"Good." Vorn left the window and returned to the solar. A room whose fire his father-king had always enjoyed but left most others drenched. Who needed a firepit in Jherako? "If they fail me as they did my brother, I hope you will cut them down as I have their predecessors."

Tarac said nothing.

They headed to the library where Vorn noted a stack of letters perched precariously on the edge of the desk. When he strode past them, the pile lost kilter and fluttered to the ground. A sergius rushed from the side and picked them up.

"What are those?" Vorn asked.

"Letters from the various realms, offering condolences . . . and their daughters."

Growling, Vorn fought the temptation to shove everything off the desk. "Burn them."

Tarac started. "Sire—"

"Burn. Them." He stretched his neck. "I do not want their condolences or their daughters. I will not marry."

"Oh, but that will not do." Vizier Balerik made his appearance at that moment. "You are the last of House Thundred," he persisted. "You *will* marry—soon—and produce heirs as quickly as possible. I have instructed the master of the harem to find the fairest virgins already under his care and—"

"Vir—" Vorn glowered. The thought sickened him—a beauty contest.

"Do not argue—it is best."

Rage blinded him to the oaths he had sworn to uphold. Right now, he simply wanted to strangle the man before him. But that was not the way of the Creed.

"You forget whom you address, Vizier Balerik," Tarac warned. "When you speak to the king, you will address him as Your Majesty or sire. You will bow in deference to His Majesty and never show him your back."

Mouth tight, Balerik seemed to take a moment to control his irritation. "Of course." His gaze moved to Vorn. "I beg your mercy, King Vaanvorn. It was not my intention—"

"Was it not?" Vorn countered, squaring his stance as he challenged the man's lie. "Did you not walk in here and dare to instruct me on what I should do? Have you not already given instruction to those of this House to take such measures as rounding up girls without broaching it with me first?" Was this man part of the canker in this House? Could it be possible *he* had helped Yirene learn where to purchase the poison? "I am well aware this is how you conducted yourself with the two kings before me, but hear me now: that will not be the case with me. All decisions, all actions will be cleared either through me or my Sword of the King, who is as my own voice."

The vizier stilled, his expression pale. "And who is that?"

Vorn removed the ring from his left pinky and handed it to his First. "Captain Tarac Mape."

Small and almost unnoticeable, the twitch Tarac gave betrayed his shock, but he shrewdly held his surprise in front of the vizier. He took the ring, inclining his head in silent acceptance, then placed it on his hand.

The vizier balked. "But he has no training! He has—"

"Been at my side these fourteen years," Vorn said. "There is no one else who can so decidedly know my will or intent. He has proven himself in combat and character."

"You mean he is prone to violence. The office of—"

"It means he knows how to deal with sniveling politicians." Vorn considered going a step further and naming Tarac a duke, but that would have to go through the King's Council. As well, Tarac had long made it clear he wanted no part of court politics, though the realm needed dukes and barons like him.

"M-majesty," Balerik said around a disconcerted chuckle. "Forgive me, but it is my duty as vizier of House Thundred to give counsel to the sovereign and uphold—"

"*Counsel*," Vorn agreed. "Not instruction. Should I find again that you have gone beyond me in any manner, you will be stripped of that robe and title."

The vizier gaped. "You jest! I have served House Thundred for over twenty years."

"Nineteen years too long mayhap, as you seem to have forgotten the very meaning of 'serve,'" Vorn suggested.

Mouth open beneath that odd vizier hat that had one side taller than the other, Balerik seemed intent on digging his own grave. "Your father put me in place, said he trusted no man more—"

"And if you do not tread carefully, I will remove you."

The man scoffed. "You cannot—"

"Tempt *not* my anger." Challenging Vorn's anger had seemed the order of the last seven days since Tamuro's death. "Dismissed, Vizier Balerik." He left his solar and moved down to the great hall where a table was set up with six parchments, a bowl of water, and a towel. On another table by the windows overlooking the bay sat a pitcher of chilled cordi, goblets, and a tray of bread. He turned and faced his Four, who had followed him. Saw in them the same ragged determination that this course was not pleasant but necessary.

"You are sure, sire?" Tarac asked.

"What if they were simply following orders?" Azyant wondered.

"Then their character is too weak. I do not want puppets in power who are easily corrupted. We need men and women of character, willing to protect this country at all costs."

"Balerik had one thing right, though," Azyant said. "With no more Thundred heirs, you need a queen to provide you one. Now." He cast a sideways glance at Vorn. "There is the harem."

Vorn growled loudly.

"I could consult the augur," Lathain offered. "She mentioned a real Lady as your consort."

Waves, he'd forgotten about that. A real . . . "You— She— A Faa'Cris?"

Lathain shrugged. "They're fierce and magnificent. Bound by honor."

Interesting. Vorn felt Tarac's dark expression and disapproval without even meeting his gaze. The reminder to eschew this trouble was burned into his conscience. But why? If she knew this would happen, if she foretold his accession . . .

"Even evil can wear a cloak of innocence."

Vorn eyed his Sword. "And in what manner has she been evil?"

"Do you not know? Felt you not her tug on your adunatos, even as she offered you the very thing you need? We both know how evil can masquerade until good tears off its mask."

"You and your cloaked words," he grumbled, knowing his man was right. It was why he was forced to cleanse corruption from those in authority over the realm. He stretched his neck, took a sip of cordi, and nodded. Time for the cleansing of House Thundred. "Who is first?"

"Councilman Greenburg."

Vorn grunted. He'd never liked the man, but that had no bearing on excising corruption from within these walls. Absently, he palmed the hilt of his broadsword. "You have the judgment signed by General Kossi?"

With a grave nod, Tarac said, "All of them."

It would not be the first time blood was on Vorn's hands. "Bring him."

Tarac nodded to Ba'moori, who went to the door and opened it.

A man in a fine blue silk jerkin and breeches entered with his head held high. That the man preferred the fashion of the north and forwent the attire of his own people said something. "Your Majesty." Greenburg hurried in and went to his knees, head down.

"Councilman Merkil Greenburg," Tarac introduced him.

"I am honored to be among the first you have called to Forgelight following your . . . accession."

Vorn stood at a table. "An honor you call it?" He turned with the document in hand.

"A-aye." Greenburg's hesitation betrayed his guilt and lie. "Of course. One of my stature could not have risen to such heights without serving this great House. As I'm sure you can tell, I have always been loyal to the king."

"Have you?" Vorn lifted the parchment signed by the general and affirmed by the Thundred seal. "I have here a signed affidavit that attests you have not only *not* been loyal to the realm, but you have taken bribes and paid them to spies among the household staff who have fed you information regarding the comings and goings of the previous rulers. Those secrets afforded you financial benefit and enabled you to promote yourself at the expense of the realm."

The man's face went blotchy red as he shook his head. "N—"

"In addition"—Vorn cut off the objection—"and most offensively, I have evidence you have conspired with others to kill my brother, the late King Tamuro."

"No!" The man shoved upward.

Before the man could fully find his feet, Tarac and Azyant collided with him. Secured him and forced him onto his knees once more.

"Earnestly, no. You are gravely mistaken, Prin—King Vaanvorn," Greenburg stammered and whimpered, but as Captain Azyant unsheathed his sword, the man's pleading turned to anger. His face reddened. "You are as much a fool as your brother. You will fall, Vorn! You will fall!"

Azyant lowered the edge of his sword to the man's neck, silencing him with the light pressure of the blade.

Impassive, Vorn said, "So that you may go to Shadowsedge in peace, know that your family will not receive the same judgment, but they will be removed from the city and relocated to a village on the border."

"No, please—it's dangerous there! They're innocent!" the man cried, his defiance evaporating. "I'm innocent—I did not poison your brother. How would I have access to fire root?" He scoffed. "Never would I do such a thing. Please, reconsider. I know you are honorable."

Smoothing his hand over the hilt of his own sword, Vorn told himself to calm. But the anger at the councilman's words . . . "I never named the poison in our meeting earlier." In a fluid, practiced move, Vorn unsheathed his sword, spun around, and drove the blade of his weapon into the man's chest. "You were to guard our people, not bleed them. So you will bleed, Merkil Greenburg."

Vorn grabbed the cloth from the table and wiped his sword, returned it to the sheath, and went to the window as sergii removed the dead body. Cleaned the floor. Once quiet fell on the room again, he drew in a breath. "Who is next?"

"Iereas Farin Looten."

He motioned for them to bring the priest in. Despite the fact that most iereas were outside their authority, because this one had served House Thundred as the mediator between the White Temple and Forgelight, he was subject to Jherakan laws, and therefore, the king.

The iereas came in, pious and quiet. Then he saw the bloodied towel and bowl. His gaze shot to Vorn. "Please—no! Send me to the White Temple. Let me face their judgment."

"Were your crime of a religious nature, I would agree." And so it was he delivered judgment against even a priest.

Over the next few hours as he and his Four dealt with the treasonous betrayals, Vorn felt the eradication of each life just as he felt their betrayal against him and the realm. He stood with cordi in hand, tired, weary. About to take a sip, he saw a sergius rush across the room to Tarac, who nodded then faced Vorn with a grim expression.

Lathain strode forward, anger pinching his face. "The commissioner is here and requests an audience to deliver news to His Majesty."

The lanky man strode forward and inclined his head. "King Vaanvorn, thank you for giving me this chance. I came at once to inform you that the vizier is in the fountain square."

"And this is worthy of my attention how?" Vorn fisted his hand, waiting.

"He was overheard to be inciting a rebellion against you by telling the people that"—Lathain hesitated, his gaze dropping—"you killed Tamuro. I have been told by sources that he is sharing the movement of your Furymark and army along the border."

Tarac heaved a breath. "This would be him tempting your anger, Majesty."

Aye. And no matter how much he wanted to take the gentler path, it had become clear the vizier would not be brought into line with mere words. "We ride."

03

VAANVORN
FORGELIGHT, JHERAKO

The door to the clockmaker's shop opened, and from the other side of the fountain square, Vorn watched. Wrists crossed on the pommel, he monitored the unfolding betrayal of the court vizier.

"Vizier Balerik, stop where you are in the name of King Vaanvorn!" Tarac's command echoed across the square.

Dressed in head-to-toe black robe and headdress, Vizier Balerik faltered on the stoop of the shop.

Vorn nudged his Black forward, taking a lazy pace toward the traitor, who glanced around as if to run.

Swarming the small structure, the Furymark made themselves known to the vizier.

"What is this?" Balerik snapped. "You kill your brother, now come after me?"

Mounted atop his Black, Vorn waited in silence as his Four filed into the shop.

Azyant reappeared moments later, holding aloft a parchment. "As reported, sire."

Vorn considered the men who emerged behind the vizier. Took note of faces, memorized names. Felt a full flood of rage again. Would it not end? Aye, it would. At his hand. He signaled his Furymark as he dismounted.

The elite kingsguard slid off their horses with fluid grace and tightened a circle around the vizier, swords out, tips pointed to him.

Vorn climbed the steps, unsheathing his longsword. "Boison Balerik, you have violated in the most odious ways the oath of the office of vizier. And here I find you conspiring against your new sovereign." Beside the man, Vorn had a two-inch height advantage. "I warned you not to tempt my anger."

"The Thundreds have destroyed this city and country," the man spat. "I believe in this city," he shouted to the people, then indicated to Vorn. "He is a murderer! He has killed six of his councilors. Let him live and you will watch your children starve."

Though Vorn thought to run the man through and be done with it, he would not create a martyr. Would not force upon these innocents the sight of a killing. "You have acted against my predecessors and myself, so as king, it is my right and duty to answer that treason. Arrest him."

Without warning, a Furymark's horse reared, its hooves raking the air. Women and men alike cried out and sought safety, causing a swell of movement in Vorn's direction. He shielded himself, instantly alert to his surroundings. The Furymark destriers were well trained and not easily spooked—something or someone had frightened the horse on purpose.

"On your king!" roared Tarac from the right.

Gold-and-black uniforms swarmed in around Vorn, blocking him from the crowd. "Do not let him escape!" Though he saw soldiers converging and the throng roiling with movement, he could not find the brigand. He hopped up on the edge of the fountain almost in tandem with Tarac to survey the chaos.

"Where is he?" Tarac growled.

A head of silvering brown bobbed, and Vorn narrowed his gaze on the man threading through the congestion like a fish darting upstream. "Toward The Iron," he shouted to his men. Even as they turned, he saw an opening to his left. Pitched himself in that direction. Sprinted through the tangle of bodies and screaming women dragging their children to safety.

Having negotiated these streets and alleys as a young man trying to avoid the security his father-king had sent after him, Vorn made quick work of closing in on the vizier. He skidded up to a corner and peered around it, nostrils stinging at the stench of waste and filth. Saw the vizier pass the alley, then double back. Duck into the darkness, his boots quiet in the silt that formed the street.

With the man coming straight toward him, Vorn stepped into his path.

Balerik faltered. Scrambled around—and found the Furymark blocking his escape.

Two boys emerged from a door, armed with fruit and papers.

"Clear out," Tarac shouted to them.

But the vizier caught one of the kids, hauling him back and drawing a short dagger. "Let me go or the boy dies."

The man had sealed his fate. Eyeing his First, Vorn sheathed his sword and moved forward, hands raised. "Easy, Balerik. I just want to talk."

"Your sword!" the man shouted. "Toss it aside. Everyone knows your skill with that thing is lethal."

It was not just his sword that was lethal. His determination was even more powerful. Eyes locked on the man, he removed the belt. Tossed the sheathed sword toward his First. Held out his hands. "Better?"

"Nothing has been better since your brother and now you took the throne," he snarled. "You've forgotten how to rule with honor."

"We had an agreement," Vorn said, indicating the boy. "Let him go."

Balerik stilled. Eyed the Furymark and Vorn's Four. "I do not think so. You've failed, Vorn. Your time will end, and soon. A stronger power is coming. They are far more wealthy and powerful than you or anyone in House Thundred. And I know how you deal with your—"

Like lightning, Vorn darted in, one hand going to the vizier's sword hand, the other to his throat, even as he kicked the boy from the man's grip. With a twist of his wrist, he disarmed Balerik. Coldcocked him. As the man crumpled against the brick wall, Vorn extracted the dagger sheathed in his boot, then drove it into the man's neck.

Vorn stared into the dull, shocked eyes. What else had these eyes seen that they shouldn't have? "Race face-first into the Eternal Embrace, and may you meet the Ancient's vengeance there for the violence you perpetrated against the innocent of Jherako."

Warm, sticky blood coated his hand, but it was not the first time Vorn had sated the thirst of his blade with the blood of the wicked. He withdrew it, the man rasping his last few breaths. "You are relieved of a world whose air you were not worthy to breathe, Boison Balerik."

He stepped back, doing his best to shield the boy from the sight of the dead vizier. But as he stood there in the alley that reeked of refuse, he felt . . . something. The hairs at the base of his neck prickled. He glanced back, behind him. To the crowd. They were watching but there was something . . . someone . . . His gaze traipsed the faces.

Wait. Purple eyes? He retraced the faces . . . purple . . . Had it been his imagination? Had he not seen something similar in the market?

"Sire, we should hasten you to the house."

Taking a thick breath, trying to shake off that eerie feeling, he let his men lead him out of the alley to where Lathain had his Black waiting.

"Errant, seek the Ladies and know their pleasure!" the craggy voice warbled from beneath a tree. "Come closer still and learn their will. Trust, trust in me, and I vow what you gain will far outweigh all else."

Gut tight, Vorn met the withered visage of the augur. Felt the swarm, the same one he'd felt in the alley. He stared at her as he passed, her words echoing in his head as he rounded the wall all the way back to Forgelight.

An hour later, hands, blade, and House cleansed, Vorn removed himself to his solar. He bathed, donned his pants, and stood at the basin while the sergius trimmed his beard. Stared into the mirror at the man looking back. The Thundred dark hair and eyes were notoriously marked with good looks. And the burden of his kingdom.

He hung his head, chin propped on his shoulder. Trying to banish the memory of the blank look in the vizier's gaze. In the mirror, he saw the flutter of the black banners behind him that bore the dark pall of death. They plunged from every palace window, reaching to the ground in which King Tamuro III had been laid. Never would Vorn have willed or imagined their lives would take this course, that he would wear the crown.

"You are well?"

His gaze flicked to the right, to Tarac there with his hands clasped in perfect calm. After a quick thanks to the sergius, Vorn grunted and wiped his face. Threaded his arms into his white tunic and undervest. "It appears opinions are varied on that."

"Opinions never mattered to you before."

"I had not the weight of the realm on my shoulders then."

"You know I speak my mind quite openly to you—"

"Aye," Vorn barked with a laugh.

"You have done what needed to be done," Tarac said with conviction. "Growth, real and true growth, is difficult, painful. Jherako needed limbs pruned so it could flourish and bear good fruit."

"Words of a master gardener."

Tarac huffed. "My words are earnest."

"Aye," Vorn conceded, then considered him. "Thank you. I appreciate your wisdom."

Each death weighed on Vorn's conscience and heart, but they were necessary—as Tarac had said. The heavy thoughts followed him into the main room, where he and Tarac joined Ba'moori, Azyant, and Lathain, who were seated at the table and rose upon Vorn's entrance.

"What have you discovered about the vizier's accomplices?" Vorn asked.

"That they are dead," Lathain stated flatly as the sergius delivered a bowl of steaming stew before him.

Vorn stilled, frustrated. "Why do they choose death over honor?"

"Pride." Tarac waved off the steamed cordi the sergius attempted to serve him. His man rarely drank anything but water.

"Both men called you the Errant, not king as is your right and title."

A laugh did little to hide how much that name indeed offended. Vorn abandoned the drink and ran a hand over his face before he let his tired eyes rest on the linen tablecloth, where a stain of cranberry reminded him of the blood spilled this day. "I care not what they call me as long as they rise from their stupor and once more believe in and fight for Jherako. They grew fat and drunk on Tamuro's complacency and unwillingness to address the rot infecting this country. Excess and corruption have been the hallmarks of this House." He fisted his hand. Slammed it on the table, startling the sergii, who scampered back to their places of waiting in the shadows of the room. "No more!"

"All told, seven put to the blade . . ." Azyant grunted quietly as he mopped a piece of bread in his stew. "No one can accuse you of complacency in your rule."

Vorn eyed the barrel-chested captain. "Seven or seventeen, I care not about numbers, only the complete eradication of corruption. I will snuff it out," Vorn said firmly. "Readily do I accept the stain of their blood if it means Jherako yet stands two hundred years from now." His thoughts wandered to his own line . . . of which he was the end. And there was no hope for a powerful alliance. A whisper teased him, bringing recall of the crone's suggestion to bind with a Lady.

Lathain rested an elbow on his chair. "With those seven dealt with and removed, it will be, Your Majesty."

Majesty. It would take time to adjust to that. Vorn dragged his hands through his hair, trying to navigate the tricky waters of turning the realm around. "Trimming branches, apparently, is the easy part. Rebuilding . . . not so much."

A loud knock came at the door and as a sergius answered it, the Four came to their feet, hands falling to their sides in readiness.

Setting down his napkin and fork, Vorn swallowed his food. Waited to see who intruded on their meal.

Commissioner Haarzen Gi's hasty entrance was slowed as his gaze hit the readied Four and the table littered with food. "Your Highness." He bowed at the waist with much more deference than he'd displayed at The Iron that fateful night on which everything had changed. "I beg your mercy, sire." Again he eyed the food. "It is well past the noon hour, and I did not anticipate you would be eating."

Vorn motioned the man forward, still not sure what to make of the sudden contrition or intrusion. He considered the man shifting in his shiny brown boots. "Are you better pleased with the realm now, Commissioner?"

Uncertainty crouched in the corners of his eyes. "I . . ." Gi glanced at the Furymark and did not draw nearer the table. "Sire?"

Head cocked, Vorn cleared his teeth of food and took a moment to gather himself. "In The Iron a week past, did you not say that I would soon be king, thereby insinuating my brother, the king, would die?"

Concern suddenly in his expression, Haarzen stilled. "Aye . . ."

"This is what you had planned?" Was that the justification for his haste in coming? Had word reached him that Balerik was dead, and he sought to put himself in that position? What was it about this man that both concerned Vorn and impressed him?

"Planned?" Gi balked with a nervous laugh. "No, sire. If you will recall, the crone spoke those words more directly. I had only to read the signs in the air. No reason existed to threaten the king, as the signs were written on the walls of this castle." He shifted on his feet and swallowed hard. "What I spoke was in anticipation of the ruin coming thanks to the egregious mishandling of the realm."

Vorn rose to his feet, irritation scratching at his mood. "You speak of my brother, Commissioner."

"Aye, sadly, I do, sire." Gi stood tall, but not in pride. Only as an intelligent man with a healthy wariness and experience. Likely, too, awareness that seven others had been felled recently. "In what way can I convince you, sire?"

"You mean, how can you keep your head?" Vorn studied the fifty-something commissioner, still trim and fit—and shrewd. He was tired of the politics, the pandering. Time was the only proof these days. "You came here with great haste, Commissioner. To what end?"

"The foundling home, sire."

Everything in Vorn tightened. "What of it?"

The commissioner took a step forward. "It has come to my attention," he said, gaze taking in the others, "and I am not sure you are aware of this—"

"Do you suggest now that *I* am mishandling this realm?"

"No!" The man seemed surprised this time. "My concern is for the foundlings, sire. Since King Tamuro ended the endowment—"

"He what?" Vorn thought of the children, the mutterings of the Sister at the Sanctuary. "Tamuro had no right."

"I agree with you, sire, but when he took the throne it was one of his first orders," the commissioner said quietly. "As you can well imagine, the foundlings are not doing well. Many are in states of starvation and disease is rampant."

Azyant cursed under his breath.

"Restore the endowment," Vorn said in a flat tone, his mind racing as he turned to Tarac and Azyant. "Take Matron Khatrione and have her assess the situation. Bring the royal pharmakeia to tend the foundlings."

"That is ill-advised," the commissioner said. "The disease is blue fever."

Azyant let out another curse.

The ravenous fever deprived the infected of oxygen, turning lips and fingers blue until the entire body suffocated. Several painful, smothering days most often ended in death.

Meeting Tarac's gaze, Vorn saw determination and resolve. Had no doubt the man would make sure things were dealt with.

"I will see it done." With a curt nod, Tarac hurried out with Azyant.

Knowing these two were setting out to secure the foundlings, Vorn felt acute relief and focused on the commissioner standing before him. "You once numbered among the Furymark, did you not, Haarzen?"

The man's cheek twitched as he cast another glance around the room, taking in the kingsguard standing sentry. "Briefly, sire."

"Twenty-three years, eight as second-in-command," Ba'moori supplied, "before you were named commissioner by King Tamuro."

Vorn winged up an eyebrow. "You call that a brief time?"

Gi almost smiled. "When one's years number fifty and seven—aye, brief."

His plan now held a shroud of concern, so Vorn had to admit to more than a little hesitation. "It is with regret, Haarzen Gi, that I remove you as commissioner."

Haarzen's gaze shadowed. He blinked, confused, again skating a look to the corners and shadows, as if waiting for a blade to strike him down. "You think me complicit in your brother's death?" He started forward, then rethought the move when hands went to hilts. "I assure you—"

"Assurances I do not need." Vorn set down his goblet. "Only fidelity."

"On my life, you have it. Never has my hand been set against the Crown."

"Yet you spoke in The Iron that I"—Vorn patted his chest—"should be the one on the throne." He held his hands out and motioned around the room. "And here we are. You stand before your king." He narrowed his gaze at the man. "I would be very careful what you speak, what you deny, for truth has a way of finding its way to the surface, and I would not have you drowned by your own words."

Haarzen Gi faltered. Swallowed.

Vorn moved to the windows. "You and the others of your private committee wanted me on the throne—to make changes." Arms behind his back, he glanced over his shoulder at the commissioner. "Did you not?"

The knot of frustration smoothed from Haarzen's brow. "Aye," he conceded quietly. "We did. It seemed most prudent and best for the realm." He relaxed in surrender. "If you feel the kingdom is better served without me, then . . ." He nodded. "Let it be so, but if Your Majesty is aware of something I have done that has grieved you, please speak so I may remedy it."

Inspired at the man's selflessness, that he would surrender his position—and thereby his wealth—for the good of Jherako, firmed Vorn's choice. "That is twice in a week you have mistaken me, Commissioner."

That knot returned—and tightened. "Sire?"

"I removed you as commissioner because, as of moments ago, we have a vacancy in the office of vizier."

Haarzen started. Gray eyes widened.

"I have need of a man brave enough to call me out and speak truth when it must be said. And after the words spoken to me at The Iron, I think you are that man." Vorn ambled toward him. "What say you, Haarzen Gi?"

A sharp, stunned nod. "I am . . . grateful. Ready to serve you, King Vaanvorn."

"Well, don't spend too much time there." Vorn sniffed. "This day I have vacated six other offices. I need candidates to consider and corruption eradicated." He placed a hand on the shoulder of his new vizier. Met his eyes. "I think it goes without saying, Haarzen, if I find out you colluded to kill my brother or father, I will show no mercy."

04

VALIRIANA
DEVERSORIA

"This day we consider the man who has very recently become king of Jherako," the Revered Mother opened the assembly as Valiriana slipped into the rear of the coliseum and searched for a seat. "Vaanvorn Thundred, second son of Tamuro II, unexpectedly acceded to the throne, and since his name has risen on the Flames, we are tasked with setting aside our intimate feelings and weighing with sound judgment facts in order to consider a Sending. It is the task of this Synedrion to determine whether the benefits outweigh the risks, but more than that—is this king worthy to join with one of our Daughters? Look here." She motioned overhead, and the likeness of the considered king hovered in the air. "Lend your ear and yield your will to the Lady and the Ancient."

Valiriana spotted Relissa, who waved her over and indicated to a seat beside her. A week ago, the Revered Mother and Kaliondre had discussed this man as they hurried from the square, and now the Resplendent were poised to set arguments—unbiased—before the general body of Deversoria. The hewn stone walls that had stood for centuries lent themselves to the long tradition continuing this hour among the many who crowded the coliseum. Though any willing to hear the facts could attend the debate, only the Resplendent would vote.

"Jherako suffered greatly under the last two Tamuros, Vaanvorn's father and brother, respectively." The Revered Mother was apparently tasked with defense of the man—a challenging assignment, to be sure. "The benefit of aligning the Faa'Cris with this new king is irrefutable—he is powerful and holds a strategic seaport. As well, Jherako borders Kalonica and Hirakys. Through him, we can help Drosero as a whole." Shoulders squared, she lifted her chin. "The Progenitor's War is coming, and this king could be vital in assisting this planet without exposing ourselves. The Thundred men have proven themselves hardy and intelligent. And if this Synedrion should deem it prudent to conduct a Sending, the Daughter chosen will be pleased to know that Vaanvorn is also not difficult on the eyes."

Despite the titters that ran around the coliseum, what the Revered Mother had presented were simply geopolitical facts. Disappointment tugged at Valiriana—surely her mother could have presented a better defense. Was she not trying? How did he treat his people? Were his affairs conducted with shrewdness and honor? Valiriana could not fathom a Resplendent providing anything but her best, and yet, she would understand if they did not. After all, had not Sendings ceased in the last twenty years? Lady Nicea had been the most recent sent from the Sacred City, and that had been over two decades past.

The Revered Mother held out her hands to the gathered. "The floor is open for reasoned debate so that we might discern the will of the Ancient in this hour."

The mighty Decurion Cybele rose, severity scratched into her ebony skin. "Vaanvorn has been a king but a week and already he has ruthlessly slain seven officials who had long served his father and brother in their reigns. One poor soul was cut down in the city square, right before women and children." Imperious, she scanned those in attendance with the cunning she had used to weigh the hastati and find them wanting, time and again. "No matter whether he is hard on the eyes, he is a man obsessed with power and bloodshed. Rumor flits about the capital city that he poisoned his brother."

"A brother deep in his cups," the Revered Mother noted.

"A man's action—no, a *king's*—should not be based on the behavior of another but grounded in truth and honor," Kaliondre challenged as she stood and glanced around. "Thundred is a man absorbed in bloodlust. Just this morning, I received word from my own scout that King Vaanvorn murdered the Jherakan vizier. Without trial. Without chance to offer a defense. Do not believe my words but see for yourself."

Replacing the image of the darkly tanned king with his long black hair held in a queue and biceps corded with leather was footage of a brightly lit street with a horde of riders barreling up on a structure. Several dismounted, including one very recognizable and forbidding shape—the king. A man stood before him, thrusting a pointing finger at him, clearly upset.

Why come at this man with so great a force? No wonder he seemed angry. That would put anyone in distress!

Valiriana startled when a flurry of activity arose that had people running and all the guards on horses moving to avoid trampling the innocents. "Terrible," she murmured. "Anyone would—" She squinted as the scene changed, grew more dim. Shadowy forms, one clearly the hunted man, blurred together. A third form darted forward—King Vaanvorn—and a struggle ensued. A blow. The man fell beneath the king's fists.

"Will they earnestly show us a murder?" Relissa whispered as she leaned closer, eyes fastened to the hovering image.

"I—"

A dull glint caught the blade that King Vaanvorn produced. Valiriana found she could not breathe as he thrust the dagger into the vizier.

Gasps and shock rippled through the coliseum.

Anger churning, Valiriana clenched her teeth. "He does not value life," she murmured, sickened by what she had just witnessed.

"I seek your mercy for such violence being displayed here," Kaliondre apologized as her powerful legs carried her around the dais, "but are we in earnest that we would consider *sacrificing* one of our own—a *Daughter*—to this monster?"

"His ways are so dissolute the people have named him the Errant," she continued. "They believe him errant in his ways, so why would we—who have but distant reports—think we know better?" She slashed a hand in the air. "No! Definitively, this Licitus is not worthy of a Sending."

"Aye," Cybele said, nodding to her Sisters, "and this is just one of the seven he has so ruthlessly slain! Lives stolen at this king's hand. No justification should be found to excuse his disregard for human life."

A raucous shout of agreement went up throughout the coliseum—right along with Valiriana's. No, he was not worthy. Thankfully, the others gathered here were of the same mind, or so the predominant tide of opinion seemed to indicate. Not *all* the others, though.

"Tell me, Decurion Cybele—the lives you took at the Battle of Kahandra . . . do they number more than seven?" Miatrenette rose and eyed those on the dais with her. "If we are to gauge worthiness by the number of lives taken, I fear all on this dais would be disqualified."

"Miatrenette makes a valid point," Cybele conceded. "However, we are the Blades of Vaqar, and as such, we war on his behalf and that of the Ancient. Thundred's taking of these lives was not done in that accordance."

"I'm disappointed, Cybele. We cannot know what the Ancient tasks to another," the Revered Mother said softly. "As well, I will point out that those officials Vaanvorn dispatched were not merely corrupt but wicked, blackhearted. One—an iereas—had violently abused children and young women, darkening not only Jherako but the White Temple. Another had colluded with others to drive the former king—Vaanvorn's brother—to suicide, and when that did not work, convinced the young Iaisonian lady bound to the king to poison him." Ma'ma paused and took a breath. "It appears by all accounts that Vaanvorn Thundred is cleaning house. With a violent hand, yes, but too long has that kingdom been in the grip of the diabolus. He seeks to make things right." She looked around, her violet eyes probing. "Thundred is ripe for our influence, to help him correct Jherako's course."

"Were we to send a Daughter, what if he sets a blade to her throat one day?" Cybele suggested, her words like daggers. "Men like this become enraged when a Daughter is conceived and taken. They want them to secure alliances. You well know this after your own experience, Revered Mother."

Valiriana swallowed, shrank in awareness that this was a reference to her own birth. Somehow it made her gaze find the hovering image of the considered king. He had strong features. Seemed formidable. Frightening. Handsome.

No, *just* frightening.

Would he be as furious as her own human father had been when Ma'ma returned to Deversoria with her yet in womb?

Her mother's eyes flashed with fury. "Do not justify the denial of wisdom and prosperity to one man because of another man's actions. This Synedrion has never accepted such flawed logic, Decurion Cybele."

"Yet, we do!" Kaliondre's argument seared the air. "In recent years, no Daughters have been sent out, though it is one of our most important edicts and purposes."

"You forget Rejeztia," Miatrenette said pointedly.

"I do not," Kaliondre bit back, "as Rejeztia was not Sent, only commissioned for reconnaissance."

"A failing, I would agree." The Revered Mother addressed the gathered. "The Ancient gifted us not for our own amusement but for the benefit of others. These abilities and our ways are not for ourselves but to serve the world on which we were set. If we continue to deny candidates, we will become as the Gray."

Dread traced Valiriana's shoulders at the mention of those creatures, lost in their emptiness. She certainly did not want that for any of her Sisters. And secretly, she again thanked the Lady she was not qualified to be sent out.

"Would you trust your daughter to this monster, Revered Mother?"

Valiriana's heart skipped a beat at yet another mention of her. Surely not. No mother would. *I would not help any man.* Especially not this one!

"If the Ancient wills it, then it is my will, too," the Revered Mother replied simply.

Too simply. Surely Ma'ma would not let them send her out.

Alas, I am not eligible, thank the Lady.

"Kaliondre," the Revered Mother continued, "answer this: Has Vaanvorn replaced the iereas?"

The red-haired Resplendent held the Revered Mother's gaze. "A new one is en route."

"And is that not the first edict we assess regarding every candidate, that they seek the counsel of the Temple, of the Parchments?"

"It is, but not the only one. Others before Self, Honor before Desire, Sacrifice before Indulgence. Ancient before all," Cybele argued. "And in several of these edicts, Vaanvorn fails. He has taken what he desired without regard to either his honor or that of others, and also availed himself of chatelaines and strong drink."

"Your information is true but flawed," the Revered Mother countered with a hefty dose of disappointment Valiriana was well acquainted with. "Those were all marks of his character before his brother's binding. In the last ten months, my sources reported a marked change in the prince."

"And that is supposed to excuse more than a decade of debauchery and wickedness?" Cybele balked. "I'm ashamed at you, Alanathina. What we do in the darkness defines who we are in the light."

"And I would also point out," the Revered Mother went on, undaunted by the truth spoken by her Sister, "that Vaanvorn's love was stolen from him by his jealous brother, a course of action that had drastic repercussions in him."

"*After* Vorn had stolen her virtue!"

Valiriana drew in a breath. He had fornicated with her? Why did it surprise when it had been proven that he had relations with ladies of the night? Her skin crawled. This king did not even deserve the breath wasted to consider him. She shifted in her seat, ready to leave. For this to be done.

"Since that night," Ma'ma asserted, "Vaanvorn has shunned female company. Attractive women may be his weakness still, but he learns to curb his desire. As for liquor—that vice was his brother's and contributed heavily to the failing kingdom and the actions Vaanvorn has since put in place to reclaim the realm for the Ancient."

Murmurs swept the coliseum. The man had violated the sacred act by tasting the virtue of a woman not his own. This was a great dishonor. No matter how formidable and handsome, he was a scourge. Not worthy of their time, Valiriana decided . . . again.

"But the lives he has snuffed out—if there is no justification—in that there is no defense. But those are answers we do not have now," the Revered Mother said firmly, then sighed. "The day has been long, and we are no closer to a decision. We will resume on the morrow."

05

VAANVORN
FORGELIGHT, JHERAKO

On the expansive green so prettily situated at the front of Forgelight proper gathered thousands of Jherakans. Sandwiches, fruit, and chilled cordi were served as the people anticipated their first glimpse and address of their new sovereign.

A dozen paces from the balcony, Vorn could see the vast sea of his people as he waited for the doors to open. Head weighted by the crown that had graced the heads of a dozen kings before him, he stood here, acutely aware that he was now alone in his line. No father, no brothers, sisters. No aunts, uncles, or grandparents. All gone.

Emptiness. Loneliness.

Those he would shoulder without complaint, along with the responsibility to help this realm succeed, to advocate for his people. In preparing his coronation speech, he had given much thought to the raiders who'd attacked the former queen, himself, and the Furymark. The councilmen he'd banished to Shadowsedge. Things and times were changing. He could not help but wonder how he would fare. What would historians say of his rule?

Waves, how had he ended up here?

At his right, Tarac stood in full regalia as well, bearing the standard and emblem of the house he served as Sword of the King.

"Did you imagine," Vorn said, "that you would stand here with me one day?"

"Hoped," Tarac confessed. "If only that the better man would rule."

He skated his Sword a sidelong glance. Did he really see him like that? Even though he'd endured all the years Vorn's name had been forgotten to the "Errant" moniker?

"And now," a voice thundered, the sound rattling through the glass doors, "the Sovereign of Jherako, Ironesse Island, and the Vantharq Ocean, Vaanvorn Thundred, Tenth Son of Aeglin of the Iron."

The doors swung open and seemed to snatch his breath and cast it on the warm, salty winds. Vorn followed it and stepped into the morning light and roar of the crowds. He lifted a hand in acknowledgement, a swell of emotion rising through his chest, not sure whether to be relieved, thrilled, or overwhelmed.

Even if he wanted to share a word with his Sword, he would not hear him until he removed himself to the amplifier and the crowds fell quiet. It was a heady, powerful moment that made him take a second to collect himself. "I am before you not for my own benefit, not to display my wit or wisdom, but as your sovereign, resolved to live and die alongside you. We are in unprecedented times, having lost two kings in as many years. For the record," he said, injecting some levity, "I intend to break that pattern." A titter of laughter flittered through the crowds. "I also intend to fight for the Ancient, for this kingdom, for my people—you. I dare any prince to invade the borders of my realm, for rather than any dishonor, I will take up arms. I will be general and judge—"

"Will you kill us like you did Balerik?"

He knew not how those words managed to reach his ears, but they did. "And rewarder," he continued, then swallowed. "Rewarder of every virtue exhibited by Jherakans in the field and at home. For it is incumbent upon you who have strength to set a right example to others. Remember that the loose- or foul-tongued cannot retain honor. Lead a clean, honorable life. Every man here knows the temptations that beset all of us in this world. At times any of us will slip. I do not expect perfection, but I do expect genuine and sincere effort toward being noble and proper in thought, in word, and in deed. Our whole focus should be on securing those qualities and virtues that make this realm unconquerable. Be strong—I would not respect you if you were not. In our decency and honor, we find strength. I desire to see in our country strong, trustworthy men, and until that is attained, we will not be as successful as we ought. Thank you. It is my honor to serve as your king."

With that, he eased back and again waved, noticing with some regret that the tenor had changed. The people did not seem as exultant now. He removed himself into the house. "What happened?"

Tarac strode alongside him but said nothing.

"I am off to an abominable start and know not why." He stalked down the passage to the stairs where a contingent waited to escort him to the receiving hall and reception now under way to celebrate his coronation.

"The *Muqqadas Ritsar* draws a select band of men, very small because few are willing to adopt such a stringent life. You as much as told them you expected the same of them."

"What is wrong with striving for honor and—"

"You told hardworking men they needed to give up their ale and respite. That they would have to fight and you would die with them—cold comfort when the end is that they and their king are dead."

"I will!" Vorn snapped. "All of us will . . . eventually." He growled and shook his head. "I am not suited for this, Tarac. Put a sword in my hand and—"

"All hail King Vaanvorn!" pronounced the caller as Vorn approached the doors to the hall.

Black seas! Could this day get any worse?

It did. He entered the den of prowling mothers and fathers, anxious to tie their noble houses to the Thundred name. He sat, received gifts, endowments, invitations, and oaths of fealty from the noble houses of the realm. Three hours and one massive headache later, he retired to his solar with his Four. And Creed be cursed—what he would not do for a tankard of ale. Instead, he gulped down three goblets of cordi before dropping into his favorite chair. "If one more nobleman offers his pampered, pale priss to me, I will hurt someone!"

"You should have just listened to the augur," Lathain said as he ate cake.

Vorn pitched his goblet at the man. "Blast you!"

Lathain leapt aside with a laugh. "What was that?"

"Be thankful," Vorn taunted, "I did not make good on my threat to hurt you."

"Ah, but see? I did not offer my nonexistent daughter. Only a—" When Vorn hoisted the entire pitcher of cordi as if to throw it, Lathain held up his hands. "I jest! I jest."

VALIRIANA
DEVERSORIA

"You have to admit—he has nice eyes."

Valiriana gaped at her friend as they sat in the coliseum, waiting for the second day of debate to begin. "I must admit no such thing." And yet, she looked to the image of the proud king hovering in the air. Wearing a leathered undervest that gathered at the waist with a wide cummerbund accentuated his muscular torso that was bared and sculpted. Blessings, that had nothing to do with the undervest. She felt a flush in her cheeks and knew she would need to recite extra prayers before sleeping.

"Why are you so decidedly set against men?" Relissa asked, her ivory skin glowing as she stared up at the visage of the Errant.

"Because they are *Licitus*—Fallen! Their only purpose is to distract and corrupt." Valiriana shook her head.

"That is not in keeping with our teachings, Valiriana. Men are—"

"They are not worthy of us, Relissa. I do not want my adunatos dirtied or darkened because of a man!" The very thought turned her stomach.

"Being bound does not sully us, Valiriana." Relissa sounded enamored with this impudent king. "It is designed to be a blessing, an enhancement."

Valiriana scoffed. "If I did not know better, I would think your adunatos already contaminated."

Her friend laughed. "Just because I can appreciate a handsome man's appearance does not mean I have lowered or sullied myself. Did not the Ancient make them as well?"

She could not argue that. But she would not concede Licitus were their equal. "Mayhap, but only for practice before *designing* us."

This time when Relissa fell into a fit of laughter, Valiriana joined her. "You should volunteer. You seem so smitten with them."

Shy brown eyes dipped low. "I already have," Relissa whispered.

With a gasp, Valiriana spun to her friend. "You did?"

"It will not happen, so make sure to bring extra cordi cakes to help me accept it."

While Valiriana could not fathom wanting to be chosen, she knew her friend would make a perfect ally and candidate for the Sending. "Why would you not be selected? You are gorgeous and sweet—and a triarii-in-training!"

"Not until Induction." Relissa sat poised and confident, then nodded to the dais where the Resplendent were again taking their seats. "I heard tell at least two decurions offered their names for consideration should a Sending be approved. Someone like me would not have a prayer."

Valiriana recoiled. "You would think those with such experience would know better."

The summoning sword clanged against the altar, bringing the debate to order. Valiriana settled in, her thoughts drifting, imagining what it must be like to abandon the glory of being Faa'Cris to condescend to the level of a human male.

That physique of the king's spoke of training, his eyes of experience. But what if Relissa did make it? She would leave . . . would be gone for decades, likely. That would be a loss Valiriana would not choose to suffer, for she loved her Sisters and Deversoria too much to leave them.

". . . but the evidence speaks that Vaanvorn's ways are changing," her ma'ma's voice rang through the coliseum, pulling Valiriana's thoughts back to the Synedrion. "What better way to influence and guide this king's transformation than under the tutelage of a Daughter?"

"Foolishness," Kaliondre snapped. "One does not send a child into battle without first teaching them to wield a sword and ride a horse!"

"Clearly," the Revered Mother pronounced sharply, "it has been too long since we have conducted a Sending, for we seem to have forgotten how to reason together and are resorting to attacks and absurdities. All will refrain from base speech and contend with facts and reason." She gave a nod. "Please resume in maturity and that which would honor the Lady Eleftheria."

"In a fit of rage," Cybele took up the argument, hardly affected by the remonstration of the Revered Mother, "he killed his own vizier in front of a five-year-old child. Is that what you would call worthy?"

"That vizier had conspired against the Crown and sought to infuse dissent and chaos into the city," Ma'ma said. "And what I call 'worthy' is a man who has renewed efforts to care for the foundlings of his city by sending the royal pharmakeia and stocking its pantry. Is that not part of our commission—to protect the weak and motherless?"

"Replacement of the iereas also speaks to his change, and as stated previously," Lady Miatrenette spoke, "he has put off debauchery and fornication. This speaks to a notable change of heart in this powerful king. Too, I have read the reports and his right hand is a man who honors the Ladies and seeks the Ancient. It is my opinion that Vaanvorn Thundred is ready and ripe for influence by a Daughter."

"To abuse a Daughter, you mean," Decurion Cybele continued with more than a little disgust in her words.

Quiet descended, and Valiriana's gaze once more flicked to the king, whose stern face and broad shoulders spoke of his formidability. When the near-silence stretched, she glanced to the Resplendent and realized they were all focused on the Revered Mother. One by one, they nodded to her.

Valiriana growled, shifting on her seat. "I hate it when they do that," she murmured to Relissa.

"*Vox Saeculorum* is the greatest weapon of the Faa'Cris," her friend snickered.

"It is decided," the Revered Mother declared. "The recommendation of the Synedrion is that we send out a Daughter to perform in-depth reconnaissance of this new king with the intent of committing to a Sending unless egregious intel is returned to us."

"That means they had at least two dissenters," Relissa muttered as they stepped into the flood of bodies moving out of the coliseum.

"Decurion Cybele is most certainly one of them. We now know there are at least two intelligent Daughters."

"Valiriana!" her friend hissed, then laughed and nudged her.

"You may laugh, but I do not." With a growl, Valiriana made her way down the spiral stairs. "I do not see what is so difficult—he is debauched, wicked. Never would he be tolerated within these walls."

"Then it is clear there is something to which we are not privy," Relissa said. "I trust the Resplendent. Do you not?"

"Of course, but—"

"Valiriana."

Startled at the snapped tone and the voice behind it, she turned to find Ma'ma there with a very terse expression. *Uh-oh.*

"See you tomorrow after training," Relissa whispered, then excused herself with a nod of deference to the Revered Mother.

After training, not *in* training, because they were in separate classes now that Valiriana had been held back.

"Walk with me." Her ma'ma extended a hand.

Surprise lit through Valiriana. Ma'ma rarely communicated with her personally during working hours in order to maintain her position as Resplendent and Revered Mother to all Faa'Cris. There was no differentiation to Ma'ma, even though they were blood related. Gladly Valiriana accepted the invitation, hoping to ferret out what it was that convinced the Resplendent to commit to sending anyone out for any reason.

Or . . . was Valiriana in trouble?

They walked in silence until they had cleared the square and city center and begun climbing the slight incline of the street to the home they had shared until Valiriana had entered training. From that time she had been housed among the other hastati in the barracks.

"What did you think?" Ma'ma asked quietly as they passed the small flower garden that had been nurtured by the touchstones.

Hesitation guarded Valiriana, knowing questions such as those were never as simple as she believed. "The testimonies were both intriguing and conflicting. The Errant has not earned a Sending. A man who can kill so ruthlessly in front of women and children . . ." She shook her head, hating how much her blood rose at the thought of this man benefiting from anything Faa'Cris. "It is my reasoned opinion that this king is not worthy of a Sending. Even without the murders—"

"We do not know that they are murders."

Valiriana gaped. "How can you say that? We saw it—"

"Perception is colored by opinion. Too, each country and people group has its own laws and rules regarding the taking of a life. In Jherako when a serious wrong is discovered, the facts are presented to the king. He is tasked to then mull them and make a decision. Jherakan law grants him unilateral authority to deliver not only judgment but punishment."

"But to take a life! That is severe and overmuch, do you not think?"

"Possibly," Ma'ma conceded in the way that said she knew more than she let on. "But he is a man who has come into rule of a kingdom that is in disarray. His own father and brother contributed to that corruption."

"And does it not suggest that he, too, is corrupt—by taking lives? How are we to know the facts were honestly presented?"

"Are you now judge, Valiriana?"

She drew up straight, seeing Ma'ma's point. "No, of course not." Neither could she so easily abandon her conviction. "But the people call him the Errant."

"And you have been called defiant."

She bounced a look to Ma'ma's eyes, knowing how much that truth had hurt them both. Ma'ma because, despite her great efforts to raise a Daughter in the nobility and truth of the Lady of Eleftheria, Valiriana remained . . . well, not defiant, but not far from it either. "I prefer 'spirited.'"

Ma'ma laughed as they gained the outer courtyard of their small home. "I have no doubt." They stepped down the cobbled path into the house. "In light of these things, do you not agree that commissioning a Daughter to reconnoiter the king is a good middle ground?"

Surprise leapt through her as they entered the kitchen and Ma'ma drew fruit from the basket in the cooling room. It was rare for the Revered Mother to inquire as to her thoughts on a topic, especially one as weighty as the eligibility of a king for a Sending. "I . . . um, I don't know. Part of me does wonder why would we reconnoiter in light of the information shared in the Synedrion. I mean, clearly this king is too Fallen for true consideration."

Holding a melon, Ma'ma leaned against the table and cut the fruit. "But is he?" She held a slice aloft. "Despite the arguments, despite feelings one way or another regarding this man, this *king* . . . how else would his name have risen on the Flames but that the Lady or the Ancient had provided it?"

Valiriana stilled, eyeing Ma'ma and resenting the truth of those words. "I had not thought of that." She worked to section an apple. "But he has the blood of his own people on his hands, and he is a . . . a *man*!"

With a soft chuckle, Ma'ma placed the sliced melon in a bowl. "It is easy to get caught up in emotion, to look down our noses at those we deem as less. But should we not give careful consideration when events conspire to put that person in our lives in the first place?" She shrugged as she washed and added grapes and the apple. She started for the sitting room, bobbing her head for Valiriana to follow. "I am not saying he will receive a Sending, but neither should we dismiss him so lightly or quickly. Thus, we reconnoiter to answer the questions that yet linger."

Curled into the corner of the couch, Valiriana tucked a piece of fruit in her mouth and chewed. Hated admitting Ma'ma was right. That a Licitus could earn any Faa'Cris attention. "They are so . . . infuriating."

"Who?"

"Licitus! They serve one purpose—to derail us from the Ancient's path."

"You are being absurd, Valiriana." Ma'ma's lip curled into a slow, knowing smile. "Sometimes distraction is not necessarily or wholly a bad thing."

Valiriana gaped. "You shock me, Ma'ma." She was not pleased things were so close to granting a Sending. But one thing that did please her made her smile. "Thank the Ladies it is not I the Resplendent will send." For once, she could be grateful she had failed hastati training. "I would be mortified to be so close to a brigand and murderer. I still cannot believe Relissa put her name in."

"Valiriana, you know not to speak with me about candidates."

"I was just . . . muttering." She shrugged. "Do not worry, Ma'ma. We all know a triarii who has just entered next levels does not have a prayer to be chosen."

"All are considered equally, and a Lady is sent regardless of her training, since it is the Lady Herself who grants the final approval." Ma'ma chewed a piece of melon quietly, then side-eyed her. "What if it *were* you?"

Valiriana choked on the fruit. Coughed. Eyes watered. She thumped her chest, then laughed. "Is that answer enough? It would kill me!"

Ma'ma set aside the bowl and folded her arms, narrowing her gaze. "What if the Ancient asked it of you, Valiriana? When you entered hastati training, you gave your life to the Lady to serve. Do you also get to dictate what she can or cannot do with your life?"

She slowed her chewing. Swallowed what felt like a boulder. "That is unfair."

"Fairness is not what serving the Ancient is about. It's about *His* will. He sees the future, the now, the past—they all happen simultaneously for Him. Despite being Faa'Cris, we are limited, finite." She squinted in meaning. "When you go into the training yard, do you not trust Decurion Cybele's instruction?"

"Of course I do."

"Why?"

"Because she's a decurion, one of our fiercest warriors. She knows from experience and—" Valiriana groaned. "I walked straight into that one."

Ma'ma chuckled. "So why wouldn't we trust the Ancient if He asks of us the single thing we do not want to do?"

The directness of this conversation, the way Ma'ma had pointedly pulled her away from Relissa and placed the magnifying glass squarely over Valiriana's heart . . . "Wait." She suddenly felt sick and sat forward. "Do you say the Errant *will* get a Sending?" Nothing was more mortifying. To think of any of her friends being forced to submit her enlightened form to remain with him—and then the whole producing heirs thing.

She shuddered, stomach queasy. "I think I should go. I . . . I need rest before training resumes." On her feet, she was met by her mother and held up her hand. "Please—no more profound words or truths. This has been painful enough."

With a smile, Ma'ma kissed her forehead. "I would have you learn that being Faa'Cris is not about being in control of ourselves or our lives. It is about surrender."

So much for no more profound thoughts.

"Rest well."

Valiriana found her way back to the barracks and the quad she shared with three other hastati. After ablutions and her nightly rituals, she crawled beneath the blanket. Imagine—her, being sent out to reconnoiter—or worse, for a Sending. Ridiculous!

The thought of being near enough to look into the Errant's eyes made her stomach churn. Why—why of all candidates, a Sending to *this* man? She stared at the dim light of the touchstone sneaking through the hall, throwing lines and arcs across the blanket of darkness. Just like his blade. The stroke of his dagger as it drove into the poor vizier.

She tugged the blanket up and turned onto her side. Burrowed into the warmth of her blanket and sleep. Closed her eyes. Whispered a hurried prayer for the Daughter who *did* end up with this terrible *missio*. She may not be experienced in the way of men and women and procreating, but she could not fathom allowing a man to touch her. Kiss her.

With a grunt, she tugged up the blanket more and gave herself to slumber.

Wings deployed, she spiraled through the air and landed, her boots sliding in the sand of the training pit and her arms lifting the sword in readiness for combat.

"I am proud of you."

Startled to hear her Ma'ma, Valiriana turned and frowned. What was she doing here? They did not converse during training. "Thank you, Revered Mother. But . . . for what?"

Ma'ma's gaze drifted past Valiriana, forcing her to look over her shoulder.

Wearing dark pants and undervest, broad chest gleaming beneath the light of the full sun, the Errant stood. He was large—much larger than she'd realized. Ebony hair shining and queued back, he was handsome. Save his black beard, which was gnarled and thorny.

"Just like your heart!" she yelled, once more returning to battle stance to answer all those he had killed.

"You are more beguiling than I imagined possible." He was suddenly directly before her. Reached out to touch her cheek.

Snapping her wings, Valiriana shot backward. Away from him. Yet he still somehow reached her. His fingers hot against her cheek. Singed. Seared. She screamed.

VAANVORN
FORGELIGHT, JHERAKO

"What kind of man allows children to starve and women to be abused?"

"Indeed I do not—see for yourself. They are fed now. Tended!" Pointing from The Iron, on whose stoop he stood, to the foundling home down the street, Vorn felt the ground shift but refused to tear his eyes from the incredible beauty.

Again, the ground shifted and he stumbled—straight into his own bedchamber. The embers of a fire struggled, and on the hand-knotted rug in all her ebony-haired beauty, hovered the woman, scorn radiating from piercing, judging blue eyes.

How could one who did not know him condemn him so wholly? Indignation roiled through him. "What right have you to speak to me like this?" Desperation rushed in, not wanting her to leave or find him lacking. Who was she? Why did she revile him, despise him? Speak so cruelly—and ignorantly!

"Is justice only granted to nobility or the king? Or is it for all?"

Justice? "You know not of what you speak."

"Do I not? What of the farmers bent beneath taxes that force them to choose between feed for their cattle or food for their children? Or the widow who must sell whatever she can find to afford a roof over their head?"

"Am I to solve all the ailments of the world?" He could not tell why, but he wanted the approval of this woman with seaborne eyes. What would it take to convince her that he was not the villain she believed?

Why did he care about this woman so strident in her rejection? A hazy recollection cobwebbed his thoughts and came to one conclusion—Lady.

She turned to leave.

A Lady! A real Lady, not of this realm but of Shadowsedge—and he did not mean Jherako's neighbor to the northwest! "I beg you—wait! Please, speak more. Tell me what to do to gain your favor and it will be done. I swear it!"

When she glanced back over her shoulder to him, she no longer had those achingly alluring seaborne eyes. They were, instead, shot through with violet, a color so bright and searing that it stung him deep within. "You do not deserve our Touch."

He was close to her now, tauntingly so. "What must I do to change your mind? You have but to speak it, my Lady." *A heady aroma like a floral crown and vine snaked around his mind and drew him closer. Their lips hovered within a breath of each other.* "Please . . ."

Icily, she stepped back. "Not worthy." *She strode down the dark stone passage, blending with shadows, becoming the emptiness.*

"No! Don't go!" Vorn lunged and felt the teasing edge of gauzy fabric. "Wait!" Hand reaching out, he blinked and found himself abed, the coverlet tangled around his legs. Desperation dried his tongue and mottled his brow with sweat. "Wait . . ." Shadows lingered where he had last seen her.

No, it couldn't have been just a dream. It felt so real. *She* felt real.

He glanced from the door—shut tight—to the hunt tapestry concealing the servant's passage.

It fluttered.

His heart raced. Vorn vaulted off the bed and whipped back the heavy covering. The small, arched wooden door behind it was closed. He threw it open and stared into the dark. Jerking around, he searched his bedchamber, breathless. "Where are you?" he called into the still darkness, frantic for it to have been real this time. To prove he was not losing his mind.

He returned to the bed and dropped back against the feather mattress. "Augh!" Pounded his fists on it.

Steps carried heavily across the solar, delivering Azyant and his drawn sword to the bedchamber door. His gaze swept the room and landed on Vorn. "You are well, my king?"

Jabbing his hands through tangled hair, Vorn grunted and stalked to the side table. Gulped a goblet of water. "A dream . . ." But was it? Was *she*? There seemed little differentiation between waking and sleeping. He looked at his fingers, rubbed the tips together. Raging seas, he did not want her to be a dream. Not again. "She stood there on the rug, the answer to all my prayers and dreams . . ." His gaze drifted there, and he recalled those piercing eyes. Her imperious "Not worthy" whispered against his mouth. Torment!

"Who?" Tarac asked as he entered, followed closely by Lathain and Ba'moori. The sergius no doubt had roused them in case of a legitimate threat.

Vorn blinked, swallowed. "Nothing. A dream."

"Aye, you've never mentioned a dream before . . ."

Feeling the fool, he poured himself another glass. "Every night since my coronation I have seen her. In my dreams, her eyes are . . . haunting, searing violet." Vorn pinched his lips. "Burning with condemnation." He slumped into a chair and huffed, motioning to the foot of his bed. "She stands right there. Sneering. Judging."

Tarac silently bent forward in his seat, elbows on his knees.

"'You do not deserve our Touch.'" Still he felt plagued by her chilled, calloused words. "Every time, she always throws those same six words at me." Misery tugged at his conscience, wondering what purpose the dreams had. "This time, she added 'not worthy' to her condemnation. For good measure, I suppose."

"It is said the Faa'Cris have violet eyes," Tarac said calmly, then lifted his gaze to him. "Do you think . . . Could the woman in your dream be a *Lady*?"

Vorn sniffed. "With the judgment she poured out, no doubt." He smoothed his hair back and tied it. "But why? If she truly is a Lady, why come just to tell me I do not deserve them? To condemn me?" His conscience squirmed, hearing again all the barbs lobbed against him by his father and brother over the years. "I am doing my best to save this realm."

Only then did he sense his First's gaze. "What?"

"You saw the eyes in the market . . . now in your dream."

"Not the same eyes, but"—he cocked his head—"the woman in my dream was a siren, magnificent and condemning. Telling me to right the wrongs."

Tarac peered at him, hesitating.

"*What?*" Vorn demanded.

"Apparently," he said, as if he did not want to voice what came next, "Lathain spoke to the augur a few days past."

The rowdy captain raised his hands. "Oy, nobody said I couldn't."

"Then," Tarac continued, "last eve, the crone was at the gate, demanding an audience with you. She insisted you hear her out. Let her help"—gray eyes found his—"find the Lady for you."

Something in him recoiled. "No."

"I told her as much," Tarac admitted, relief in his exhale. "Sent her packing."

"Which is a mistake," Lathain grunted. "Think about it, sire," he pleaded, going to a knee in front of him. "Last eve, she was here because she knew you were having dreams."

Vorn shoved to his feet. "You had no business consulting with that creature!" He trudged to the balcony doors and flung them open. Salty air rushed in, brushing back his hair. "I reinstated the iereas and the foundling endowment. I work, day in and day out, to do right, to cleanse this kingdom of my father's ambivalence and my brother's debauchery."

"Talk to her," Lathain said. "She can guide you—"

"Having an augur counsel me defiles everything I have worked to set right," Vorn growled, looking to Tarac. As if he needed affirmation that this path was poorly set. "It is wrong!"

"What if this is more than a dream?" Azyant suggested.

"Aye, the augur said—"

"Enough!" Tarac snapped.

There. His Sword had spoken. Definitively answered the question begging Vorn's attention. "Wait." Stomach churning, he had a thought as he returned to the solar and stood before his Four. Eyed Azyant. "What do you mean, more than a dream?"

Excited, Azyant stalked toward him, hands held before him as if he carried something valuable. "What if this siren from your dreams *is* a Lady, and she's visiting you, speaking to you even now?"

"Then already I am doomed because she scorned me." His pulse sped, and he resisted the urge to search his chambers for her again. But he had to admit that thought sprouted hope. "Is that even possible?"

Lathain gave a cockeyed nod. "The augur suggested it is."

So, the one with seaborne eyes could be real? His heart thudded at the thought, the possibility. Even in her scorn, she was bewitching. He would have moved Ironesse Island had she asked.

Groaning, Vorn turned to the ocean, his thoughts laden with her. The whisper of a touch against her cheek, her gauzy gown . . . "She's painfully beautiful, even her voice. The memory of her has haunted me since waking. I feel her in here." He thumped his chest. "The purity of her . . ." He shook his head, feeling dirty, unworthy, just as she had judged. "Already I want to avoid tonight's sleep because I do not want to hear that siren condemning me yet again." He growled. "And yet I long for it, too. What grievance has she against me that I am already rejected? And if it is legitimate, how do I remedy it?"

Lathain inclined his head. "The augur said she would wait at The Iron for you. Let us go—"

"No," Tarac argued, his objection strident. He moved to Vorn and tucked his chin. "Sire, you asked me to guide you in the way of the *Muqqadas Ritsar*, and this goes against everything we adhere to. Open our doors to the crone and we are open to—"

"At least hear her out, sire." Lathain shrugged. "That is all I ask."

Vorn hesitated. Temptation rose to the fore, recalling how close they'd been, the thought of a kiss lingering before she darted away. *Hone honesty. Develop discipline. Seize sacrifice.*

"If she is right," Lathain said, "then she can guide us in finding this Lady and bringing her to you, to Jherako. What could be wrong about that? You will have your queen and heirs. Powerful men of renown."

He made sense. Vorn needed—wanted—heirs. And a virtuous queen who would not choose another man over him. A Lady would stay true to the integrity that guided his own steps, yes?

"Vorn—please reconsider," Tarac warned quietly, urgently. "Desperation should not drive our actions. Augurs do not assist without their price. And that price no man can afford to pay. She seeks your very adunatos for darkness. The dreams alone should tell you—"

"Forget you whom you address, Captain?"

Tarac stiffened. Lowered his gaze.

Frustration thudded in Vorn's chest. He had no idea why Tarac aroused his anger, other than that desperation drowned reasoned thought, the very reason that Tarac supplied.

But he did not need reason. He needed heirs. Though doubt lingered about consulting the crone—the very antithesis of the Lady—Vorn could not release the thought of having the dream woman so close. Knowing he would have someone as dedicated to honor and the realm—even if there was no love between them—was a temptation too great to ignore. And yet, the thought of bringing the augur into his house, this house . . . "Let's go to her."

It was not so simple, of course. Duties filled the morning hours, but by noontime, he was entering The Iron. Even as he moved toward his room at the rear, he felt something different, something strange in the air. He scanned the patrons and landed on one in particular.

Steady eyes held his. Strange attire—unduly clean and crisp—kept the stranger stiff, and his hair was cut in a peculiar fashion, close on the sides and longer atop. He gave Vorn a solemn nod.

Tarac and the others shouldered in, not used to him slowing in his progress to the back room. "You know him?"

"No," Vorn muttered, continuing course. "Never seen him before." Unsettled, he refocused on his mission and sat at his table. "Is the crone here?"

"No," Azyant said. "Lathain is searching for her."

Searching the streets . . . drawing attention. Coming to The Iron as a prince not intended for the throne was one thing. Coming as king . . . not so smart. And for *this* reason? Had he lost his faculties? What was he doing, leaving the safety of the castle when—

The newcomer loomed in the doorway, snagging Vorn's gaze.

"Private party," Ba'moori barked, using his tall, broad frame to block the stranger. "Move along."

The man did not. "A word . . . King Vaanvorn?"

Amused the man would dare intrude on his time, Vorn indicated to a seat across from him. "If you dare." As the man joined him, the air swirled and brought in an odd smell that told Vorn one thing. "You are not from here."

The blond smirked. "Not hardly."

His accent—Vorn hadn't heard one like it before. "Where then?"

"Doesn't matter right now." The man hunched his shoulders, and only then did Vorn realize he was pulling something from his vest pocket.

In a heartbeat, Vorn snatched up his dagger and held it along the edge of his outer wrist, ready to fight. "Do not make me regret—"

"Easy, friend." One hand up in mock surrender, the man slid a metal black box across the table. "I'm not here to harm you."

Maintaining his grip on the dagger, Vorn eyed the box. "What is it?" He used his free hand to lift it. Made of a strange material, it was hard but did not seem as sturdy as steel. "What material is this? How does it open?"

"Plastic, and it doesn't." The man sniffed. "Voids, it amazes me what I have to explain to downworlders."

"Downworlders?" Vorn narrowed his eyes, recalling that term from his father's talk of the Accord. "Where are you from?"

Another smirk. "Not anywhere around here."

"Mayhap you are used to speaking to other . . . downworlders"—the word was odd on Vorn's tongue—"but clearly you have not presented yourself to a king before. Intrusions are not looked upon kindly, especially not rude ones shrouded in mystery."

"Point taken." The man shifted closer, lowered his head and voice. "Surely you are educated enough to have heard of the planet Cenon. My planet. It's—" His gaze struck Vorn's and then he waved a hand. "Never mind. I'm here because I've heard your coronation speech about progress."

How had he heard the speech if he wasn't even from this planet? Vorn had known, of course, if somewhat vaguely, that some men must come from elsewhere, or the Accord would not exist. But how could he verify this man numbered among those? "We have an Accord with—"

"Outdated." The man shrugged. "And considering Symmachia already interferes with business on this planet, including right here in Jherako, ineffective."

Vorn scowled. "How—"

"And I can almost guarantee that interference is more pervasive than you might want to believe. Therefore"—he winked and took in a breath, then exhaled—"I have a proposition that might help."

Nonplussed, Vorn considered him. "Your name?"

"Revalor." He pointed to the box. "Watch that, and I'll be in touch."

"What?" Vorn looked at the item. "Are you concerned someone may abscond with it?"

Revalor snorted. "No. Voids." He reached across the table and touched the box no bigger than Vorn's palm.

Tarac had his sword at the man's throat even as Revalor depressed the center.

A blue ghoul comprised of light danced over the surface, sound crackling.

"Easy, friend," Revalor said, gently guiding aside the blade, his gaze striking Vorn's again. "This is what we call a vidscreen. Press here to start and stop it." He glanced into the main area of The Iron. "But maybe wait till you're home." He shrugged. "Less attention. It acts as a communications device as well. I can reach you and vice versa through it."

Vorn swiped the slim box from the table, studied it then the man who stood to leave. "How long did you wait for me to come?"

A shoulder lifted in a shrug. "Couple days." With a nod, he turned—putting his back to Vorn—and walked out.

"I do not like him," Tarac muttered.

"I am of the same mind, yet . . ." Vorn considered the device. "Maybe progress designed on another planet may succeed here." He eyed the space the man had vacated. "He may be what we need."

Lathain reappeared. "There is no sight of the crone."

Just as well. After this encounter, he was even less sure it was wise to seek out the augur's words. "I need to return to the house." Watch the device. See what was on there, what message the man from another planet thought could help them.

Awful, terrible man. He had invaded her waking and sleeping with his forbidding bearing and gruff words. His audacity in touching her, speaking to her as if she must obey. Days and she still could not shake the tangibility of the dreams, especially the most recent one.

Shuddering, Valiriana scooted the baked roots across her plate, reveling in how she'd angered him, scorned him to his face. Face . . . She felt a strange tingling in her cheek, the same place he had touched. When his fingers made contact, she'd felt a zap in her belly. But then she'd rebuffed him. It had been glorious!

Granted, it had all been but a dream, but the satisfaction was thick. One day, mayhap, she could say it to his face.

"What are you smiling about?"

Valiriana straightened and met Relissa's gaze across the table. "Nothing." She dropped her fork on the plate and pushed it aside, grateful for the distraction. "Are you ready for triarii Induction?" Jealousy needled in, wishing she would be in that ceremony, too.

"More than." Relissa seemed morose as she took a bite of bread and cheese. Sad green eyes met hers. "Have you heard the latest on King Vaanvorn?"

If her friend was so affected, this must be good news for Valiriana. "What?"

"Apparently, he is doing experiments on the children in the orphanage. A pharmakeia coming and going at strange hours. Bodies being removed to a pauper's grave late at night."

"No," Valiriana said in disbelief. "But at the debate, it was said he had *helped* the foundlings!"

"Of course he did," Relissa insisted, her expression devout. "He is a *good* king. These are just poorly drawn conclusions based on assumption and prejudice."

"You always see the best in others." Regardless, Valiriana felt vindicated in her judgment against him in the dream. "Such a man should never have been considered for our Touch!" As she had told him. "This—*this* is what the

Resplendent need in order to understand that no *missio* or Sending is needed!"

"The Resplendent are divided in their opinions. Some are moving to cancel his name from the records."

For some reason, shock rocked Valiriana. It was a strident thing to strike a name from the Parchments, a blistering and permanent judgment. No heirs from his line would ever be allowed consideration.

Something niggled, but she shoved it aside. "Good. He deserves as much." So . . . why did that feel like a mistake? No man deserved it more than he.

Relissa considered her. "You don't sound convinced."

"Of course I—"

"Lady Valiriana?"

Irritation scraped her wing ridge as she dragged her gaze to the left, where a Licitus waited. Men. Always intruding. *Be gracious*, she chided herself. Did children not need instruction? "How may I assist?"

With a shaky hand, he slid a card across the table. "From Resplendent Kaliondre."

Valiriana stared at the missive. Picked it up, wondering at the obscure delivery method. "Thank you." What had she done now?

Once the Licitus turned to leave, Relissa leaned in. "What did you do?"

That her friend echoed her self-condemnation, Valiriana did not like. She waited until the Licitus was far from earshot and then opened the note.

"What is it?" Relissa scooted closer.

"She says . . ." Scanning the words, she stilled, then gasped. Sat straighter. "I'm to be promoted to triarii." Bulging her eyes, she looked at her friend. "I can't believe it. Why would they do that? I was failed because of the Licitus. No one advances after failing the trials!"

"Will you question it?"

It would be the right thing to do. "No," Valiriana decided. "I would rather not give them a chance to say they had made a mistake." Then she wilted. Groaned. "Oh, I must, mustn't I? If it is a mistake . . ."

"Aye, you should." Relissa caught her hand. "Come on. I'll go with you and will pray the whole way over that it's not wrong."

They hurried across the cobbled streets to the Academia and made quick work of reaching the main offices, only to nearly collide with Kaliondre coming down the stairs.

"Resplendent Kaliondre," Valiriana said, donning as much deference as possible. "May I have a word, please?"

The Resplendent stopped and scowled. "Should you two not be going through petitions and preparation before the Induction?"

Valiriana faltered, acutely aware of Relissa grasping her hands tightly with a sharp intake of breath. "Then . . . it's true? Real? Right?" She sounded like an idiot. "This missive—I am truly advancing to triarii levels?"

A smile slid into the Resplendent's face. "Would I have sent it otherwise?"

"I just thought— No." She would not argue. "But . . . why?"

"Are you saying the decision is wrong?"

"I failed trials."

Kaliondre gave her a long look. "Sometimes, things happen that are beyond our making, beyond our control. We must accept them and continue on."

"Oh." That did not explain much, but she had given the Resplendent a chance to correct the mistake. She would not press her to change her mind. "Thank you." She ducked her head and backed away. "Thank you, Resplendent Kaliondre." Catching Relissa's hands, she bolted back down and outside.

Relissa gaped. "What did that mean?"

"No idea. But . . . I'm in!" For a moment, she forgot she was Faa'Cris and did something entirely human—squealed and jumped on her toes. Hugged her friend.

"Okay, okay. Induction is in just a couple of hours. There is much to prepare and many things to do. You have the instructions?"

Valiriana nodded.

After another hug and squeal, Relissa kissed her cheek. "See you there. Don't forget to thank the Lady during your petitions!"

Mm, yes. Petitions—maybe she would petition the Lady or the Ancient to remedy the problem of the Errant, so the Faa'Cris could return their attention and energy to all things *parabellum*. Even as she hurried to her quad and went through ablutions, she wondered how and why this had come to be. It did not make sense, and the Resplendent rarely—she actually knew of no instance— reversed decisions on training.

So what was going on? What if . . . what if this decision to allow her to graduate with her class, be promoted to triarii, was a sign that her strident views regarding the Errant, regarding the Sending, were correct? That the Resplendent agreed with her stance.

Her heart skipped a beat.

That had to be it. Why else would they reconsider?

So. The Errant was *not* worthy of their attention or efforts. Feeling smug—

she would ask forgiveness later—she prepared for the Induction.

Later that evening, triarii lined up in the lavacrum that had a dozen sanitatem bays flanking a central aisle set off with arches and marble pillars. Each new triarii stood before a sanitatem, dressed in a ceremonial gown, which was really only a more embroidered version of a nightgown. Barefoot on the marble floor, Valiriana smiled at Relissa, who was positioned directly across from her, both ready to lay their lives in the Ancient's hands.

Decurion Cybele clapped hard. "Stand straight," she demanded. "Earn the place you have been gifted. All of you!"

The Resplendent glided into the room.

"Congratulations," the Revered Mother said, her voice carrying easily in the marble lavacrum. "You have worked hard and are now ready to enter your next level of training. To advance another step toward becoming a full praelia—warrior, Blade of Vaqar and the Ancient. The cost is high, the commitment required higher." She scanned the line of triarii as she spoke. "The transformation is not easy or pain-free." Her gaze landed on Valiriana and anger flashed. "In fact, it will be excruciating."

Excruciating because at this point in the development of a Faa'Cris, the clypeus—the ridge that mirrored their spine—would be fully freed. Their adult wings would be released from the membrane that held them safe and protected young Faa'Cris who had not been trained in how to deploy and control their full double span without ripping apart their backs. Pain would usher in a much more powerful span and abilities.

"You may think you have won a victory."

Why was she still staring at Valiriana? Did she condemn her for advancing when she had failed the trials? This had not been her doing, but Kaliondre's.

"But this is the first of many sacrifices. Of yourselves, your wills, your lives." The Revered Mother nodded. "Step into the bath and repeat after me."

Heart racing, Valiriana moved to obey, noting the handspan-deep, gelatinous liquid that already filled the bath. "To the Ancient," she repeated with the triarii, their voices echoing in the lavacrum, "I commit my life. I step from this moment of training and into the next." The djell was cold as it cocooned her legs to her calves. "I set aside old ways."

She let the thin sheath that covered her fall away as instructed and lay in the sanitatem, her heart pulsing a little fast, excitement and dread urging it equally.

The Revered Mother stood at the elevated control bay, clearly displeased.

Had she no voice in allowing Valiriana to advance? But she was the Revered Mother—nobody superseded her authority. So . . . what was going on?

Confusion choked her as she lay in the sanitatem, gooseflesh rising on her arms and shoulders. "I lay down my will and life," she whispered, eyes still on Ma'ma as she eased back, "to be used by You, Ancient."

The thick substance clogged her ears even as the lids thrummed into place, vibrating the djell like a gentle massage. She tried not to think of it as a tomb but as a more complicated bath. It ensconced their bodies, save the face. The gel-like fluid would repair her human body and enhance her enlightened form—her full wingspan would be freed and firmed, her armor imbued with a special alloy to protect her in battle. The anticipation of the coming pain made her breathe a little heavier.

"It is important," Resplendent Miatrenette intoned, "that you relax. You spoke words of surrender, now you must enact those words. Elevated heart rates will make the process more excruciating."

Relax, relax, relax, Valiriana warned herself even as Ma'ma appeared next to her bath, extending a hand of blessing as she whispered words in the ancient Faa'Cris language.

"Settle your thoughts, Daughter," came a firm voice in her head.

Immediately, Valiriana experienced a sudden realization of peace and belonging. She breathed out the tension and held Ma'ma's gaze. *"Did you grant my promotion?"* she asked via the *vox saeculorum.* *"I did not earn it."*

"You did not," Ma'ma pronounced. *"Think not that this is an honor but a duty."*

A duty? What did that mean? Sure, it was the duty of each Faa'Cris to advance. That process alone honored the gift the Ancient had given them, but this, Ma'ma's words, sounded like more. *"I do not understand."* Drowsiness soaked into her bones, compliments of the bath. *"Why would you—"*

"The Lady Eleftheria was the first to surrender her life to the Ancient, to serve Vaqar, whom she later embraced as her *compleo.* As Ladies of Basilikas—Faa'Cris—we strive to be as Eleftheria, not seeking our own desires but striving to serve. Repeat: Her will is my will. My will is to serve."

"Her will is my will . . . serve . . ." Heaviness weighted Valiriana as the sanitatem lowered her head and shoulders. She tensed but remembered the key—surrender. Let it lower. Felt the thick water slide up her neck, lap at her ears . . . then her cheeks . . . over her face . . .

But three wills superseded the Revered Mother's—those of Eleftheria, Vaqar, and the Ancient.

Even as the startling thought came to her, Valiriana felt a force exerted on her body. Shocked, scared, she tried to breathe. Tried to move. But her limbs would not cooperate, her legs would not move. Frozen—her entire being was frozen stiff. The force pulled her backward.

She shot a look to the Revered Mother, whose gaze widened in surprise.

Yanked into blackness, Valiriana entered a shrouded sleep.

There in that billowy slumber waited a solitary figure with a warm, tender fragrance that washed away fear and doubt. Whispers of courage and strength ribboned through Valiriana. She pulled in a breath and was drawn deeper, following a pinprick of light that slowly grew . . . brighter . . . brighter.

She blinked and found herself staring at a gorgeous blue-green ocean. The sight stole her breath—and she heard her own gasp. Wait, how could she hear that? It was not echoey like being submerged as she was a moment past. So, was she aboveground? How? Turning to take in her surroundings, she gaped. Towering over her, a massive stone structure loomed like a specter, the black sheets hanging from it making the specter seem to float and move. "What are those?"

"Banners of mourning."

She glanced over her shoulder and startled. Sucked in a hard breath. "Magna Domine!" Eleftheria Herself! The realization sent Valiriana to her knees. "Gracious Lady—"

"No, no. On your feet, Daughter." Her voice was clear, delicate, and yet filled with authority.

Still in shock, Valiriana somehow struggled upright. Dared not look into that wondrous face. "I—I am honored. But I . . . what am I doing here? I do not understand."

"Sometimes, that is best. We learn the most when we are open and curious."

Curious?

"What do you see?"

Forcing herself to lift her gaze, she realized Magna Domine—whose profile was lovely and perfect—was not looking at her now. Her gaze rested on the shore, water leisurely lapping at the sand. And there stood a man.

"A Licitus," Valiriana spat.

"Look deeper, better." Disappointment saturated the Lady's words.

She felt the remonstration acutely. Grieved that she had already let down the Magna Domine, she did as instructed and with all her heart, looked at the . . . man.

Holding something, he stood by the water's edge with stooped shoulders and a downcast head. From him emanated a deep, bitter scent—grief.

"He is sad." She craned her neck to see better—and suddenly found herself within reach of him. She started. Stepped back, the rocks and sand crunching as she scrabbled away.

Scowling in her direction, he came around.

Something lodged in her throat when she saw his face. *"No."* It was—

"Are you ready, Valiriana?" Magna Domine asked.

Ready? Ready for what? Her heart stammered. There could be only one purpose that she was here. *"No . . . No, I don't think so."* Oh Mercies—this explained so much. Why she had been promoted. Why Mama seemed so upset—and in the seconds before she had transferred, shocked. Had she seen the Lady Herself in that instant?

"Say you that I chose poorly?"

"No!" A pause. *"You chose* me?"

Eleftheria smiled. *"Good."* In a blink, they stood in the middle of a square with a dancing fountain. "Your work begins here, Daughter."

"My work?"

The Magna Domine touched Valiriana's shoulder.

Something warm erupted in her chest. Fire rushed across her clypeus and firmed in her spine, forcing her to draw in a breath.

Smiling, Eleftheria faded from view. *"Fac fortia et patere, Daughter."*

VAANVORN
FORGELIGHT, JHERAKO

A heat not born of the sun radiated on the shore where he stood. Vorn felt that buzz along his nape again and, sensing an intrusion, carefully scanned the area. An attack. Or . . . something. Behind him, he'd heard the sand grate beneath a step, yet when he turned, he stood alone save Tarac and Lathain waiting a good ten meters distant. It was not their movement he had heard so close. Then what? Who?

Though neither inquired if all was well, his men readied themselves to face a threat, hands going to pommels, stances firming. But that's when he noticed Tarac was not as calm as he'd appeared. Recalling that he'd dispatched his man earlier to see that food and stores were delivered to the foundling home, he singled him out. "How were the foundlings?"

They climbed the hill in quiet for a moment.

"Most are well, but there was indeed an outbreak of the blue fever," Tarac said quietly. "A few are still quarantined, and a couple succumbed, so they were buried under the cover of night to expose as few as possible. The pharmakeia believes he arrived in time to stave off more fatalities."

Swiping a hand over his mouth, Vorn nodded. So, his brother, in ending the endowment, had put children in the grave. And to think, if not for Haarzen Gi, Vorn might not have learned of the desperate situation for the home. He spotted the new vizier waiting just outside the house. "What's he want?"

"The goodwill ride to the festival."

"Waves," Vorn growled. "It was so much easier when I could go to The Iron and laugh away the hours."

"Easier, but not healthier," Tarac said.

"Granted." He shook his head and strode toward Gi. "Vizier. Ready to ride?"

Mounted up with his Furymark and the vizier, Vorn made his way to the park just north of the docks, which hosted the annual harvest celebration.

"Have you watched the box?"

"No."

"Will you watch it, considering what technology on the planet means?" Tarac asked.

Vorn nodded. "I have asked myself that as much as I've thought of the Lady."

His Sword gave him a long look.

"Do not cast judgment."

"But the Accord . . ."

"Aye," Vorn grumbled. "I feel as if possessing that thing is as treasonous as Belarik's actions. Yet, I wonder . . . what if the Accord *is* outdated? What if Revalor's words are true?"

"You believe what he said about Symmachia and the Accord?"

"Believe—not yet. But I would be a fool not to weigh his words carefully."

Cheering silenced their private aside as they rode down the street, people converging from the field where they had been enjoying games and sweets. Children waved flags and shouted his name.

"At least, they are not shouting 'Errant' as they once did."

Not exactly the expected reception, but he was glad for it. The Furymark formed up on him, blocking the people from reaching him. Vorn guided his destrier to a clearing and dismounted. The kingsguard and Tarac were with him in an instant.

"Long live the king!" a man shouted, the phrase quickly becoming a chant echoing around the field.

Striding toward him, Vorn extended his hand. "Thank you."

A boy of five or six escaped his mother's hold and rushed him.

The Furymark, ardent in their conviction to protect him, started to intercept, but shrewd Tarac indicated for them to let the boy pass. Vorn met the child with a grin. "Hello, brave knight. What is your name?"

"I'm not a knight," the boy argued. "We are farmers. Not fighters."

Vorn laughed. "Ah, but see? That is just another kind of knight—you fight the pestilence, the drought, to yield good crops. We have great need for those who plow the fields and harvest."

A young girl offered him a fake crown. "You need this."

"Wise you are, my lady." He took it but then set it on her head. "For your generosity in protecting your king, I dub you Princess for the Day."

Face bright, she gasped and rushed back to her papa, who apparently was in charge of a sweets stand.

Amazed at the reception here, that he was not decried or set upon, Vorn wandered the various stands, shaking hands, talking with the people who wanted his help with more donations for the poor, fixing the streets, cleaning up the docks . . .

"King Vaanvorn," a woman said, her manners kind but jittery.

So much so that Vorn felt his Four form up.

She drew a young girl no more than fifteen toward him. "This is my Celie."

Oh no.

"Majesty," Tarac called, his voice authoritative but not rude. "You are needed over here, Sire."

Thank the seas. "My apologies, ladies. If you would excuse me." Vorn gave the woman and her daughter a smile and pivoted in the direction of his Sword. "If I get offered one more daughter as wife—"

"Ah, sire!" Vizier Gi rejoined him.

Sunlight stabbed through the trees lining the little park.

"It will take time for the country to trust you. They have, after all, had two lackluster rulers before you." The vizier took a leisurely pace across the lawn toward the side streets. "However, people appreciate the change, even if it is first met with reluctance. Your changes have the nobles unsettled, looking over their shoulders."

"Not a bad thing, that."

When they came to an area partially blocked by a spilled cart, Vorn turned aside, but Gi grasped his arm. "Sire, it is but a bit of debris. Let us continue." He picked his way through the detritus, only pausing a moment when he stepped in a puddle of what looked like pudding. Vorn reluctantly followed and noted with annoyance that two councilmen joined them just beyond the mess. But at least these would not offer a family member for Vorn to marry. He hoped.

"But once we get the trade routes altered to encourage more traffic, more revenue, they will be glad. Shadar, Waterflame, and Saigo will not agree," the vizier warned. "Your father was no friend to our neighbors."

"We must convince them otherwise." And yet Vorn wondered if merely altering trade routes would be enough to pull this realm from the brink. They needed a bigger venture, something daring to spur the economy. Something to bring not only wealth but power, redevelop Jherako into a force to be reckoned with.

Vorn caught sight of something ahead—shadows where there should be none. Shifting. Angling. "Hold," Vorn muttered.

Apparently having seen the same, Tarac edged into his path, blocking him, protecting as he lifted a hand in warning to the Furymark.

An arrow whistled toward Vorn. He ducked, the missile carving a line across his baldric before it *thunked* into Azyant, knocking him backward. Angry, Vorn sighted the man fleeing. Threw himself onto a horse nearby and barreled down on the attacker.

The wily brigand tossed aside his bow and darted between two tents. Vorn pursued.

"I'll come up the other side," Tarac shouted, breaking off.

Vorn kept the man in his sight as they raced through the celebration, children and women darting out of the way. He spied Tarac eliminating the brigand's options. The man hesitated, skidding to a stop near some carts.

Closing the gap, Vorn leaned to the side and threw himself off the mount into the man's back. They sprawled into the grass. Rolled, Vorn's shoulder slamming into the cart's wheel. But he seized the man. Pinned him.

Screaming, the man twisted, trying to free himself.

Vorn held him fast, yanked him onto his back, avoided the punch the brigand threw. Missed the next, which connected with his jaw. With a roar, he reared and slammed his fist into the man's face. Grabbed the man's head and shoulder and twisted in opposite directions.

The brigand collapsed in a heap as a communal gasp hauled Vorn around. Another man rushed in with a weapon. Vorn met him, caught his hand. Drove it down, expertly forcing the blade into the man's own stomach, deep and up. When the man finally groaned and slid to the ground, holding his abdomen, Vorn straightened. Found dozens watching, mothers pulling their children away from the ghastly sight.

Breathing hard, Vorn stood, eyeing the Furymark who raced toward them, keeping at bay a circle of onlookers who seemed to think the attack a demonstration of Vorn's power. Which . . . he supposed it was.

"My king!" The vizier pushed through and scanned him. "You are well?"

Vorn gave a sharp nod as he scanned the brigands for marks that might identify who they worked with. Who wanted Vorn dead this much. But he found nothing. He eyed Tarac, who ordered the Furymark to cover the bodies. "Azyant?"

"En route to the pharmakeia," Tarac said, breaths heaving from giving pursuit. "Clean hit through the shoulder."

Vorn rotated his own shoulder, feeling the ache from the collision with the wheel.

"Mayhap it is time to return to the house. Have the pharmakeia look at—"

"No. I—"

A presence swooped up from behind.

Pivoting, Vorn caught the interloper by the throat and registered the face. The one with more visible veins than the secret underground tunnels. "Augh!" He shook her off, his adrenaline still high after being attacked. "What do you here?"

The augur seemed to grow in stature, eyes flaring to violet and years falling away as if she were no mere human. "She is here!" she shrilled, wagging a hand at him. "I told you she would come."

A jolt rang through him. His gut burned, and instantly he recalled the feeling at the shore of being intruded upon. Of being seen yet finding no one watching. "Where?" He turned, searching the crowd.

"Here. Even now, I sense her." Her eyes darkened once more. "You did not take seriously my words before—just as you shook me off, so you did with my warning. Now she is here, and you are ill-prepared for what this Lady brings."

Heart thudding, Vorn probed the faces huddled around him. Ignored yet another woman pushing her daughter forward, begging him to take her.

"I will lead you, my king. Listen to me, swear to hear my counsel and—"

"Where?" he demanded. "Where is she?"

"Trust me, and I will lead—"

"No!" Tarac's bark echoed on the street as he surged forward. "We should go, sire." He glowered at the augur as he shouldered in between them. "There are too many. The crone does not know what she speaks. Please, sire."

Vorn frowned, hearing the tension in Tarac's voice. Feeling it in the air even as he checked face after face, not sure what he was looking for or even where to look. He imagined she would be glorious, outshining the rest. Surely. But mottled browns and grays clogged his line of sight. Why did he feel so desperate and ready to believe the crone over his oldest and truest friend? More credence should be given to his Sword, who had long adhered to the guiding words of the Creed. Lived a life that left Vorn in awe. Would it not soil his name to be connected to her, to believe her, trust her?

"Hear me, king," the crone insisted, her voice raspy and resonant, "you will not find her without me. Your whole kingdom will fall if you do not trust my wisdom. Have I not already shown true?"

Tarac shifted closer to Vorn, and in that single move, betrayed his own nerves that his king might listen to another. "Sire. Vorn."

Go with his Sword and he went back to the castle emptyhanded. Listen to the crone . . . And what? Miraculously bound to a Lady? He sniffed and nodded to his friend. "Let's go."

When a Furymark guided his Black to him, he gripped the reins of his destrier, hiked his boot into the stirrup, and gripped the pommel. With one last glance over his shoulder to the crowds, his gaze collided with those fair violet eyes—pure and steady—that delivered in the waking world the same judgment he'd experienced in the sleeping, remonstration and reproof. Scorn. *You.*

08

VALIRIANA
FORGELIGHT, JHERAKO

They had given him the wrong name. This man was not just the Errant, but also the Vicious. The Murderer. His heart was as black as his horse. He deserved no favor from Vaqar or anyone!

Recoiling as he snapped the neck of the first man and drove a dagger into the second, she stared in horrified shock as he straightened, her gaze transfixed on the blood spilling over the blade and his hand.

Cries chilled the air, the grief of the people whispered and frozen like dew on a petal, acrid as revulsion should be when so heinous an act is perpetrated.

Unable to move, she stared in disbelief. She had been sent to investigate this king, learn if his name had been duly earned. So much for fearing she would come and discover her presuppositions had been wrong, that the Errant was a good man. Ha! Once again, she was proved correct by Licitus. And yet both her attitude and the depravity of men grieved her. This was not as the Ancient had wanted it. A man who so easily shed the blood of another could have nothing to do with justice and truth, the hallmarks of the Ancient.

Guards rushed in, pulling the Errant from the man he had stabbed. He stood for a moment, then spun and grabbed a woman by the neck.

A shudder traced her spine. Did his violence know no bounds? Appalled, she grieved for the people who had died at his hand, their bodies already being removed from the street by local authorities. Grateful for the hood that shielded her from view, she watched him exchange words with the woman he had accosted, whose back was now to her. Watched as even his man, the one reputed to be so honorable, turned harsh eyes on the poor old woman. Something about the exchange sickened her, clouded her adunatos with a miasma of disgust.

"*His heart is as black as is the Void,*" she said to the Revered Mother, already anticipating her trip back.

"*Only the Ancient knows the heart.*" Ma'ma's reply sailed across the distance.

"If you could but see what he did—"

"Give care and trust not what you see."

Trust not what she saw? Ludicrous! How else was she to assess him?

Dark brow rippling, the king angled to the side, his broad bared chest and bloodied arm glaring evidence of his savagery. How could a man be so vicious and yet have a face like that? *"I hope the Ancient disciplines you for your dissolute ways!"*

The man wore pants and boots, but on his chest nothing more than a long, belted vest made of hide. Seeing this display in person was markedly different than in the coliseum. Surely if the Daughters saw how his eyes—

Eyes! Jarringly, she realized he was looking in her direction. Afraid she might give herself away, Valiriana dared not stir.

"You!"

Me? Surely he did not mean her—she was hidden, her face concealed. And yet, the scent assailing the air spoke of deep admiration, attraction, and anticipation. Mercies—he *did* see her. Move! Yet she found her legs as anchors, her heart climbing into her throat at the realization she could not budge.

"There." He pointed straight at her. "Bring her!"

She sucked in a hard breath, unable to look away. Unable to think. She had thought her visage would be concealed as she chose. So she'd been taught. Regardless . . . *Move! Go, now!*

"Sire, who?" The man to his right started forward, glancing back to his king.

"The gray-hooded woman by the baker's shop. Bring her to me!"

Valiriana backed away. Spun around, her mind racing. What had she done wrong? It did not matter. She must get out of here. Focusing as she aimed toward a dark alley, she folded, transferring herself from here to . . .

She stumbled.

I'm still here. Why am I still here?

She closed her eyes, hearing acutely trained on the thudding of boots racing in her direction. Once more she attempted to fold.

Nothing.

Panic lit through her. *"I can't fold,"* she cried out to the Revered Mother. *"Help me!"*

Silence met her distress.

The Lady Eleftheria said her *missio* started here. Obviously to find out about this king. Not get captured. Terrified, she hunkered into her hood, only then recalling the way he'd shouted her description. Wondered if she could switch cloaks. She rounded a corner and scrambled down the street.

"It's you," a gravelly voice said as a man blocked her path. "You are the one the king wants."

"N-no," she stammered, stricken when his hand coiled around her wrist. "You are mistaken." Wh-why had the Ancient not protected her? He should not be able to accost her. What was this? What was wrong?

For such a small man, he had a ferocious grip. Held her. "Furymark, I have the girl."

"No!" She pulled against the man. "Release me!" Glancing over her shoulder, she spied the black-and-gold uniforms flooding the crowds, which parted preternaturally as they advanced. A strangled yelp clawed up her throat as she wrested free and shoved past the older man, feeling terrible for treating an elder so poorly. "Mercy," she whispered, "mercy."

She rushed on, shocked, sickened that her gifts were not working. That she was weak, trapped here. *What is happening?*

A woman bowled into her, their arms entwining as the woman kindly helped steady her.

"Sorry," Valiriana whispered. "Thank y—"

"Here!" the woman shouted and caught Valiriana's hood. "Captain Mape—here is the girl!" A stern, caustic expression clouded the woman's gray eyes. "I don't know what you done, love, but you need to face the music. Can't have no wastelander upsetting the burgh and bringing trouble on me and my own. It's better this way."

"Done? She hasn't done a thing," a yellow-toothed man said with a leer as he shuffled toward them. "Look at her. The Errant don't want her for trouble. He wants her for his wife!"

"Never," Valiriana vowed. Shock and panic thrashed her veins, a foreign, paralyzing concoction. Training forgotten, she staggered in the grip of terror. Stumbled and came up, free of her cloak.

The woman balked, looking at the now-empty cloak. "Oy, you!"

Valiriana found an opening between two buildings. Dived into the shadows, hearing the citizens betraying her to the soldiers.

Panicked and on the verge of tears, she ran, the space narrowing until she was forced to shuffle sideways. It grew so tight she struggled to breathe. Looking up, tears blurring her vision, she tried to shut out his face. Those eyes. That formidable bearing. His bare chest glaring from beneath the leather vest. But the most startling . . . the way she'd heard his voice in her head.

"O Lady . . ." She shuddered a breath. *"Help me."* She stumbled out onto a street shadowed by trees and tall buildings. Straightening, she glanced to her right. Far at the end of the cobbled street glittered the sea. To her left—

A hand clamped her arm like a vise.

Valiriana sucked in a hard breath at the man towering over her, his black jerkin and leather vest marking him one of the kingsguard. She stepped back, her training suddenly refocused, and aligned her body with his. Drew up her arm and rammed her elbow onto his. Though she felt blinding pain ricochet through her arm, she had no time for it. Her hand went to the sheath that had—in every sparring match in Sacrum Lapis—appeared, but found only air. A tremor of panic nearly made her falter. But they were trained for mishaps, too. Her mind readjusted, noted the sword at his hip.

"Easy now," the man grumbled.

She twirled in front of him, catching his hilt as she did. On his other side, she lifted the blade and aimed it at him. The tip touched his throat just as a blinding pain shot through her back. She cried out and went to a knee, the sword clattering to the ground.

A heavy weight plowed into her, sent her sprawling on the cobbled road. Pain scored her cheek. Pressure pinned her to the ground.

"What's it going to be?" a man asked. "Do we take you to the king unconscious or standing?"

She felt no strength. No courage. Only defeat and terror. "I . . ."

Two resounding thuds sent the men tumbling to the street, unmoving. Behind them stood a woman and man.

A boy of about six darted to her and grabbed her hand. "Hurry! This way."

Weeks had passed since he'd set eyes on her and discovered the siren delivered into the waking realm. Since his killing of the brigand had cost him notable goodwill with the people. Not exactly his wisest move, ending a thug in front of women and children. Some knew the truth and understood the need for such violence, but rumor did not need accuracy to spread like wildfire.

But . . . the woman. Who was she? *Where* had she fled to? Why had the Furymark not found her yet? With each passing rise, he grew less confident of ever locating the siren. He wanted to abandon his duty and scour the city himself, desperate to bring what still infested his dreams back to the tangibility of reality. But he had alliances to secure, especially since it seemed Hirakys was sending raiders into the city to kill. And there were kings to entertain.

"You have experienced much loss, Medora Zarek." Vorn walked the Kalonican king and his entourage to the docked HMS *Aetos*. "Yet you have persevered, and your kingdom is stronger than ever for it."

"It is not loss that defines us but what we learn from it." Dark hair threaded with silver, Zarek had a commanding presence. "Your hospitality has been appreciated."

"My pleasure! I would enjoy more conversations like this."

"Agreed. A good beginning," Zarek said stoically. "Seek peace, Vorn."

"Swift waters . . ." The blessing died on his lips as he clasped the king's arm. After farewells, he watched the foreign delegation climb the ramp up into the ship. He could breathe a little easier now that this alliance with Kardia had begun, but now to figure out how to get—

"Errant!" screeched a voice from the crowd. That dark, piercing sound belonged to only one foul creature—the augur. "She is here, yet you waste time pandering to kings. They are not your answer! Come to me!"

"Silence her," Vorn hissed to Tarac, refusing to look around. *Something is wrong with that creature.* He hoped Zarek had not heard the crone. One such as he would surely disapprove.

"She is here . . ." her warning crooned in his head.

Since seeing the Lady in the city a month past, he had thought of little else, sent men into the city to find her, seek her out. Just as powerful, honorable rulers of the past had done.

Honorable. He sniffed. No such claim could be made of him, considering his debauched life before the crown had been set upon his head. Yet hope dangled now that he had seen her. Though he had neither introduction nor acquaintance, he needed her. Wanted her. Despite violet eyes that chastised him . . . firm lips tightened with disapproval. Revulsion clearer than her unparalleled beauty.

He marveled that the one who infested his dreams was real. The timing of her arrival and his dreams of her was no coincidence, of that he was sure. Still, how did one persuade a pure immortal to join forces with a struggling king with a sordid past?

As the *Aetos* cast off, he waved one last time to the Kalonican medora and shifted left, spotting Tarac striding toward him, freshly returned from taming a shrew. Of a sudden, he was gripped by a violent fear that his last hope of diverting this realm from ruin was lost. That could not be. "Where is the creature? Take me to her."

Tarac stilled, gaze uncertain as he considered him.

"Quick," Vorn growled, "before good sense seizes me."

Amusement radiated from Azyant, who yet guarded his side that had taken the arrow. "She said you'd say that. She waits at The Iron."

"We ride!" Vorn cursed his predictability as they started for the stables. Mounted with his Furymark, he made his way through the city. Hated himself for lowering to this level to achieve his goal. He'd wanted to be a better man than his father and brother, a better king. Was this that route? Taking counsel from one whose ways were dissolute and connected to the diabolus? *What am I doing?*

When Tarac quietly cleared his throat, Vorn woke from his thoughts and realized he'd stopped on the stoop of the public house. His man opened the door and Vorn ducked inside. Air thick with the scent of fermented drinks, the firepit, body odor, and the piquant fragrance of chatelaines' perfumes designed to disguise other smells lessened his tension. Somehow, compared to the sanitized halls of the castle, this was comforting. It was a twisted realization.

"Welcome!" the barkeep called cheerily and lifted a hand in greeting, then hurried to flick open a rear door. "Your room awaits." He muttered something to a tavern wench, who scurried into the room.

As Vorn stalked to the room, his men moved ahead to verify it was safe, and he scanned the public house, taking in The Iron's patrons. Trying to rout the crone, who had the audacity to instruct him on what he should do.

"My prince," crooned Tarielye who slid her bosomy form toward him, resting into his chest. "It has been too—"

"Not now, Tarielye." He shrugged her aside, unwilling—

"Oh come," she purred. Her hands slid along his shoulders.

And for the first time since he'd taken advantage of her more than a cycle past, he had no stomach for her. "Leave off, woman!" Thrusting his arm up had the inadvertent effect of pitching her back against the wall.

She started, eyes wide. "What—"

Ba'moori moved in, blocking her path as he took her elbow and ushered her into the care of her matron.

Vorn scowled, then let the men guide him into the room. Had she always made such a nuisance of herself—and he'd failed to notice because he'd had one thing on his mind—or was he just in a particularly foul mood?

Both, he decided.

The barkeep delivered a tray of tankards and bread even as Vorn rounded the long table. He tugged back a chair, and a rush of foreboding crawled up his spine and the back of his neck. Though he should adhere to the Code, the sense of crackling bugs crawling beneath his skin made him seek relief. Never had he been as good as his Sword anyway. He turned to the tavernkeeper. "The crone—"

"Hmph. That old hag ruins my business." The wide-bellied man thrust his chin over his shoulder. "She's there, in the corner."

Darkness seemed a shroud that coddled the crone, her graying hair like a twisted halo. Even as he set eyes on her, Vorn felt that rancid stench in his adunatos.

"I told you," she said in that grating voice of hers, "if you did not adhere my words, you would fall. And look at what has been happening!" She cackled, and it was truly one of the most malevolent things he had heard. "Hear my words, cleave to my side or you will not find her!"

How dare the witch call him out. Suggest that if he did not take her counsel, he'd fail the realm. As if her word alone protected the realm. Anger pushed him across the tavern, and he sensed his men flank him, the Furymark fanning out and taking up position around The Iron. The darkness he had perceived around her seemed thick and damp, like dew on the grass, only this was . . . rancid. Sticky, as if it clung to his adunatos. There was something amiss in her gaze, something ominous. Dangerous.

Never had he cowered and neither would he now with this haggard wretch.

"Come down from your throne, mighty Vaanvorn," she intoned, "and find the gift the Ancient laid at your feet! I told you she would come, and you listened—now she is here. And you let her slip between your fingers!"

He placed both fists on her table and loomed toward her. "Why don't you bring her to me, since you know so much?"

"So you admit you need me, that without me, you are unable to find this Lady?"

"No."

"Then you *have* found her?"

He gritted his teeth. "What game do you play at, crone?"

"I am not a crone," she sniveled. "And no games—the times are much too important for such. But if you keep coming to me for help . . . and now you want me to hand her over to you—does that mean you would hand me the benefit of her, too?"

Curse this foul creature! She played him as the fool in front of his own people, loudly proclaimed his inability to locate one woman . . . But no, he could not—*would* not—plumb these depths and hand over whatever benefit came from it. He and Jherako needed the Lady's blessing. "You know well the answer to that and seek to lord it over me."

Again, whether some trick of the lighting—no, it was much more—some majuk, she seemed young again, almost pretty. But her eyes—her eyes stayed dark, with no hint of purple lightening the murky brown. "I seek to aid you, King Vorn."

"No man—or woman—does anything that does not directly benefit them first," he countered. "What do you want?"

Brittle eyes glittered as she aged again and suppressed a smile. "To be your counsel. To guide your steps as you rule—"

"No!" Tarac caught his arm. "Please, sire," he hissed almost in Vorn's ear. "Give not yourself to this wickedness. You are a better man than this."

Head cocked to his Sword, appreciating that reminder of who he was—or wanted to be—he nodded to the augur. "I already have the position of counselor filled."

"Tell me," she rasped, "whatever you would have me do and I will do it, if only you would let me see this Lady in your court."

This Lady in his court . . . Those eyes meeting his every day, having her at his side, seeking her wisdom each day, her passion each night . . .

Vorn drew up, surprised at where his thoughts had gone. He frowned at the crone. "What are you doing?"

She swooped her hands out with a flourish. "Me? I am doing nothing but talking to you, encouraging you to take my words to heart, to trust." The last word she drew out, hissing like a serpent.

His head felt odd. His heart ached, wanted to include her . . .

A lean chest pushed closer. "Sire, I fear for your adunatos if you strike an oath with this one."

His man was not alone in that fear. Fists balled, Vorn knew the desperation to have the blessing of the Lady on his realm and in his home demanded satiation. But he sensed something heavy descending as he dealt with this augur. If he obeyed her. He would be a fool to follow the instruction she gave. Yet, mayhap no greater fool than one who would try to lure a Lady into his net—and that, he was convinced, was a mission he must not abandon.

Her cackling began again, as if she knew she had won. That she had him caught in *her* net.

No, this is wrong. He could not . . . would not bow his knee to this crone. His head . . . his head felt so strange. He shook it and saw in her gaze a reveling. She knew—*knew* he felt disoriented. She was toying with him.

He banged the table, making the shriveled woman shrink. "Enough. You toy with me." He pivoted and started away.

"By the swalti fields, living in a barn." Crooked, gapped teeth flashed as she lifted her chin, knowing she had him. Knowing he could not turn back now. "See? I have told you what you wanted to know. Surely that is proof I only want to serve you. So, King Vaanvorn. Tell me how I may serve you."

"This is wrong," Tarac muttered, voicing aloud Vorn's earlier thoughts.

"What manner of creature knows these things?" When she did not answer, Vorn felt his gut clench. It wasn't just that *this* was wrong, but . . . *that* she *is wrong.* "What are you?" Even as he asked, he felt a heaviness in his gut. A tugging at his core that made him take a step back.

She sneered and again suddenly appeared much younger. "Why care when you will soon benefit from the warmth of a Lady and the wisdom I can offer?"

"Because honor is a prerequisite to aligning with a Faa'Cris." *A little too late to have recalled that one.* "If I have sought counsel with . . . a Fallen . . ." He would not hesitate to protect the interests of the realm against such a vile being.

Something dark glimmered in her eyes. Challenge. Smug satisfaction. "You are ensnared now in a web of your own making, Vaanvorn Thundred, and I own you."

His head . . . it felt wrong . . . it wasn't . . .

With a roar, Tarac unsheathed his sword and drove it into the crone.

The band tightening around Vorn's head snapped loose. He stumbled and looked wide-eyed around him, locked onto his Sword. "What . . .?"

"She sought control of your adunatos, sire." Tarac stared at the dead crone. "I could not let it happen." He inclined his head, wiping his blade clean and sheathing it. "Shall we rout the Lady now?"

Vorn considered him, the opportunity. Felt a shift in his gut, as if the death of the augur had healed a canker he'd not fully recognized. Yet he had involved the crone, and now he wanted to be sure he was doing the right thing. Wanted true, good guidance. "At first light. Prayers first."

VALIRIANA

Smothering. The heat in this country was absolutely smothering. The sweat sliding down her back made her ache for the perpetually cool passages of Deversoria. And yes, she could admit that the heat and ever-vigilant sun could be invigorating . . . at first rise. Before it had a chance to spread its steaming breath over the tightly packed city.

Which would be why Valiriana had taken her daily constitutional into the market shortly after dawn. Tucking her hair up into the traditional cap, designed to keep ladies cool and hair off their napes, did little to conceal her identity, but in the weeks since her encounter with the king she had grown adept at avoiding authorities and kingsguard. Early on, she had also learned to avoid men in general. She'd been warned, of course. All Ladies knew the powerful effect of their adunatos on human males and therefore, also knew to expect attention out of measure—especially in the early weeks after departing Deversoria, since her Faa'Cris nature was flush with its holy and healing authority—and to be careful. Still she had not realized how great the influence her kind had over human males. Once, she had merely been laughing and watching a farmer's goats frolic, and she came home with a jar of milk, compliments of said farmer. Another time, she had admired a necklace at a gypsy's stall, and the woman's husband insisted it would not look good on anyone except Valiriana. That incident had become very awkward and embarrassing, so she'd taken it and hurried off. Dropped it in the river as she crossed the bridge. Were all men truly so weak-minded?

Would Vaanvorn Thundred be as easy to ply? What if she went up to the castle and convinced all the guards to let her see the king? Then, once granted audience, she would tell him how wrong he was, to correct his ways.

"What can I do for you, my lady?" a man in a wide white apron asked.

With a small yelp, Valiriana twitched, realizing she had stopped in front of the bakery. "Oh." She tucked her chin, feigning deference. "I apologize. I was . . . distracted." *And who is weak-minded?* With a quick nod, she hurried on.

Her *missio* here was to assess the king, and talking with the people and listening to their stories as they went about their lives would have to suffice since she did not have direct access to him—and no, she was not idiotic enough to test the Ancient by attempting some ridiculous plan to infiltrate the palace. Even if she would love a nicer dress and shoes. And a bath—mercies, what she would not do for the warm, thick waters of the sanitatem to heal her aches and blisters.

"—the king?"

"Better than the last one," a tall but stout woman said with a bit of a laugh.

The words plucked at Valiriana's ears and she moved to the fruit stand to hear better.

"It is early in his rule, but I believe Vaanvorn will be leagues better than his father or brother," the woman said as she set apples into her basket.

"But what about the chil'ren? We heard he's been experimenting on them."

The woman laughed. "Ridiculous! The king has sent funds and the royal pharmakeia to undo what his brother did when he ended the endowment for the foundlings home. I daresay King Vaanvorn has a soft spot for children."

"Think he'll be looking for a queen to give him some?"

"I know the vizier has it at the top of his list. Um, cordis, please—he does love those in the evening." The woman set her basket down and brushed her hair back. "But I will tell you this—whoever marries that Vaanvorn will not be sad to wake next to him."

Titterings carried around the stand, and Valiriana blushed.

"And what about the taxes?"

"If you want a full rundown," the woman said with a rueful eyebrow, "you can go to the vizier and ask him yourself. As for me, I'd best get these back to Cook before she is looking for them."

What did that mean?

"Here, miss," a man said.

Valiriana felt something being pushed into her hand and looked there, finding an apple, then to the man who'd given it to her. "Oh, I—"

"Take it. Has nothing on the apples of your cheeks and probably isn't as sweet." He grinned.

Humiliation acute, Valiriana accepted it with a whispered thanks and turned into the busy street where sellers had their wares lined and early-morning shoppers were strolling. She banked right—

A horse reared, hooves snapping at her head.

Sucking in a hard breath, she leapt away. In the split-second wherein she released her ridgeline, Valiriana caught herself. Knew it would be a terrible mistake to embrace her true form in the middle of the market. Halfway over a crate, she lost momentum and crashed against it. Nailed her tailbone even as she heard the rider's shout.

"Whoa, whoa!"

Scrambling out of the way, she absently thought about the apple. Started for it only to hear the thud of boots hitting the ground. And in that instant saw the black and gold of the kingsguard uniform.

Oh, Ancient, help me.

"Waves of providence, Lathain. What are you doing running down pretty girls on the street?" came the voice of the woman who'd bought the apples for the king.

"It was an accident—she walked right into the street!"

"So you're blaming the poor woman for your running her down?"

"No!" The guard's eyes widened, and he glanced about.

Many were watching. Too many. She did not need this attention. Valiriana tucked her chin and turned away. Started walking.

"You there," the guard—Lathain—called. "You are well, my lady?"

"Yes, fine," she muttered and kept moving.

"Lathain!" Another voice. "I think that's her."

"Who—" His gasp warned of recognition. "Oh! Lady! Stop!"

The ardent pleas sent her racing around the corner of the last stand. Up the street. Hiking up her skirts enabled her to run faster. She shimmied to the side and slipped into a shop. Prayed he had not seen her.

She wandered down the farthest aisle and strode to the back. Swallowed against a dry mouth and tidied her hair. Smoothed her skirts. She set her hand on a sack to steady herself and catch her breath.

"She went down there," a boy shouted, pointing down the street. The kingsguard gave chase in the wrong direction as the boy looked through the window and grinned at her, glanced down the street again, then back at her with a wave before he vanished.

Valiriana closed her eyes and stifled a laugh. Saved by a child. Again. What a—

"Do you need grain?"

She started, shifting aside and looking at the man who stood in the narrow aisle. "Sorry?"

Quite handsome and pleasant demeanor, he indicated to the shelves before her. Sacks of grain lined one portion and two barrels with lids offered varying grains.

"Oh, no. I, uh . . ." Again she looked at the window, still uncertain she was safe. What if they came back?

"Here." He stepped over, lifted a scoop from a hook, and proceeded to fill a bag with yellow grains.

"I, uh . . . I have no—"

He pivoted and thrust it into her hands, eyes shining. "A gift." Color rose into his tanned face moments before a smile.

And she felt a tug of regret that her Faa'Cris nature exerted itself so powerfully over a man who seemed so very kind. She looked into eyes of heather and hesitated. "Why?"

"Isn't it obvious?" he said with a smile. "We have too much grain and you have none."

"Oh." That was not the case at all. "But this is your means of income. And if—"

"Please." With a nod, he winked. "And I hope you continue to evade the kingsguard."

Valiriana faltered. So he knew. "You . . . you are not fond of them?"

"Fond?" He snorted and folded his arms over his chest. "The king ran my father into the ground with his taxes, not to mention the workload. We had to supply the palace with bushels every month."

"That . . . is not fair." She frowned, her mind adding up the facts. "But King Vaanvorn has only been on the throne a short while. Do you mean one of the Tamuros?"

"Aye," he said with a shrug, "but they're all the same, right?"

"The taxes," she said, deciding to be bold with this man, grateful for the chance to glean information. Honest information. "The ones from King Vaanvorn—are they heavy?"

Scratching the side of his jaw, the man exhaled. "No—in fact, he's reduced them to pre-gorge days."

"Pre-gorge?"

"Bakri," a voice called from the back, "where are you? We have this order for the Sanctuary to deliver before ten bells."

"Right, coming!" He gave her a sheepish smile. "Well, enjoy. And when you do have coin, remember who helped you."

"I will. Thank you."

She slipped out of the shop and kept to the deep shade cast by buildings in the early sunlight, thoughts weighted by what she'd learned about the Errant. Odd. All good things today. But then, she had only heard from a few people. There were *thousands* in the city. Which meant she simply had not found the right ones or the truth yet. So the quest must continue.

"The city is quiet this morn," came a gruff voice, boots thudding in her direction.

Valiriana pressed herself into the anemic alley that stretched between two buildings and edged backward, afraid the kingsguard had backtracked. She should've thought of that. It had been a tactic used in their hastati training. She knew better—

Rapid footfalls drew closer. "Sire, she was spotted in the area, but we lost her."

Breath trapped in her throat, she feared her thundering heart would betray her location. Brick dug into her shoulders, and she fought the urge to fold. This was her chance to spy on the king, to learn firsthand what he was like . . .

"Again?" he growled and resumed course. "Keep looking! Never thought one woman could be so elusive against an entire Furymark regiment."

"I beg your mercy, sire."

He huffed and started walking again, a lanky figure pacing him up the hill, followed by kingsguard.

Where were they going?

She eased out of the alley and skimmed the buildings, staying far enough back that, should they look, their eyes would be confounded by the intermittent shade and sunlight between them. That was her hope anyway.

A cat hissed and sprang from the curb. Heart skipping several beats, she watched the feline arch its spine and did her best to avoid stepping on the critter.

"I heard it, too."

At the voice of the king's man and the ensuing footfalls drawing nearer, she searched for a place to hide. Spotted a fence enclosing a small courtyard beside the cobbler's shop and tucked herself inside, the slats affording a narrow view of the men in the street. Watching them draw closer, swords silently coming free of scabbards, Valiriana thought of how easily she could deal with any threat they presented. But that . . . she couldn't. She was to recon . . .

She shifted back.

Creak.

The sound was loud. Obnoxiously loud.

King Vaanvorn stopped short, his gaze snapping in her direction.

"What is it?" his man asked.

"Heard something . . ." Probing eyes traced the fence, the building. He drew closer, head cocked, wariness in his expression. Closer . . .

Valiriana held her breath. She would fold if she must, but she wanted to know what he was doing in the city this early.

"Sire?"

The Errant came to the fence, his shoulder seeming to touch it on the other side as he looked into the courtyard. Tested the gate. His gaze again traced the fence, his eyes a dark, fathomless brown. She prayed he could not see her, that her form would be lost among the various sacks and crates piled along the fence. Yet she studied his face, his bearing, with unabashed curiosity. The planes of his brow and cheeks were firm and strong, right into that thick, trim beard that seemed to amplify his intensity and . . . handsomeness.

Aye, she could not conceal that thought. He was handsome. Quite. And there was the scent of him—not just the efflux that was heady and strong, but the scent of his soap or cologne. No, soap. He did not seem the kind to want to smell pretty. But this was a cool, woodsy scent that wafted over her nostrils. Curled her belly into knots.

"We should go," his man said quietly—yet the words resonated as a gong.

Which made her twitch. She felt the wood bump her. Oh mercies!

He joined the king as actual bells began to toll nearby. "It's started."

After one more perusal, his gaze unknowingly dancing over hers, the Errant grunted. His sword tip lifted to the fence.

Valiriana drew in a breath, ready to fold.

The tip tapped the wood. "The air feels different here . . ." With that, he turned and sheathed his sword. "Come. We tarry too long." The group of six then stalked up the hill.

Knees quaking, adrenaline racing through her veins, Valiriana sneaked from her spot and watched from a distance—she dared not draw closer again—as the contingent made its way to the Sanctuary and entered through a side door.

He went to . . . worship?

No, he must be there to rob the coffers.

It was a wicked, unfair thought. But she realized at that point she must follow. Through the stained glass she could see figures moving. Six walking to the front . . . four stopped . . . two continued. Then knelt.

Somehow she was at the window. Peered through a clear part . . . and stared in confusion. What she saw could not be comprehended. The Errant was praying?

All the long day, she tried to make sense of the king, and she tried still even as she fell asleep.

His touch on her cheek was gentle. Warm. Charged. "Why do you condemn me?"
    "Look around you, at the blood you've spilled."

A rough hand jarred her, snatching her from the dream that would not let her alone and plagued her into the dawning day. "From where did yeh get the grain, Aliria?"

Valiriana sat up, blinking over her shoulder at the woman in a cotton dress and head covering. "What . . .?" She shifted around and sat on the edge of her cot, eyes adjusting to the sunlight slanting through the slats of the barn. Regardless of how roughly she had been awakened, she would remain respectful to this woman who had given her shelter in this hovel of a barn after the Errant's men had chased her through the city.

"The crock!" Jan'maree Eknil snapped, holding the ceramic container and lid in opposite hands. "Where did yeh get the grain? Tell me yeh did not steal it."

Taken aback by the accusation, Valiriana held her anger and rose. "I did not steal." Life here these weeks had been hard, the pace unrelenting. Exhaustion tugged at every muscle in her body, and she wanted to shout that she had done nothing wrong. Then again, neither could she explain how she had gotten the grain.

"The crock is again full!" Jan'maree exclaimed, face wrought, holding the lid aloft as she angled the crock at her. "How?"

Jan'maree would never believe that the miller had pushed it into her hands. Valiriana steadied her racing heart. She had concealed her identity this long. Surely—

"She's a *Lady*," little Jorti proclaimed, tugging at his mother's brown skirts. His perceptive assumption made Valiriana start. It had not been the first time he had asserted that truth, but she'd always managed to divert his attention.

"Don't be daft," Jan'maree snipped as she replaced the crock in the cupboard. She shook her finger at Valiriana. "If we are found out and taken to the magistrate for stealing—"

"That will not happen," Valiriana promised as she moved to help prepare the meal to break their fast. "As said, I did not steal. Never would I bring harm or danger to you or your home. Ever have you been kind and generous to me, and I am grateful."

Weariness tugged at the woman's face. "I know . . . But how do yeh explain this?"

Should she tell them?

"What if she's doing something less . . . honorable to gain the goods?" Shimeal accused as he entered the small area that served as both kitchen and sitting room.

Valiriana drew a shocked breath. "How dare—"

Thunder shook the ground, drawing their attention to the ceiling and walls as dust sifted down. The goat they owned bleated at the sudden intrusion of noise, and chickens clucked. It seemed as if the whole structure would come down on top of them, but more than that, Valiriana detected the strident effluxes of more than twenty riders. Men. Warriors.

"What is—"

"Horses," Shimeal growled. "A lot of them." He indicated to the cupboard. "Cover it! Jorti, yeh know what to do. Cover the beds, Aliria."

She started toward the stalls.

"Furymark!" came a shout from outside as the thundering softened and plumes of dust coiled through the slats of the barn.

Grabbing a sack from his wife, Shimeal scowled at Valiriana. "Yeh've brought trouble on us by steal—"

"The only thing I've stolen is hunger from your bellies." She shouldn't have accepted the bag from the miller, but their hunger had demanded otherwise.

"See?" Jorti insisted. "She's a *Lady*!"

"Give over with that, Jorti!" Jan'maree hissed.

"If you will remember," Valiriana said, trying to calm them, remind them that at one point they had believed in her, defended her, "you knocked out two guards when you saved me!"

He grunted. "Clearly a mistake. Should have left you to the guards."

The words cut deep, but Valiriana swallowed them. Her conscience squirmed. *Had* she endangered them? Jherakan law forbade people from squatting on property that did not belong to them. But what was this family to do when they had lost everything in a fire? There was no help for people in dire situations, a failing of that insolent king with his dark eyes and thick shoulders, which still infested her dreams.

Nightmares, more like.

And the arrival of his Furymark could mean imprisonment for this family. Surely Vaanvorn Thundred would not be so cruel. *He has bloodlust, remember, Valiriana!*

"You, in the barn!" The gravelly shout stabbed through the timber shelter. "I am Captain Mape, Sword of the King, Commander of the Furymark. Present yourself at once."

Jan'maree yelped. "We'll be cut down for sure."

"You won't. I promise." Valiriana would not let them be harmed.

"Yeh are a foundling with no power to make that promise," Shimeal warned somberly as he looked to his wife. "Told yeh we should have left her on the street. Violence is the way of the Furymark."

"Not since King Vaanvorn was crowned," Jorti argued. "And not with a Lady—"

"*Cease*, Jorti!" Jan'maree said, defeat in her words and expression.

"Stay here," Valiriana urged the Eknils, determined to make sure this family was not punished for sheltering her. "I will go out front and—"

"By order of the king"—the captain sounded irritated—"come out *now* and you will not be harmed."

Order of the king . . .

Heart thumping, Valiriana looked toward the sliver of light pressing through the slats and sensed the Errant, but not danger. Somehow, someone must have seen her come out here. Reported it to the king. Her presence could save the family that had shielded her, since the king had so obviously still been looking for her. Perhaps he would accept a trade.

"Stay here," she said calmly. "I will do what I must to ensure you are not harmed." Determined, she strode into the morning light. Her breath arrested at sight of the kingsguard arrayed before her in an arc, their polished black-and-gold armor glittering in the early sun. Swords and daggers. Gazes sharp with experience. Held erect by ferocity.

Almost as impressive as the triarii. The sight infuriated, so clearly was it a display intended to frighten or impress. Neither affected her. Slowly, she let her gaze slide over each kingsguard. Reached out and tested the air around them. Enough to make her flinch inwardly and know should she need to wield against them, a violent response would be not only necessary but justified.

"What is this?" she demanded. "How dare you—"

"Give care, my Lady." It was the gravelly voiced captain. *Sword of the King.* "You address the kingsguard and no demands are made of us." He crossed his wrists on the pommel, clearly confident in his role as commander and none concerned that he faced a threat. "You have evaded the kingsguard these many weeks. The king seeks you, and I am here—"

"Seeks me? To what end?"

"Lady," he said with a low growl, "one does not question the king, but I will tell you that he would but speak to you."

She sniffed a laugh. "I am here. Where is your king?"

He scowled. "You—"

"And is it commonplace," she challenged, aware of the people gathering along the road, "to send the Sword of the King and twenty warriors to one woman exhausted by honest work?" She appraised the man, taking in his Signature, which was filled with honor and loyalty. "One would think such a trivial matter beneath someone of your station, Captain."

"No matter that concerns our king or this realm is beneath me." His manner of response suggested boredom and his efflux—irritation, then amusement—made her wary. "Will you come of your own volition, Lady?"

"I will not." Most likely she should not take such pleasure nor such an imperious tone, but it gave her more satisfaction than it probably should to see his sharp eyes glint in the sun.

"Very well," the captain said tersely, and his gaze shifted to the barn. "Shimeal and Jan'maree Eknil of Oakton, you are commanded to present yourselves—"

"What do you?" Valiriana asked with a start. "Why do you harass these honest, kind people?"

"Kind?" The captain angled a look to his left. "I doubt Hiertuk of Maropoli would agree. He had three stitches after she assaulted him. And Mikriel saw double for two days."

Swallowing hard, Valiriana recalled how Jan'maree had cracked the vase over the guard's head in the market. How she and Shimeal had stood over the two guards they had felled, looking terrified and resolute. She paled at the thought of a Furymark taking those blows.

"An attack on the kingsguard is taken as an attack on the king himself."

"No," Valiriana said, the word half choking her. "That is not—they were only trying to protect me."

"That will be determined by the magistrate, Lady." His gaze again shifted to the barn. "Eknils, do not make this harder on yourself. Come out at—"

"You cannot do this," Valiriana balked and surged forward. "What right have you to twist this—"

Swords sang free, and two of the outer guard swung down from their mounts, bringing Valiriana up short, heart thundering with both fear and indignation.

"Hold," the captain growled to his men who advanced on her, his expression implacable, but those sharp eyes never left her. "As Sword of the King and these men"—he indicated with a jut of his jaw in a half circle—"his kingsguard, we do not tolerate subversion. How—"

"*Subver—*"

"*However,*" he dragged out with more than a little impatience, "I extend grace, as your accent betrays you are not from here. But any further acts designed to subvert our efforts here *will—*"

"You cruelly manipulate me and this entire situation," she argued, again lifting her jaw and feeling that twinge of rebellion boiling in her belly.

"Enough!" the Sword barked. "Surrender yourself to us or stand aside and let us deliver judgment against the Eknils."

Valiriana clenched her teeth. Felt her ridgeline burning, aching to be freed so she could fight this injustice. But no . . . she must yield her will . . . But by the Ladies, she could not bring herself to speak her surrender. It was not in her to do so, except to the Ancient.

Without warning, the two Furymark closest the road spurred their horses forward. It was then she saw Jorti start for the road, see the beasts, then double back—sprinting straight for her. She gathered him to herself, searing the captain with a glower. "You would harm a child?"

Walking backward—slowly—she sought to return Jorti to his parents, who stood on the remnant of a home that had once stood here decades earlier, the large foundation stones now props for weeds and saplings. But he would not release her skirts.

"Lady, you test my patience."

Thankfully, his use of "lady" was that of propriety, not an inference of her nature, which a Licitus like this would never understand.

"And," he continued, sounding bored, "you have given me time to think—

this barn . . . it belonged to Baron Farook. He vacated this land a decade past. Do you or this family have proof of letting?"

Oh mercies . . . "That is unfair."

"That," he said, "is the law. The magistrate will determine guilt. I must bring the entire family in for questioning, I think . . ."

Up the three stone steps to higher ground. Should she fold away? Escape this insanity? No, she could not leave this family at the mercy of the kingsguard for protecting her. "Is this how Jherakans treat their own? How the Furymark of the king treats his people?" But was this not her chance to be before the king? To find out how he did treat his people? What if—

"We answer to none but the king," sneered the one who'd had stitches—Hiertuk. His efflux was rank, humiliated, desiring revenge.

"Where is this king who finds children so grave a threat that they must be abused in a public street?"

A destrier shifted forward, and her gaze rammed into those familiar, haunting eyes that made her heart and stomach squirm . . . then rage soared. His attire was insulting as well, half-dressed as he was with his leather vest gathered at the waist and no proper shirt.

The Errant himself. "My Lady."

He dares! The undercurrent in his words said he understood her true nature, but that was impossible. He could not possibly know that she was Faa'Cris. And *never* would she reveal her true self to someone like him. She despised this man. This king who condoned such horrid treatment of others. Had killed two men in her presence. Anger charged through her veins, but she would not be so easily manipulated this time. "Am I so vicious a creature that you come at me"—she tucked Jorti behind herself, holding his hand—"with sword and so great a number?"

"*Come* at you?" Amid a laugh and a smile that twitched his dark beard, he dismounted in a display of rippling, raw power. "My Lady, this"—he motioned to his Furymark as he slowly stalked forward, removing his gloves finger by finger, step by step—"is your escort."

Jorti tightened his grip yet could not stop himself from peering around her to see the king.

The gentleness about the king's words must be deception, like thin ice on a frozen pond. He was dangerous. And handsome. Dangerously handsome.

"Escort?" she scoffed, hearing her hollow voice and knowing her own words had lost their edge. She told herself to look at his eyes, his face—

anywhere but his well-muscled chest and arms.

"We are here but to guide you to safety. The streets present certain dangers."

Her gaze again fell on the warm eyes and rugged features of the king. *Even poisonous flowers have their beauty.* "Smooth are your words and shrewd the game you play, but how is your heart, Vaanvorn Thundred?"

"Give care," one of the guards barked. "You address your king!"

Eyes still on her, the Errant held up a hand, silencing the reproof of his man as he closed the distance.

He had dared call her Lady, so he must know the power she could wield. Granted, not on the level of a Resplendent, but he did not know that. "Stand there, hold true, King Vaanvorn."

He stilled his approach and seemed aggrieved. "How can I assure you, my Lady, that I intend you no harm?"

"Let the boy go."

Amusement brightened the Errant's eyes as he set a boot on the first stone step. "I do not believe I am the one holding him."

Cursing herself for the mistake, Valiriana sought a particularly strident response. "It is my hand that secures his safety in this moment, but should it not be your hands providing that security, Vaanvorn Thundred? Is a king not charged to *serve* the people, not lord over them, abuse them?"

Head cocked, the Errant considered her and those words. "Rightly spoken, Lady."

Surprise squirreled through her chest. What was this, a concession?

A trap!

She would not be lured in by his smooth words or good looks. Yet he had opened a door she must put to use. "Allow the boy and his parents to go free. No charges."

Left hand resting on his thigh, Vaanvorn peered up at her, the sun piercing his left eye to a glittering amber. "They attacked my guards and are living on land not their own." He indicated to the barn. "That cannot be overlooked, especially the former. Surely you understand that a price must be paid."

"I will pay it." Her heart thundered more than she'd anticipated at handing herself over to these men, their brand of justice. "Release them, and I will go with you to the magistrate." Justification wove through her. "They were protecting me, sheltering me. In that, I own the guilt of their actions."

He grimaced. "You do not help your case, my Lady."

Blood and boil, how many mistakes would she make? Valiriana glowered. "I—"

"Stay your defense, my Lady." He ran a hand over his beard and considered the gathering crowd on the streets. "Captain Mape, have I fulfilled my quota of benevolence for this rise?"

The Sword of the King had not changed position with his crossed wrists and confident seat on his destrier. "You have not, my king. I believe you are one short."

They mock me . . . Let her manifest her enlightened form, snap her wings and ridged tips at them, and see who they mocked then. Alas, no. She must be the picture of grace and mercy. They must learn from her, not be fueled by her. No matter how much they deserved a flogging.

"Ah, see?" The Errant lifted his hands in mock surrender. "There you have me—I have a benevolence quota to fill." He shrugged as if he had no choice. "Three crimes have been committed against the Crown." He bobbed his head side to side and pursed his lips. "I see no need for *four* people to pay. The boy can go."

"And his parents," she insisted.

"I am extending generosity but will not disregard the laws my forebears put in place to guide this realm, nor will I fail to protect the men who—"

"Leave Shimeal and Jan'maree out of this, and I will go with you."

Without a word, he pushed up the next two steps, the air seeming to rush from the stone foundation as he drew nearer. An exotic mixture of nuts and cordi swarmed the man, his heavily tanned chest glistening in the afternoon light. It seemed the sun itself shrank from this man as his large form shaded her from its light. Eagerness marked a line from his eyes to the smirk twitching his beard.

Ha! She had succeeded—he would grant her demand. It had been so easy to bend the will of this Licitus to hers. But then, was it not always so when it came to men? So craven and carnal. How had any Lady endured—

"No."

She blinked. "What? But—"

"You are granted benevolence—see? There I have fulfilled my benevolence quota." He angled his head but not his gaze to his Sword. "Make a note, Captain Mape."

"Note made, sire."

"You toy with me." Anger trembled through her.

"Two criminals remain. The man and woman. Choose—"

"No." She flared her nostrils, willing her heart to slow.

His eyes sparked with both anger and amusement. "Lady—"

"Transfer my benevolence to Jan'maree," she whispered, her words nearly catching in her throat. "I will serve her sentence."

"Tempting," he said with a grin, "but the Ancient would tear down the walls of Forgelight were I to put one such as you in the dungeons."

"Please." Valiriana caught his hand. "*Please*—she is with child. She and the babe would not survive if she were put in such a place."

"Realize what bargain you strike? It would be for one full cycle."

Frustrated with herself for not seeing a way around this, Valiriana again thought to fold away from his chaos, this man of ill repute. But she could not abandon those who had sheltered and protected her these many weeks.

"Lady?" He tucked his head, their faces improperly close, those indecently rich eyes taking her in as if he could not stare long or hard enough. "What say you?" His words were unfairly soft, husky, teasing her ears.

Her mind reeled, thoughts shifting and colliding. Blood and boil—a full cycle! How she had already failed, a terrifying realization. She swallowed and immediately regretted it, for in his gaze, she saw his exultation. That he knew he had won.

Hating the conclusion of this—she was defeated—she shifted her gaze to Jan'maree and Shimeal, thought of what this beast was willing to do to them. Had she not intervened, he likely would have done the same to their son—a child! She drove her anger and gaze back to the Errant. "You are self-serving, wicked, and blackhearted, Vaanvorn Thundred." Mercies, the pleasure it gave her to say that to his face, to see how his cheek twitched. "You are not worthy."

Eyes darkening, he remained unmoving. "Do you go, or does she?"

Another swallow. "I will."

The Errant gestured to his man, who barked an order that was lost in Jan'maree's shout of objection. Valiriana stared past the king, stunned as the guards shackled Shimeal and pulled him from his wife. There had been no way to bargain for his sentence, but she had not expected to be so unsettled by the sight of his arrest.

Jan'maree threw a fierce glare at Valiriana. "How could you? You know he is not well! You promised this would not happen, and now he goes to his death!"

"See?" The king's breath feathered over her neck, sending chills down her spine. "You take her punishment, yet she decries you. Now, mayhap, you know what it is to rule. The unwinnable impossibility of every decision. Oh. You asked how is my heart?"

Dying and charred, I hope.

His height forced her to tilt back to see into brown eyes that were as inviting as the caverns of her home. "It is yours, my Lady."

No, not inviting—the lure of the diabolus. She despised him. "Would you not have to possess a heart to give it away?"

Dark eyes widened almost imperceptibly before he barked a laugh. "This will be an entertaining year. I look forward to getting to know you, my Lady, over our many dinners together."

"What say you?" she breathed.

"Your sentence." The Errant paused and gave her a wink. "One year at Forgelight Castle. With me."

She was here, in his house, bound by a deal that required her to remain with him for one year. More than enough time to win the siren to his side, convince her to stay. Bind and rule with him. He strode across the bailey, removing his gloves and wiping the sweat from his brow.

He glanced over his shoulder to where Ba'moori was reaching for the carriage that held the Lady. "Bring the Lady to the lesser hall."

"Aye, Majesty."

Inside, he was met by a bustle of house staff, the word clearly having already spread. "I want Matron Khatrione and her four best ladies-in-waiting in the hall at half past."

A guard hustled behind him and down a hall that led beneath the stairs to the royal residence. Vorn took them two at a time to gain the solar. "I'll change into dry clothes"—the heat of summer months always baked him— "then I want the steward and house heads in the hall as well."

Tarac nodded to the kingsguard at the solar doors, sending him off to carry out the orders.

Vorn changed into a clean undervest and tucked it beneath a wide black cummerbund. In his sitting area, he eyed the box sitting on the mantle. Rubbed his jaw, debating with himself yet again over watching it. Violating the Accord. He grimaced—that had been broken just by taking this piece of technology.

A soft rap preceded Tarac's entry. His Sword slowed, noticing what Vorn studied. "You watched?"

Vorn picked it up. "Not yet." He recalled the instructions Revalor had given him. Swiped. Tapped. The black surface surrendered to variations of gray.

"What is it?"

Shaking his head, Vorn continued watching. It seemed to be backing away—the object growing smaller . . . smaller . . . "A sky ship."

Tarac pointed to a corner. "That looks like Vysien."

"It is," Vorn growled, anger tightening his chest. "What is a sky ship doing in Hirakys?"

"Revalor spoke true," Tarac said with more than a little disappointment in his tone. "The Accord *is* broken."

"Aye," Vorn acknowledged gravely. "I had hoped it untrue. It would have made things so much simpler."

"You must address this."

Vorn grunted. This meant trouble, likely meant war. "I want more intelligence on this."

"Think you will seek out Revalor for more?"

Eyeing the device, Vorn recalled the stranger saying he could communicate through it. Why did things have to keep getting more complicated? "The Lady . . . I will see to her first."

When his Sword said nothing, he gave him a sidelong look as he gathered his hair and secured it. "Speak your mind now while we are yet alone."

"I am conflicted," Tarac said quietly as he waited. "We discovered this girl—"

"Lady."

His Sword gave a conceding nod. "Perhaps. Regardless, the means by which we happened upon her were not in keeping with the Codes of the Brotherhood."

"But?"

"If she is what is claimed of her, then she has a connection to the Ancient that you and I could never hope to attain, no matter our prayers or petitions." He raked a hand through his hair and grunted. "But the augur directed us to her. I cannot . . ." Tarac sniffed. "I almost want to encourage you to seek a concubine from the harem rather than this."

"Almost," Vorn repeated his Sword's word. "Those left in the harem were brought here by my father and brother. I want none of that. In fact, if I did not know it would disgrace them, I would send them back to their homes." He sighed and shook his head. "I want a wife and queen. After our time in Sanctuary yestermorn, I am at peace."

"The vizier offered to scour the country—"

"No." Vorn planted his hands on the wardrobe doors. "No, I will not disgrace *myself* by holding a beauty contest."

"Yet you will hold a Lady of Basilikas hostage—"

"She's not—" Frustration gouged the hope that swelled in his chest, knowing she was here. "She offered to pay the sentence for the woman. I agreed."

"Readily."

"Aye!"

"In the hopes she would become your personal chatelaine—"

"No!" Vorn glowered at his First. "You are as a brother to me, so I will overlook that accusation. You know me better."

Tarac gave a weighted breath. "I know you have accepted the favor of more than a couple chatelaines at The Iron."

"You know I gave myself to the Brotherhood after Yirene," he said, hating himself. Hating his past.

Tarac considered him, judgment plain on his face.

"You think so little of me?"

"Nay," Tarac said, more than a little miserably. "But I have been here. I know your passions . . ."

"On my honor," Vorn vowed, "no one will share my bed until I take the Lady to wife."

His First straightened. His expression smoothed. But he still looked forlorn.

"Still you doubt me."

"No," he said firmly. "I doubt her."

"A Lady?" Vorn balked, then sobered. "How so?"

"She is far younger than I expected a Lady would be and far more imperious. That is not the way of the Ladies I learned about. If she is so wholly consumed with herself and her plans, then keeping her here will serve no one. And I fear what a Lady may do when angered."

Changed, ready to leave, Vorn was slowed by the heady realization. "You are right . . ." He thought of Tarac's words about how they had come to know about the Lady's location. "Were right—about the crone. Thank you, brother."

"I am your Sword, figuratively and literally," Tarac said.

Vorn clapped him on the shoulder. "Now, my Sword, let not your heart be troubled. We have sought the Ancient's will—our way is clear. And she is here! Come."

Downstairs, they made their way toward the lesser hall that served well to host a small number of guests. As they approached, an eruption of chaos— screams, shouts, and meaty thuds—rang through the house. Vorn sprinted through the doors, which were flung open by guards, and rushed forward, around the corner, through the receiving hall, right into the lesser hall. Skidding to a stop, he struggled to process what he found.

A pool of humanity lay at the Lady's feet on the palace floor, kingsguard groaning and debilitated.

He spotted the four he'd assigned to the Lady, who moved with a lethal beauty, sparring Hiertuk and newcomer Irascil, both of whom sought an advantage—and failed. She delivered a near-lethal strike to Hiertuk, who dropped to a knee, his wound blooming crimson across his tunic.

Shock held Vorn captive. He had heard Ladies were warriors, yet it stunned to see her skill played out, his best conquered. He shook himself. "Hold!" he demanded as he moved closer, despite Tarac's urging to stay back. "Stay your weapons." He motioned to the Furymark.

The elegant whirlwind slowed to a stop. Beneath a canopy of black strands, violet eyes struck his, and he soundly felt their impact. Recalled stories long told. Wondered what wrong his men had perpetrated against the Lady for her to retaliate in this manner.

Tarac seized her distraction and expertly delivered the Lady to her knees. Cuffed her wrists and hooked an arm around her throat.

"No!" Vorn ordered, expecting the sting of death any second. "Release her!"

Tarac frowned. "But sire, she—"

Expecting his First to be dead any instant, he demanded, "Now!"

His man drew back, angry, confused. Unhanded her.

Slowly, she straightened, mouth tight, brow furrowed.

"*Never* set hand to her!" Vorn glanced at the Furymark, battered—not dead, thank the seas—and furious. Wait—no, one lay motionless. Who . . .? "What happened here?" It had been but minutes since he had left them in the bailey. "Azyant, speak!"

"M-Mikriel, sire," Azyant grimaced as he nodded to the dead Furymark. "He was charged with seeing the Lady to her chambers . . . and . . ." Expression grave, he struggled to his feet, guarding his previous injury, which seemed to have reopened. "It seems he sought retribution for the attack in the market by the Eknils."

Waves. "You have my deepest apologies, my Lady. It will not happen again. You have my protection, and all here give witness to what I have spoken. Be at peace. Please."

Wariness guarded an oval face, youthful as Tarac had pointed out, but also filled with experience one her age should not have. She seemed to ripple as she straightened. Squared her shoulders and lifted her chin.

Better. He could take an even breath now. "Captain Gormon, see that those involved in the attack upon the Lady—" He stopped short, realizing he did not know her name. "Do you have a name?"

"Do not all creatures?"

Vorn fisted his hand. No doubt she tested him. That she dared speak to him, the king, with no deference, would—if she were any other—have had her at least removed from the house. And yet she stared openly, so he returned the favor, studying her. Noting how her complexion, so smooth and creamy, glowed beneath the caress of the touchstones. Her blue-violet eyes could safely guide any ship to harbor like the Ironesse lighthouse.

Would she do that for him, guide him through this storm of saving a failing kingdom? He had a year to convince her . . . But this was a terrible start.

And strange—he'd fathomed her so much taller, larger than life, yet she stood before him with the elegance her kind so fully defined—a head shorter than he. And small—so small. Fragile.

Exactly what she would have me think. Underestimate an enemy . . . A terrific warning screamed to tread lightly. "May I have your name, Lady?"

She shifted, making the Furymark twitch—a reaction she clearly enjoyed. Those blue-violet eyes found his. "Aliria." On the one hand so fair and delicate, yet on the other, she radiated iron strength. "Vow you will not harm Jan'maree, Shimeal, or their boy."

Vorn lifted an eyebrow. "You insult me, Lady. I have given my word regarding this family, and a deal was struck between us. Do you suggest I would break that—"

"It is common for Lici—" She seemed to reconsider her words. "For *men* to break confidence once their demands are met."

"Demands." Raging seas, he had never endured so many abuses of his character from one person in so short a time, and his men were not accustomed to it either, judging by the hands going to hilts.

Lady Aliria shifted her gaze to the men, seeing the same. "Are your men always this ready for blood-violence?"

"His men," Tarac bit out, "are not used to one from the street repeatedly shaming our king and behaving in so poor a manner for a Lady."

"Captain," Vorn chided quietly, holding a hand to his Sword. Clearly it surprised them both that a Lady of Basilikas did not know how to conduct herself in a court. But as his guest for the next year, she would learn. "Stru

Maron, Miscil Duz, Tozet Chaiy, Glon Chilzovko, stand forward." Vorn waited as the four kingsguard stepped up in a tight formation. "Lady Aliria, when I chose my Four, these Furymark were the next highest ranked among the kingsguard." He nodded. "They are now your detail. They will go wherever you go and protect you at all costs. They will do as you request under one condition: that it does not countermand my word." He eyed the men. "Lady Aliria is a guest of House Thundred with limited freedoms. I place on you the responsibility of ensuring she does not leave these grounds without me or my express approval. If any harm should come to her, your failing will be treated as if harm had befallen your king. Are my orders understood?"

"Yes, Your Majesty." Though they accepted the instruction and new commission in unison and without complaint, he saw the question in their eyes about who this Lady was and why she was given so much.

He signaled for the room to be cleared, save his Four and the ladies of his staff. "Matron Khatrione, this is Lady Aliria." He liked the sound of that. "She will be our guest for the next year. House her in the gold apartment and assign her your best lady-in-waiting." Deliberately did he set his gaze to appraise her, taking in the oversized dress belted at the waist, doing no justice to a figure that he even now admired. Dirt smudged her cheek. "And get her fitted into attire more appropriate for life here. Order some gowns and day dresses, whatever other frivolity women need these days."

"As you will, Your Majesty," Khatrione said with a bow of her head.

Her Imperious Highness gaped. "I need no friv—"

"You will have shelter, food, clothing, and a modicum of freedom." Vorn moved to stand before the Lady, taking in the vision that she was. "Are *we* understood?"

"I comprehend your meaning," she bit out, "but if what I am is truly understood, you know these men are not only unnecessary but pointless."

Vorn smirked, appreciating the challenge she set. "All the same, they will be on duty day and night. Besides, Lady Aliria, are we not both bound by honor? Would your people look upon you as honorable if you harmed men merely carrying out orders and protecting the laws of the land?" When her mouth tightened, he inclined his head, knowing his point had been made. "They are your guard, *should* you need anything."

The Lady watched him, seemingly curious and mayhap a little annoyed.

And he wanted to know . . . A few paces separated them, and he reduced that to two. Recalled the men she had leveled. Not just men—but hardened, trained kingsguard. "You came to Jherako," he said just for her ears, "watched me from the crowd at the celebration . . . I daresay you were judging me, assessing me." He quirked an eyebrow. "For an alliance."

She scoffed. "You think too highly of yourself."

"Lore tells of Ladies coming to rulers, offering alliances . . . and heirs." Raging seas, his heart beat fast at the hope of convincing her to remain after the year and give him—

"Never." Aliria's nostrils flared with her defiance, and around gritted teeth, she hissed, "*Never* will I give you either." Triumph glittered in those alluring seaborne eyes.

Shocked at the brutal truth of what and who she was, what she vowed to withhold, Vorn struggled against a rising fury. "Then why come to Jherako at all?"

"To prove to them you are not worthy."

"I can be very persuasive," he said. "And I have a year to change your mind. A year where your freedom is in my hands. Where I will control your comings and goings."

"Mayhap," she all but growled, "but not the workings of my mind or heart. You will never force me to convince the Synedrion that you are worthy of having a Lady in your life."

He cocked his head. "But do I not already have one in my life?"

Expression tight, she let the four lead her away.

VALIRIANA

"These are your chambers, my lady," the tall, strong-shouldered matron said as she pushed open the door and strode in. She crossed the room and thrust back heavy curtains, revealing a large balcony with an expansive view of the sea beyond. "Yieri will serve you night and day. Should you need anything, let her know, and she will present it to me for consideration."

Valiriana stood in the middle of the apartment, taken aback. It was far more than she had imagined when she surrendered herself on Jan'maree's behalf. A dark chamber in the lower reaches of the keep with musty air and little more than bread and water had been more in keeping with her expectations. This . . . this was—

"Morning fasts are broken at half seven. Midday meal is served at two, and if you are not otherwise engaged, dinner is served at seven as well." She clasped her hands at her waist and nodded to another woman who entered. "This is Simika, our seamstress. She will take your measurements."

"Meas—" Right. Clothes. It was still an adjustment to have someone touch her so intimately. The armor she wore manifested of its own accord— but they did not know that. Nor would they understand.

"As the king stated, you are to remain in chambers, and please understand that defying the king's order comes with severe consequences. As well, if you would take a walk, you will have your guards and Yieri with you. Receive visitors in this sitting area, eat over there," Matron Khatrione said as she pointed to a corner near the balcony with a table, buffet server, and chair. Then she started toward an interior set of doors. "Your bedchamber is here. If the mattress is too firm, let Yieri know, and she will remove the topper. Pillows can be switched out as well."

It was all so luxurious, so . . . much. "All this is for me?" Most certainly not the prison she had imagined.

Khatrione lifted an eyebrow, her gaze raking over her. "Of course it is."

Feeling awkward, under inspection, she forced herself toward the glass doors of the balcony. Appreciated the warmth of the sun streaking through them. The view was unprecedented. Waves and water glittering like crystals in the river caves outside Deversoria. To either side of the doors, the walls were painted with floral vines. She touched them and realized— "It's paper."

"It is," Khatrione said. "Queen Yirene had landscapes of her country done for the walls. If you want it altered, I can inquire of the king."

"Queen?" She blinked. "These were the queen's . . . rooms?"

The matron bristled. "Of course. Gold for the queen, as it has always been."

Her heart crashed against her ribs. "But I am not . . ."

"No, you are not," the matron snipped, then seemed to catch herself. Inclined her head. "If you have any need, let Yieri know. Cook has word to send up a meal."

Two women entered just then, carrying steaming buckets of water. Heads down, gazes never quite meeting hers, they hurried to a smaller room off the bedchamber where a large bath was set into the middle of the room. By the time she turned, the doors were closing and the matron was gone.

"She does not care for me."

"That is my job," Yieri said, her lined brow furrowed.

"I meant—" Valiriana deflated. Rubbed her shoulder. This *missio* was not going as she had anticipated.

"Come, let us get you bathed."

She started. "I do not need help—" But Yieri and the other two women took her to the bath chamber and began undressing her, Yieri's crepey hands working surprisingly deftly. "No, pl—"

"My lady, the king will be most displeased with us if we do not."

Frustrated, she yielded to the humiliation of being undressed, helped into the bath, and cleansed. They then helped her into clothing that had a better, closer fit with nicer, more supple fabric. An hour later, seated at the table with the remnants of her meal before her, she smiled out at the glittering waters. "It is so beautiful. I've never seen anything like it."

"Have you not seen the sea before?" Yieri asked.

"No," she said, realizing it was probably best not to go into where she had come from. It would only lead to confusion. "No seas or oceans. There is a river . . ."

"Would you like to go down to the shore?" Yieri suggested.

Valiriana straightened in the chair. "Could I?"

"I'm sure of it. Come." She led her to the doors and opened them.

Four black-and-gold-clad guards turned their way.

"The Lady has asked to see the south lawn," Yieri said.

"You cannot enter the main halls. The king is entertaining," the guard said. Entertaining?

"Is there another route?" Valiriana asked.

"Oh," Yieri said, glancing nervously at the guards, "the servants' passage . . ."

The guard shrugged. "As long as we avoid the main halls."

"That way is not pretty," Yieri warned.

"It is the sea I want to see, not the passage."

They slipped into a small panel door set in the wall and entered a musty stone passage that was little more than the width of a man's broad shoulders. "I doubt the king could fit in here."

"I would be aghast if he tried," Yieri said quietly, her voice still rattling along the stone walls and steps. Down, down they went. Then along a lengthy corridor. "There, at the end, is the door."

They were nearly there when a child darted out of a room.

Valiriana laughed when he saw her and bolted back inside. She peeked in as they passed . . . and what she saw pulled the smile from her face. The room was not even as big as the chamber in which she'd been bathed. Yet the walls were lined with bunks—three high. Narrow slivers of sleeping space. Lines crisscrossed the room, dividing the area with dingy curtains. "This . . . this is where you live?"

Looking stricken, her gaze bouncing to the guards who stood behind them impatiently, Yieri motioned her onward. "Come, my lady. This way." She hunched. "Please."

The lady's maid's efflux was cluttered with nerves and fear. In other words, *Do not cause trouble.*

Reluctantly, she followed, very aware of the other three rooms that mirrored the first one. All packed. Valiriana trailed the lady-in-waiting out into the evening and onto the lawn, hugging herself. She verified the guards were keeping their distance. "Yieri," she said, looking at the sea, which she found she could no longer appreciate, "speak true—is that where you live?"

"After many years employed here, I now have my own room. Most are either two or three to a room. Please, lady," she said, motioning to the sea. "Enjoy what you came for."

They had so little, worked so hard, and there Valiriana was with a room fit for . . . a queen. So, the Errant spoke shrewd, smooth words and yet treated his people abominably.

"We must go," Yieri stated hurriedly, whispering. She took Valiriana's arm. "The king is on the lawn. We are not allowed . . ."

Valiriana let the lady-in-waiting lead her back to the house but stole a look over her shoulder. Spotted the king in a clean vest and pants, standing with two other men. He sipped from a short glass, and his gaze never left hers.

Good. He would see that she entered through the servants' passage and know she had found him out.

"Who is the beauty?"

In his solar with the skycrawler and his Four, Vorn eyed the stranger. So he had seen Aliria on the shore earlier.

Revalor winked and grinned. "I do not blame you for tucking her away—that raven hair and sky-blue eyes . . ."

"She is not tucked away." Yet he recalled watching her emerge from that rear passage door. Servants' entrance. What had Yieri been thinking? He made a mental note to chastise the lady's maid for taking a Faa'Cris through an area that was clearly beneath the Lady. And yet, he had no doubt Aliria would rebuke him regardless. In fact, he was fairly certain that had been reproof glinting in her eyes. What fault had she found in him this time?

"I see, then—keep your secret. I would not want to share her either."

"She is a guest of the king," Tarac bit out.

"I am sure." Revalor chuckled.

Enough entertaining. "The device you gave me—"

"You finally watched it."

Vorn set down his glass on a table and considered the man with his wiry hair and build. "I did." He swiped a hand over his beard and sighed.

"And did you like what you saw?"

"You know I did not."

"Fair enough," Revalor said.

"The sky ship—"

"A Symmachian Fast-Attack craft called an Interceptor," Revalor corrected, and though he had a bit of smugness in his expression, it fell away. "It's an older model, but still—you clearly can see that I was not lying to you. Symmachia is here, interfering on your planet."

"But to what end? And why Hirakys? They are the least of the realms on the continent."

"Perhaps they were the most desperate to get a leg up on the others."

Vorn pulled the device from his pocket and considered it. "Hirakys and Jherako have always had tense relations, but now, knowing they have broken the Accord . . . I am alarmed. Is there a way to monitor their actions?"

"To a certain extent my ship has been doing that from orbit," Revalor said as he produced another device. "This data channeler is tied into our satellite. For as long as the life of it, you'll be able to see what's happening as it happens." He shifted around and showed Vorn some of the controls. "See, here— Voids!"

At the hissed word, Vorn flinched. "What?"

Revalor worked the data channeler quickly. "Look," he said over his shoulder and aimed the device toward Vorn. "An encampment . . . That wasn't there when I dropped." He shook his head gravely. "And according to our intelligence, your border is that blue line."

"An invasion?" Tarac balked. "They would not dare."

"Not an invasion. Reconnaissance," Vorn said, sliding his finger over the screen, learning to manipulate it even as he evaluated what the image showed him. "There is at least a brigade waiting on the Hirakyn side. If the infiltrating force returns . . ." War. How in the black seas was he already facing this?

Because Tamuro was weak, as was Father.

"We have to send a messenger to General Hiro right away. How did his scouts not catch this?" Tarac looked tormented. "If what you said is true and the Hirakyns manage to return with their intelligence . . ."

To have power and not be able to wield it. Yet . . . Vorn lifted the data channeler. "This device—do you have another I might use?"

Revalor smirked. "I have a dozen if you want them."

"What are you thinking?" Tarac asked, brow furrowing over his gray eyes.

"General Hiro has the Fifth Infantry doing training maneuvers in the west."

"Aye, he's based out of Lighthold north of Rebel's Bay where the Admiral Suruk is anchored," Tarac said. "But that is more than two days' ride."

Vorn grunted. "That can't be helped. We send this with our fastest rider. I can communicate with him this way and eliminate further delays. Tell him to run down any Irukandji or Hirakyns who dare to put a toe on Jherakan land."

"I could do it," Revalor offered. "I could use my ship—"

"No," Vorn barked. "If we do this, it must be with the utmost care. If anyone sees the ship and ties it to us . . ."

Revalor gave him a conspiratorial grin. "When did you see me land here?"

The realization made Vorn pause and give the man a stiff look.

"Exactly," Revalor chuckled. "This is not my first covert mission. I can deliver the device to him before midnight."

"It is one thing to learn Hirakys has violated the Accord," Tarac said quietly, "quite another to violate it ourselves."

"And what is the Accord except a measure to protect your world?" Revalor said. "This communication device is not a weapon—"

"Is it not?" Tarac argued. "It is a tool used against our enemy."

"No," Vorn said, feeling justified in sending the device to Hiro. "Not against them. For us. We use this to protect ourselves, communicate faster."

"Sire, it is a breach of the Accord."

"Which is already broken." He patted his friend's shoulder. "If it would appease your conscience, send the rider as well." Then he nodded to Revalor. "I will prepare a message for the general, who will no doubt be as suspicious of you—if not more—than I was when first we met. Take the device to the general and tell him raiders cross the Diabolus Mesa. Show him how to communicate with me."

"Begging your pardon, sire," a guard said as he slipped inside. "The lady . . ."

Vorn scowled at the guard. "Not now." He again focused on Revalor. "Keep me informed."

"Of course," Revalor said, his gaze skipping to the guard, who was still lingering at the door.

"I said not—" But then Vorn noticed the ajar door. The green gown . . . Finally, it registered. *Her* guard, here. His gut spasmed, and he felt a need to hurry along the offworlder. "Thanks, Revalor. Azyant, see him out."

As the two left, Vorn did not miss the way the offworlder eyed Lady Aliria. "Let her in," he instructed.

The door yawned open, and she filled his field of vision. And in her eyes was a blaze. Not unlike the fierce glower she'd lobbed at him across the rear lawn. "Lady Aliria, to what do I owe—"

"You claim to be a king who values honor and integrity, yet you live in luxury while your sergii are relegated to squalor."

Feeling as if she'd slapped him, Vorn tightened his jaw. "Close the doors, Tozet." He fixed his gaze on hers, turning the ring on his finger. Doing his best to calm his anger. He was very likely facing an invasion—war! Perhaps for their very survival—and she wanted to talk about living conditions.

"Have you no response?"

Tarac shifted forward. "You address the king. Give care how you speak, or you will be removed. Possibly punished."

She cocked her head as if his Sword had just proven her point. "Are you so afraid of a question that you would punish me for asking?"

"He is not," Tarac barked, "but neither does he deserve disrespect."

Vorn held a hand to Tarac, then motioned to the settee. "If you please, Lady Aliria."

"No. Thank you."

Mercies, would every conversation with her be a round of sparring? "Your choice." He moved to his chair and considered her. "Squalor, huh?"

"Yes," she said definitively. "I saw the rooms—there are six bunks in a room smaller than this space." Her gaze roved the receiving area. "And there are just as many women and children living in there. Yet, here you sit in your leather chair, with your wall of books and luxurious rug—one of you in a space large enough for at least twenty of them."

Vorn could not help but get lost in the fire of her eyes—until that imperious and remonstrative tone destroyed any illusion that he was even close to winning her over. "You really do believe me the diabolus, don't you?"

"What I think of you"—she seemed to bite back acidic thoughts—"does not matter. The care and conditions of living for those under your charge does."

"You are right." Vorn rested his elbows on the arms of the chair and steepled his fingers. "These bunks . . . you saw them?"

"I did," she said, lifting her chin.

"Did you ask anyone what they were?"

Consternation did not look good on a Lady of Basilikas.

Vorn shifted, wishing she had given him more credit. He straightened and stood before her, appreciating how she seemed to resist cowering, though he would vow she had to defy the instinct to take a step back. "Rarely do I explain myself or the way in which I run my house, but since you are a guest for an extended time and"—no, he should mayhap not mention that he hoped one day she might be Lady of Forgelight—"not from this country, I will indulge your impertinence."

She started. Mouth opening, no doubt to object.

Vorn pressed a finger to her lips and held her gaze. "There are over a hundred staff on property." He rested his hands on his cummerbund. "Many have spouses, children. Rather than see families split up, they are given priority for private rooms. Last week the sergii quarters were heavily damaged during a storm, so the sergii are crammed." Waves, she was formidable, and he was glad to see some of her imperiousness fading away. "Would you have preferred I put them all out while repairs were made?"

"The larger apartments abovestairs could have been utilized—"

"I understand you are new here, that you do not know how a royal household is managed, and for that reason alone will I forgive your continued impertinence. Sergii will not be housed with the royal family or visiting guests and nobles. Regardless of your sensitivities." He leaned into her space. "That will not change, and there are reasons I do not expect you to understand on your first week in residence." He motioned Tarac to them. "The Sword will see you back to your apartments. I have business to attend."

VALIRIANA

Rude, insufferable man! Valiriana stood on the balcony watching the sun break the power of darkness and spill its glory over the sea and land. Though she tried to appreciate the growing warmth from the sunlight, since last eve, since seeing the state of living conditions, a chill had pervaded her bones and heart. He justified the inhumane living conditions because of storm damage, but was there not plenty of room to temporarily accommodate those who so fastidiously served in his house? This was . . . unacceptable! Hugging herself, she grieved that she had been right about this king, but worse—that being right meant others suffered.

"Will you not eat, my lady?" Yieri asked—not for the first time.

Eat in luxury when those below sat on cots in dingy, musty bunkrooms?

Clearly this Licitus did not deserve Faa'Cris aid. She had longed to communicate with Deversoria many times, but she should not seem petulant or inexperienced by racing to report every injustice she witnessed.

"Revered Mother." She spoke using the *vox saeculorum.* Her giftings had been inconsistent at best since the barn, so she hoped—

"You are well, Valiriana?" Ma'ma's voice held a charge of concern.

"I am not." Far from it! *"Had I not intervened, the Errant would have imprisoned a child! Now, he demands my compliance. Holds me hostage, against*

my will." It was not a whole truth—she had agreed to the bargain, perhaps a little hastily, not fully comprehending what she'd committed herself to. Ma'ma would understand, issue a recall. She would return.

"Perhaps against your *will, but clearly not against the Ancient's."*

The words grated, but truth sometimes did. She shifted against the railing, eyes closed, hearing the roar of the surf below her. *"I saw him attack a young man who did him no wrong. Then another. He has an entire palace yet relegates sergii to cramped quarters with naught but sheets for privacy. Surely we do not condone this. I cannot stand the Licitus!"* Never would he convince her of his honor. To do so, he would have to contain some.

"This missio *to gather intelligence is not about* you, *Valiriana."*

"Did you not hear the grievances? He—"

"Remember whom we serve—not our whims. His will is what we should seek."

Whims? Jaw tight, she knew she must yield. The points were valid. But . . . if the Revered Mother would not hear her complaints, then how was she to convince them he was not suited for a Sending? The thought of his life being joined to a Lady's sent a repulsed shudder through her. *"He does not deserve us."*

"Do you say the Lady Eleftheria was wrong?"

Valiriana lifted her head, opening her eyes to gaze across the ocean vista. No, the Lady was not wrong—she was never wrong because she sat with the Ancient and Vaqar, so her words were wise and well-reasoned. How desperately Valiriana wanted the Lady to be wrong.

"You know what you must do." With those words, the *vox saeculorum* closed.

She must remain. Continue the mission given her by the Lady. She slapped the railing, bruising her hand. She yelped and rubbed the sore spot. One thing was certain . . . she had to adjust her perspective. Blood and boil, she did not want to. He had taken her freedom.

Correction: she lost her freedom by standing in for a friend who had protected her. She had made the bargain with the Errant, which meant she must also endure her sentence and remain here with him.

One year, a prisoner to this savage.

Prisoner . . . Her gaze took in the chambers. Papered walls, marble floors, a receiving room with chaise and settee, a bedchamber with an enormous raised, canopied bed and bedcurtains, a dressing room, a bathing room. While she resented the restriction on her movements, she must concede it would be a year spent in extravagance. Far grander than the much simpler life within Deversoria. Or perhaps not grand but . . . wasteful. Everything looked pretty here, but how were their hearts?

Corrupt. Errant. Foul!

A thunderous knock drew her around. Hugging herself, she returned to the bedchamber as Yieri scurried across the cream stone to the apartment doors, which she tugged open.

The Sword of the King stalked into the receiving room, his expression impassive and stonelike. "You will sup with the king tonight."

In Deversoria, she had taken her meals in the great hall with the other trainees. This sounded . . . different. He only mentioned the king—did that mean they would be alone? *Not if I have any say.* Holding her robe tight to her throat, she eased into the receiving room. "And if I refuse?"

"Then you will be hungry and lonely."

Adjusting her robe, she held her position.

"Suit yourself." Captain Mape made for the door. "His Majesty is better without you."

She remembered some of the first words Khatrione had spoken to her and called after the Sword of the King. "Does not disobeying the king's command have repercussions?" Her own guilt squirmed in her belly for wanting this man to pay for his seething comments.

But he did not falter as he grabbed the handle. "Aye."

Disbelieving he had not seen the wisdom of her words, she again called to him, "And you would have me suffer it."

He jerked around, his dark eyes alight with anger. "I would have my king seek a woman who deserves him, not a Lady whose detestable arrogance would shame the greatest of her Sisters." He slid his gaze to Yieri in the corner. "If she comes, you know how to dress her." Then he was gone, the door rattling beneath the force of his haste to abandon the room.

The arrogance and disrespect! "In earnest," she said, spinning to the lady's maid, "how could he think *I* do not deserve the king?" The suggestion infuriated.

"Then . . . yeh are a Lady, a real one?" Sweet innocence wreathed the old woman's face.

Valiriana realized her mistake too late. Looked to the woman assigned to her. "I . . . I spoke out of turn."

"Then yeh are not?"

She could not lie to her. "Can it be our secret?"

Face alight, Yieri nodded with the excitement of a child. "Imagine—me, serving a real *Lady*!"

Suddenly, Valiriana's actions and attitudes seemed to scream. She *was* a Lady, and as such, she was a representative of the Daughters, Eleftheria, Vaqar, and ultimately the Ancient. She now stood charged with a *missio* that would irrevocably alter lives. Regret over her response to the captain drew her attention to the door.

"Give no mind to him," Yieri said softly, coming to her with a comb. "He is overprotective of the king. They are like brothers."

"Like brothers, but . . . *not* brothers?"

After seating Valiriana in a chair, Yieri went to work on her hair. "The captain was brought here as a ward, the eldest son of a nobleman deeply in debt to King Tamuro II. To clear the obligation, the baron offered his son as companion for the young prince."

Valiriana frowned. "Why would Vaanvorn need a companion? He had a brother already."

"In blood only."

She frowned, confused at the way that sounded so . . . distant. Cold. "I do not—blood is the greatest of bonds."

Yieri clucked her tongue. "Prince Tamuro hated his brother, always saw him as a rival for the throne and their mother's affection. So, when the queen died, the king had young Prince Vaanvorn relegated to the farthest reaches of the castle and focused all his energy on training the crown prince."

"Men truly are the most wicked of creatures," Valiriana murmured and reminded herself that those words included the current king. She shoved aside the attempt of pity to dig into her focus. She could not be weakened by sad stories, but she could glean one valuable nugget from Yieri's tale: "So if anyone knows the king, it would be Captain Mape?"

"No one knows him better."

Which meant the Sword of the King would be her best chance to learn the true character of Vaanvorn Thundred. Yet the captain did not like or approve of her.

One year.

Valiriana spent the day wandering from balcony to bedchamber, receiving room to balcony, wrestling with her situation and praying for guidance. A hundred times she softened. A hundred times her heart grew hard.

The afternoon was far gone when she rose from her chair on the balcony, the shadow of the castle stretching out over the lawn to touch the waves. At last she knew what she must do. The Lady Eleftheria had chosen her for this delicate mission, to rout the inner workings of this king's adunatos. Valiriana would not fail her. But she could not learn of the Errant and his goings-on if she remained locked abovestairs. She glanced at her lady's maid, who sat dozing just inside the doors to the bedchamber. "Yieri. I will go to the dinner."

Eyebrows lifting, Yieri straightened. Her face brightened. "Oh, very good, my lady. Let us get you ready."

After ablutions and hair plying, Valiriana eyed the ornate gown hanging ready for her to don. "No. I cannot wear that."

Yieri faltered. "But my lady—"

"No. Find something . . . simpler." She refused to be made up into something she was not. "Whatever is suitable for any one of the ladies on the street, for a farmer's wife like Jan'maree, perhaps."

The woman went white, hand to her stomach. "My lady, please . . ."

Valiriana strode to the wardrobe and prowled through the gowns . . . gossamer, gauze, satin . . .

"Please, my lady. You do not understand. He will be angry if you are not properly attired."

All the better. She found a nice burgundy one. "This one!"

Yieri gasped. "No!" She yanked it from her and hurried into the far corner and stuffed it in a basket, then returned, her pallor extreme. "That is an *evening* garment, my lady."

"Aye, and that is exactly what this is—evening!" Valiriana drew out another similar to the first and started dressing. Eyed her lady's maid, who looked ready to cry. "Be at peace, Yieri," she said. "I agreed to his term of one year, but make no mistake—I am not here to adorn his arm." After a glance in the glass, she started for the door.

"Please, my lady, do not."

She turned and set a hand on the older woman's shoulder, faltering when she realized how thin it was. "Fear not. All will be well. I assure you." So what if Vaanvorn were angry? She could bear anything he threw at her. Out the door, she nearly laughed when the guards stumbled to catch up with her quick pace.

"Lady, where do you go?"

"To dinner," she pronounced. "I am ordered to join the king."

"My lady, would you not like to dress for dinner?" the guard asked.

She held out her arms as she glanced at her dress. "I am attired."

"Would you like to return to chambers and dress *appropriately*?" the guard insisted.

She lifted her chin. "What is your name?"

The guard shifted, sharing a glance with his cohort. "Tozet Chaiy, my lady."

"Well, Tozet, am I to tell the king I was delayed because of you, or will you show me to dinner?" She touched her stomach. "I do find myself suddenly famished."

He faltered. "I . . ." His throat processed a slow swallow, uncertainty in his gaze.

"As thought." Valiriana continued on, relieved when they finally led her to the hall.

"Please, Lady, it is not—"

The kingsguard outside the hall scowled as she approached and shifted into her path. Blocked the door.

"The king said I am to join him," she said, nodding to the heavy barriers behind them. Over her shoulder, she addressed her guard. "Tozet, tell them—"

Cocking his head in apparent displeasure, Tozet sighed. "The Lady Valiriana comes at the pleasure of the king." He muttered something else she could not decipher, but apparently the guards could, for they moved aside and the doors opened.

A heady, spiced aroma drifted from the room and made her stomach growl. Valiriana strode in and looked around.

The casual din of chatter in the room died . . . fast. And was soon followed by murmurs and titters. Hushed mutterings. A form popped up on the far side and several long strides hastened Tarac Mape toward her, his face a veritable storm.

"Ah, Sword of the—" Shock ripped through her when he clamped onto her arm. She hauled in a breath. *What is this?* The pain of his grip was startling. "Release me," she bit out. "Do you not recall the king said never put hand to me?"

"*What* do you?" he hissed as he pulled her toward the doors.

"Dinner—" Her gaze collided then with the king's. What she saw there made her falter.

Brows furrowed, lips thinned, he tucked his bearded chin and glowered. She did not recall his face being so ruddy before. Anger . . . and something dark moved through his expression, stealing her voice.

Laughter tittered through the room.

What was he doing, removing her from the hall? "You said the king asked me to join him for the meal," she mumbled, glancing around the tables and noting the way the women pointed at her, sniggering. Some shook their heads dismissively. The men scowled in disapproval.

Even as Tarac hauled her out, she heard cruel words spoken. That she was a chatelaine, that the king was desperate, that he could not control his own house, so how would he rule the realm?

Valiriana sought the king as she was drawn through the doors, which were already closing. She again found his gaze. Tight. Furious. What . . . what had she done so wrong? Her feet tangled on a rug as she was yanked around a corner. She tripped but the captain jerked her upright, his grip unmerciful.

She cried out, surprised. This was cruel of him, so uncalled for.

"What idiocy infects you that you carry out a stunt like that against the king?" Tarac pulled her onward.

Valiriana pitched forward, breaking her fall as she canted into the plastered wall. "Release me, *Licitus*!"

His grip only tightened. "I warned him you may not be Faa'Cris—and I am correct. Your actions this night prove it." He was unrelenting in his fury, forcing her back to her chambers. "You show up to a state dinner dressed like that? A real Lady would never make a mockery of those they would protect."

Down the hall, two guards thrust open the door to her apartments, all too happy to let the room swallow her.

The captain flung her toward the settee.

"How dare you!" Valiriana spun, twitching her spine to free her clypeus. Though heat rushed down her vertebrae, her span did not deploy. What . . .?

"If you ever attempt to humiliate King Vaanvorn again, I will make sure you feel the full stupidity of your actions!"

"What have I done wrong except choose my own attire?"

"Atti—" He bit back a curse, and his gaze shifted. Landed on Yieri, who stood to the side, hands clasped before her and head down. His gaze darkened and nostrils flared. "You know where to find your letter."

Yieri twitched, her eyes widening—but not lifting—almost imperceptibly.

The captain gave a sharp nod and the lady's maid left the room without another sound. Was that a tear sliding down her cheek?

Valiriana felt something corkscrew through her. What was this?

The Sword looked to Tozet and the other guard. "She is not to leave this chamber without the express permission of myself or the king. Understood?"

"Aye, sir."

Heaving a breath, his anger apparently abating, he shook his head at her. "The more I know you, the more I am convinced of your humanity. No Lady would so cruelly and unjustly abuse a man as you have done."

"How dare you! I am a Lady of Basilikas, raised among the Faa'Cris for the entirety of my life!"

"Then prove it!"

"I—"

"Not with words," he growled. "Show us what one who honors the Ancient and the Lady behaves like. Let the words from your lips drip not with condescension but integrity that comes from said life spent among the Faa'Cris, serving the Ancient!" He drew in a ragged breath and let it out. "I pray the damage you have done this night is reparable. If not . . . I will make sure it is repaid against you ten times over, immortal be cursed."

Damage? What had she damaged? "I am not immortal."

He gave her a dark smile. "All the better."

Stunned, she watched him back out of the room, tugging the doors closed as he seared her with a terrible glower. "It is but a dress!" she shouted at the door, even as a heavy *thunk* sounded on the other side.

A tremor of fear raced through her, and she hurried to the doors. Pulled. Found them secured tight. Locked. She banged on the heavy wood. "Let me out!"

The doors remained closed.

I am Faa'Cris. You cannot hold me! With smug defiance, she flicked her spine and released her span. Only . . . it did not release. Wings remained tucked into the clypeus.

Valiriana rolled her shoulders again and made a more dramatic outward push to release the clypeus.

Nothing.

Panic choked her. *"Revered Mother,"* she spoke into the *vox saeculorum.* Silence.

"Revered Mother, we must speak." Still nothing but empty distance. *"Please."* The hollowness of that gap grew chilled, hard. *"Ma'ma! Please—I must speak with you!"*

When only more silence met her pleas, Valiriana told herself to calm down. Quiet her fears. Settle her heart. She tried again. *"Ma'ma, I need you."*

The clanging of masts on the harbor and the call of gulls were the only response to her cry.

"Ma'ma!" she shouted. Dropped back against the door. Kicked her heel back against it. Scream-squealed her outrage. Her panic. What had she done wrong? Where had she gone off course?

What did one dress matter? It had been an innocent mistake.

No . . . not quite so innocent, for she *had* rebelled against the instruction of her lady's maid. Even when Yieri had begged her not to wear it.

Valiriana straightened herself. *I must apologize to her.* She nodded to herself as she climbed into the bed. On the morrow when Yieri brought food to break the fast.

Lying in the quiet of the night, the sheets cool, her anger still hot, she ached to talk to the Revered Mother. No . . . to Ma'ma. What did it mean that she couldn't reach across time and space to talk with her? And her wings—why were they being stubborn and not deploying? She so wanted to snap her ridge at that impudent Sword of the King. She had heard of times when stress and strange circumstances made it so a Daughter could not access the *vox saeculorum* . . . but not her span? That was strange.

Stress. It must be stress. And anger. She was Lady enough to confess her sin and anger. But the king was so . . . infuriating!

More than ever, she despised Licitus.

I should never have come.

But she was here. And she would fulfill her duty and deliver a report. "You will never have a Lady, Vaanvorn Thundred. Neither you nor any in this realm." She gritted her teeth. "I vow with my life you won't."

Light stabbed her corneas. Valiriana groaned and shifted, dragging herself from a heavy sleep. Blinking, she sat up, wondering why she felt as if she'd failed trials a dozen times over. But it all came back to her in a rush—arguing with Yieri about the dress. Going to the dinner. The humiliation. The Sword of the King dragging her back here and locking her in.

Then the *vox saeculorum* . . .

It had been a dream, aye? A bad, bad dream. Had to be.

Valiriana drew in a ragged breath. Touched her temple as she reached across the distance once more. *"Ma'm—"* She swallowed. *Do not be a child.* *"Revered Mother, I need your help."*

Emptiness gaped.

No . . . *"I beseech you, Revered Mother. Ladies."* Tears stung her eyes, a darkness yawning between her and home. *"Please, I—"* A panicked sob choked off her words. *"Talk to me!"* Burying her face in her hands, she cried.

Why had she thought she could do this? Did she not have enough proof of this king's unsuitability? Then why was she shut off?

Rebellion. She had rebelled against Yieri's admonishment to dress nicely.

A creaking startled her out of her mourning. She glanced to the side and through the partially drawn bedcurtain, where she spied a young girl hurrying into the room with a tray of food.

Valiriana pulled herself upright.

"Oh." The girl stiffened. "Forgive me, Lady. I did not mean to wake you. I . . . This is not my usual—"

"Do not distress yourself." Valiriana wiped her tears and pushed her thick black hair behind her shoulder. "Where is Yieri? Is she well?"

The girl's expression went slack. "She . . . she is gone."

"Gone?"

"Got her papers."

Papers. Valiriana recalled the Sword saying something about that. "Papers for what? Will she return soon?"

The girl frowned, confusion marked in her young face. "No, my lady. She is removed from the palace, her employment terminated." She bunched her shoulders in a shrug. "*Gone*."

"Terminated?" Valiriana shoved from the bed and hurried to the girl. "Why would she be terminated? What offense was so great to deserve that?"

Anger scratched through the tawny features, then washed away in a hasty, blank mask. "She failed to carry out her duties."

"What duties? She was *my* lady's maid."

"Aye." The girl ducked her head. "She was supposed to ready you for an audience with His Majesty."

Shock struck her dumb. Valiriana could not move. Her mind viciously replayed the maid's pleading, her fear that the king would be angry. Valiriana insisting there was no concern, thinking she could bear the king's ire. She'd been a fool. "This . . . this is my fault."

"No, my lady. It is our—" The girl snapped her mouth closed and dropped her gaze. Went preternaturally still.

"It is your what?"

The girl did not move.

Valiriana edged nearer. "Why will you not speak to me?" The Daughters were silent. Her ma'ma. Not this sergius, too. "Pl—"

"A moment, Karistni," a deep voice intruded.

With a nod of deference, the girl scurried through the door by which she had entered earlier.

Valiriana pivoted to find Captain Mape there. "You—you did this! Why? Why would you terminate Yieri?"

Handsome and severe, he did not falter. "Because she allowed you to appear before the king in nothing—"

"That was my doing—"

"—but a dressing gown."

"Why is she blamed—" Her mind caught up with his words. "Dressing gown?" she repeated numbly. "What is that?"

The Sword averted his gaze, as if the explanation alone might shame him. "A gown donned by a lady preparing for bed."

Mortification crashed through her. "*Nightclothes?*" She had worn nightclothes to the dinner hall? "She said they were evening garments."

Hard eyes found her again. "They are the same." He swallowed. "And appearing in the king's hall, in the king's house, in such attire implied to his guests that you and he . . ." He cleared his throat. "That you are more than simply a guest, if you take my meaning."

She frowned. What meaning? More than a guest?

"That you and he share more than passages and meals. That you share a bed."

Gasping, Valiriana recoiled. "I would never . . . That is . . ." Heat scorched her cheeks. Overcoming her humiliation, she hugged herself. Fought the instinct to shrink. She was Faa'Cris, and Ladies did not shrink from any Licitus. "Th-that was my mistake. My . . . ignorance. I was unaware of its purpose when I wore it. Why would Yieri be terminated for my mistake, such a silly—"

"It is her job to make sure you are properly attired, regardless of your choice. Yieri should have informed you of the indecency of your choice and prevented you from humiliating yourself and the king."

"What she laid out was too pretentious. Bulky," she tried to explain. "I wanted something simple."

"The damage done to the king's name and reputation last eve is extensive."

Damage. Last evening he had said as much, and it did not pinch any less this morn. "Even so, it is my fault. Bring her back. Punish me. I own the guilt—I should pay."

"Agreed." His answer was sharp, definitive. "But the hour is past, and as said, damage done. I challenge you to think carefully of your actions and heed the instruction of those in this house before you cast off our voices as an encumbrance, deeming yourself so much the wiser."

The animosity in his words cut like a dagger. "I erred—"

"Aye!"

She jerked back a step, startled. Had she not owned her guilt? Yet still he railed at her. His disdain for her was plain.

"And so help me," he snarled, "if you do any more harm to the king, you can be sure—"

"The king?" she balked. "An elderly woman is tossed out and unemployed from this *house*. How is such an aged person to find another position? To provide for herself? To feed herself? Yet here you stand, worried about a king whose only concern is how a woman dresses when she comes to—"

"*Give care*"—his voice boomed over hers—"what you speak against the king."

"Is he so fragile that he fears my words?" Taunting him was below her, and it disappointed how quickly she had fallen into such infantile behavior. Then she recalled the maid saying this man was as a brother to the king. That may explain his behavior, his defensiveness. "You . . . you are close to King Vaanvorn. And as a ward, surely you—"

"Do not think to ply me against my king. How dare you!" The Sword stalked toward her but pulled up short, his gaze slamming to the right. He snapped to the side and lowered his gaze. "Majesty."

"Leave us, Tarac."

At the resonating voice behind her, Valiriana whirled to face the king even as the Sword strode past her and made a quick exit.

Powerfully built, tall, he wore his unruly black hair slicked back in a queue down his spine. A wide leather cummerbund secured his cream undervest. His olive skin seemed to glow along corded muscles that ended in a series of leather bands on his wrist. Why must he forego shirts? But there was no mistaking that this man trained hard and regularly. Never had she seen a man's abdomen so . . . well-defined.

"Do you approve?"

Valiriana twitched, coming to herself and realizing the king stood with his arms to the side and a cocky grin that said he had caught her staring. "No." She blinked. "I mean—" She clamped her mouth shut and flared her nostrils. "The manner of attire here is . . . bewildering." It was a natural segue, was it not? If she offered apologies, would the *vox saeculorum* reopen to her? She kept her gaze down—let him think it deference if he must, but it was more to maintain her focus. "Which explains my mistake last eve. I did not understand the garments were"—best not to mention nightclothes before this errant king—"inappropriate. Had I—"

"*Listened* to the lady's maid, none of this would have transpired?" he supplied with more than a little amusement.

She met his gaze, surprised at two things—that he had so perfectly read her thoughts and at the tinge of mockery in his words. Though she thought to snap back at him, it was hard not to think of all that had happened, the mess she had made by reacting rather than responding. In truth, it was hard to think at all considering the man before her, the attire he wore that did nothing to conceal his torso. Absently, she wondered if it would feel more like leather or satin.

Blood and boil, her thoughts were straying! She banished the images from her mind. Pushed her attention back to her mistake. "Aye."

Now *he* looked surprised.

Which put her in remembrance of Yieri. She ached for her former lady's maid's bearing the punishment due Valiriana. "I would beg you—return Yieri to her position."

The smile vanished from his visage. "No."

Tilting her head, she frowned, convinced he misunderstood what she asked for. There was no possible justification for refusing her request. "In earnest, she should be returned. The mistake was mi—"

"Leave off this subject, Lady." His beard twitched as he wandered to the window, twisting the ring on his little finger, his mood much altered now. "Quickly will you learn in this castle that our actions do not affect us alone. What you have done, your disregard of protocols, impacted another. Gravely." His expression grew grim. "Perhaps Yieri's suffering will teach you something, but as for retracting my decision . . . I will not be moved."

"Because you have no heart to move?"

His gaze snapped to hers, and she felt the ferocity of it to her marrow.

Why was she so quick with her words and so slow with wisdom? Had she done more *damage* to this situation now? She must don contrition. "Please—I beg you let her return. She is aged and—"

With a huff, he speared her with an acidic expression that silenced her. When he ran a hand over his queued hair and beard, she could not help but notice the way his muscles rippled. Hands falling to rest on his cummerbund, he stared out to the water and went silent.

Valiriana struggled to remain where she stood, watching, knowing she had done harm where she meant to do good, knowing her actions were undoubtedly tied to the silence of the *vox saeculorum* as well as to Yieri's dismissal. She struggled to find a solution. Ma'ma and her mentors had always said she had a quick mind—if only she could apply it here. Because at the moment, her conscience quailed.

"Why will you not set aside your"—she searched for the right word, her heart drumming—"arrogance"—*no, no, wrong word but it is out, spoken, so*—"and listen to me. It was my error. Punishing her is unfounded and ridiculous."

Silence shrouded the powerful man as he stood there, feet shoulder width apart, his frame . . . admirable. He did not speak for a while and her nerves grew. Concerned she had already done more harm, she reached out and tested his efflux.

"You think so highly of yourself," came his gruff remonstration without turning to address her, "yet you claim—"

"Only because Faa'Cris are far superior—"

"They *should* be, but what I have seen is far less."

Shock anchored her feet to the floor, her mouth to silence. Staring at his back, she had to strangle her desire to fly at him. Drive her boot into his spine. But her clypeus hadn't exactly been cooperative the last couple of days, so that was unlikely to happen.

There arose something that stayed her irritation—a strange scent in the air around him. The sudden awareness made her realize his words had pulled her from processing the air, the scents. As she finally did, she felt a twinge in her adunatos. Well, that was . . . unexpected.

Frowning, she considered him. Why was the Errant sad? Somehow, though she could not fathom why, she sensed that sadness might be connected to her actions. His words about the Faa'Cris being *less* made her cringe. That was her fault, was it not? She had stained the name of the Daughters and that invariably shadowed the Ancient's as well.

Arguments fell away. She had disappointed herself and the Lady Eleftheria. Disappointment swelled through her regarding her behavior. He was right—Ladies were supposed to be better. Because of her, in his view, they were now less.

The heaviness drew her toward him, toward the window. She gained his flank and did not miss how his gaze slid toward her—but didn't quite meet her—then back to the water. Determination to make amends forced her to stay. "I—"

"There is a feast in a few days," he said as he pivoted and strode away. "I would have you attend." He paused. Shifted to her. "*Properly* attired this time. I realize you care little for me or this realm, but I would ask that you respect our customs and not unilaterally offend every guest this time." His rich, dark gaze held her hostage. "Mayhap I should point out that if you abandon our deal, there will be no choice but to remand Jan'maree Eknil into custody."

Why did his every word make her want to defy him? Not trusting herself to speak, she inclined her head. When she looked up again, he was gone and the door closing behind him. But the sadness that had infested his adunatos remained, lingering in the warm air. Chastising her for her part in its creation.

And now, she had a chance to redeem that error.

VAANVORN

Sun beat down on the training yard where Furymark worked to perfect their skills. From the elevated observation deck that ran the perimeter of the yard, Vorn gripped the rail that did little to stop him from pitching himself down into the fray. Were these the best Jherako had to offer in defense of the realm and Crown? And with Hirakys defying boundaries and borders. Jherako must do better. Be stronger.

"They are green," Tarac muttered from his right.

"They are *weak*!" Vorn hissed, shaking his head, straightening and folding his arms as he scanned the trainees. "Hirakys could invade blind and drunk, yet emerge victorious."

His mood was befouled by what had transpired last eve. He rifled through his thoughts, options, doing his best to harness the anger. Seeing her walk in dressed like that . . . hearing the derisive comments of his guests—*his guests*! It was just like the celebration in which Tamuro had taken Yirene all over again.

"So," Tarac said quietly, "no word from Hiro yet?"

"Nothing," Vorn conceded. "Revalor said by first light, and here we are oras past breaking our fast." It did not bode well.

"You fear something happened to him?"

"No . . . I know not." He roughed a hand over his face. "But what other explanation is there?"

"That he is an offworlder, that he plied our vulnerable position against us to gain access to the palace, to you . . ."

All thoughts that had plagued Vorn throughout his meal. "To what end? Think you he betrays us to one of the other realms?" It could be. But, again, to what end? He straightened and folded his arms. "I do not know which frustrates me more—the Lady's actions or Revalor's silence. I spoke with her this morn, as you know, but I have no idea if it will help or hurt."

"I confess I lost my temper when I delivered the Lady to chambers," Tarac said, palming the ledge of the observation wall. "If she is a Lady—they are shrewd, powerful, so I cannot take her actions as ones of ignorance."

"Aye, yet she is all wide-eyed, beguiling innocence when confronted with her transgressions."

He let his gaze track to the recruits, his thoughts skipping from them to Aliria to Revalor. At least Vorn had been able to court Kalonica, who had been a hesitant-but-willing ally. Sasada had so many protocols that sparked offenses if not respected, it felt like trying to walk on coals. Iaison would forever be considered subjugated to Jherako for Yirene's murder of Tamuro, but the strained relations did not help. Avrolis was jealous of its water boundaries and too competitive in shipping trade to be reasoned with . . .

I am failing. Mere months on the throne and I already—

A barked laugh drew his attention to where two recruits who'd earned their first color sparred in the corner, but they were spending more time laughing and giving a halfhearted effort than preparing themselves for battle.

"Strip their color and make them run the gauntlet against the kingsguard," Vorn growled.

Tarac hesitated, but then sent hand signals to Ba'moori, whose face went slack, but then he scowled and jogged to the two, whose gazes swung to their disapproving king before they sprinted out of the practice yard toward their grueling workout.

A scrawny youth thrust upward to block an attack and stumbled. Fell into the dirt.

"Black seas," Vorn muttered, "he tripped over his own two feet."

"And that's Creel's nephew," Tarac said with a trace of amusement. "I keep telling him the boy doesn't have the makings of a warrior, but—"

"Guard!" Vorn shouted when he saw the direction of the pup's overhead strike—straight toward a Furymark training another pup. "Waves of providence!" *Why does Azyant coddle the boy?* "For the love of—" He vaulted over the rail, dropping the ten feet to the ground with the expert precision of a warrior with decades of training and combat experience. He stalked across the sandpit.

"Stand clear for the—"

Vorn flicked a hand to Ba'moori. He dared someone to try to cut him. He motioned to the weapons master, who hefted a longblade and flung it to him, hilt first. Vorn caught it deftly, never breaking stride. His gaze punched into the pup's. "Ready yourself, Recruit!"

With a vengeance, Vorn threw himself into sparring with the young man, who had not even shown the first signs of a beard. The kid repeatedly overreached, offering his side for a critical strike. So Vorn took it. Drove his blade just below the kid's ribcage.

"Augh!" The boy stumbled, gripping his wound, blood sluicing between his fingers. He tripped. Went down hard, jaw slack.

Creel gave a shout and rushed to where his nephew bled. He shot a furious glance at Vorn. "What did you do? Pharmakeia!"

Rage coloring his vision, Vorn hauled Creel up. "Whom do you address?"

The man blanched, apparently remembering himself. "Y-you, Majesty—K-King Vaanvorn."

"And who do you train?"

"The kingsguard."

"And who do they defend?"

"The king and the realm."

Vorn pitched him backward. "Dare speak to me like that again, and I will have you running the gauntlet, too, minus a few waves." He steadied his ragged breath and looked to the pup. "I taught him a lesson he will not soon forget—that battle and defense of this realm are very real and very dangerous." He slid his blade to the pup's throat, then his gaze to Creel. "You serve our enemy well by coddling our soldiers." He lifted his voice and turned a circle, taking in the Furymark assigned to training the next generation. "Train them hard, Captains. Train them well, and they will live. Our enemy will not be forgiving nor"—he purposely glanced at the bleeding boy, who now also had a pharmakeia tending him—"will he avoid key organs that you might live to train another day."

Creel started, looked at the pharmakeia.

The Furymark physician nodded as he packed the wound. "He is correct—it would seem no vital organs were damaged, but we will need to remove him to the hospital to review his wound and let him convalesce—"

"One week," Vorn pronounced. "Then he will resume training."

"But—"

"We are Furymark! Not children playing at war." Vorn exhaled heavily. "Back to sparring. Let's go!"

The men complied, their moves taut and uncertain. Scared. Scared that Vorn would join their pairing, injure one of them. A pair of second-years chose hand-to-hand and soon went to ground. One had the other—a blue—in a chokehold, which he struggled against but then made quick work of not only freeing himself but neutralizing his opponent.

"Well done!" Vorn shouted. "Again!" When it happened again, he motioned to a training captain. "Secure the blue's arm behind his back."

The blue's face washed of his arrogance.

"Come out of that victorious and we will talk."

The kid ate up the challenge. He launched into the next round. Vorn knew he'd master it, but it'd take time. He strolled a few paces to the next pair.

"Sire!"

Vorn glanced back, just in time to see the blue extricate himself from a reverse chokehold. He whipped around on one knee and in a blink held a dagger to his partner's throat.

Okay. This had his attention. He moved back to the blue. Considered him, still saw a spark of arrogance. "What is your name?"

The young man's gaze flicked to Tarac, then back to Vorn.

"I'm sorry"—Vorn gave a chuckle he did not feel—"did Captain Tarac ask you the question or did I?"

Twitching back into decorum, the blue ducked. "I beg your mercy, King Vaanvorn."

"Your name," Vorn demanded.

"Dezan . . . Mape."

Surprised, Vorn looked at his captain in question.

Tarac gave a sharp nod. "My little brother."

"That explains much. Captain Gormon!" Vorn shouted across the yard.

In a tick, Azyant was at his side. "Yes, Majesty?"

"I think this blue needs a challenge," he said, appreciating the way Dezan Mape now sported a different expression. "Run him into the ground."

The burly training master grinned. "With pleasure, sire."

Vorn shifted to his Sword. "You should've told me."

"He needs to earn his own way."

"That he does." Vorn returned to his inspection of the recruits, feeling Tarac swing up on his right. He angled his ear to him even as he watched two teen blanks training with wood swords.

"You have an audience," Tarac said quietly, and with the barest of indication lifted his gaze and brows upward.

In that instant Vorn felt the warmth of her gaze. He searched the inner bailey to the upper balconies. There she stood at a third-level window, dumping her disapproval with a severe expression. "At this rate, my grandson is more likely to win her approval than I am."

"At last there is someone's disapproval you will weigh longer than a heartbeat." Tarac followed as Vorn left the training yard and headed toward his library. "If you were to deploy that method of . . . strengthening all the recruits, we would have none left. They would all be in the infirmary recovering from your *instruction*."

Curse the man for amusing him. "I may have been . . . aggressive in my determination to correct their course." Likely born out of too many frustrations pounding him all at once—his brother's betrayal and death, Hirakys testing the border, no word from Revalor, the untried weakness of his own Furymark, the Lady here but a petulant—

"King Vaanvorn."

At the voice of his vizier, Vorn growled and focused on his destination. "Not now, Haarzen."

"I think we should talk. The ambassador expressed concern."

Raging seas, would he get no break? He stormed into his library. "Let him in." He considered the selection of liquor on the sideboard. Felt the thirst he needed to quench . . .

"I think," Haarzen Gi said quietly amid the sound of the door closing them in, "you will want a clear mind for what lies ahead."

Vorn huffed and pivoted. "And what is that?"

"The intrusion of your . . . guest . . . gave the ambassador of Giessen concern."

"He has been looking for an excuse to break the alliance since my father died."

Haarzen gave a slow nod. "That is true, but we do not want to exacerbate the issue, nor do we want him to win others to his cause. After your departure, he suggested if you cannot provide for or control those within your own house, you were unlikely to be able to do so for the people or for other provinces."

It did not surprise that Nindrol Brikorn would defame him in order to gain an upper hand in negotiations. Vorn muttered an oath and moved to the window. It was his mistake—he had been so proud that he'd negotiated her into coming to Forgelight that he'd given her too free a rein.

"Who is she?" Haarzen asked.

Vorn considered the tall, stately gentleman he'd hand-chosen. A man he'd trusted enough to make vizier to administer the kingdom and manage the financial affairs of the realm. But did he trust him enough to share this secret?

"I do not mean to pry, Your Majesty, but there may be damage done from her appalling intrusion last eve," Haarzen said somberly. "Who is this girl that she is cloistered here and tended by your staff?"

He did not like the way the vizier questioned him. "Do I now answer to you, Vizier Gi?"

"Nay, Your Majesty, but as vizier, I would like to know how to respond to those who are inquiring and who pose risk of rumor."

Vorn dropped into his seat. "She is a guest of the Crown, and that is all you need know."

Haarzen studied them for a moment, then focused on Vorn. "You named me vizier and asked me to look to the kingdom's affairs. I cannot do that if I do not know—"

"In time, Gi," Vorn said. "Thank you—"

A knock at the door preceded Major Alen. "Sire, I thought you should know the Giessenese staff have called for their ship."

"Augh!" Vorn shoved everything off his desk. Paced to the window, then faced Tarac. "Go. Do whatever it takes to keep them here. We need their pockets. Tell them I will consider the arrangement to marry the princess."

"She's *nine*," the vizier objected.

"I did not say I *would* marry her," Vorn said, rubbing his forehead. "Only that I would consider it. But if they leave, our coffers will suffer. We need an injection of gold if we are to hope that we can rise above the stagnation and slump of the last decade. We *cannot* lose another ally! Tarac, go."

His Sword nodded.

"Vizier, thank you for your help today. If you will excuse me."

Understanding the dismissal, Haarzen stilled, then cocked his head in acknowledgement and backed from the room. Alone with his thoughts and anger, Vorn paced. Tried to find a way to salvage the mess. Long did he consider the cost of last eve. The humiliation. He leaned on the balustrade and eyed the stars.

He had half a mind to storm into the Lady's room and demand to know what idiocy possessed her . . . first the dinner fiasco, then standing over him in judgment as he trained his men. With fervor had he bought into the augur's story—in spite of her poison—that finding the Lady would help him heal the blight that infected Jherako. He had believed she used that truth to try to entrap him. But a few days here and the Lady was bringing the realm down brick by brick.

He'd been a fool to believe things would improve. Would the waves of providence *ever* move in his direction?

"I was too late," Tarac said when he returned. "The ship had already set sail."

Vorn glanced over his shoulder to where Tarac stood on the threshold between the solar and the balcony. He took in the sun sparkling on the water. "I brought her here to make things better, and they're worse." He grunted at the painful memory. "I did not sleep last night. Her disastrous performance plagued me, brought back bad memories . . ."

"Of Tamuro's feast."

He nodded absently. Humiliated all over again. "Now Giessen sees it as an excuse to break faith with us. Yet a skycrawler sees the benefit of helping our realm when our own allies do not. There is something inherently wrong with that."

"She destroyed a dinner in which we hoped to firm alliances. Lost us Giessen. Put two kingsguard in the infirmary and one in the grave and displaced a trusted and faithful sergius. Is she really worth it?" Tarac asked quietly, his tone earnest.

"I believe she will be." Vorn dragged a hand over his beard, thinking, realizing there was no way he would surrender her without a violent fight. Already she infested his heart and mind, beguiled him. "Give her time to adapt."

Tarac studied him, his jaw muscle jouncing.

Seeing his Sword's hesitation, feeling it in his own bones, Vorn could not help but think his entire rule had been a lesson in defeat. "I . . . I cannot give up. I want—need her to be the hope our country needs. To help turn the tide. Trust me. Please, Brother."

On his feet, Tarac met his gaze evenly. "I am and will always be your Sword."

14

VAANVORN
FORGELIGHT, JHERAKO

Tarac had been right—consulting the augur had been a mistake. Already Vorn regretted bringing the Lady into the castle. Aye, she held beauty beyond compare, but the trouble she had brought . . . Sitting in his solar, staring into the small fire, he rubbed his temple and forehead. What had he been thinking? When Father and Tamuro had sat on the throne, he'd been so sure he could do better. Yet it was much like trying to wrangle a squid into a boat with his bare hands. The thing would probably strangle him.

Legs stretched out, he sat back and let his head thump against the leather chair. Stared at the mantle. The— What was that? A strange light glimmered over the papers and reflected off the mirror.

The channeler!

Vorn leapt up and spun toward the library where he'd left it. He hurried there and pitched open the doors.

"Your Majesty? Are you there?" a voice crackled in the air.

Heart in his throat, Vorn threw himself toward the device on the table. For a second forgot how to use it. "Hello?"

"Majesty!" Hiro's stilted accent carried through the electronic device. "I . . . I am confounded."

"General Hiro, is that you?"

"Aye, Majesty. I must beg your mercy—I did not believe the man who came—"

"He held me prisoner!" Revalor shouted over the general. "Two days in a wood cage!"

"This man, sire—he is sent by you?"

"He is," Vorn said. "He, uh, is not from Drosero but he had a quicker way to reach you than we could manage. With the Hirakyns on the mesa, we felt it urgent to communicate the situation with you."

"How is that possible that you can know this about Hirakys—"

"He can explain, but I need you to listen to him. He has intelligence that Hirakys may be violating the border."

"Aye," Hiro said. "We tested his message by sending scouts to the mesa, and that is why we are so delayed, why your man was held so long. We have been routing the savages from the caves in the mesa. Roughly fifty so far."

Fifty. Fifty were trying to get in . . . how many had already succeeded? "You've dealt with them?"

"They will not be bothering anyone again."

"Good," Vorn said, relieved to know the incursion had been headed off. He poked his head out the door to speak to the Furymark standing guard. "Bring Captain Mape at once." He then turned toward the balcony. "Hiro, do you need reinforcements?"

"I don't believe so, sire. I called up the entire division, and we're now encamped along the mesa. Your man has shown me recent images from this . . . satellite? At this time, there are no more Hirakyns crossing. Our show of force seems to be deterring them."

"Very well. If you need another battalion, let me know. Use this device to expedite requests, but as you can imagine, others may frown upon the use of technology."

"I do, sire. This is most—"

"I understand. But times are changing. Hirakys has broken the Accord and breached our border. We cannot afford to be lost in policies that need revision. Understood?"

"Yes. Majesty."

"I well understand your concerns, General," he said quietly, calmly. He understood how violating the Accord even in this small way accosted the man's honor. "And I appreciate your dedication to Jherako and protecting it." He spotted Tarac slipping into the solar. When his First's eyebrows lifted in question, he pointed to the device. "General Hiro, unless you have more questions for me . . ."

"Not at this time, and apparently, I can reach you when needed."

"That is what I understand, too," Vorn said. "Good work, General. I appreciate the peace of mind that comes with knowing you are there and dealing with this. Thank you." How exactly did one dismiss a general over a communications device?

"It is an honor to serve you and Jherako, my king. If you are done with me, the . . . skycrawler would have a word with you."

"Of course." That would make it easier to end communication with the general. "May the waves of providence guide you and yours."

"Swift winds at your sails, sire," the general finished the blessing.

"Hey, uh, Vor—King Vaanvorn."

"Revalor. We were concerned. I hope you were not too offended at the security precautions my general took."

"Well, when you put it like that . . ." The skycrawler huffed a laugh. "I would meet you, if you have time, at the caves on that island off your southern shore. The one with the lighthouse. I believe I have shown myself to be trustworthy, and as such, I have a proposal for you."

"I will hear you. When?"

"How long would it take you to reach the island?"

"Ironesse?" Vorn said, his gaze swinging to the windows, where he could see the lighthouse even from here. "Two hours."

"Okay, then. Two hours." The screen went black.

"I never thought I would see the day when we would talk to a plastic box over a face," Tarac said with a rather sour smile. "So you are content that he is honorable?"

"I cannot speak to his honor, but he hasn't led us astray yet." He jutted his jaw. "Ready to take a boat ride?"

Disembarking hours later, Vorn spotted the skycrawler and gave the man a long look. "Is there a reason this could not take place in Forgelight? We draw attention to our movements by setting sail."

"There is," Revalor said, smirking. "I'm glad you figured out how to turn on the vidscreen again. I thought I might be in that cage forever."

"More wisdom can be found in not mocking the sovereign you seek to convince to break a long-standing accord."

"What I want to convince you of," Revalor said as he motioned them even deeper and around a winding bend, "is to seize an opportunity to be the first to stand against an entity that is gobbling up the Quadrants and dominating the skies, and has—as the screen clearly revealed—given little regard to that Accord you and most on this planet cling to like a security blanket."

"Dominating the skies," Tarac muttered with a hint of mockery. "The heavens are vast and cannot be dominated."

Experienced eyes gave him a bemused look. "One day, you will see how wrong you are. And regardless of the crowding, it is the inevitable crush of trade options that concerns me, pushes me to make inroads on this planet.

Symmachia will control it all, and if they decide we are on the wrong side of an issue, they can easily cut us all off."

"Why come to Drosero? What are we that you risk violating the Accord?"

Revalor paused and faced Vorn, sincerity bleeding from his eyes. "You tell me—what is it about this planet that you've signed an Accord? Why have you blocked technology?"

Vorn considered this man and the question. Glanced to his Sword with hesitation.

Tarac gave a grim shake of his head.

"You don't know?" marveled Revalor. "You eschew technology and deprive your people for some reason you don't—"

"Knowledge is behind our silence," Vorn growled, irritated. "You would do well to consider showing respect—"

"You are right. This is no way to win you to our side." Revalor held up his hands. "But that you remain in the dark when technology could be—"

"The Vale of Zarisem." Vorn cursed himself for letting this man goad him into answering.

"Sire," Tarac whispered, his tone urgent and warning.

Holding up a hand, Vorn stayed his Sword and focused on the man. "The vale was once the most charming spot on Drosero. Through the centuries, many made a pilgrimage there. Said it was there that the Lady Eleftheria and Vaqar chose as their dwelling. Lush and fertile lands, clear waters, perfect temperatures . . . A paradise. My own father journeyed there when he was a boy and stepped beneath the Andrelian Falls for a blessing from the Ancient."

Cautious, Revalor glanced between Vorn and Tarac. "And I suppose there is a moral to this story?"

"Having come from the skies, you no doubt are familiar with the topography of Drosero. Aye?"

A firm nod.

"The Fire Gorges."

Revalor had the decency to look grieved.

"Sasada is half the kingdom it used to be since that disaster."

"What happened?"

"An overzealous Symmachian wanted to demonstrate a weapon," Vorn explained, feeling an ease of burden as he talked. "They were courting the western countries, trying to buy their loyalty with promises of wealth and military might to overtake the rest of the continent and eventually, the planet."

"Let me guess—it didn't turn out well."

"Besides the ruination of the vale, ocean waters were contaminated, species made extinct. The effects were so far-reaching that every ruler on Drosero signed the Accord to keep technology—and Symmachia—from our planet." Vorn folded his arms. "Understand that we are not against progress, but it will come in our time, in the natural order of things."

"Afraid not," Revalor said with a click of his tongue and a shake of his head. "As you've seen, Symmachia is already interfering with your buddies to the west. When I broke atmo, there were two ships in the valley and a cruiser in orbit. Had to waste a lot of fuel to come up in a direction they couldn't see. However." He cocked his head in the direction they had been walking. "Let me show you something that might even the score."

Nerves afire, Vorn moved in the direction of the nearby cave mouth, trusting his Four and the Furymark who had escorted him to the secret rendezvous. He stopped short when he saw a hideous hulking structure in the gaping maw of the cavern. "Black seas," he hissed.

"An Interceptor, just like the one you saw on the vidscreen before you sent me off to get locked up like a dog." The skycrawler gave one resonating clap, then laughed. "But much, much larger in person."

"Incredible." Vorn swiped a hand over his mouth and beard.

Revalor stepped back and put his hand on a man's shoulder. "This is Jubbah Smirlet, my business partner, and I hope in the coming days yours as well."

"You overreach, Revalor," Vorn said, good sense taking over once more. "You said if I was interested in hearing your proposition to come to the island today. I am here—interested to hear your words. But there has been no agreement."

"What will it take for you to grow a brain?"

Vorn was not used to this manner of speech, but he could tell by the man's tone that he intended a slight. "Is this how you convince all your allies—mockery and bullying?"

The man steepled his hands. "You're right—sorry. I . . . I'm trying to rush past the small things because I don't think your planet has time for indecision."

"Neither does it have time for rushed indiscretions that break a decades-old accord."

"Void's Embrace, I didn't think you people would so thick-skulled! They are *here*! At your door, and you worry about a document—"

"Aye! One of grave concern," Vorn snapped. "Jherako already sits on the edge of a war, and dismissing careful consideration of a decision to defy every country on this planet whose rulers signed that Accord is not something I take lightly. I beg your mercy if my care and concern for my people—"

"That!" Revalor said, his voice cracking in the tunnels. "That is what you should be concerned about. Symmachia *is* here. They are breaking— *have* broken the pact. Those ships in Vysien"—he again extended the device he had removed from his vambrace—"are proof. You can play to the tune of honor but if you don't act now to level the field, this whole planet will succumb. Technology will be shoved down your throats, because I promise, whatever Symmachia is doing across your border, it's not to help anyone but Symmachia."

15

VALIRIANA
FORGELIGHT, JHERAKO

"Is it true . . . that you're a . . ." Wide green eyes hesitated and stood guard over the word that hovered behind Karistni's lips.

It surprised that in the days since being placed under the girl's care and that fateful night she'd made her terrible mistake, Valiriana had not already faced that question. Especially considering how much time they spent together, the lady's maid guiding her around the castle, showing her the stables and amphitheater, learning routines of the staff and changes of shifts. And yet, Valiriana would not supply the missing word to Karistni's question, nor did she confirm what the girl sought. Her *missio* here was not to bring attention to herself but to determine the worthiness of the king for a Sending. May and true, she also feared confirming her identity as Faa'Cris when she had already brought such humiliation to the king and forced an older woman from her vocation.

"I beg your mercy," Karistni said, keeping her head low. "I should not be intruding into your business. It is simply that word has spread of a Lady who helped a farmer and his family, then the king took this person hostage . . . and here *you* are."

"I am no hostage," Valiriana said quickly, though she was not sure why she argued the point. Had not she even called herself that many times since entering these luxurious halls? Was she not confined to these grounds? "A bargain was struck between the king and me in exchange for leniency upon Shimeal and his family."

"You gave yourself as prisoner," Karistni whispered in awe. "I heard what you did to the kingsguard when they treated you poorly. And I saw the pharmakeia tending their wounds."

Ah. Valiriana's breath struggled through her chest. She had forgotten about that. In the heat of the moment, the indignation of being hauled into this castle as if she were a dog on a lead and the aggressive reaction of some guards had unsheathed Valiriana's anger and abilities. "Are they well, the ones . . . injured?"

"They are, my Lady," the girl said. "Already returned to duty."

Relieved to hear it, she let out a breath.

"Most of all, I was impressed by what you did for Madam Yieri . . ."

Valiriana winced. "It was not my intention that she lose her position here—"

"No, my Lady," Karistni said. "I referred to what you asked of *the king*."

What she asked . . . Yieri's reinstatement. How had the sergius heard of that? Valiriana had been alone with the king during that conversation. "The king refused my request."

"It was brave of you to speak to him so boldly on behalf of a sergius. Few here would dare do such a thing."

Uncertain why, Valiriana felt her skin begin to crawl. Experienced an unsettling in the center of her being that she could not explain. Why did the girl's words—meant as praise—feel like an intrusion? Was it common for sergii to spy on the guests? Karistni was a lady's maid—it was her duty to remain cognizant of the happenings within Valiriana's chambers so she could respond when needed. So why did it concern her so much?

"For the dinner this evening," Karistni said, moving on smoothly, "I have been instructed to have a dress prepared for you, one befitting your station and position as the personal guest of the king. Might you have requests or preferences I need to consider?"

Another dinner. Valiriana wrung her hands. In Deversoria, Ladies did not concern themselves with frivolity like differing attire for various meals. A standard uniform was worn during training. Outside that and Academia, they remained in simple attire. Thus her confusion previously with "evening garments." The very idea of getting dressed up to accommodate the Errant . . . Yet would not this be a good time to hear the thoughts of others regarding this man and king? Her hope to learn from the Sword had died with their last encounter.

"Also, respectfully, my Lady"—her wary eyes darted to Valiriana, then back to the floor—"I was told that under no circumstances can I allow *you* to choose your attire. Please understand that I follow the Sword's instruction, which came from the king himself."

"In other words, you do not want to lose your position as well?"

Guilt bobbed in the girl's eyes. "If you please, my Lady . . . I would not want to be in the poorhouse again."

Startled at the bald truth of the girl's existence, Valiriana nodded. Rubbing her temple, she tried to knead away the stress headache. "Nothing red, black, or provocative." She ushered the words quickly into the space between them before she could reconsider.

Karistni's face brightened. "As you will, my Lady." She inclined her head and backed away. "If you do not have any particular needs, I will see to this immediately."

"I am well able to tend to my needs, thank you."

Karistni moved toward the sergius passage.

"One thing, Karistni."

The girl stopped and held her hands together. "Yes, my Lady?"

"Will you speak truthfully to me?"

Furtive glances spoke of the girl's nerves.

"The king . . . what do you think of him?" Why did her heart hammer when she asked the question? "Simply put—is he a good man? A man you deem honorable?"

Karistni wrung her hands. "He is the king, my Lady. It is an honor to serve here—"

"Of course." In other words, the lady's maid would not speak against the king who paid her wages. "Thank you."

"But if you want to know of the man, not the crown . . ."

Valiriana stilled at the words.

"You might want to discover his errand in the city this day."

"I see." But she did not. What was that to mean? Valiriana waited till the girl left, then moved to the balcony. Appreciated the salty air from the ocean. Enjoyed a small bowl of fruit and cordi as she relaxed in the afternoon shade. A while later, she heard a commotion to the far left. She peered there, where the castle swung around in an arc toward the bailey, and spotted the king with his men. Mounting up. Leaving.

Her heart skipped a beat. This was her path to learning about him, according to Karistni. She thought to change into something simpler but feared she would make another mistake, even after weeks here, she was still only vaguely familiar with their customs. Instead, she found a light cloak in the wardrobe and swung it over her shoulders. Hurried to the door and opened it.

In a flash, two Furymark stood before her, hands extended in a gesture that clearly said "stop."

She drew up sharply. "I would go into the city."

"Sorry, Lady Aliria," Tozet said crisply. "Orders from the king—while he is out, you are to remain in your chambers."

Bristling, she frowned. Reminded herself of her role as Faa'Cris. *Very well then.* She acquiesced and closed the door. Leaned against it. There must be a way out. But how, when she did not trust folding with its hit-or-miss madness. She went to the balcony. Eyed the ledges . . . Could she use them to get down to the bailey? No, far too wide apart and high up.

So, folding . . .

After rolling her shoulders, she tucked her chin and arched her spine.

Nothing happened.

With a groan, she tried not to get frustrated. *I* must *go. This is my* missio. "*Lady Eleftheria, please assist me. You tasked me with finding out about this man. Please free my span and gifts.*"

Inhaling deeply, reciting the oaths, she made herself relax. Stepped back, arched spine . . .

Nothing.

"Augh!" She stomped her foot and felt every bit the child then. "This is my *missio.* How am I to complete it if I cannot give witness to the man's deeds?"

Determination dug into her. She closed her eyes. Tried once more.

A burn radiated up her spine. Her clypeus thickened, rolled. She gritted her teeth, the fold taking entirely too much energy, but something—

Valiriana pitched forward.

And collided with a solid mass—a man. Something clattered to the floor.

"I beg your mercy," Valiriana muttered quickly even as his curse seared the air. She bent to retrieve the object, a small square thing with a strange symbol—but then her gaze flicked to the—brick! It was not a marble floor but a cobbled street. She had folded! With a gasp, she shot up. Her head cracked against the man's. "Ow!"

The man let out another curse. Snatched the object from her. "Give me that, tavern wench!"

She sucked in a breath and scowled at him. "How dare—" Dark eyes seemed to roil with fury and wickedness that forced her to take a step back. Drop her audacity and feign deference. "I beg your mercy," she repeated. "I—"

"Look where you're going next time!" After a shove, he stalked away, his black cloak billowing like the shadows of the alley that swallowed him.

Bewildered, more than a little affronted, Valiriana stared after him. Then gathered her senses and pulled to the side to get her bearings. Only then—finally—exulting that she had folded. She let out a tremulous laugh that died as she realized how much her back ached. That had taken entirely more effort than usual. The bigger question and concern was her location.

Where am I? Taking in her surroundings only confused her more—an alley that reeked of . . . well, things she would rather not name or continue to inhale. Not wanting another encounter with the angry man, she went in the opposite direction. Caught a scent . . .

Wait. I know that efflux—

A small body slammed into her. Clamped around her waist. "Aliria! It is you!"

Stunned, she touched the boy's arms. "*Jorti?*" She squatted and looked into his eyes. Cupped his face. "What are you doing here?"

He frowned. "Ma'ma and I live near here now."

"Where is here?"

Jorti gave her an incredulous look. "Forgelight, the inner city."

"Of course." Relieved she at least had not folded into another country, she straightened and shook off her confusion—at least, tried to. "Where is your ma'ma?"

"Working. We ain't working the farm no more, thank the seas."

"Indeed." She could suddenly smell those two chickens again.

He wrinkled his nose, as if he could, too. "What are you doing here? I was sure when the king took you we wouldn't see you again."

"I thought the same." She hugged him again. "And you—what has you scurrying around these alleys?"

He paled. "I . . . I'm going to get the key from the king and free my dad."

"Key? Key to what?"

"The prison! Days back, I finally got to go with Ma'ma to visit, and Dad couldn't even come out and hug us proper!" He pouted. "He shouldn't be in there, so I'm going to get him out!"

Valiriana faltered. "Oh, Jorti. It would not be safe for you to attempt that—" Wait. She frowned at him. "You say the king is here?"

Jorti nodded excitedly. "At The Iron." He started hustling backward. "We have to hurry. It gets crowded fast when he is there."

Valiriana trailed the spry little boy through alleys and straights right up to . . . "A tavern?" she said incredulously. *This is what he does with his time?*

"Here," Jorti said, ducking around a handful of people trying to get inside. "There is a better way." And with that, he led her down another alley, up another, and then rounded a corner.

"Slow down," she hissed, struggling to keep up. When she cleared the corner, she stopped short. Jorti was gone. The thud of a door snagged her attention, and she rushed there. Stepped inside.

Darkness dropped on her—and a cacophony of smells and noise that made her withdraw into the shadows for a moment to get her bearings and steel herself. Hesitating to move, to be seen, she reached for scents to guide her, to make up for the momentary loss of sight.

"He's always at the back," came Jorti's loud whisper as his small fingers caught her own. "Come on." He tugged her forward.

Valiriana eased into the acrid room that reeked of yeast, bodies, smoke, and the rancid stench of vomit. Shielding her nose, she slipped around the throng. Never had she seen so many bodies so close together.

And in a blink, she felt the loss of Jorti's touch. "Wait—"

Two large men shoved past her, muttering something about new entertainment in The Iron as their lecherous gazes slid over her. She tugged the cloak tighter and shouldered around them. Squeezed between some women who seemed to be falling out of their clothing. Though she was from Deversoria, she was not ignorant of what went on here. And that the Errant chose to come here . . .

A raucous laugh shot into the air.

She faltered, pulling into the shadows. That was *his* laugh—Vaanvorn's. Tucking herself against an alcove near the stairs, she found a line of sight on him. And her heart beat a little faster at the casual manner in which he talked and laughed with those around him. This did not look like the king who had challenged recruits in the training yard, commanded his men and even her . . . Yet—odd—when had he started wearing tunics in lieu of the undervest? Was he trying to be incognito? If so . . . why? Her gaze skipped to the man with him. He did not seem familiar. Her attention returned to the king—his hair hung almost loose, the queue nearly untied at the back. It let his black hair touch his shoulder as he leaned an elbow on his leg. A fist on his thigh. He straightened and resecured his hair, the muscles rippling. So impressive . . . and . . . beautiful.

Startled at her own thought, she shook her head. Touched her temple. *Focus.* Eleftheria would be ashamed. Even as she felt the heat in her cheeks, she saw Jorti . . .

Oh no.

The little guy was navigating people and tables, earning more than a few stern glares. But then he was on his hands and knees, scooting under tables and between chairs. She recalled his words about getting the key to the prison from Vorn. It had to be a misunderstanding—she could not fathom a king carrying around a key to a prison. But if the boy truly believed that . . .

Heart in her throat, she considered intervening but knew she was too far away. What if she presented herself? As a distraction.

Right, and earn another scathing rebuke from the king?

"I said no!" Vorn's voice carried like a whip through the tavern.

Valiriana's gaze snapped in his direction, and, in that instant, she noted two things—first, a woman with entirely too much cleavage and her right leg exposed by her skirts tied up around her waist reaching for the Errant.

And he chided Valiriana about inappropriate attire?

Then again, here it was probably very appropriate.

Was that what he wanted? A woman like that? Decurion Cybele had reported that the Errant indulged his pleasure with chatelaines—or had until relatively recently. Face afire, she realized the stories were true.

Mayhap, but did he not rebuke the woman? That differed so very much from the relayed accounts . . . Still, the woman clearly had engaged in intimacy with him to think she could touch him so inappropriately. Proof— was it not?—that he did not deserve a Sending. Just as suspected.

So . . . why was she so disappointed, sad? She averted her gaze but remembered the second thing—a small child's arms reaching toward the king's pocket.

A shout went up.

The Errant launched upward after a small child—not Jorti—in a dingy shirt bolting out of the tavern. "Stop that thief!" Face a rage, he shoved his way through the crowd, which parted quickly, fear evidenced in their expressions.

The people here clearly knew that angering the king would bring a terrible punishment. Well, she would not let him harm this child.

The Errant barreled out the door, a storm in his face. "You thief! Stop!"

Captain Mape and two other guards rushed after them.

Emboldened once the king and his men had exited the room, the other patrons hurried to see what was happening. Valiriana slunk from the shadows, desperate to make sure the Errant did not abuse the boy. A crush of bodies made it impossible to reach the door, let alone see what was happening.

"Likely, he'll have that boy thrown in the pauper's prison, he will."

"Nah," a woman said. "Tamuro might have but not Vaanvorn."

"But he's the Errant," another said.

"Aye, but he's changed."

"You watch—it'll be the dungeon for that one."

Valiriana determined to intercept him and folded.

Nothing happened. "Oh Ancient, help." Fisting her hands, she tried to press forward, stretching on her toes to see out the door. When that failed too, she determined to exit via the alley Jorti had brought her through.

She shifted to move around the crowd, lifted her foot—and when it touched again, she stood in a dirty, dark alley, so narrow that the late-afternoon sun only showed as a distant square of golden light marking where the alley opened to the street. The instantaneous movement stole her breath. The fold was a little late, but she would not complain. She jerked around and appreciated that she was no longer in the same alley. Though similar, this one seemed dingier, more threatening. A small cluster of people stood looking in the direction of some row houses. The Errant and the boy were nowhere in sight. Had she been too slow?

Soft voices reached her.

Valiriana hesitated, listening. The murmur drew her gaze behind and to her right. She shifted, the late hour making it hard to see. Another corner led into a narrower alley still. Gently, she inched closer as the voices grew louder. She peered into the shadows.

On the landing of the steps that traced the side of a building, the boy sat, dwarfed by the gruffer, beefier king, but at rest—no longer fleeing, no longer even fearful. In spite of the dim light, she clearly saw the Errant hand the boy a piece of paper, then draw out a small package tied with twine. "Will that help?"

The boy's eyes were wide. "Ain't you gonna put me in jail? I stole your dagger."

The Errant flipped the dagger around in his hand. "*Borrowed*, you borrowed it." With another revolution of the blade, he slid it into a sheath inside his boot. "But I promise, Eroc, if you ever were to steal from someone, I would have no choice but to turn you over to the magistrate."

"But we ain't got no food. Now that me dad's gone . . ."

"The palace kitchens, remember?"

The boy squinted one eye skeptically. "That's for real? You ain't saying that to make me get in jail, are you?"

Vaanvorn ruffled the boy's hair. "No. To give you hope, but remember our deal?"

Eroc nodded.

The king stood, the rickety steps creaking. "Go buy food for your ma'ma with that. I'll know if you don't. My spies will tell me."

Did he really have spies who would turn in a child?

The words seemed to have the desired effect, because the boy darted off even as the king stalked down the wooden stairs and returned to the alley.

Two shapes peeled from the shadows of the buildings—so very close to where she herself had hidden—and morphed into Captains Mape and Gormon.

Valiriana drew in a breath as they fell in step with their king.

"You won't punish him for stealing the dagger?" Tarac inquired softly.

"No," came the gruff answer of the Errant as he reached the juncture.

Something snaked around Valiriana's waist and yanked her back. With a yelp, she slammed hard against a solid form, her vision blurring from the impact. A gloved hand smothered her face and nose.

Awareness shot through her of the terrible situation she'd gotten herself into.

"Watch the alley," the man growled as he hauled her backward. Another shape rushed to the corner.

She struggled against the man, fought to break his grip. But paralyzing fear worked against her. Limbs heavy, mind sluggish, she panicked. A strangled cry crawled up her throat as she rammed her head back against his. Heard and felt the whack, but it did not do any good. *No!*

With a grunt, he hauled her aside. Shoved her to the ground.

Pain scored her side. She screamed, the sound sputtering out as his weight dropped on her and knocked the breath from her lungs. Hands moved on her body, going where no hands should. One hauling up her skirts. "Stop, get off me!" Understanding of what he intended shot through her, panic acute. "Ancient!"

Thwat-thud!

With a grunt and impact that radiated straight down to her, the man slumped.

Valiriana's instincts returned. She thrust him aside and whipped onto her feet, one hand drawn back, the other aimed at the man sprawled on the ground, a cutlass in his back. Her vision was still blurry. Her head aching. More confusion clouded her mind as she realized she had acted as though she bore armor and the gifts of the Ancient. Her lightsword.

But she did not. She was in a gown. Useless. Her legs trembled, and she staggered.

"Easy," came a warm breath along her neck.

"No!" she balked as hands pulled at her.

"*Easy*, my Lady."

"No, no—" She found herself pinned between a chest and a building. "Release me!"

He muttered something and backed off, lifting his palms as he considered her with concern.

Though he said something, her drumming pulse drowned it even as she registered his face, the beard. The dark eyes. "Vorn." Heart pounding, she strangled a sob as she realized he had not pinned but braced her trembling body against the wall to stop her from falling. She turned away, shamed by her inaction, by the abuse she suffered, for forgetting her training. She saw Azyant jerk his cutlass free from the man's back with a wet, slurping sound. The man groaned.

Nausea roiled. It was one thing to train, to practice for combat . . . but to hear it, see it, smell it . . . The very real nature of what had nearly happened. The man intended to take liberties with her, steal her . . . Tears burned and she moaned, focused on the grimy stone wall beneath her palms. Took comfort in the solid strength.

"My Lady . . ."

He had been right—she was *less*. Less warrior. Less brave. Finally, she let her gaze stumble back to the Errant. His gentleness washed over her with his concern. His hands braced her shoulders.

"N-no," she stammered, pulling back before realizing how the entirety of her being quaked.

The king remained close, though he complied with her wishes and removed his touch.

But she regretted it. Felt herself wilting.

Arms came around her, supported her. Held her.

Valiriana caved to the desire to sob. Covered her face, her shame. She should be stronger.

The king bent in, his beard brushing her cheek as he urged her face to his shoulder. Held her for a moment while she cried. He reached to lift her into his arms.

Aware of what he intended and unused to being touched by Licitus so much, she planted a hand on his shoulder. "No." But then she had no idea what to do next. What to say. She was too shocked, too rattled. Too ashamed.

16

VAANVORN
FORGELIGHT, JHERAKO

The Lady trembled worse than a branch in a winter storm. Vorn had dared touch her to give aid and had not been killed on the spot. A good thing, that.

At his shoulder, her fingers coiled into the fabric of his tunic, as if she struggled to remain upright, in control. Her breath bloomed over his chest as she fought for strength. This fierce, formidable siren who defied and challenged him seemed ready to crumble. Her arm tremored as she tried to hold him off, her fear no doubt a remnant of the blackguard who had attacked her.

Spotting the pale blue marks on the man's arm, Vorn moved closer.

Azyant knelt next to the man he had run through. He swore. Looked at Vorn. "Raider."

Vorn signaled his Furymark. "Search the alleys for more." He focused on the Lady again. "Please, my Lady," he whispered against her cheek. "We must be away."

"I will walk," she said, her voice thick from crying.

He hated the sound, one of weakness, pain. It should not come from one such as her. And truth be told, he resisted releasing her. He wanted to help. Hold her close. Yet, he feared violating her will, sensing some test of his mettle and character happening by a source greater than them both.

"As you will." He eased off, hand still on her back—his selfish allowance.

She took a step and her spine rippled. Legs buckled.

Vorn scooped her off her feet and turned toward the alley.

With a shudder, she dropped her head against his chest, burying her face in his neck and sniffling. It undid something in him to see this strong, amazing creature broken so quickly. So easily.

"Your cloak," he said to Tarac, who hurried beside him. "Throw it over her."

His Sword did as told, then skipped ahead. "I'll get your horse."

By the time he reached the end of the alley, Tarac and Ba'moori were there with the horses and reports of the assailant's lookout being in the custody of the magistrate. The rest of the kingsguard grouped up, swelling around them to protect him and the Lady. Outraged that anyone had dared touch her, Vorn determined to meet this aggression with his own. He pointed to the man on the ground. "Execute him!"

"No." Amid that raw proclamation, she lifted her head, the cloak sliding down, mussing her hair. Red-rimmed eyes held his. So very close. Those glassy irises reached right into him and took hold of his heart. "Do not kill him. Promise me."

"He—"

"No." She touched his face, fingers like warm honey against his beard. "Please."

Vorn gave a curt nod, wondering if there were a way to reassure her and yet sever the life from that savage. "I will not touch him." He allowed Tarac to support her as Vorn climbed atop his destrier, then received the Lady into his arms. He spurred his horse and raced back toward the palace. By the time he reached Forgelight, the pharmakeia waited on the steps.

Vorn released her to the Furymark, dismounted, then leaned close to gather her up again.

"No," she murmured. "I will walk."

"My Lady—"

She held up a hand even as she swayed.

Vorn steadied her, then passed her into the care of the pharmakeia and his attendants. She moved slowly, head up. By the Mercies, she ignited something in him. Her strength, her courage.

"I want updates," Vorn demanded of the pharmakeia. He halted when she continued without a word, something strange twisting in him at how she abandoned him. Never thanked him. Never looked back.

Tarac and Ba'moori rode up as Vorn extricated himself from the heaviness of what had transpired. His Four converged as he made his way to the royal residence. Once in the safety of the solar, he eyed his men. "What of that blackguard?"

Ba'moori nodded. "He didn't make it, not with the wound Azyant gave him."

Feeling something rattling in his head, his anger stirring, Vorn poured himself a glass of cordi. Never would he forget turning and seeing her there in the alley. How it'd thrilled—then terrified him when the brigand yanked her backward.

Why? Why had the Ancient not protected her?

That's what you're here for.

"Your Majesty," Tarac said as he returned.

"What?" he gritted out, working to temper the squall rising through him.

Head inclined, his Sword went on. "Revalor inquires about the meeting."

Vorn roughed a hand over his face—they had again met with the skycrawler at The Iron, but then the boy made off with the dagger and he had given chase. In the events that followed, he'd forgotten about Revalor. He would not risk leaving the castle until he was assured of the Lady's condition. "Bring him here."

"Very well, sire." Tarac said.

Wanting to be alone and gather his thoughts before becoming entrenched in talks about the ships, Vorn nodded to Ba'moori. "I won't keep you. No doubt there is much to do before the dinner tonight."

"Aye, Majesty." With a curt bow, Ba'moori and the other two left.

Staring at a small fire that kept the solar free of dampness and mold, Vorn could not shake the memory of her in his arms. Her cheek resting against his chest. The delicate lines of her face etched in confusion and distress. Her touch like fire, igniting something in him. The teasing whisper of her words against his lips—so close, they'd been *so* close—as she pleaded for the life of the man who'd been a part of attacking her.

A rap came at his door sometime later, and his agitation rose. Mercies, could he have no peace? "Come!" he bellowed, moving to the dressing closet where he tugged off the stiff jerkin and tossed it aside.

The door to the solar opened as he chose a cream undervest and brown cummerbund. When he heard the steps were not the confident stride of his captain nor his other men, he pivoted, listening to the softer, quieter movement. What was this? A sergius? He stalked to the solar and stopped short. "My Lady."

Her gaze yanked downward, and he then remembered himself, his state of undress. Threaded his arms into the undervest. By the way her long, black hair fluttered loosely against her back, she must have come straight from the pharmakeia.

Concern pushed him toward her. "Should you not be resting?"

"I am well." Her chin lifted—and by the Mercies, she radiated an admirable fire. But then a swallow rippled that graceful neck, and she looked down with a sigh, a move that drew his gaze to the bruised knot on her temple. Violet-blue eyes rose to his again. "I am here to thank you, King Vaanvorn." Breath seemed to stagger through her chest, as if this took effort for her to say. "For your intervention"—her voice wavered—"and your protection."

"My Lady, you are a guest in my house, so that protection is understood."

Some confusion flickered through her sparkling eyes.

Was it possible his answer disappointed her? It was almost too much to hope. "But the intervention . . ." he said, drawing nearer. "Few move me to act in such a manner."

Pleased that she did not refuse his presence or tense at his approach—there was the slightest of reactions, but this time seemed less irritation or derision, and more uncertainty—he dared close the gap. Touched her temple. "That you were injured ignites my rage."

Her lips parted, eyes widening ever so slightly. Waves of providence, how bright and radiant were her seaborne irises. He trailed his fingers down her cheek, appreciating her quick intake of breath. What he felt, what he saw was not just a rush of attraction. There was something deep and incredible here. In her.

He had known Faa'Cris were said to be magnificent, powerful, but his breath had been stolen, seeing her shove the blackguard off. The way she whirled through the air like an aetos, landed in a fighting stance with little more than a slight wobble—no doubt compliments of the knot on her head—had solidified his awe.

And here she stood—able to do incredible feats—allowing his touch. Was that a flush rising through cheeks yet marked with innocence? His gaze traced those delicate lips the color of the sunset. They lured him closer. Dared him—

She shivered and drew in a breath.

Vorn caught himself halfway to her mouth and hesitated. Saw alarm in her gaze, along with an intense warning that said any violation of her person would be met with the fiercest retaliation. As his guest, she was under protection. Even from himself.

Despite how desperately he wanted to seize that kiss perched on her lips, he drew back. Hauled himself under control by turning away. To the table. Cordi. "You can go."

Quickly, before I compromise us both.

Purposing to put his thoughts elsewhere, he took the goblet of cordi and went out onto the terrace balcony. Chastised himself for attempting to do what the brigand had done—take something from her that did not belong to him.

Think of other things. The Vantharq Ocean and Ironesse Island to the southwest. The site where he may very well host his most audacious attempt to save the realm. Being able to maintain an aerial patrol of the border, monitor the movements of the savages . . . would it be worth the cost? Potentially becoming the enemy of every realm on the planet . . . They already called him the Errant. How much worse could it get?

Roughing a hand over his face and beard, he ached for wise counsel. Who was there to help him sort the tricky waters of this venture? Eyes closed, he muttered an oath. Wished his rest had been longer, more beneficial.

"Who was he?"

Her voice was soft and a lure that made him pivot. Surprised that she was yet here in his chambers, he was glad she had not left. Although, it would be better—easier—if she had. "I told you to go."

"No," she said, her elegant form gliding to his side at the balustrade. "You said I *can* go." With a shrug, she added, "I chose not to." She turned her gaze to the glittering ocean, and for a long while savored the fresh air coming in with the tide. Her blue-violet eyes came to his. "Who was the man you were meeting with in the tavern?"

Vorn sighed and leaned back against the rail and crossed his legs at the ankles. Thought to rebuff answering her, but had he not just been wanting wise counsel? Who better than a Lady of Basilikas? "A skycrawler who has convinced me to break a very sacred accord." He watched for a reaction, but her expression remained implacable. "Why do you ask?"

She swung her gaze to him then away just as fast. "Curiosity—why would a king attempt to dress as a commoner and meet with a mysterious man in a tavern? The entire affair was suspicious."

Were her words a remonstration? *"Attempt* to dress?" He considered what he had worn earlier—no attempt to disguise himself. He had simply dressed down. But he enjoyed this interaction and would not have her leave so soon. "What of it?"

Again her eyebrow arched at him, and—black seas!—she was too close. He took a step away, feigning indignation.

"The weave of that jerkin was too rich for a commoner, not to mention the silk. And then there is the man himself—"

"Me?" Annoyed that she had picked apart his attire, he was also impressed that she had noticed those things. "What is wrong with me?"

"Where would you like me to start?" Her imperious tone seemed to dance the edge of a smile on her lips. "Your appearance or your mannerisms?"

He laughed. "Mannerisms."

"Your royal blood starches your neck and your attitude. While wearing a commoner's garb, you treated everyone as your minion, your lesser." But her gaze zipped to his, as if she remembered something. "Except the boy."

Ah, he'd wondered how much of that encounter she'd witnessed. "How long were you spying on me?" He straightened, sliding black strands of hair off her shoulder before he realized what he was doing. "Forget that. I would know how you got out of the palace. I told the Furymark—"

"I go where I am needed." She rested her palms on the balustrade, standing tall and confident as she took in the ocean, its waves nearly as dark as the ones that rippled down her back. She defined elegance.

So, she would not answer how she'd gotten out, but he still did not want this time with her to end. "What of my appearance?"

A smile teased the edges of her lips as she gave him a sidelong glance.

"That bad?" he laughed.

"It was perfect—*too* perfect, with your perfectly untrimmed beard and your perfectly unstyled hair, not to mention the eyes that betray the handsome king in his castle even though you were lounging in a tavern."

Vorn shifted close. His mind on the kiss he'd wanted but hadn't taken. "You think me handsome, perfect?"

That rattled her. She darted a look in his direction but retracted her gaze, wetting her lips. "I only meant—"

His slid his hand around her neck and cupped her face, her clarification falling away as she aimed those mesmerizing eyes at him. He traced her lower lip with this thumb. "What is it about you, Aliria, that tells me to defy my right to have you?"

A cool breeze swept into her irises. "You have no right to me, Vorn."

Truth, he must concede. But, encouraged that she used "Vorn" and not some honorific, he eased in closer, tempting. "You speak those words so easily, yet I see in your eyes the same desire burning in my gut, proof that you want this as much as I do."

"Want what?"

He bent to capture her mouth.

"My lor—" Tarac called from the solar, the scritch of his boots betraying the moment he likely saw the near-indiscretion.

Aliria spun away from him, moving to the other side of the balcony.

Never had Vorn so badly wanted to kill his captain. "Waves of providence, Tarac. What is it?"

"Forgive me, my lord." His Sword moved into the salty air and offered a nod to Aliria as well. "I did not—"

"*What* is it?" Vorn growled, stalking back into the solar.

"The . . . ambassador is in the library, waiting."

He set down the goblet and noticed his man had quieted, his gaze now on the balcony. "See her back to her quarters."

His Sword spun, his expression wild. "I interrupted—"

"It was . . . best."

Oozing disbelief, Tarac angled closer, awe in his expression. "You *kissed* her? And you yet breathe?"

Vorn glowered. "Thanks to you, there was no kiss." He started for his dressing room. "I lost track of the time. Return the Lady to her chambers so she can prepare for the dinner." He started moving but noticed his Sword hadn't. "Is there a problem?"

Tarac hesitated, then shook his head.

"Good. And find out how she left the palace without guard or notice."

As he left, Vorn was struck with the audacity of his actions, but more so—of hers. She had not left when he'd granted leave. Instead, she had come to him, inquired about Revalor. Listened. Why? And why had she been in the alley in the first place? To spy on him?

The possibility seemed ludicrous. And yet . . . what other option was there? Did this mean she did not find him trustworthy? How could they ever advance to the possibility of an alliance if she felt the need to spy on him? She might find him handsome, perfect—as she had said—but at the core of any relationship was trust. As much as he wanted to think he might actually win her, Vorn feared, like most every other person he had chosen to put hope in, there was a darker, less favorable reason for her actions. A deep, terrifying chance for another betrayal.

"You are sure?" Valiriana asked as she smoothed a hand down the violet crushed-velvet gown. In the mirror, she took in the dress, the beauty of it. The extravagance. The scooped neckline was embroidered with silver flames that descended down her middle, as if reaching for the wide belt of deep purple, violet, and silver brocade. An emblem held the middle and allowed purple ribbons to hang down to her toes. From the elbows, a band of the same brocade grasped long lengths of sheer violet fabric that also draped to her toes. Glittering gems hung around her neck and matched the forehead chain that draped diamonds and pearls into her raven hair, which had been gathered on the sides but hung loose down her back.

"It feels . . . much. Clothing should be functional, not ornate."

Matron Khatrione clucked her tongue as she gave the sergius instructions. "Not when you set yourself before the king and want to win his favor."

"I do not want to win his favor," Valiriana bit out, but even she heard the lie. Thought of the moment on the terrace when his whiskers had tickled her cheek. His breath, feathering over her mouth . . . How she had been entranced and . . . hopeful for that kiss. When he retreated, she had felt the chill of his rejection—and the same for being wanton. The things he made her feel and think . . .

"You should be right proud that you have his eye."

"I do not have his eye," Valiriana protested as Karistni smoothed perfumed lotion on her arms and hands. "I am his prisoner, bargained myself into this." Oh, Ladies—Jorti! She had forgotten to check on him after the incident in the alley.

The matron sniffed a laugh. "If the king wanted you in prison, you would be *in prison.*" She chuckled something to herself. "A man that handsome who rules a kingdom sets you up in the queen's chambers, and you think he only regards you as a yardbird." She was laughing more now. After another cluck, she bent and adjusted the medallion that held the hip band, tightened it some.

Valiriana felt the heat in her face and swallowed. Of course he had more than a passing interest—clearly he knew she was a Lady. Powerful men wanted Ladies for alliances. She just had not expected him to want *her*—she was here but for a preliminary *missio*, to determine his suitability for a Sending. *She* had not been sent. Another Daughter would be sent. She was merely a scout.

In earnest, was this dress not immodest with the way it fastened itself to her every curve? It was like wearing an undergarment, she felt so naked.

"One last touch," the matron said as she straightened and slid a ring on Valiriana's right index finger. The black gem glittered so brilliantly it seemed the stars themselves were contained within the stone.

"It's incredible."

Khatrione nodded and stepped back, tugging Karistni with her. "There." The clock intoned the top of the hour, and both women gave a nervous laugh. "And not a moment too—"

Thud! Thud!

Karistni jumped. "Great seas," she muttered. "No doubt that is the captain come to fetch you."

Suddenly queasy, Valiriana wondered if she could refuse.

"You are well, Lady?" Karistni asked.

"I—"

"Lady Aliria!" a deep voice boomed into the room. "Present yourself at once!"

Indignation wove through her, shoving aside the brief insecurity. Head up, spine straight, she glowered at the wall separating her from Captain Tarac. *He really is not fond of me.*

Could she blame him?

"Go," Matron Khatrione murmured. "He only seeks to protect the king."

Mustering her courage, Valiriana stepped off the small box she'd stood on for alterations and preparations. Lifting flowing skirts, she started for the door. Faltered for a brief heartbeat.

"Lad—"

She pushed herself into the open.

The captain snapped his mouth closed, eyebrows winging up. "Waves of providence," he muttered. Then seemed to shake himself. Took control once more of his expression. "Better." He moved to the door and tugged it open. "You are late."

"You can thank—"

"Hurry." He strode out the door, not waiting for her.

Hustling to keep up, she noticed the guards the king had assigned her stayed unusually close as they wound their way through the passages. She wondered if they had gotten an earful after her escape to the city.

"Recall," the captain's voice echoed in the stone halls, "when you enter, bow and wait for the king's acceptance of your presence. Once you hear your name, you may gain his side—on his right. They are already in hall and seated—awaiting you."

She skated him a glance, understanding then why he was in such a testy mood.

"Tonight is important to him. Please do not humiliate him—again."

"I have no intention of doing so," she whispered, realizing only then how true those words were.

"Dinner will be served, then there will be a small reception in the adjoining hall. It is strongly suggested that you remain with the king."

"Why? I do not—"

"Because you will be seated at his right."

Those words had meaning beyond what lay on the surface. She frowned at him as they turned down into the passage that led to the great hall.

"It means you are his personal guest."

Stomach aswirl with nerves and another painful realization—as his guest, she should have already been seated.

"In light of your . . . presentation, undoubtedly nobles will seek your favor for their houses, their sons. You will receive invitations to visit their estates." He frowned. "You are to refuse."

"Why—" She swallowed the question and answered it herself. "Because I am *his* guest."

"You learn fast." The acid in his tone hurt, but it was appropriately applied after the damage she had done at the last dinner. "As well, accepting an invite is akin to welcoming their attention and interest. It could even be seen as bestowing the king's favor."

A short man in full regalia stepped forward and met them.

"Considering your limited knowledge of Jherako, you are encouraged to smile often, speak rarely, and decline all invitations."

Valiriana stewed—she had a vast amount of knowledge. "I did not come here ill-informed. The Great Libr—"

"Just ill-behaved, then."

Her mouth fell open at the rebuke. "That was unkind."

"But not untrue." He seemed less acidic, more resigned as he angled toward the other man. "The Lady Aliria."

The man pivoted and the doors were flicked open by Furymark. He marched forward, his bearing crisp and precise.

Her first peek into the hall unsettled her stomach. This was not a small gathering like the previous one—there were easily a hundred guests seated, chatting and laughing. Decadence, wealth . . . camaraderie.

I do not belong.

Fool! This was not about belonging. Being here among the Jherakans was about determining . . .

Somehow, her gaze immediately found the king, as if her adunatos had been attuned to his, to the unique Signature that was both woodsy and spiced. Exotic. On a dais at the far end, he was ensconced between a noble and an empty chair. Her chair. Where she should have been. The gaping obviousness of her absence squeezed her stomach.

The trill of a horn startled her.

"Go," the captain grunted as he gave her back a small nudge.

Awakened to the way she had frozen, Valiriana glided forward, her thoughts blurring, colliding with each other. The king watched her without a word or movement.

"The Lady Aliria," the caller announced, the hall falling silent and making her steps echo across the stones.

She found her way to the spot marked with the flame and stopped. The swarm of effluxes proved surprising, though it should not have been. Perhaps it was more the variety assailing her—intrigue, attraction, curiosity, animosity, and even outright jealous contempt. Tracking the scents, she found the one spewing the latter, a pretty young woman with auburn hair and brown eyes. She wore a tiara and fairly bristled—and that irritation was clearly aimed at Valiriana.

A charged emotion raced through the room and startled her. Alarmed her. Reminded her she was supposed to bow. Even as she recalled this, she detected a swift rush of air from the left. Sensed the autonomic response of her clypeus to the incoming blow from a Furymark, who were determined to put her prostrate before the king.

Another kingsguard advanced from the right.

"No!" Vaanvorn barked, his voice stilling the guards as his chair groaned against the stone floor, pushed back from the table as he stood. "Touch the Lady not."

Attention fastened on the king, Valiriana let her anger and frustration roll away. Felt the swelling in her ridge recede.

Admiration sailed toward her from the handsome king as he made his way around the tables to her. With his hair down, he wore power like a talisman. His features were rugged like the outer reaches of the underground city of Deversoria with its stone walls. Whereas some men wore doublets and breeches, the king wore a linen undervest and his black cummerbund was secured with a gold medallion.

Vorn remained focused solely on her. "My Lady."

"I would beg your mercy, King Vaanvorn," she said quietly, her gaze taking in the hall. "My . . . order prevents me from bending a knee to any other than the Ancient."

"Rightly so." With a twitch of his cheek, he smirked. He held out his hand and slid his gaze over her dress and face, then shook his head in appreciation. "Lady Aliria, you are . . . resplendent."

"I am not." Did he think she numbered among so revered a group of Faa'Cris?

"In this," he said, drawing her from the middle of the room, his gaze greedily inhaling her from the jewels on her head to the slippers on her feet. "I must hold my own counsel." Clasping her hand aloft, he led her to the table, where sergii attended the two empty chairs.

She appreciated the way he guided her and the calm, steady pace . . . or was that his heart? As she stepped to the place and looked out over the room, she started to find all attendees standing and watching her and the king. Anxious to have the attention removed, Valiriana sat in the chair, the wood frame smoothly meeting the back of her knees, thanks to the sergius who seated her.

Gasps and whispers skidded around the room, shocked effluxes flinging at her. What mistake had she made this time?

VAANVORN

It was impossible to think or give ear to any conversation when such a vision sat to his right. He was fair certain his heart had stopped when she glided into the room like the ethereal she was. Then to see the Furymark moving to assault her for not bowing—he had feared a bloodbath instead of a feast.

The lady's maid had done well in dressing her for tonight's gathering. He had not missed the drool of nobles splatting the tables when the Lady entered. Or how his own jaw had struck the floor at the sight of her. Even now—after her error of sitting before he had taken his chair—he noticed the gazes and quick, hushed words among the eligible nobles. Mayhap he should have kept her under lock and key abovestairs. Silently, he thanked the steward for seating the noble of Faals Valley—who was forty years Vorn's senior—to the right of the Lady.

He reached for his goblet, only to strike hands with hers.

She withdrew her hand to her lap. Dipped her chin. Rubbed her temple, her brow furrowed.

Vorn leaned toward her, his protective instincts rising. "You seem distressed."

The Lady swallowed and touched the edge of the table. "This is not . . . In Dever—" Wide, uncertain eyes came to his. "We are not so formal."

"It can be overwhelming at times," he conceded.

"I fear I have made many mistakes already." She watched as he eased back and allowed the sergius to set his napkin on his lap, then did the same. "I pray I have not done damage or shamed you again."

Stirred at her words, at her concern over his name and reputation, Vorn cocked his head. "You have not, my Lady."

Her blue-violet eyes danced over his face, seeming to take in every nuance. Wary but curious, she did not seem to mind that she stared, and in truth, neither did he. In what lifetime could he have ever guessed that he would be the object of a Lady's scrutiny? And one so stunning. He welcomed her gaze.

She opened her mouth as if to speak but closed it. Looked at the table and then lifted her goblet. Took a sip. Set it back down and once more rested her hands in her lap. "The emblem on our brooches," she said, her fingers tracing the one fastened near her hip as she looked at the one beneath his heart. "What is it?"

Would she be offended? "The cypher of House Thundred."

Understanding spread over her face. "Your house . . . Family." Her expression clouded. "Then why do I wear it?"

If she needed to ask . . .

Her eyes widened almost imperceptibly. "I—"

"Where are you from, Lady?" the baron of the valley asked as their dinners were set before them.

Resistant to being drawn into another conversation, she faltered. Then surrendered the debate clear in her expression. "Shadowsedge," she said.

Vorn wondered at her answer but was relieved to have her distracted from the cypher conversation. For a few moments, conversations dimmed as the guests began eating. There was something incredible about having her at his right, her presence bathing him and even enhancing him. Bringing beauty to the implacable front he presented. He appreciated the delicate ways of her manners as she ate, clearly aware of her presence at his side. They both suffered that attentiveness, did they not?

"Shadowsedge, you say?" the baron said as he lifted his goblet to wash down a mouthful of food. "Afraid I'm not familiar with that one."

"Most are not," the Lady said quietly. "It is small by comparison to Jherako."

"Smaller than Forgelight?"

"Not that small."

"Then how surprised I am to have not heard of it." The baron puffed his chest. "I am quite well traveled, and there is little I have not seen or experienced. Ask our good king if you do not believe me."

"Never did I speak such words," the Lady said, agape.

Vorn reached over and took her hand, wanting her to relax, for the baron to stop monopolizing her time and attention. "Your meal meets with your approval?"

Her glittering violet-blue eyes met his for a fraction, then flicked to his hand on hers and back to his gaze. "It does."

Waves, she was incredible. Beautiful and soft, yet also commanding and formidable. Such a dichotomy.

After slurping more drink, the baron pressed his lips together and scowled in thought. "In what direction is this Shadowsedge?"

This edged into dangerous territory.

"North," she pronounced firmly.

Vorn did his best not to laugh.

"North, you say?" the baron persisted. "Would that be north of our border—it must, for I know all villages and towns of our great realm—in Kalonica, perhaps?"

Enough with this line of inquiry. Vorn caught Tarac's eye and nodded even as he touched the Lady's shoulder, appreciating the way she startled but then relaxed. "We leave."

Tarac gained his feet. "Friends, Nobles, Guests—we now adjourn to the side hall for a short reception. Please remain seated as the king and the Lady Aliria make their exit."

Vorn stood and seamlessly, as if she had done it her entire life, the Lady rose and turned toward him.

Those seaborne eyes glittered like that single gem at the center of her forehead.

He extended his hand without thinking. After a brief pause, she accepted his offer. When their hands met, there was no jolt of electricity or giddy sensation. Just . . . warmth. Rightness. It washed over him as they made their way from the hall.

An hour later, the reception was in full swing with laughter, tea cakes, and drinks. Some more lively guests were dancing and enjoying the evening. Though he talked with his nobles, he never lost awareness of the Lady's location or with whom she spoke. The kingsguard assigned to her were never more than a length from her.

"She's remarkable," the Faals Valley baron said, his thick fingers around a goblet. "Wherever did you find her?"

"Common street criminal I'm reforming," Vorn taunted, just to see that look—the one yet manifesting on the baron's round cheeks. He knew if he remained, the man would ply him with an endless stream of questions. "Excuse me, Baron. I see the Sword has need of me." He navigated the crowd to Tarac and met him with a sigh. "How is she doing?"

His Sword arched an eyebrow. "You may not want the answer to that question."

Vorn studied him and that smirk beneath a sandy beard.

"She asked me about the cypher."

"And?"

"I told her she would need to inquire of you."

He grunted.

"As well, every person who presented themselves to her was asked their thoughts of you."

With a quiet groan, he roughed a hand over his face. "I should have remained with her."

"She asked me once if you so feared what people thought of you."

He considered his captain. "I do not, but neither would I want any to speak of some rumor that would convince the Lady to leave Forgelight."

"Forgelight? Or you?"

"We are the same."

"Not to her."

Grunting, he decided to intercept her. Mayhap head off any damage too-honest words might cause. As he drew closer to her, he was not surprised when she straightened and looked over her shoulder—right at him. "My Lady." He wanted her away from these catty women. "A dance?"

She inclined her head, excused herself to the others, and placed her hand in his. Let him lead her to the terrace, where a small orchestra had set up on the lawn.

Vorn turned to her and drew her closer, setting his hand on her waist. She stiffened slightly, and he half expected a bolt of lightning to strike him. Instead, they fell into the rhythm of the music, and for the first time in many days, he felt he could breathe easily. "You know I will answer all your questions about me, do you not?"

Hand on his shoulder, she maintained a proper distance. "Aye, but would they be honest answers?"

"You suggest I lie?"

"Truth is often not pretty."

"And lying is?"

Lips flattening, she shifted her gaze over his shoulder. "The Lady Shahryar said your father-king had suggested an alliance between your houses." Uncertainty marked her expression. "That you were to court her."

This almost sounded like jealousy. Vorn barked a laugh as they turned another circuit on the terrace. "She exaggerates. I doubt there is a noble house with an eligible daughter that my father-king did not speak to about an alliance. Were I to be committed on that account, I would have twenty wives by now."

"I heard there are over a hundred in the harem."

He tightened his jaw.

"See? The truth is not pretty."

"Would it absolve me of the guilt if I explained all currently in the harem were brought by my brother or father? None are here at my hand."

"But at your hand, they remain."

"Because if I send them out, they and their families are shamed. Deemed rejected by the king—me." He bored into her gaze. "Is that what you would have me do? Destroy a hundred families?"

Regret marked her delicate-but-fierce features. "No, and I thank you for correcting my mistake."

Now it was his turn to be both surprised, and regretful. "You confound me, Lady."

A hint of a smile played on her lips, then a small giggle that was the last sound he expected from her. "Ma'ma often said the same."

"Will you tell me of her?"

She considered the question, then gave a slight shrug. "Earlier, you called me resplendent."

"It was—*is*—the truth." It was hard to keep his thoughts on her and their conversation, not the curve of her waist moving beneath his touch.

"That term, Resplendent, is a title reserved for our leaders, the most senior Faa'Cris, and my mother numbers among them. They guard and protect our lives. Having lived as long as they have, they are filled with wisdom and experience that guides us."

"And how long *have* they lived?"

"Some own centuries."

He twitched. "Centuries? In truth?"

"You suggest I lie?" she said, tossing his words from earlier back at him.

"Apologies, I did not mean to imply that. It is just—so you are immortal."

"No. We can die, and with that knowledge ever before us, we live in accordance with strict statutes and Guidings to safeguard our hearts and lives so that our legacy is protected. Daily, we pray, learn, and train."

"I can tell." There was nothing slight or diminutive about this woman in his arms.

The song ended and they stepped apart, clapping in appreciation of the music.

"Walk with me?" He indicated to the path that trailed around the lower gardens toward the water.

She inclined her head and moved with him away from the din of the assembly. "Will you explain the cypher to me? One of the women I met—she said it meant you claimed me." Incredulity marked her words.

"In essence, yes."

She stopped and faced him, hands at her sides. "How dare you! No man claims Faa'Cris!"

He held up his palms. "Please hear me, Lady Aliria." Though she seemed annoyed, there was more than that in her gaze. "I know what it is to be in your presence, to have my wits flee out the door and my words tangle as clumsily as if ropes bound them."

Her mouth closed and she hugged herself. Started walking, as if his words were . . . uncomfortable to her.

"I know what you are, why you are here—the men who encounter you do not. I felt it foolish to allow you around them without somehow making sure the waters were not muddied by invitations to balls, to visit estates, to be courted. I knew if they saw my cypher, they would leave off. Believe you were—"

"Yours."

He held her gaze as they rounded a corner and found the ocean before them, rushing up onto shore, then gracefully gliding back out. "Aye, but only for the purpose of protecting by thwarting unwanted advances."

"Is that truly all? You merely wanted to protect them . . . from themselves?"

What was this? He faced her, cocking his head. "What would you have me speak?"

"The truth . . ."

The way her words faltered and faded, dove off the edge of their meaning, stirred something daring in him. Did she really want him to confess to wanting to make her his own? "You know the truth, Aliria."

Her chin lifted—whether at hearing her name spoken without her title or at what he said, he did not know.

Vorn inched forward, but as he did, he heard those same internal alarms from the last time he'd nearly kissed her. "You are here to judge me, ascertain if I am worthy of . . . assistance."

"*Assistance* is not what you want."

"No," he conceded, then turned to the waters. Strolled out toward the glittering waves. "Not that alone. Jherako was once a mighty kingdom.

Far exceeded Kalonica in wealth and power, but my father"—he shook his head—"was not a ruler. He was an enabler. Corruption dug deep roots into the Council. Nobleman set blade to nobleman, attempting to steal lands and titles. The kingdom began dying from within. Upon his death, my brother, Tamuro, was crowned. He swung in the opposite direction, heavily taxing the people"—he sniffed—"crushing the very ones who needed his help, relief. He called in debts left and right . . . all while drinking himself to death.

"I was never supposed to be king. In truth, I did not want to be—the ones before me were corrupt and self-absorbed. Life was already cruel enough that I did not want that burden."

"Yet the burden fell to your shoulders all the same."

"Aye," he said, staring down at the ebb and flow of the water.

"And he took your true love."

Vorn started. Scowled at her. "Who spoke that to you?"

"A few people," she said with a small shrug.

He strolled the beach again, needing to move. Not look into her eyes that held judgment and condemnation. "In truth, my Lady, I am not proud of the man I was before coming to the throne, but after losing Yirene simply to spite . . ." He shook his head again. "Then she killed my brother."

The Lady caught his arm. "What say you? It is said he fell."

"The official word from House Thundred." Sorrow leeched through him. "The truth is that I had made her my own, taken what I should not have, and the next morning vowed to set petition, only to learn that my brother—the king—had already set petition and her father accepted." He dragged a hand down the back of his neck. "She brought me to her bed knowing on the morrow she would be his."

"She wanted to know love first."

Vorn started. Held her gaze. Wondered that there was no condemnation there now. "I dishonored her and myself . . . there is no justification—"

"No, of course not."

The compassion she extended confused him. "Regardless, my dishonor spurred her to kill my brother." He had put this out of his thoughts for a long time. "Shortly after she became queen, she poisoned Tamuro. The Furymark caught her trying to flee. She was wild, broken . . . but she killed our king. The penalty was death. But I could not do that, so I banished her with her family. I had no choice. They left at first light the next morn."

Confusion and concern dug into her face. "That is terrible."

"So, you see," he said around a forced smile, "it is my fault. Had I not violated my honor, she would not—"

"Untrue." She tugged his arm again. Stepped in to face him and hold his attention. "The lady's actions were not your fault."

Desperation wanted her words to be right. "You were not here."

Her hand still rested on his arm. "No, but I understand the condition of the heart. Killing another is not a simple act. Even when done in a fit of passion or distress, a darkness must have existed well before she did this horrible thing."

"Oh, Lady, I would love your words to be true . . ."

Aliria stepped even closer, her free hand coming to rest beside the first. Then she touched the side of his face, and he was stricken. That she was here, touching him, showing him compassion . . . *Touching me* . . .

"Hear me," she said, her voice taking on a hollow effect, her eyes—waves of providence!—violet, "the stain is washed from your hands, Vaanvorn Thundred."

Shock riddled Vorn. Awed, he mentally took a step back but could not move his physical body. "Lady . . ." By what authority did she say his stains were gone? Except . . . mayhap the Ancient had inspired her words. Could it be?

Normalcy returned to her voice and eyes, but that ferocity, the authority in which she had spoken lingered. She seemed surprised to find herself touching his face but did not withdraw her touch. Instead, her fingers trailed down his beard, then back to his cheek.

His hand slid to her hip, drew her even closer. Cupped the back of her head. And he set his mouth to hers as he tugged her into his arms, leaving no distance or propriety. Her fingers curled into his undervest, and her curves so rightly set against him unleashed a cacophony of passion and warning bells.

It seemed that holding her, kissing her, was not unlike trying to tame a cyclone. He eased off, finding her gaze—as hooded and hazy as his own, no doubt—and then teasing her lips once more.

This time her hands pressed against his chest, pushing him back. Off. Away. Clearly embarrassed, she turned in the other direction—twitched when she saw Tarac. Stepped back and drew her spine straight. "I should— we should not have done that."

"But Lady," Vorn said with more than a little petulance, "you asked me what I wanted. You have my answer."

That imperious chin lifted again, and the fierce, feisty Lady returned. "As said when first we met—that will never happen." Was it his imagination or was her chin trembling? "I was not sent here for a joining but to weigh your character. In conducting ourselves as such, we have compromised the situation, ourselves, and now my judgment cannot be trusted."

Another step back. She stiffly nodded, turned, and fled.

18

VALIRIANA
FORGELIGHT, JHERAKO

Weak, imbecilic girl!

Thumping the heel of her hand against her forehead, Valiriana rushed from the lawn and up the touchstone path to the house. Hearing the guard behind her, she darted through a side door. And found herself in the middle of a boisterous gathering. Recoiling, she spied another door farther in and hurried toward that, doing her best not to run and draw attention.

She was a fool! So arrogant, so convinced she could bring down the mighty Vaanvorn Thundred, only to end up with his charms and good looks causing her fall—right into his arms. Her body buzzed with the remembrance of his touch. The way he crushed her to himself, kissed her so ardently that she lost herself. Savored the warmth of his touch and kisses. So commanding and—

"Idiot!" she hissed.

A sergius gasped and jerked to the side, head down as she passed.

"No—sorry, not you," Valiriana said, hurrying past. Too embarrassed to stop. Too afraid the Furymark would find her. She would have peace, solitude to her prayers and penitence. After that encounter with the Errant, her ablutions might take weeks!

Holding her skirts, she hustled up the steps. Disbelief that she had made it this far without being stopped kept her moving, half expecting an intrusion any moment. When she reached the top, she banked right toward the hall that led to her apartment. One more turn and she'd be there. Yet even as she started in that direction, she felt as if she'd walked into a sauna of tension, the air thick with both raw anger and visceral fear, peppered with a dark emission.

What . . .?

Each step thickened the miasma that struck her receptors and made her want to stop. She had not before detected so deep a resentment or so dark an efflux . . . But what—who—could be the source?

A stern voice filtered around the corner and lured her into glancing around it to the left. There she found Karistni standing beneath a stiff rebuke of the vizier—Haarzen Gi, she thought, was his name.

"You were to report all her comings and goings directly to me!"

Head down, cowering, she shrank from him as she held out her hand, palm up, exposing a small black object.

"That is too little, too late!" He slapped it aside, the item clattering to the stone floor.

Breath backing into her throat, Valiriana couldn't help but notice the piece was just like the one the man in the city had dropped when she'd folded and stumbled right into him.

"But I did what you asked—"

"And it has not helped me! Think you the skycrawlers will care?"

Skycrawlers? Valiriana straightened her spine at the odd discussion. And though she hated conflict, neither would she abide this man striking the girl. "It seems," she said, stepping into the open, "that the girl cannot control what does and does not help another."

Startled at her intrusion and—apparently—the audacity she exhibited in interrupting their confrontation, Gi skewered her with a look. He took two fast steps in her direction, a ferocious expression twisting his features.

She may not like confrontation, but she was well-equipped to handle it. Instinct had her spine rippling, and by the stalled pace of the vizier and his shocked visage, she guessed the more supernatural side of her glimmered around her, though she stopped it to prevent an obvious display, since his aggression seemed to subside.

The vizier seemed to bristle as he gave a shaky nod. "Lady."

Valiriana squared her shoulders. "Karistni, I have need of you, please." Deliberately, she held the vizier's gaze, daring him to counter her request, as the girl moved past him and the dropped object. "If I see further demonstration of your low character, I will be forced to report such directly to the king."

Mouth tight with indignation, he said nothing. Merely gave a cockeyed nod then a glower at the girl.

Valiriana stood there, knowing if she left first it would be a loss of power and position she could not afford with this man. As well, she would not give him her back—she would not be surprised if he threw a dagger at it. But then he crisply retrieved the device and departed. Relieved, she strode into her apartments. Heard the door close behind her. And wilted.

"How can I help, my Lady?" A cold chord rankled in the girl's tone as she came near.

Valiriana removed the head chain and dropped it on the dressing table. "Are you well?"

Karistni frowned as if nothing had happened. "Aye, Lady. Why would I not be?"

"What did he knock from your hands? He seemed quite aggrieved."

"He often is. The pressures of his position are great."

Valiriana paused, studying the girl. While Karistni was shaken, she was also angry. Why? And why defend the bully who had abused her? Other elements of the scene returned to Valiriana's mind. This girl had been spying on her for the vizier. To what end? She would ask, but the rankness of the girl's efflux warned her Karistni would not speak, or would not do so truthfully. She must think on this some more. "I would like to take a warm bath. Would you draw it, please?"

"It will have to be a quick one, I—" When Valiriana arched an eyebrow at the girl's casual tone, Karistni snapped her mouth closed. "It is just . . . the cook . . . she does not work after dinner."

"The cook prepares a bath?"

"N-no. of course not." She hurried to relieve Valiriana of the formal gown and helped her into a comfortable dressing gown. "I will return in a moment with the water."

Concern lanced through Valiriana as she watched Karistni leave. Through the main door, not the sergius passage. She glanced at the bath, trying to sort what had just happened. It was not a sergius's place to argue her will. While she was not a royal member of this house, it had been understood that the king wanted her to have the same respect they showed him. Would this sergius tell the king it would have to be quick? Make excuses about why that would be the case?

Within the hour, the bath was poured, petals perfuming the steam that rose from the waters, and towels set out. "Thank you, Karistni. It is clear you have other duties needing your attention, so you may leave for the night."

Again, the girl's mouth opened . . . then shut. With a curt bow, she left.

Valiriana set the screen around the tub, shed her clothes, and stepped into the waters. Submerged herself and bent forward, hugging her thighs, forehead on her knees. She willed her racing mind to quiet. Felt the tears welling even as the first whisper of penitence crossed her lips.

I confess before You, Ancient, and my Sisters, the Daughters, Eleftheria, and Vaqar, that I have greatly erred and fallen from the path set before me—in my words, in my actions, and what I have failed to do through my fault, through my most grievous fault. Therefore, I ask, Ancient, grant me wisdom to know Your will. Show me and let my heart be right before You that I can hear and see the straight path before me.

That prayer finished, she repeated once, twice, three times. Ached for the mistakes . . . and cursed herself that more than once she found her thoughts wafting back to his kiss and passion. The force with which he held her—

"Blood and boil," she hissed, fisting her hands in the water. "You are Faa'Cris—a warrior! A Daughter. Not a—" Chatelaine. It was time to focus. She was here to reconnoiter and judge. And she should have been prepared for any battle that came. But, clearly, tonight was proof she had not been. "Ancient, when I am afraid, in You I will trust. For You have not imbued me with fear but with power, love, and a sound mind. When doubts infest my adunatos, Your strength and comfort renew hope. I submit myself to You, rebuke the enemy, and when I do, he has to flee."

After a few more prayers and feeling released from her errant ways—ironic, considering whom she had come to reconnoiter—she climbed from the bath, dried off, and donned the clothing laid out. In bed, she again went through her petitions to the Ancient, determining even then to remain abovestairs, far from the Errant and the dangerous temptation he posed.

VAANVORN
DEVERSORIA

Dark was the hour and foul was his mood since the gala last eve. As they set out across the Vantharq toward Ironesse Island, Vorn looked back across the inky water to the dock, where he saw a thick throng. Heard shouts. The clang of steel.

"It's getting worse," Tarac muttered.

Just as it had with Tamuro and their father. He had tried. Mercies, he had tried to make a difference, set things right. And wait until the people learned of his dalliance toward breaking the Accord. Sky ships that would be definitive, turn them into the scorn of the entire world, and give them every reason to put him to the stake.

Vorn nodded, just then seeing a man fling himself into the air like some crazed beast.

A blur of pale blue trailed him.

"Raiders," he seethed. They truly had gotten deep into Jherako, and in that, they'd managed what the legitimate Hirakyn army had not—infiltration. Now more than ever he needed supernatural help. Yet now mayhap he had ruined all with his rash act last eve.

"Irukandji dogs," Ba'moori growled as he trudged to the stern and stared into the distance.

"Let us hope they do not spot this boat," Azyant said. "Then again," he added with a grin, "it'd be good reason to put those dogs down."

Shouldering in closer, Tarac eyed Vorn. "Have you sorted what to tell the skycrawler?"

"The truth." What else was there?

Tarac frowned. "Aye."

Truth was, Jherako needed the skycrawler's ships, but in their previous meeting, Revalor had at last disclosed the details of the deal. And the cost was . . . daunting. Vorn gripped the rail of the ship and stared at the skies. Where the airships had come from. Where the Lady had come from . . . he guessed. Yet, this eve, the sky was as black and void as his hope. Why had he ever believed he could steer the rudder of his realm into calm waters?

Due to rough seas, the journey to reach the island took over two hours. It should have been plenty of time to work out how to make amends with Lady Aliria, and yet he had nothing when he reached the island. No ideas, no Lady, no funds. With his men, he hiked up to the cave opening, and already he could detect the acrid odor that—according to Revalor—was the smell of burned fuel.

"Good King Vaanvorn," greeted Revalor as they delved into the heart of the island. They shook hands, and the skycrawler led him deeper into the tunnels. "I've had a team mapping these tunnels, and we have good news!"

"At last," Tarac muttered, "something goes right."

In his black attire with a weapon strapped to his thigh, the skycrawler glanced uncertainly at the captain, then Vorn. "Should I be worried?"

"In this accursed country, if you are not, you have but yourself to blame."

"That's not at all alarming," Revalor said. "The good news is that the cave system is huge. Far more extensive than first believed."

This did not surprise Vorn. "Legacies suggest the caves reach all the way to Shadowsedge."

Revalor lifted his eyebrows. "That—that's near Sasada?"

"And the Fire Gorges," Vorn said with a sniff. "But it is my strong advice that we avoid those."

Surprise lit through the skycrawler. "Agreed!"

Vorn moved toward the ships. "Come—let us forget the troubles for a tick and focus on the brilliance before us." He climbed into the nearest ship and sat in the cockpit, as the skycrawler called it. He scanned the dials and screens, buttons and knobs. Had no idea how any of it worked. "I would love to learn one day."

"I would encourage you to train with the pilots," Revalor said. "It is a thrill!"

What he would not give to learn, but considering the sobering truth that he had no heir, he could not risk putting his life in danger to experience a thrill. "I will leave that to the Furymark who have volunteered." He again scanned the instrumentation. "For now."

"What of the payment?"

Vorn ran a hand over his mouth and beard. "That was what I must speak to you about."

"Well, don't concern yourselves," Revalor said as he nodded to Jubbah, who directed the Four toward another ship. "You have a sponsor."

Eyeing the man, Vorn was not sure he liked the sound of that. "Charity?"

Revalor shrugged. "Or an . . . investor. Call it what you like, but someone has learned of our talks and our efforts to buoy your realm, and they agreed to fund what you cannot."

Vorn scowled. "To what end? What does this sponsor want in return?"

"He is of the same mind as Jubbah and I—he wants to put measures in place to prevent a total takeover by Symmachia." Revalor folded his arms over his chest. "He does have one request."

Vorn sniffed. Of course it was too good to be true.

"That you convince the country north of you to join your efforts."

"Kalonica?" Vorn barked a laugh, thinking of his meeting with the austere Medora Zarek, a formidable, stiff-lipped man. "You truly are ignorant of the goings-on here. Kalonica's king is the most strident supporter of the Accord."

"All the same, do what you must to get them on board. Do that, you have your armada."

Kalonica had no reason to join the effort. They were wealthy, powerful, and had a well-trained army and navy. What need would they have for sky ships?

"I know what you're thinking," Revalor said as he drew Vorn aside. "What we're doing here—it's not just about adventure. You saw the ships in Hirakys. Symmachia is starting small to ignite a wildfire. One spark . . . Think of what we do here as an investment in the future of your people and your planet. A protection against a fleet that you may not have seen in person, but they have seen Drosero. They are targeting your planet, even without you knowing it. In fact, it has been brought to my attention that they are *fixated* on your planet. You have something they want." He paused, looking from Vorn and Tarac to the Four beside the other ship. "And I'm betting you don't even know what it is. I sure don't."

"It is an incredible tale you bring to my shores," Vorn said solemnly. "I do not take any of it lightly, but I would know how you have come by all this knowledge."

Revalor grinned. "That's not all I know. That beauty we spoke of before? I know she's a Faa'Cris."

Taken aback that he would know this, Vorn stared at the man.

"Oh, c'mon—you can't think I'd have all this technology, this ability to get ships into your atmosphere without having details on the man I'm doing business with." He tapped Vorn's shoulder with another grin, this one cocky, knowing. "What's she like, the Lady?"

This time, Vorn scowled.

"You know, most planets in this quadrant have heard rumors of the Ladies of Basilikas, but I don't know a soul who has seen one."

Soul?

"But you have."

Vorn kept his scowl in place.

"That face tells me I'm right. I heard men lose their minds and sell their souls just for a taste of—"

"You dare!" Vorn lunged. Pinned the man against the wall.

Revalor laughed—hard—as he lifted his hands. "So it's true. Because this?" He motioned with another laugh, despite being choked by Vorn's forearm. "*This* is a man losing his mind."

"My king," came Tarac's calm, focused words, "we should set out to return. The hour is late."

Shocked at his own ferocity and the fact he had let himself be goaded, Vorn lessened the pressure. "Well played, Revalor."

The man ducked his gaze. "Where there are Faa'Cris, big things are in play. It was unfair, but I had to know."

"No. You did not," Vorn said, moving toward his Four, who were all guarded, hands on hilts. But then he glanced back. "If you knew the prowess, power, and authority of a Faa'Cris, you would not make so light of her appearance. You would fear her, respect her. Not reduce her to physicality."

"Sire!" A shout echoed through the caverns.

Vorn turned toward the tunnel that led to the opening and saw Lathain shuffling rapidly down the incline.

When his gaze met Vorn's, he stopped, his feet sliding a meter in the silt. "Boats coming, sire—raiders!"

Morning, noon, and dusk slid across the horizon as Valiriana sat with her legs folded and hands resting in her lap. Whispering petitions. Reciting the Guidings. Anything that would push the thoughts of the Errant from her heart and mind, that would fix her mind on the Ancient and this *missio* Eleftheria had assigned her.

"Speak to me, please. I am desperate to hear your voice, to know I have not so lost my way, that I have not so thoroughly failed this mission, failed you." She paced her chambers.

Felt the warm air stir around her.

Still sensed heat where his hand had rested on her hip . . . his mouth on hers, the firmness, the warmth and how his chest, strong and solid, had crushed the air—

"Stop, stop, stop," she growled, putting her hands on her temples as if that could block the thoughts. She quickened her pace. "Please! Help me!"

"Help you what, child?"

Valiriana whirled, stunned to find an older woman, hair in a plait around her crown, delivering a tray of food to the serving table. "What . . . Where is Karistni?"

"No idea where that girl has gotten to—vanished, she did. I'm Brissa, but you can just call me Cook."

Vanished? "Mayhap, she is visiting her family in the poorhouse."

Cook cackled. "Poorhouse? That girl might have it hard, but her family owns a bakery. A favorite among the nobility, in fact."

Valiriana frowned. "I . . . but she . . ."

"Anyhow," Cook said, "I did not want to face the king's wrath for your food arriving cold, so here you go."

"I am sorry for the trouble—"

"Not at all," she said with a grunt. "He gave very strict instructions on your care."

It surprised . . . and stirred those longings that had duped her into kissing him, awakening feelings she should not have, considering the mission. And yet, she found herself still dreaming of him, only now there were kisses and— *Pure thoughts, Valiriana. Pure thoughts.* She rubbed the back of her neck. "He impresses me—" *Wait, that came out wrong.*

"I 'ave always liked the prince—well, now king. Always so clever that one. Never asked for a thing, so when he comes to make the request, I gave him a good ribbing." She clucked her tongue and stepped back, appraising the spread she'd created on the table, then gave it a nod. "And never has he been so particular. You are to have the best meals, always served warm. Any treats or dishes you desire, we are to deliver."

The woman finally seemed to remember she was talking to a person and looked at her. "I can definitely see why you caught our Vorn's eye. Count yourself lucky, Lady." Cook shook her finger as she moved back to the tray. "He is the best, and he 'asn't looked upon any of the ladies who 'ave sought his attention and favor." She lifted the tray and started for the door. Hesitated, then glanced over her shoulder. "And I hope you don't mind me saying, but if you are not going to become his queen, quit the palace now. Do not toy with him. He does not deserve it, and I will be fierce angry if you hurt the prince—I mean, king."

Surprised and startled at the ferocity of Brissa's words, Valiriana nodded. "Your words are heard, Cook. I thank you for your honesty."

Wariness crowded the woman's expression as she narrowed her eyes. "But?"

"I am not here to be his queen. Another, more important than myself, has sent me to inquire about his character."

"Hmph." Cook ambled to the door and eyed Valiriana again. "Then 'ow come I saw you kissing 'im for all the world?"

Heat blazed through Valiriana's cheeks. "I . . . it was an . . . indiscretion." She swallowed. "That will not be repeated. I have made ablu—"

Cook laughed as she reached for the door. "Keep telling yourself that, love."

"I beg your pardon?"

She shook her head. "You may be a Lady what puts men to fits, but that Vorn—he puts every lady he meets into fits. The gala last eve? I heard no less than five ladies were furious you were in attendance." She clucked her tongue. "If you are so ready to toss aside our good king, then do it. Either move in or move on. There are plenty to take your place."

Mouth agape, Valiriana stared at the door as it eased closed. How dare she! Who did Cook think she was, telling her how to behave, to either *move in or move on?* Aghast, she turned to the food. Hmph! It could go cold for all she cared!

You are being churlish.

Aye, she was. And it seemed this place brought out the worst in her. Bristling, frustrated, she just wanted to return to Deversoria. If she had failed, so be it. She would face the punishment. Face remastering hastati training. Whatever it took to strengthen herself, not be so weak in the presence of a man.

Valiriana climbed onto the bed and curled in on herself. *"Ma'ma?"* Though she reached out, she knew the *vox saeculorum* would fail her again. *"Please . . . just let me come home."* Clearly she had not been prepared for this. Hugging a pillow, she screamed into it. It had been a good lesson, coming and learning how ready she *wasn't.*

"I am so very confused." Her feelings . . . she had never been driven by them, not really. Until this Licitus.

She cringed. How she had thrown that word around like a rotten piece of fruit. Allowed bitterness to root in her heart. "Show me, Ancient . . . Show me Your will," she whispered around a yawn before falling asleep.

"Have you seen the north training yard, my Lady?"

Valiriana turned to find deep, rich brown eyes glittering at her. Breath stolen at his closeness, she somehow knew it was a dream. And she seized the chance to study his face. Like the way the corners of his eyes pinched in an ever-ready smile that seemed to always rest on his lips, too. Pleasant, happy—gregarious. She had seen little of that side of him since arriving in Jherako, but had not most of the people she'd inquired of said the same about him—he's a good man, poor soul is up against an entire country, better than his brother and father, any lady would be lucky to be his queen . . . many were lined up to be candidates. Unrest was digging into the country, but its root sprang from a threat not born of the king alone.

Had she wronged him with her harshness and—dare she admit it—arrogance?

"Show me," she replied.

With a grin that rivaled the sun, he took her hand. A swirl of giddiness rushed through her, and though she thought to fight it—was she not Faa'Cris?—she decided, since it was a dream, to let loose those feelings that had no place in reality.

They stood on a sandy stretch between towering walls.

His hand came around her waist, and she did not object.

"There," he said, pointing to a large basket filled with training swords. "Pick

your weapon, Lady."

Strangely, she did not want to go to the basket. It meant leaving his side. Finally, she made the six-step trek and bent to peruse the offerings. "They all seem so old and . . . abused."

"In truth, are not we all?"

"Well, you are not," she flirted, lifting the wood sword that was least dented and moldy. She turned to face him. "Will this—"

"Augh!"

Valiriana started, hearing his screams but not seeing him. "What?" The spot where he stood was blurred, ruined by streaks of water rushing down . . . down . . . even as his screams and shouts continued. "Vorn!" She liked the sound of that name better than the Errant or Vaanvorn. But it did not help her find him. "Where are you?"

"No, stay back!" he said, his words sounding warbled, as if he were gargling them. "Behind you!"

A meaty thud echoed through the yard, followed by a thump.

Dirt and water plumed toward her, both wet and dry as she made out a body. Her breath backed into her throat as those rich, smiling eyes stared up at her, empty, vacant. Smiling no more. The king was dead!

"Vorn!" Heart racing, she threw herself at him.

Valiriana landed with a thump on the hand-knotted rug. "Vorn!" A strangled cry lurched up her throat, where panic thrummed.

He's in trouble.

The door flung open. "My lady—what threat?"

Aware of her improper attire before Tozet, she hugged herself. "The king—where is he?"

He faltered. "Away."

"Where?"

"I am not to speak of it, my lady."

"Well, speak to someone because he is in terrible trouble." She knew it. Felt it. Somehow keenly, irrevocably attuned to his adunatos. *"Lady,"* she cried out to Eleftheria, *"please—let me help him."* Head tucked, she closed her eyes. Felt the approving warmth of the Lady's presence and the swell of her ridge. Conviction and purpose rose through her, and just as in the dream, Valiriana folded, throwing herself toward his adunatos.

"Ready your arms!" bellowed Tarac.

Sword drawn, Vorn readied himself for battle. Gritted his teeth that any had discovered his efforts on Ironesse. Determined nobody would make it to shore with that knowledge. "They cannot live," he called over strong winds that swelled ahead of a storm.

From his position on the upper aft deck and with the aid of lightning streaks, he could see the swarm of raiders coming. The Irukandji's telltale pale blue marks betrayed their position, and he thanked the Lady for that mercy, for it was said She had carved their sins into their bodies since they had so wholly chosen a path of savagery and violence.

Vorn and the Furymark had set off from the caves in a deliberate attempt to draw the raiders away from the tunnels, away from the ships. The last thing he needed was Hirakys making that discovery.

"Furymark, portside!"

Turning, Vorn spotted a handful of savages climbing up the side of the ship as if they were spiders, not humans. Their snarling around daggers clamped in their teeth spoke to the kind of battle this would be.

Not waiting to be attacked, Vorn rushed forward. Cracked his hilt over a raider's hand, the fool dropping into the churning waters. Another raider scaled the rail, toed it, then launched himself up and over Vorn.

"Waves." He spun, his blade seeking the movement his ears detected. Blade met flesh and dug in. With a growl, he drove the sword through the chest and ripped it back. The raider dropped where he stood. Another vaulted over him. Vorn squatted and came up, drawing his sword upward. Connected with tendons and severed an arm. A feral scream pierced his eardrums. Tightening his shoulders and stance, he worked to brace against the excruciating sound. Winced—saw a dagger a fraction too late. Felt it bite into his shoulder.

Whipping around, he caught the raider's hand, shoved in and twisted the hand, forcing the raider to impale himself. Feeling the slick warmth of blood, he maneuvered around, needing more room in which to drive his sword. The raider seized the opening and lunged at him.

Vorn hit the deck hard and felt the impact radiate through his spine. Being down meant being dead. So he hiked himself up, drawing his sword and perfectly angling it at the chest of the raider who flew at him. Felt the vibration of steel on bone.

"Augh!" Vorn delivered the raider to Shadowsedge, then turned, ready for the next attack. He shouted as he staggered back and thudded against the wall of the upper deck. Drew in a ragged breath and swallowed. Swiped his bloodied hand over his pants. Realized there were no raiders to deal with. He shifted out and scanned the deck. Saw only bodies, blood, and rain . . . When had it started raining?

Shouts from above drew him around. On the upper deck, he saw Tarac struggling against two raiders. He pitched himself up the ladder to even the odds. Boots sliding along the deck, he dove between Tarac and the sword. Drove the raider back. As he did, he angled, enabling Tarac to deliver a death blow.

"My thanks," Tarac said as he took in the deck.

Heaving a grunt, Vorn dragged the body of the raider and pitched it over the rail. He took a moment to catch his breath—and in the split second that lightning struck, he detected two things: the scream of a raider too close to avoid and a winged form erupting in the blast of light that was not lightning.

The Lady!

A fragranced blow told him the raider had been dealt with, but by the second heartbeat, he heard the splash. Realized the Lady had not landed on the deck, but in the water. "No!" he breathed as he rushed to the rail. Gripped it as he peered over. Saw a glow in the water that faded as she plummeted. A strangled cry rushed from his lungs as he grabbed the rail to throw himself in after.

"My king!" Tarac was there with a rope.

Vorn grabbed the end and dived into the water, following that fading light. He felt the teasing tendril of something. Grabbed at it. Nothing. He kicked hard. Hiked himself toward it. A brush of fabric. No no no! Come on!

He felt the sea's smothering, crushing power increase.

The light was gone, but he felt a stirring of the water. Snatched at it and caught fabric. He yanked and felt resistance . . . then nothing. It'd torn!

Fighting a scream, he surged again. Felt a thwack against his wrist. Flipped the grip. Caught her arm.

Not waiting for a better hold or for her to grip his hand—he cursed that she was not responding to his touch—he wound the rope around his arm and tugged. Instantly, he felt the upward pull of the line as the men hauled them to the surface.

Please, Ancient . . . please . . .

They broke the surface, and Vorn hauled in a greedy breath, pulling the Lady up with such force she nearly bobbed out of his reach. He lunged at her and caught her waist. Shook his head to clear the water from his eyes and searched for the rope. Catching it again, he let the men draw them to the sloop. A basket dropped over the side, and he shoved it beneath the water and stuck in his legs. Hooked his arms around her waist and pulled her inside.

"Go!" he shouted to the men, who would have to work together to maneuver them aboard. But Vorn was already focused on her limp form, her open mouth. He bent her over his arm and pounded her back.

The basket scraped the hull as it was dragged over the rail and onto the deck. They tumbled over, and Vorn flipped her onto her side, hating that she was as limp as a dead fish. "Aliria!" He jerked her against himself and forced her to bend. Hit her back. Hit it again. And again. Again. Desperation choked him. "Lady!" he bellowed and yanked her backward, free of the basket.

She contorted. Coughed.

He shuddered a laugh born of relief and shifted the Lady onto her side. She coughed again, then vomited onto the deck.

Furymark shouted in exultation.

Vorn massaged her back. "That's it, Aliria."

On all fours, she vomited more, the ocean itself seeming to have come from within her. Choked and coughed. Weary eyes came to his, her hair limp around her face. She collapsed onto the deck, shivering in the rising storm.

Warmth draped his shoulders—a blanket from the hold. Vorn took another Lathain proffered and settled it over her. "We should get you out of the rain. Are you well enough to walk?"

She nodded, levering up, her arms shaky beneath her weight.

Though Vorn reached in to lift her, knowing she was likely too weak to support herself after nearly drowning, he registered weakness in his own limbs, too. He nodded to Tarac, who moved in and lifted the Lady without further instruction. Lathain and Ba'moori gave Vorn a surreptitious assist, and they all went belowdecks. The thick, briny scent permeating the small interior made his head ache. Or was that from diving into the ocean and being deprived of air?

"How do you fare, sire?"

Hunched, tugging the blanket around his shoulders, Vorn nodded. "I will be better once I am dry." He trudged down into the small captain's cabin. As Tarac set Aliria on the bed, Vorn slumped into the chair.

"Under the covers, my Lady. We will rout dry clothes for you," Tarac said, drawing back the blanket.

"I am f-f-fine."

"Your shivering speaks otherwise. Please," he insisted, "so you do not get sick. If that happened, I would have to answer to the king, and that is not something I wish to endure."

A shudder stole the humor from Vorn. She had nearly died, and he would have been to blame. Why could she not exercise caution, think through her actions?

When Tarac shifted aside, Aliria was lying back and her wary gaze found his. The men cleared out, and he followed to get changed, too.

"Thank you," came her soft, vulnerable words.

Hand on the door, he hesitated. "*What* were you doing?" he growled as he turned to her. "You could've drowned! Then your death would've been on my head!"

"You were in trouble. I folded to help—"

"How in the black seas could you possibly know I was in trouble? Besides, I was not—we had it well in hand until you plummeted into the ocean, forcing me to go in after you!"

Clinging to the blanket, she swung her feet over the edge of the bed. "Next time I will be sure not to help and let you die at the hand of savages!"

"Good!"

"Good!"

Vorn closed his eyes and tucked his chin. Groaned. "I have no idea why I thought having a Lady in Jherako would be a benefit. Your presence has brought nothing but trouble. And I nearly killed myself trying to keep you from drowning, yet all you can say is you'll let me die next time." He grunted and pivoted to the door. "If I haven't said it before, you can leave. You do not have to fulfill your term at Forgelight. This is trouble no man—or king—needs!"

She shoved to her feet, the blanket dropping. "I will not!" She fisted her hands, and Mercies of the heavens, the wet gown was still plastered to her perfectly designed form. "I will give you no reason to imprison—or execute—the Eknils."

"Exe—" He bit off the word. Muttered an oath. "You really do see me as the savage here." He stepped out and threw over his shoulder, "Clothe yourself, Lady. You're indecent."

VALIRIANA

Snatching the blanket back around her, Valiriana was mortified that she had forgotten the damp clothes plastered to her body. Horrible that she had once again been improperly attired around him. This time worse, since she was well aware of what wet fabric might reveal. Worse—she might as well stand naked before him for the injury done him.

"Magna Domine, I continue to make a mess of this. Please, release me from this. Let me return—"

A rap at the door silenced her as she tightened her grip on the blanket, ensuring she was modest. "Come."

The door opened, and Captain Mape appeared with a bundle. "I fear these are not as comfortable as one of your gowns, but it is the best we can manage. You will be dry and warm." He inclined his head. "You are invited to join us in the galley for food."

"Food? We are but an hour from shore, are we not?"

"We are," he said, his annoyance clear regarding being questioned, "but the storm ruins visibility, so the captain cannot navigate the dangerous shoals that guard Jherako's shoreline."

She gave a nod. "I thank you for the explanation."

Surprise held him fast for a tick, then he angled toward the door.

"It was not my intent to endanger him," she said, her throat raw. "I woke from a terrible dream in which he was being attacked. I had to help . . . so I folded . . ." Her eyes burned from unshed tears.

"What you mean and what you do are quite different, my Lady." He stepped around the chair and closed the gap. "The man you torment, taunt, and belittle is a *good* man. The best I have known. And you have repeatedly put him in danger, ridiculed, and disrespected him. I beg you—leave if that is all you are here to do."

She stared up at him, stunned into silence that so many were telling her to leave. That two men did not want her . . . What a confounding, crushing realization. But not half as devastating as realizing she did not want to go. "I am sorry. It was not . . . I did not . . ." She deflated.

"You are blue—still too chilled." The captain tapped the clothes. "Change. Then come down the gangway for warm broth before you catch your death."

Left alone with her thoughts and their rejection, Valiriana ached for things to be different. To have not made a complete disaster of this *missio*. Oh, it had been so much more difficult than she had imagined to come here, watch, learn, reconnoiter. Discover what lay in the heart of the Errant. Her heart had gotten twisted up, involved because of Jorti and Jan'maree.

No, her prejudices were formed well before then.

Disappointed in herself, she realized she had not come here to learn but to prove what she had already decided before leaving Deversoria.

Oh, Lady, how could You have chosen so poorly? Though she had ardently rejected the thought when Lady Eleftheria asked her that same question at the beginning of this mission, she wished she had given an emphatic 'yes' and saved everyone the heartache of her mess.

Changed into the rough, near-sackcloth trousers and oversized tunic, which she belted at the waist, Valiriana wrapped herself in a dry blanket and made her way down to where she heard men talking, laughing. Easing closer, trailing one hand along the wall for support against the sway of the ship, she did not enter but took in the goings-on.

The room was several times larger than the small room in which the king had delivered his rebuke. Two long tables were filled with men, eating, talking, and wet from the rain. But not soaked through as she and the king had been . . .

Because of my idiotic attempt to think I *could* save *him.*

How had she made so grave an error as she'd folded? It was an almost instantaneous relocation through time and space, but Faa'Cris were able to use the gifts granted them by the Ancient to judge that distance and land safely.

How did I so terribly misjudge?

A round table at the far side hosted the king and his men, who were hunched over bowls and maps. He was still wet.

"My Lady," Lathain said, shuffling to her. "Come." He drew her inside to the end of the nearest table where a large pot was secured, with bowls and ladles beside it.

Unfolding her arms and bracing her legs, she picked up a bowl and spoon. Felt very much the way she had the first day of hastati training—small, insignificant, off-balance. She ladled some broth into the bowl, along with a few chunks of roots. When she straightened, she found her gaze colliding with the king's. She drew in a sharp breath. His hard, disapproving glower shoved her gaze back down. With a slight stumble, she slid into the nearest open spot on a bench. Took the first bite and felt the benefits of the broth to her bones. She sighed and took another bite, then focused on finishing it . . . and figuring out how to get back to Deversoria when there was no answer from the Ladies nor Lady Eleftheria. Had she not repented? So why did they withhold access?

Because you try to flee . . .

Upon first arriving, she had wanted to return simply to get away from the Errant, believing he did not deserve the presence of a Lady. Now, she wanted to leave because she was ashamed and had failed. Failed the mission, failed . . . him. She wanted to leave because she could not endure what lurked in Vaanvorn's beautiful eyes when he looked upon her now. Or hear the way his scorn altered his rich, deep voice when he accused her.

I am not merely ruining things with my inexperience but also with my arrogance. Truly, she never should have set foot outside Deversoria.

A throat cleared, pulling her attention to the present, to this galley of sorts. Nervous glances skated to her. Why were they standing and looking at her? She looked to the side—and then felt the presence. Even as she turned, it was not hard to determine who hovered behind her. "Oh." She looked up at him—felt her stomach squeeze because for all her bravado, all her callous conjecture, Vaanvorn Thundred was a truly beautiful man.

"Lady, come sit with us at the head table."

"No, thank you." She lifted her bowl and rose. "I am done. Thank you, but—"

"My table," he bit out, the invitation now a command.

She swallowed, disconcerted at his tone. Inclined her head. Followed him over to where the Four were also standing—deference to their king, even on a rolling ship! A chair had been added to the table, and Lathain tugged it aside for her.

With a nod of thanks, she stepped between the chair and table, but this time remembered to wait for the king to take his seat. They settled and conversation resumed. What was that all about?

Seated, hands in her lap, she remained poised, quiet. In truth, her thoughts were heavy with her own failings. With her desire to return to the Daughters. Seated between the king and Lathain, Valiriana noted when the Furymark captain tugged a piece of paper, shuffled some others, then shifted one to the Errant. When he did, she saw . . . Wait . . . She eased forward, squinting to see a page that bore a small symbol stamped in the corner. It looked like . . .

As the men continued reviewing the attack that had been interrupted by Valiriana's arrival, she slowly moved her fingers toward the parchment. Drew it closer. That was the same—

"A problem, Lady Aliria?" Vorn's voice had the power of a gale.

"No." She dropped her hand to her lap again. "I am we—"

"Does that symbol mean something to you?"

She met his eyes. Swallowed. What if she was wrong? "I . . ." Had not she already made enough of a mess?

"Where did you see it?" Captain Mape asked firmly.

There was nothing for it—she had been found out. "In the city, I"—telling them she had folded badly then would not help her case—"bumped into a man. Knocked something from his hand. Despite my retrieving and returning it to him, he was none pleased. That was the first time I saw an object with that emblem."

"First time?" Vorn asked, concern in his eyes.

She nodded. "Last eve I heard some harsh words in a passage at the castle and followed them—found my lady's maid with the vizier. He said something about crawling the skies and slapped something from her hand. It was an object similar to the one outside The Iron. Both had that emblem on it."

"Craw—do you mean skycrawlers?"

She startled. "Yes, that's it."

Eyes darkening, the king reached into his pocket and pulled out a small black box and turned it over. "Did the object look like this?"

Valiriana drew in a breath. "Yes, quite similar. In fact, mayhap exactly that. What is it?"

"A powerful communication device," Captain Mape said. "Symmachian in origin."

"You are sure?" Vorn edged into the space between their chairs. "This is what you saw?"

It proved difficult to think and breathe normally with him in such close proximity, but she forced herself to focus. "Quite."

"And Vizier Gi is the one you saw with it?"

Grateful that he spoke to her with more familiarity, less resentment, she wanted to keep this communication open between them. "In the castle, yes. He took the device and left. But his manner and what I detected from him left no doubt he was not a good man."

Vorn turned the thing over between his fingers. "It appears we must needs speak with the vizier."

"Sire." A Furymark hastened toward the table, his boots thudding loudly across the deck. "Captain Herrigan says the visibility has cleared. We should make dock within the hour."

"Thank you, Alak." The Errant propped his elbows on the table and palmed a fisted hand as he stared at the emblem. Abruptly, he rose. "If you'll excuse me . . ." He strode from the galley without another word or look back.

The others dug into conversations about contingencies and possible strategies. Valiriana listened and waited as the topic shifted to purging the inner city of raiders. When Vorn did not return, she quietly slipped out and made her way back to the room. She banked right—

Vorn was propped against the wall, head down, eyes closed.

She stilled, then took the three steps to reach him. Touched his arm. "You are well?"

He started. Straightened, then sank back. "It's all . . . slipping through my fingers." Shoulder against the wall, he faced her.

"No," she said quietly, feeling her Faa'Cris nature rise with the power of the truth—and knowing from the way Vorn's eyes sharpened on her that her irises were going violet. "That is a lie designed to distract and deter you."

"Would that you were right, Lady."

Somehow, her fingers found the hair at his temple. She brushed it back. "I would not be here if there were no purpose. Though, if you want me to leave . . ."

He straightened. Caught her waist in a move so fast and urgent that it took them both by surprise. "Losing you is the last thing I want."

The words melted something in her. Warmed her core. She framed his face, his beard scratchy yet soft. "I am glad," she whispered. "When you were angry with me for trying to help you—"

"No," he said, his words thick. "I was angry because I nearly lost you. The thought of you dying . . ." How was he closer? His arm encircled her waist.

She drew up and felt the world shift. Was she debased to want him to kiss her? To feel his passion once more?

His knuckles grazed her chin, then his lips teased hers. He groaned. "I do not want to cross a line. I cannot lose you, Aliria."

"I know," she whispered, her words blooming warm against his beard. A breath shuddered through her. "But . . ."

His dark eyes carried the smile that was buried between their lips as his mouth caught hers. She released herself and felt him rotate and hold her against the wall. Deepened the kiss that had teased them both.

"Sire—whoa."

Vorn eased away, smiling down at her. "What is it, Azyant?"

"We're pulling into dock, sire. Lady."

Relieved as she was to have peace between them, when Valiriana stood with Vorn on deck while the ship pulled into harbor, she realized with a sense of awakening the terrible truth of the dark time in which Vaanvorn Thundred had been set to rule. His earlier complaint that he had hoped for a Lady's help and ended up with her shamed her. Keenly she felt her mistakes now. Her *missio* to reconnoiter did not involve judgment but rather clear assessment. Which she had failed to execute.

Watching the sailors tie up the lines to secure the vessel, Valiriana had a niggling sense that something was not right. She could detect chaos and animosity, but she often caught those scents in this busy city. This was something else.

"Something feels off," Vorn said from beside her, hand resting on the rail.

"I sense it as well," she agreed.

They disembarked, and she was kept amid the cluster of Four and the king as they made their way down the gangplank.

"Take the Lady back to her apartments," the king instructed.

"What, no!" Valiriana startled. "Where do you go? I would remain with you."

Vorn edged toward her, his hand instinctively going to her waist. "I have longed to hear those words, but I yet know it is not for the reason I had hoped."

You are wrong, she thought to herself. She feared being apart from him.

"As well," he said, diverting around his own vulnerable words, "we go to confront the vizier, and that is not a place—"

"I was not scared of him then, and I am not now," she said. "Besides, it would save me from folding poorly again if I remained at your side."

At her threat of escape, he held her gaze and took her hand. "Stay close."

In moments, they were mounted on Blacks and riding through the city to the vizier's house on the square. There, Vorn dismounted and immediately moved to her destrier.

Valiriana slid from the horse right into his hands, which skimmed to her waist. For a moment she stood, locked in a gaze that held her hostage and made her heart race. A smile rushed through her. *How mistaken I have been.*

But a cool, menthol note in the air made her draw in a breath. She whipped around, searching the shadows.

"On your king!" came the shout from Captain Mape.

A suffocating press of bodies startled her. Made her realize she had taken hold of the king's arm. "Wait. It is not trouble," she whispered.

"I intend you no harm," came a resonant, authoritative voice as a cloaked figure strode from the shadows of the night.

Heart alight, Valiriana thrust herself forward, pushing to get past the Furymark.

"My Lady!"

She broke through and set eyes on the tall, formidable figure and let out a tremulous laugh. "What do you here?"

He took in the kingsguard around them as he caught her in a hug. "Mayhap you should inform your escorts who I am before they run me through."

Valiriana laughed. "As if they could!"

"My Lady." The king's tone was not as kind or as cordial this time. In fact, it was hard as steel. Anger roiled through his gaze as he moved into the open.

To her surprise, she saw and detected jealousy.

He is jealous? Ohh . . . Why did that make her heart sail? "King Vaanvorn, I would like to introduce you to this Kynigos Master Hunter—most importantly—my uncle, Roman deBurco."

"Your Majesty," her uncle greeted. "It is an honor, and I wish there were time to address the concerns and questions I yet detect in your efflux, but there is not. I know not what madness possesses a king and his guard to stroll the streets at this hour—"

"How dare you!" Captain Mape growled.

"—but I admonish you—there is dark trouble at your door and—"

Boom! Boom!

A faint rumble drew their gazes north as the distant sky turned from night to day.

"I am too late."

Vorn surged toward the man. "Speak, sir! What do you here? For the sake of your"—his gaze skidded to Aliria, more than a little confused and concerned—"niece, I will stay my blade, but—"

"I beg you, King Vaanvorn, to—"

"Now is not your turn, Lady Aliria." He hated the hurt and shock she shot him at the remonstration, but he had been sidetracked by this siren too many times. He eyed the tall, broad-shouldered man in a long black cloak, black boots, and gold cords that swung across his chest. "I know not what a *kinn . . . gose* is, but the Droseran-Tertian Accord—"

"Kynigos," the man corrected with more than a little disapproval in his expression. "Intergalactic bounty hunters. We have been granted hunting privileges across the Quadrants to retrieve fugitives. Even here. Please feel free to reference that Accord. Your *broken* Accord, King Vorn"—his look was pointed and accusatory—"which keeps technology and Symmachia from your planet also makes an exception for my hunters to track here." He huffed, giving Aliria a forlorn expression, his gaze narrowing for a long moment on her before settling again on Vorn. "By the dolor in the air, I am too late to save one king, so I would beg you, return to your castle so I don't have the weight of two on my conscience this dark hour."

"I understand you want your niece safe—"

The hunter barked a laugh that emphasized his formidability. "What uncle does not? But she is capable of defending herself far more than you, and mayhap even she, understands."

"You forget who you talk to," Captain Lathain growled.

"I do not," the Kynigos said firmly. "If you would have pandering, look to someone else. You will not find it from me. I have long trained pups who needed truth and challenge. As well"—his gaze rose to the skies in a generally northern direction—"with what has happened this hour, I have little tolerance for politics." He touched the Lady's shoulder. "I would have a word with you, Niece."

She inclined her head, and Vorn clenched his teeth when the two moved to the side. The hunter, taller by a couple hands, bent toward her, whispering in her ear. She gripped his sleeves and inclined her head, some strange emotion playing over her features.

Instinct had Vorn taking a step toward her, but even as his boot hit the cobbled road, she straightened. With a whispered word to the hunter, she turned and started toward Vorn. What played havoc in her face one second had vanished the next.

"Are you well?" he could not help but ask.

With a cockeyed but silent nod, she regained his side and positioned herself there, facing away from her uncle.

Vorn wanted to put an arm around her, again inquire about her change, but she was a Lady, he a king. And they were in the open. "If you don't mind, we have business—"

"I beg your pardon, King Vaanvorn, but it would be my strongest advice to return to the castle at once and not persist in the—"

"Your suggestion is appreciated," Vorn bit out, displeased with this man for upsetting Aliria and for his audacity in instructing them on what to do and where to go.

"I have angered you," the hunter said, his expression betraying dismay. When Tarac started to argue, the man lifted his hand. "I have heightened senses, and that gift enables me to read emotion as easily as one might read words on a page. My intention was to protect, not instruct. Much is at play here, and I fear for your life, Majesty. Do not think your endeavors with ships have gone unnoticed. Please—be prudent and return to your house. For now." His shrewd blue eyes locked on Vorn. "I sense what you feel for my niece, and I beg you—let that be your guide in your decision. I know you would not want her harmed."

"You play his affections against him, uncle."

The hunter smirked. "Only if it works." With a curt nod, he said, "For honor," then sailed off into the night. Scaled a wall better than any monkey.

Vorn might not appreciate the way the man had spoken to him, but anyone who could move like that deserved his admiration.

"Sire," Tarac said, angling toward him, "may I recommend Lathain and

Ba'moori escort you to the castle. Azyant and I can take a contingent and address . . . the problem."

"No," Vorn said. "I put the man in office. It should be my hand by which he is delivered of it." He glanced at the Lady, of a mind to send her back as the hunter had suggested.

She firmed her grasp in his hand and gave a nod telling him she was okay.

Siren. "What we go to do will not be pleasant."

"I belong with you—er, I am safest with you." She faltered at her own words, as if they surprised her, too, and though she seemed embarrassed, she did not retract them.

At that, Vorn felt a swell in his chest. And prayed neither of them regretted it. "Stay close and ready."

Catching the pommel, she hiked up onto the destrier with the aid of Tarac's knee. Astride, she peered down at him and nodded. Never had she seemed more confident in her person.

Vorn flung himself atop his Black, and soon they were en route to the vizier's residence on the square. As they slowed to a stop by the foundation, he watched the Furymark fan out around the two-story structure that was as wide as it was deep, neither of which was very large, making their task that much simpler.

He dismounted and felt the men form up on him, the Lady Aliria tucked into a phalanx of Furymark. Even as he gained the stoop he saw the door swing open by a sergius, who moved out of the way and bowed low. "Where is the vizier?"

"He . . . left only this moment, sire."

Vorn pulled up short. "Where?"

"The ba—"

Shouts outside came from the rear of the residence, Furymark bellowing as hooves thundered and clattered on the road.

"Protect the Lady!" Vorn shouted as adrenaline drove him around the side. He was yet on the steps when he spotted a shadow spiriting along the garden wall. Before he could respond, a blur sailed past him. Lathain! His man collided with the skulking figure.

A woman screamed as Lathain hauled her up and pinned her to the wall.

"Karistni," Aliria gasped.

Vorn growled. "Where is the vizier?" He looked around, the gathered Furymark and his Four seemingly as confused as he was. "Where is Gi?"

The defiant girl spat at Vorn.

Azyant slammed the hilt of his sword into her temple. When she crumpled to the ground, he almost looked regretful. But then he shrugged. "She would not have helped us."

"Search the alleys and roads," Captain Mape shouted. "Find Haarzen Gi and bring him to the king!"

Vorn exhaled heavily, disappointed to learn how close the enemy had been all this time.

VALIRIANA

She slept better that night than she had in weeks. Then again, almost drowning did that to a person. Disheartened for the king, who had not been able to capture the vizier who betrayed him, Valiriana readied herself in haste the next morning. Donning a simple gown—oddly relieved not to have someone dressing her—she then secured her hair in the standard hastati plait and knot.

A rap at the door interrupted her. She moved to the middle of her chambers and clasped her hands. "Come."

The door opened and a page appeared with a tray of covered dishes.

Right. A meal to break her fast, which had normally been delivered by her lady's maid. Who was a criminal and traitor. "Thank you. You may place it over there," she said, indicating to the table by the windows.

He set down the tray, placed the plates and glass on the table, then removed the lids. Faced her and gave a curt bow. "Anything else, my Lady?"

"No, that is—" Valiriana stopped and glanced at the door. Then back to the boy. "Do you know where I might find the king?"

The boy frowned. "I wouldn't be knowing. They don't let me go there."

"Of course." She nodded to the food. "Thank you. That is all." She felt pretentious uttering those last words, but she had learned quickly that if she did not, they would stay.

Though she was anxious to seek out the king, she felt her stomach rumble and recalled the substance-light soup of last night. She sat down to eat, biting the biscuits first.

"Good rise, Valiriana."

The sudden, unexpected intrusion of the *vox saeculorum* into her thoughts made her suck in a breath—and choke on the bread. She coughed and thumped her chest. *"Ma'm—Revered Mother."* She swallowed. *"It is good to hear your voice. It has been an age!"*

"I am relieved that you are well integrated into Jherako and the king's affection."

Heat flamed, and she mentally growled that Roman had relayed the news to Deversoria. *"It was a surprise to see Uncle on the streets last eve. I should not be surprised that he has informed you—"*

"He has not," Ma'ma said firmly. *"Do not think we were unaware of your efforts or trials there."*

She tossed down the bread. *"How? I was shut off, could not hear or speak to you!"*

"You mistake silence for obstruction, child."

"But you would not speak to me!"

"What has light to do with darkness?" Ma'ma stated flatly. *"You were absorbed with yourself, Valiriana. You grew bitter and focused on self, rather than the* missio *for which the Lady Eleftheria chose you. Your bitterness and anger blocked you, not us."*

Hearing Ma'ma state so plainly not only the truth that Eleftheria had chosen Valiriana but that her guilt presented an obstruction in communicating with Deversoria proved difficult, unsettling. Though Valiriana bit into the sausage, it tasted bland. She was sure her entire meal would taste the same and moved it aside. Accepted her guilt. *"I am ashamed of my actions and attitudes. They were so contrary to what we have learned. I was so caught up in proving him unworthy that I was not considering the facts."*

"It is a hard lesson to learn, but I am proud of you. And relieved to hear you once more."

"Much trouble brews here, Ma'ma." She must bring herself to mention what her uncle had voiced in the streets. *"Sad news has come from Kalonica—"*

"He told me," Ma'ma said quietly. *"You may not have known your father, but he was a very good man, Valiriana. We are all grieved at his loss, me especially."*

"I would think so, if you gave him three sons before me."

"It is rare," Ma'ma conceded, *"and I would have returned to Deversoria sooner, but when your uncle took our eldest to the Citadel for training, Zarek was so heartbroken I could not bear to leave him."*

She had not heard this tale before. *"Uncle said all was lost last night. Does* this mean . . . I alone remain of my father?"

"You are not alone."

It was strange, curious. She knew none of her brothers, not even her father, yet she felt as if they were a part of her, an anchoring to some past she had never experienced. Knowing she yet had a brother left Valiriana with a thick sense of relief. *"So all is not lost for Kalonica, then. His heir can come and take the throne, help—"*

"You must not speak of Achilus to anyone, Valiriana. He has his own path. It is imperative you leave him to it. He will change the world."

Mind racing, she struggled to understand the cryptic, daunting words of her mother. *"That carries such an ominous note, almost . . . prophetic."*

"It is a troubling time," Ma'ma said. *"However"*—she suddenly sounded cheerier—*"I reached out to you for another reason, Daughter."*

Daughter. Not Valiriana. Thus a shift in their conversation, from mother/daughter to Revered Mother/triarii.

"Laborare pugnare parati sumus," she replied via the *vox saeculorum*, knowing it was the only proper response. *To work, to fight, we are ready.* At all times, Daughters were to be ready to carry out the will of the Ancient.

"The Lady sent you out for reconnaissance."

"Aye."

"But the Flames have revealed your missio *is now an official Sending."*

Breath caught in her throat, Valiriana could not move. Could not think. *"What speak you?"* No, no, no. *"I was only here to assess him. Report back—"*

"And you have—what radiates from your adunatos speaks to the character of this king."

"My adunatos? But . . ."

"Considering your vocal and spirited rejection of the Errant, in truth all Licitus, prior to your going out, and that now your efflux clearly reveals a softening and even an affection—"

Inwardly, she groaned. Her own heart had literally betrayed her to the Resplendent.

"It has been decided that it would be a good match for you and this king to be aligned."

"Ma'ma, no." Her voice wavered. Tears stung. *"I need more training, more discipline. I failed so badly, have made so many mistakes. And as you stated, my adunatos has been* contaminated *by my attitudes. I folded straight into the ocean last eve! The* ocean! *I have never made such a terrible miscalculation.*

Very nearly drowned myself, but thankfully, I did not because the king—" She snapped her thoughts closed. Would not give them more reason to persist on this terrible path.

"The king saved your life."

"I put him at risk!" she bellowed into the *vox saeculorum*. *"I am not fit for this! He deserves someone with more experience and wisdom."*

Ma'ma's melodic laughter carried thickly through her thoughts. *"You are perfectly suited for this king, and I could not be more proud—"*

"Proud? I have failed. Repeatedly! Made assumptions, mistakes." Even now her eyes burned, remembering all the injury she had done him, as well as that kiss . . . *"He deserves someone who could benefit him and this realm!"*

"That you say he deserves *anyone tells me you are in the right place,"* the Revered Mother said. *"With the affirmation of the Sending, you have permission and authority to make an offer to Vaanvorn Thundred."*

"No! Please—"

But even as the word left her lips, she felt the withdrawal of the *vox saeculorum* and the Revered Mother. "Of course." She sighed as the loneliness seeped in, bringing with it utter confusion and anger. This was not supposed to happen. There were still things she took exception to regarding Vorn— one, the imprisonment of Shimeal. Two, his former indulgence with ladies of the night. But, her concerns aside, there was an expectation that when Sent, one was bound to the Sendee. This meant the Ladies all but expected her to bind with him. The Errant king. Vaanvorn. Vorn.

Last night in the shadows of that house where the vizier managed to escape, Vorn had looked so fierce, so raw and powerful. He reminded her of the paintings and parchments portraying the ferocity of Vaqar in aid of the fire-wielding prince. Of Sir Jaigh and his fight for the hearts and minds of Tryssinia, before the mine plague ravaged his people and he left to join the Lady Rejeztia in serving the very entity that Vorn would now fight— Symmachia. Not as those complicit, but as spies behind enemy lines—under the command of a certain admiral, who had been the husband of Lady Miatrenette. Now there was a powerful, inspiring partnership.

Without the distraction of Karistni in her apartments, Valiriana quickly grew restless. She wanted to get out of the chambers. Or mayhap it was her itch to escape what the Ladies had thrust upon her. It seemed as if they had pushed her into a well-laid trap.

Oh, Mercies. That would include the Lady Eleftheria, and while she often did not understand Her instruction, Valiriana knew to trust the Lady.

So . . . she sent me here . . . for this? Or were the Resplendent wrong in transitioning this from recon to a formal Sending? *Me. Sent here . . . to marry this king.* Provide him an heir . . . And the Ladies a Daughter. Would their eyes be dark like his or blue-violet like hers?

Why am I not finding this repugnant?

In answer, the memory of his whiskers on her neck and cheek, his kiss passionate and . . . wonderful, sent a charged thrill through her.

She should be ashamed.

Why?

Shouts and laughter mingled with the resounding clack of wood on wood, along with the singing of steel. Valiriana glanced around, surprised to find herself nearing the windows through which she had seen the king before, sparring and chastising his soldiers. He had seemed so angry, so punishing.

Two sergii came toward her, and Valiriana diverted to a side hall. She was not sure why except that she felt guilty. But why would she feel guilty?

Because I search out Vorn.

The thought pushed her into a small passage between two wings of the castle. The entire left stood open to the training yard below and boasted a series of six arches. This was why she could so clearly hear the sparring. Cautiously, she eased to the balustrade and peered over. Immediately below the balcony were a handful of boys who were no more than ten or twelve, learning swordsmanship with training swords at the instruction of a burly man. In the center sparred Furymark, their strikes and parries lightning fast and more about instinct than rote practice. Mayhap both, but she could not help but admire these men who protected the king, who had protected her last night during the vizier's escape.

A loud bang echoed from the side of the yard she could not see, but all the Furymark turned instinctively toward the possible danger. Then one lifted his hand, hesitated, and pointed to a wall, it seemed.

Soon, a man strode across the yard, bearing a large hide bundle . . . Swords. He met a man at a side door, knelt, and set down the swords. He laid out another hide strip, then glanced back toward the Furymark.

"Shimeal," Valiriana gasped, seeing his face. "Shimeal!" How was this possible that he was here? "Please, wait—I will come to you."

She hurried down the passage and found the stairs, then rushed to the door to the training yard. At first, she thought to bolt inside, but reminded herself men were sparring, amped on adrenaline and the thrill of the fight. She knew that feeling well from her time in the coliseum, so she opened the door and entered carefully. Spotted him directly to her left and rushed to him. "Shimeal! It does my heart good to see you!" Without a thought, she hugged the man who had given her shelter, provided for her in the weeks the king and his men were searching for her.

Shimeal's face reddened. "My Lady." He gave a curt nod, his gaze skimming the training yard. "A surprise, I am sure."

Valiriana smiled but inched closer, lowering her voice. "I am much relieved to see you freed of prison."

"Prison?" He recoiled, frowning at her. "Wha—"

"Aye—I happened upon Jorti in the city, and he said you were in prison. Said he was going to get the keys from the king so he could let you out."

The burly man sniffed a near laugh. "That boy . . ." He shook his head and then leaned in and lowered his voice. "Lady, I was in no prison. I have been serving here with the castle smithy. Learning the trade, even. Work hard and well enough, and I might earn an apprenticeship."

Valiriana considered him, surprised and confused. "No prison? Even after breaking the law as the king declared at the barn? But Jorti . . . he was so earnest in his belief."

He shrugged, then his eyes brightened. "I recall now—Jorti came through the west foot gate with Jan'maree once—the bars were locked because it was late. I couldn't go out, so I hugged him through the bars. No matter how many times I assured him, Jorti insisted it was a prison." He indicated to the far door. "He is here, if you would see him. Jan'maree sent word he'd been summoned to train with some other boys here."

Valiriana started. "Jorti? Jorti is *here*?"

"Aye."

"In the castle?"

"Well, likely in the schoolroom or training yard, depending on the hour," he said, his chest puffing a little.

Valiriana caught his arm, stunned. "What say you? Truly? But—"

"Come, I will show you."

Mind reeling, Valiriana followed him out of the yard, too aware that she had made a grave misjudgment about the king. "You have been here the whole time?" she asked quietly, still unwilling to believe she had been so wholly wrong.

"Aye, and despite the rough treatment when I was taken into custody, it was the king himself who ordered that I be set to work here." He grinned—a nice, real smile that she had not seen in some time. "Jan'maree and Jorti are set up in an apartment not far from here. Far nicer than I could have afforded trying to farm. But working here, my income—"

"Income?" Valiriana stopped as they stepped onto a green field. "But you were arrested."

"Aye." He gave her a sheepish look. "The king bought my sentence."

"You're a slave?" she balked.

"Technically, I suppose," he said with a shrug, "but I am not treated as such. King Vorn bargained with me to work here for one year. At that time, he will consider my oath and sentence fulfilled. I'll be free to rejoin my family and still have a good job here at the castle."

Agape, she stared at him. Could not fathom . . . "Fulfilled." The same length of time as her deal she had struck with the king.

"With the caveat that I break no more laws." He gave a wistful bob of his head. "After all I have been handed, I would be a fool to defy him." As they rounded a corner, he paused, worrying a stretch of leather that hung from a belt at his waist. "I would ask your mercy, Lady. I was hard on you—"

"No, no—"

"But there is no doubt in my mind that the king gave me this chance because of you, so you have my deepest thanks. For myself, the boy—Jan'maree. Thank you."

"If I were responsible, you would be most welcome. You and Jan'maree did much for me at a critical time, but this . . . this is not me. I cannot fathom why the king would be so . . . benevolent."

"Have I fulfilled my benevolence quota for the day?" Had he been serious?

Shimeal smirked. "Can you not? Have you looked in a reflecting glass of late?"

A child's laugh assailed the day, drawing her gaze toward a tall hedgerow. Then shouts and a smaller voice joined in.

"That is Jorti—unmistakable laugh, that. Sounds like he needs to blow his nose." Shimeal led her across the lawn.

Something strange was happening. Her life was being upended. All she had thought—coming here to reconnoiter the king, to prove him unworthy, believing him guilty of cruelty . . .

A barrage of laughter snapped her gaze to a small, sandy pit. The boy threw himself at the shirtless man training him, catching his legs and flipping sideways, snaking his legs around the man's ankles and holding on tight until his opponent went to his knees. With a laugh. "Again, well done!" Both sweaty, the man straightened, hair in a queue down his back, as he turned.

Valiriana drew in a sharp breath. Stepped back. "Vorn."

His gaze whipped in her direction, no doubt in response to her squeaking his name.

"Papa!" Jorti exclaimed, and though he started to run to Shimeal, he stopped short. Faced the king. Clapped his hands to his sides. "Your Majesty, permission to be excused to see my papa?"

Vorn touched the boy's shoulders. "Of course."

Jorti bolted to his dad, nearly taking him down with the impact of a son missing his father. It was heartwarming and . . . completely not what she expected. Seeing the father and son hug and talk moved her to tears. They were well fed, healthy, and . . . happy.

"You are well?" Vorn's voice was husky, soft—close.

Valiriana turned to him, registering immediately he was still without a shirt. She did not stare this time, but with his quickened breathing and the way the sun glittered on his tanned torso, it was impossible not to at least notice. "I . . ." She gave a light shake of her head. "Aye, I am." Facing him, she studied the bronzed, sweaty face. So handsome and . . . kind. Good. "Thank you." But her thanks was not in response to his question but to what he had done. How he had provided for this precious family.

Vorn slowed, his hand resting on her upper arm. "You are changed. Are you sure you're well?"

"Papa, did you see us sparring? I took the king down!"

Shimeal, holding his son to himself by the shoulders, gave a nervous laugh. "I would not say that quite so loud." He nodded to the king. "Thank you for spending time with him, sire. We are honored."

Vorn flicked his hand. "A pleasure. The boy has talent and will one day, no doubt, serve in the Furymark."

Jorti gasped elaborately. "Did you hear, Papa? I'm going to be in the Furymark."

"Only if you master the sword," Vorn said, his eyes carrying that trademark smile. "Can you do that?"

"Yes—I will!" Jorti's eyes widened at his mistake. "Sire." He stood stiffly. "I am already really good at the *Zornhau!*"

"Show me," Vorn challenged.

The boy gave a curt bow, then hurried to the yard.

Valiriana recalled the way the king had trained, the way he'd railed at the Furymark. "Go easy—"

Vorn winked at her and cocked his head to the side, inviting Shimeal to join him. "I hear congratulations are in order, Shimeal—another babe."

"Aye." The father smiled. "Due before the harvest celebration."

"I envy you a family. It is good fortune." With that Vorn hefted a sword and stepped into the training circle with Jorti. They tapped swords and then readied themselves.

It was a quick round of strikes and parries, Vorn giving the boy instruction, expertly avoiding Jorti's thrusts. He tapped the boy's back with his blade and laughed.

"Not exactly a fair battle against one so small," Valiriana mused. "Jorti, you are doing very well."

"Thank you, Lady." His bright expression turned to the king. "She's a Lady—a real Lady, you know, of Basilikas. With wings and all."

Vorn slid an appreciative glance her way. "Wings, eh?" He squinted at her. "Not a fair fight?"

"He is but a child, you a grown man," she said with a near laugh.

"Then, are *you* challenging me, my Lady?"

22

What are you doing, idiot?

Simply providing a way for a Lady to continue to admire his physique for a little while longer. He had not stopped thinking about their kisses, the feel of her in his arms, of pulling her from the ocean. Having trained many a kingsguard, he knew how sparring changed people—it either cemented their connection or severed it. Offering to spar with her could put an end to any chance of kissing her again. Was that a risk he wanted to take? It seemed both irreverent and foolish. Then again, were Faa'Cris not the most renowned of warriors?

"You called my honor into question," he said, easing closer.

Though she straightened, the Lady did not remove herself. "That was not my intent."

He set a hand over his heart. "All the same, I am wounded."

She rolled her eyes. "Then I must further wound you, for if we were to spar, you would be at a disadvantage, King Vorn, and that is not a shame I would will on any man, especially in front of a young protégé."

Shock thumped his chest. "My Lady," he said with a laugh, confounded and entirely amused at the change in Aliria, "I accept your challenge." Rolling his shoulders, he stepped aside and motioned to the wall of training weapons. "What will be your choice?"

Her gaze took in the wooden training instruments. "Afraid I will hurt you?"

Waves of providence, he was in love! Eyes locked on hers, he angled to the side and lifted the scabbard he had shed to spar with the boy. With a flourish, he brandished his sword. Gave a singing crisscross slice. "Better?" He indicated toward the hedgerow. "But I am afraid there is no weapon for you. We can have a sword—"

The Lady, who had been standing with her feet together, watching him, squared her stance, rolled her shoulders, and then stepped back. In the split-second of that move, she no longer wore a gown but . . .

Vorn froze. Gaped.

Armor, glittering, glowing. Form fitting. "Wings," he muttered, hearing the boy shout in triumph.

"Papa, I told you she was a Lady!"

Aliria settled into her place, confident in . . . everything—her armor, the wings, the glowing sword that now extended from her firm grip. Boots melding over very shapely, muscular legs. The attire blended into her armor and kept her decent.

But he did not need to see skin for his imagination to roar to life. "Black seas," he muttered, knowing he was in trouble. "You were right."

Obviously enjoying what was happening, she tilted her chin up and to the side with a near smile.

"This *is* an unfair fight." He wanted to laugh but sincerely wondered if he was about to be handed his manhood on this field.

"So you withdraw?"

In answer, Vorn launched himself forward. He reached for her—only to find empty space where she had once stood. He stumbled around in time to find her alighting. "Cheating."

Indignation sparked in her eyes, which were full violet now.

Vorn thrust his sword, determined to put her on the defensive.

She drove upward with that glowing blade. They were in full-on sword fighting for several long minutes. He rarely tired, but apparently neither did she. Aches wove into his arms and shoulders as they parried and danced around the sandy pit, moved onto the grass, a bit more of a challenge with the dampness from the nearby sea.

Aliria was amazing—fierce, relentless, her prowess with strategy and the timing of her strikes near perfection.

The contact rattled up through his arm bones, right into his shoulders. He relaxed his form and sliced sideways—even as he felt a cold crack of something against his cheek. Stunned, he stared at her—now a solid two meters back from him—and touched his cheek. Felt blood. "What—"

"Her wings," came Tarac's shout. "They are as formidable a weapon as her blade, it would seem. Give care."

Aye. A little late with the warning.

Vorn stretched his neck and rotated his arms, working the fire from them.

"Tired?" she asked coyly as they circled one another.

Mercies, she was a sight to behold. Why hadn't she—

She dove at him. Vorn braced but did not have time to defend. He was knocked to the ground even amid shouts and some laughter from the boy and Tarac. Humiliating to be losing to the Lady and have an audience give witness. She pinned him on the ground, a strange pressure against his legs and hands. Only then did he notice she used the bony protrusions from her wings to secure him. She drew back her fist to strike him. Met his gaze. Faltered.

Vorn seized the mistake. Used it to flip her, thought it was not unlike trying to upend a rhinnock, the force of her strength so great. But as he was flinging around, something felt . . . wrong. Light. He frowned at her and saw a greedy gleam. Shouts were distant. That's when he realized she'd taken to the skies. Propriety went out the proverbial window as he clung to her, knowing any slip and he would spatter the ground.

He muttered an oath, tightening his grip. Finding her eyes glittering with mischief and delight. "Again, you cheat."

"And yet you smile."

"How can I not?" he asked, telling himself not to think about how high up he was. "I am in the arms of the most amazing woman in the world."

She seemed shy all of a sudden. "And that is where you want to be?"

Something very different lurked in her question, and he almost missed that they had alighted back on the training yard. "Absolutely."

Laughter from the men shocked him out of the moment.

"I thought you were done for," Tarac said. "One loose grip and you would—splat!"

Vorn chuckled, his gaze not leaving the Lady's, whose question had not been rhetorical. Even as he considered her, she returned to her human form. To be honest, he could not say which form he preferred because they were both stunning in their own way.

He watched as she accepted an exuberant embrace from Jorti, then Shimeal.

They were all awed by her. And he suddenly found he did not want to share her time or her attention.

"Return to your duties," he instructed the father and boy. As she said farewells, Vorn moved toward her. Extended his hand. "A sparring session like that deserves some sustenance. Will you join me?"

She nodded and took his hand.

He led her into the house as Tarac set off to some errand of his own. "You are quite the warrior. I had heard Ladies were renowned for their battle skills, but to see it, experience it . . ."

"You are much impressed but would not be if you knew that when I was sent out, I had only started second levels."

"Only second?" He grunted and walked her down to the kitchens, where he spied the cook. "Ah, how are you, Cook?"

"Sire! I was not expecting you." She gave Aliria a peculiar look that seemed to weigh and assess. "It is yet early and preparations are underway for dinner."

"Please, do not concern yourself. The Lady and I are going to sneak a bit of bread and cordi." He reached for a tray.

"Tsk!" Cook kindly shooed him away. "You two go and sit. I will bring a tray."

"You are sure?"

"When have I ever seen you bring a lady to the kitchens?" She clucked her tongue. "Of course I am sure. Go. Entertain your lady."

Heat swarmed in Vorn's chest. He liked the sound of that—*your lady*. "You are too kind, Cook. As always." He turned to Aliria and found her smiling, shaking her head. "Here, we will sit back here. It is the one place as a lad that I could escape to, beg a cookie, and be left alone."

A round booth table sat tucked into the corner at the rear of the kitchens. A picture window gave them a view of the gardens and beyond them, the sea. She took a seat on the curved, padded bench, and he joined her.

"Again, it seems I owe you an apology," Aliria said as she folded her hands on the table.

He could not resist setting his hand over hers. "No. No more apologies. We both came at each other with presuppositions."

"Mayhap," she said, "but what you did for Shimeal and Jan'maree far exceeds anything I could have dreamed. I accused you—"

"It was understandable."

"No," she said with a disbelieving laugh, "it is not. I was abominable to you."

"I am not sure I would go that far, but we can agree that I questioned before your arrival if I could ever save the realm." He nodded. "Now that you have come and we have found common ground, I have hope."

Something played in her expression, her gaze bouncing over his face, and though it was hard not to speak of it or flirt with her, he let her explore what she willed. "Hope?"

Cook delivered a tray piled with fruit, pastries, nuts, and chilled cordi.

"I may not have room for our evening meal," Aliria said with a laugh.

"A meal with the king far outweighs any abovestairs with those smelly Furymark," Cook said.

Aliria skidded a look at him as a blush climbed into her cheeks.

"Thank you, Cook," he said. "You can have that day off as promised for that compliment."

Cook popped his shoulder. "Don't you go telling fibs. I speak what is true, not what is bribed." She shook her finger at him as she started back to her duties. "You be nice to this lady. Likely the only one who could endure your mischief."

"Too true," Vorn said with a chuckle, watching as she left. Though he saw other kitchen staff bustling about, he was glad they only stole glances and did not linger.

"You have known her long?"

"Cook has been here since before I was born," Vorn said, picking a pastry off the mound and biting into it.

As he ate, she retrieved two small plates that had been on the tray and set one before him, then a linen napkin, then a goblet.

She was serving *him*. In most circles that would be acceptable, but not with a Lady of Basilikas. He should be on his knees, begging her aid and favor. He half wondered what she would do if he actually did that. "Lady, I think—"

She stayed his hand that moved to intercept hers. "Aliria." She looked at the food, then back to him. "Or Valiriana, but please—no more title."

What she offered him was no small measure. "Valer—"

"Va-*lir*-i-ana."

His pulse sped. "That is your *true* name."

VALIRIANA

It surprised how much he knew of the Faa'Cris. With a soft nod, she offered him the one thing he could never have known on his own—*her*. Did he understand what it meant?

"And it is a gift."

Her heart thumped as he answered her unspoken question. She caught her lower lip between her teeth, debating how much to reveal. "Yes." And more . . . so much more.

The king studied her for several long seconds and in those rich, dark eyes revealed that he may very well comprehend what else giving her true name meant. He shifted his gaze to the platter of food. Took a nut. Ate it. "I think I will stick to the name I can pronounce, if that is okay with you."

She laughed, relieved he had not gone to that conversation. "That is fine. Besides, I like the way you say it with your Jherakan accent."

"I was not aware I had one," he said, bemused. "So, what you did out there—the wings and glowing sword—"

"Lightsword." She would never forget his expression, his awe in that moment on the field.

"Lightsword." He processed the word. "How . . .?"

"What you saw is my enlightened form, my true form," she said, finding safe harbor in explaining things. "You know the history of the Faa'Cris?"

After a gulp of cordi, he shrugged. "I have been researching since your arrival." When her eyebrows winged up, he chuckled. "Know your enemy, aye?"

That broke her heart, made her realize afresh how she had mishandled this *missio*. "I would not be your enemy, Vorn."

He stilled, his beard twitching. "And I would not have you be, Aliria."

She smiled. Maybe too broadly, but it felt good. As if they had locked in a connection they did not have before. She tucked a grape in her mouth and chewed slowly. "I was not supposed to be eligible to come here at all, but . . ." Mercies, she had failed and they had passed her. Then the Lady came . . . and now . . . now she was commissioned for a Sending. It had been intentional all along, had it not?

"What is it?" he prodded, covering her hand once more.

His touch ignited a swarm of nervous jellies in her core. "I can see now how all this was set in motion by the Ancient. The Lady commissioning me, the Se—" She bit off the word, somehow still afraid to mention it. Put the offer on the table. She bounced her gaze to him, then cleared her throat.

He brushed the hair from her face and shoulder, clearly feeling bold. "I am so very glad you came."

She studied him. "Why did you want a Lady to come to Forgelight?"

"The realm," he said plainly. "As you have seen, it is in desperate straits. It has floundered under the rules of my father and brother. Since taking the throne, I have been routing corruption. A crone suggested a Lady could help. I never would have considered that without her intrusion."

"A crone?"

His smile faltered but he nodded. "An augur."

Valiriana drew in a sharp breath. "You consulted an augur? You who visits Sanctuary and utters petitions to the Ancient? Do you understand that augur are vile manipulators—they have turned from the path as surely as the Corrupt?" She pulled up straight and edged in. "They are Fallen—once Faa'Cris, now traitors to the Ancient, servants of His enemy. I beg you—tell me you did not do this wicked thing and bring her into your circle."

Guilt hung heavy in his gaze. "At first . . . a little."

Anger wove through her—not at him, but at the Fallen. "They tempt you with what you desire so they may control you, seize your adunatos."

"I sensed as much. She was put to blade."

"You killed her?"

"My Sword—Captain Mape—did."

It was not a method she would have advocated, but it was a relief to know he was no longer under the creature's control. "I should have known you would act with honor."

"I nearly did not. But I learned something valuable in the near miss." He touched her face, his thumb stroking her cheek. "No man stands alone. Without the grace of the Ancient in putting good men at my side, I would have fallen. Now I have a chance."

The way he traced her jaw was awakening something in her that proved intoxicating. "What chance?" Had she moved nearer, or had he?

"To have you in my life. Being here with you, laughing with you, sparring with you—it is far more than I could have dreamed. When I prayed for a Lady, I thought only of the good she might bring my rule and my realm." He grazed her lips with his. "I did not imagine I would love you as well."

Valiriana drew in a breath, but as his face hovered over hers, machi-wood eyes asking permission, she tilted hers closer. Gave him what he sought. What she sought. His kiss was gentle, caressing, teasing. She let her fingers trail through his beard and liked that his kisses grew more confident, more ardent. Realizing she could lose herself in this and that they were sitting in a public setting, she shifted and put a bit of space between them.

Gaze hooded, breathing a little ragged, he looked at her. "I . . . You are too hard to resist, Aliria."

She smiled. "Then do not."

He frowned. Drew back. "I would never dishonor you or myself—"

"I am glad to hear this," she replied, touching his hand, "however, I meant something else."

His gaze settled on hers for several long ticks, no doubt his mind running the gamut of possible meanings behind her words. Then his eyes widened. "Do you mean . . .?" Shock and exultation soaked his efflux that had roiled with passion and longing.

"Though when I first came here, my *missio* was simply to reconnoiter and report, I was recently informed that my *missio* is now an official Sending." She straightened and considered him with a long sigh, half disbelieving they were at this point. "King Vaanvorn Thundred, if you are amenable, the Resplendent—in accordance with the will of Vaqar, Eleftheria, and the Ancient—offer a Sending of a Daughter to bind with you. If you are inclined to accept—"

"Done!"

She breathed a laugh. "You need to hear the terms."

"Earnestly, I do not. Especially not if it means you are mine and I am yours."

Her heart stumbled at his words, hearing them, seeing the elation in his gaze. "I appreciate your enthusiasm, but I must continue so there is no doubt in the future. By entwining my life to yours, I will bring all the wisdom and knowledge of the Faa'Cris. And, by the strictest terms, I am to provide you with one male heir," she said around a tremulous breath. "Once that is fulfilled, I will receive a Daughter. Once she is conceived"—mercy, that was embarrassing to speak—"I will depart back to Deversoria, where my Daughter will be born among my Sisters."

"*Our* daughter," he said as if in correction. "What if a girl is born first?"

This edged dangerously close to betraying sacred truths. "That will not happen."

Hesitation guarded him. "You know this for sure?"

"I do."

Uncertainty worked through his handsome visage. "So, a son first."

She nodded. "To you, the male heir so important to this realm, and to me, a Daughter with my giftings and abilities to help perpetuate the Faa'Cris."

"A Daughter . . . whom I will never see or know." When she nodded again, he snorted. "I am to be okay with that, with never seeing *our* daughter?"

The emphasis he put on that word made her pulse stutter. "Your concern regarding a Daughter is not unusual or uncommon," she said, trying to convince herself as well. "However, I assure you that Daughters do not lack for guidance or affection."

"It doesn't make sense, though. Where she lives does not alter what she is," he said, "so why can you both not remain here?"

"Faa'Cris not born in the sanitatem and reared in the company of their Sisters often—though not always—go mad, lose their ability to reason and determine reality from fantasy. It is neither pleasant nor kind to the Daughter or those who love her."

"I cannot fathom not ever seeing her, not even her birth." He seemed mortified. "My own flesh and blood and—" He swallowed. Wiped a hand over his mouth, staring at the food. Disconcerted.

And Mercies, how it affected her, that efflux so quickly altered from elation to grief. She felt a compulsion to offer him two sons but bit her tongue. They were yet on the precipice of a new alliance, and she struggled to accept the change that had infected her life.

"And this"—he jabbed a finger at the table—"this is how you were born. In Deversoria. Taken from your father—"

"It is."

"And it does not grieve you to be separated from him, from your brother—I assume your mother gave your father an heir as well."

"She did," Valiriana said. "I cannot grieve what I never knew. He was not in my life—I was raised among the Daughters, trained, educated, loved. I did not feel his absence." Though she did often wonder after him.

"And you never wondered what he was like?"

How did he so often answer her unasked questions? "It would be a lie to say I did not."

"Have you ever gone to him? Would you go now, if you remained with me?"

She swallowed. "He is now among the dead in Kalonica."

He started, his mind processing the facts. No doubt connecting that Ladies aligned with powerful men, rulers . . . He balked. "Your father was *Zarek*?"

She nodded.

"I met him!" he said with an incredulous laugh. "He was here in Forgelight for a diplomatic meeting. He is admirable, a steady ruler. I enjoyed our time together."

"So," she said, a thickening in her throat, "you have had what I never will."

His brows knotted. "I ache for you, Aliria. He was an incredible man."

"I have no doubt. There would have been no Sending with Ma'ma had he not been. Just as . . ." She swallowed again. Wet her lips. "Since your name arose on the Flames and as it has become clear to me that you are a good man, this invitation is made known to you. There are sacrifices to be made, for certain, but what I offer you . . . it has withstood the test of centuries." Why did she feel so desperate to convince him? When he glanced down at his plate, she drew his gaze back to hers, fingers on his beard again. "Is it not better to have a few years with me—or however long it takes for a son and Daughter to come—than none at all?"

"Unfair," he groaned. "You know I cannot resist you." He framed her face, holding her in place, and rested his forehead on hers. "It is cruel to say you will give me your love but only for—"

"Vorn, a Sending does not entail love." Why she bit that out, she was not sure, for the thing that beat in her breast and made her dream of him . . . Could that be the beginning of love?

He looked stricken.

"I . . ." She saw his hope and desperation and wanted nothing more than to assuage those emotions. "I sense feelings for you that I had not expected. You have surpassed every objection and expectation. Your laughter . . ."

He muttered an oath. "This sounds like a business arrangement, not a courtship—falling in love and wanting to be together from the depths of our adunatos."

"It *is* a business arrangement," she countered with sincerity. "You want the benefit of Deversoria's knowledge and wisdom to save your realm and an heir to secure it. That we can appreciate each other beyond that is . . . a blessing."

Misery clawed itself into his eyes. "Our son would not even know you."

"No," she said quietly. "Not for long anyway."

His demeanor changed, stiffened. "Wait—Zarek was your father. There were *three* Kalonican princes."

"Well . . ." Nerves quailed at the direction he'd taken. Things were changing too fast. "You're right. Ma'ma had given him two sons, which was outside the norm, but when one showed certain abilities and was destined to be taken from them, she gave him another. He was a babe when Achilus was taken. It affected Zarek deeply, but he still had two sons, two heirs. Then I came."

"So, staying longer"—challenge hung in his brown eyes—"additional heirs . . . That is allowed?"

"It is frowned upon."

"But not illegal," he said, his expression like that of a pup anticipating a treat, "or forbidden."

Valiriana hesitated, not wanting to overcommit. Was a little overwhelmed that they were even talking about binding . . . "Please." She held up a hand. "I—I am overwhelmed with where this conversation has taken us and would prefer not to . . . strain the common ground we have."

Expression tight, he nodded. "It is a lot to consider. Granted, we have known each other but little time; however, I want my queen to rule with me till I am laid to rest. Not until—"

"You can refuse the alliance."

He managed a smile, though his efflux told of both sadness and acceptance. "Understood, my Lady." Grief scratched at his handsome face. "I know what it is to live without a mother's love. It is no trifling wound, and I must weigh carefully what I would impose on my heirs. I confess the feelings I have for you are strong, and I would have them grow and bloom, but . . ." He shook his head. "It already makes me resent the thought of being abandoned."

The words tugged at her heart and adunatos. "You wanted me here to save your kingdom, but now you speak of love? It is too soon."

"Nay," he said firmly, mayhap even tersely as his gaze traced her face. "I knew at that first kiss after the gala that what I felt for you was no simple attraction." He seemed to withdraw, gather his emotion.

Taken aback that his efflux matched his words, that he felt so deeply about her already, left her breathless. Aching. But this was a diplomatic agreement, a political— "So, you reject this, me?" Why did that thought crush her?

Those rich eyes explored her face, his brow furrowed and thick with heavy thoughts. "I know not, Aliria. I want this, Jherako needs this. But not simply long enough to give you a Daughter. I must think."

Startled—shocked—that he was seriously considering refusing the Sending, she blinked. "I—"

A throat cleared. "Your Majesty."

Vorn shifted, though his gaze did not yet leave her face. "What is it, Tarac?"

"Sire, I beg your mercy, but you must come."

"What—"

"We have word of the vizier."

"Where?" He was already moving out of the bench seat.

Leaving me . . . rejected.

"At the gates, sire. There's a riot."

23

"We should get you to the lower passages. You can flee through—"

"I will not flee my own home," Vorn growled as he stalked from the kitchen. He felt the air behind him swirl and hesitated, turning back to her. Instinctively, he extended his hand.

She glided toward him.

"I suggest sending the Lady to the caves—"

"I will not go," Aliria objected.

Tarac's jaw muscle jounced. "Sire, wisdom would not have your attention divided—"

"King Vaanvorn." Aliria dressed her words in authority and business, but not familiarity, not the woman who had so ardently responded to his kisses, providing hope that it could be possible to convince her to remain with him longer. She adjusted her position to stand before him, peering intently into his eyes. "This is part of why I was sent to you—not to be an adornment for your arm or bed, but as a warrior."

Conflicted, Vorn gave a terse nod. "The Lady Aliria remains with me."

Tarac started. "Sire—"

"I hear you, Captain." Still locked in the power of those seaborne eyes, Vorn held up a hand, staying the objections already cutting the air. "You saw what I saw in the training yard today, what she is capable of. You know that sending her from us at this time would be foolish." He eased forward and kissed her temple. "Stay close." As he started walking, he clapped Tarac's shoulder, knowing his Sword did not appreciate being countered on this situation. "Trust me, Tarac. You will see. You will see."

"My trust in you, sire, does not waver. I beg your mercy. It is just— the danger of these rioters. The Lady means much to you, and I would be aggrieved if something happened to her."

Vorn considered the man as they pushed through the doors and shuffled down the stairs. "Then be sure nothing does."

"The assumption is that *I* am the one who will need protecting," Aliria said as they reached the door leading to the bailey. "What if something happens to you and I must intervene?"

At the irritation plain on Tarac's face, Vorn could not help but laugh. "You will have my most enthusiastic gratitude."

The doors shoved open, and a swell of light and uproar slapped them. Chaos and shouts proved deafening, the assault on his ears stilling him on the portico steps. Two units of Furymark in full armor jogged toward the large bailey gate, which was bouncing beneath the people trying to force their way in.

A kingsguard ran toward the steps. "Sire, there are more at the front gate as well. I saw some taking to boats."

To slip around the break wall.

"There!" The voice of Haarzen Gi rose over the din. "There is your traitor— Vaanvorn colludes with the skycrawlers. He has broken the Droseran-Tertian Accord!"

"Someone shut him up," Lathain groused, as he, Ba'moori, and Azyant fell in with Vorn.

"No," Vorn said. "I will not become my brother." Tamuro had silenced too many of his opposers.

"Silencing dissenters only foments the lies," Aliria agreed. Then she touched his arm. "I have an idea. I will find you." And with that, she rushed back into the house.

It stunned—and stung—that at such a critical time, and after he had vouched for her to be at his side, she had fled. Concerned that he could not know her location and therefore could not protect her, and yet hoping she remained safe within the house, he faced Gi.

"What do you, Vizier Gi," he challenged, "that you bring this rebellion to my gates? Are you not yourself guilty of the very sins you lay at my feet? You have colluded with Hirakys and its new ally in the most despicable betrayal. Those raiders you arranged to bring into the city—they killed your people in the streets! Innocents! Civilians! And even now Hirakys steals across our borders, the puppets of that master you now serve."

A skirmish erupted between Vorn and where Gi was struggling to get through. It was a lost cause, trying to talk to him. *I cannot believe I handed him that position.*

Tarac gave a cockeyed nod and pursed his lips, as if to say *I told you so.* Then he indicated to the gate. "Should we go out there?"

What had Aliria gone to do? How long would it take? He could not wait long, not with the way that gate was bucking beneath the force exerted against it. "No, not here." The bailey gate was large and thick. "To the front. I will address them there."

"I think we are beyond that," Azyant shouted over the chaos.

Most likely, but Vorn must try. This is what he had worked so hard to avoid. He started down the steps.

"On your king!" the Sword commanded.

The kingsguard and his Four converged around Vorn, herding him through the bailey. Shouts and screams raked the day, drowning his words and communication with his men, who herded him to the left. Across the way, the green stretched in what seemed like silent repose beside the rage of the people held at bay by stone and iron.

As they moved through the narrowing footpath, he felt something in the air that made him pause. Glance back. "Wai—"

Crack! Boom! Grooooaaaan!

Screams and shouts rang through the afternoon. Even as a *whoosh* of air struck his face, Vorn saw the wide, heavy gates fly inward and collide with the bailey's stone wall. What in the black seas could make *that* happen? His gaze skidded back, and he sucked in a hard breath. An enormous beast—

"Rhinnock!" Azyant shouted.

Kingsguard rallied to stop the monstrous beast as it careened into the bailey, trampling the Furymark and their horses as if they were rats and dogs beneath its massive hooves.

Sickened at the spray of blood and death, Vorn felt fury and outrage course through him. He started forward and found himself staring at the wild eyes of a spooked destrier bolting straight at him.

Hands hauled him backward—Tarac and Azyant leapt in front of him as a swarm of bodies scrambled through the yawning hole left by the rhinnock. "Raiders!"

Jherakans surged after the beast, as if they too wanted to get away from the blue-marked savages.

Amid the crush of bodies and battle, his Four thrust him toward the front of the house.

"Inside to safety," Ba'moori shouted.

Safety—did it even exist at this point?

Sword drawn, frustrated, angry, afraid for his city—fed on the betrayal of his own vizier—Vorn glanced to the main gate in the distance. Saw citizens and savages scaling it, a wave of rioters flooding across the gardens and gravel, aiming for the cobbled path of the main house.

Waves of providence . . . how has it come to this?

"Sire, please—we must hurry you to the lower passages. There is yet time to—"

Air swirled behind him.

Vorn pivoted, his sword arcing up, the move instinctual and not a moment too soon as his blade rattled against another. The surprise of his opponent, who apparently had not expected so swift and violent a response, gave Vorn the advantage necessary. He shoved the man and drove his blade through him.

Around him erupted a struggle that consumed his Four and forced them to fight to stay alive. But in tandem they worked their way toward the great front terrace steps. More rioters and savages were flooding in, the civilians either unaware or uncaring of the enemy they fought beside, wrapped as they were in their suffering and rage. He must do all he could to protect his people, even those who set themselves against him. Their need to fight for better lives was understood because he knew they had endured years of deprivation and atrocity under the rules of his father-king and Tamuro.

"Defend your king!" Azyant bellowed as he drove two savages to ground with an unrelenting fury the burly man was known for.

Furymark attempted to converge around Vorn, but the effort proved futile as their enemies were numerous and a great number of the kingsguard were yet within the bailey.

In his periphery, Vorn spied the incoming tide of people.

Black seas—there is no hope. At least Aliria was safe within the castle, but how long would that last? Fire seared down his arm and shoulder. Warmth slid down his hand and side. "Augh!" He delivered a lethal blow to the assailant, striking hard and true. As the attacker fell at his feet, Vorn assessed the damage he'd taken even as his gaze roved the chaos. He stretched his hand, testing it. No nerves seemed to have been affected. No critical veins, though the wound released a steady stream of blood. He tore off a length of tunic and tied it around the arm, even then seeing raiders targeting his friend. "Tarac! Behind you!"

Tarac drove his sword through one savage, pulled his cutlass out, and stepped back, driving it into another. Only then was the gaping wound in his shoulder noticeable. Despite that, he fought. But after fending off yet a third savage, he staggered.

Snatching out his dagger, Vorn darted toward the group. As he swooped in to interdict the swordfight, he drew his dagger along a raider's throat. Felt the pressure of bloody contact and focused on the next. The rattle of steel on steel vibrated down his arms and spine. With a roar, he drove the man backward. Saw another come from the left. Too late, he realized Tarac must be down for the remaining fighters to converge on him. "Brother!"

As he parried, contacting the flat, and came around, his sword drove into the side of the first man's neck. Vorn saw the second savage coming at him and ducked, whirled in a crouch as the Irukandji advanced with a downward cut. Vorn blocked and turned, stepping in and cutting at the man's head. This one anticipated it and parried. It gave Vorn the chance for an undercut, which he drove into the man's belly.

Steel chomped into Vorn's thigh. He felt the sluice of warm blood slide down his leg as he moved forward, the man falling dead into his path. Gritting his teeth, Vorn stumbled to the side. Saw a horde of fighters coming.

His kingsguard rushed in to meet them, but it was a nightmare.

Ba'moori went to a knee beside Tarac. Stanched the flow of blood from his side. His worried gaze found Vorn. "'Tis not good, sire."

Considering the field, the bodies, the stench of death . . . "No." He shook his head but saw onslaught. "Ba'moori, get him inside. Azyant, Lathain, with me."

"No," Tarac barked. "I will not leave the battle with breath in my lungs."

"You cannot even stand!"

A strange howl carried over the property, and Vorn straightened and looked in the direction of the sound. His heart climbed into his throat as an entire line of Irukandji, howling as if criemwolves, ran in tandem toward them.

"Plagues," Azyant hissed.

"Gather our guard," Vorn ordered.

Tarac lifted his hand and bellowed a cry, drawing the Furymark to him.

For a split second, Vorn wondered what had happened to Aliria. She had said she had an idea—had it died with her? For he could not imagine her being so long gone from his side. Or mayhap she had returned to her Sisters.

He would prefer the latter to any other option, for in truth, he did not even want her here with him, not if it meant she could be harmed.

Vorn hefted his sword, eyed the incoming storm, and then nodded. Lifted his sword. "For the Ancient and the Ladies!" He charged toward the hundreds rushing toward them.

A great, violent clash went up as bodies slammed into bodies. The loss— Vorn seemed to feel each one. Grieved each one. Wished he had time to tell them how he saw their future. The future of Jherako.

Pain exploded through his side, and he bellowed, went to a knee. Struggled upward. Parried with the edge and staggered up in time for a strike to the head. Was there somewhere he was not bleeding? Hands slick with blood, exhausted, he struggled.

He saw Azyant's expression for a second—it mirrored his own. Exhaustion. Sadness. Fury . . . defeat.

And the enemy seemed to have no loss of strength or intensity. They came. They slaughtered.

A body slammed into him, bowling him backward. Vorn shuffled, fighting the very real demand of his body to collapse, rest. He knew one thing—if he went down, he would not get up.

Gi stalked toward him, surrounded by four men. "I will take your throne, your lady, and wipe your lineage from the parchments!"

He could not let this man win. Kill the last hope of Jherako . . .

The vizier seethed at him. "You were so easy," Haarzen Gi hissed. "So caught up in your own pleasures and vices, you could not see the enemy before you."

Shielding his injury, sweat dotting his forehead, Vorn fought to stay upright. "Was it worth it? Betraying your country?"

"I *defended* my country—fought to free it from the hands of the Thundred bane!"

"Into the hands of Hirakys? Or for the Symmachian skycrawlers?" Even as the man scorned him, Vorn had the wherewithal to retrieve his dagger from his boot. "You are—"

Behind came a blur of raging, swirling blue and snarls. "Of all that's hol—"

Gi sneered. "You call them savages, but even they know who the enemy is here."

"Do they?" Vorn was not so sure. They were swarming toward them . . .

straight on.

In a display of skill and power that left Vorn breathless, Furymark descended on the savages. Took down a dozen or more. But three . . . three made it.

Vorn braced himself. He would go down fighting. "Gi—"

The first raider hit—not Vorn.

"Not me, you imbeci—augh!" A deep ribbon of red slashed over Gi's chest. "Get off—" Then his arm. "No!" Two more Irukandji slammed into Gi. Took him down. And like wild dogs on a fresh carcass, they threw the vizier into the far reaches of Shadowsedge.

With a growl, Vorn saw the first one dive for him. The creature bared his teeth as he gave a hard shove and drove a dagger into Vorn's shoulder. "Augh!" Fire tore through him, along with terrible panic. He thrust and slashed in the manner taught the recruits, a series of well-placed strikes that left his hand slick and the savage dead.

Vorn rolled out from under the dead man. Spotted his sword and snatched it up. Pain, excruciating and demanding release, fought to keep him down. He noticed then the slaughtered body of the vizier, taken down by the very savages he'd attempted to bring to bear against Jherako, against Vorn.

But when his gaze rose to the green, the gardens where he had sparred with Jorti . . . Bile rose in his throat. So much death.

Mercies, Ancient. Please!

Pain exploded, and Vorn felt it. That moment a blade pierced his back. Experienced the strangest contortion of his heart as it was defeated by steel. Blackness crowded the edges of his vision. Voices grew distant. His body disconnected from him. As if he were no longer a part of it.

No no no! Please!

Light erupted, searing his corneas. A shrill noise, melodic yet somehow terrifying, filled the air. In those last moments before being dispatched to Shadowsedge, Vorn saw her . . . Aliria in all her enlightened glory. Radiating light, spinning it. Armored, lightsword in hand, fury in her eyes as she snapped her large expanse of wings, pitching people from her path.

So beautiful . . . perfect way to die, seeing her come to war on his behalf.

Her voice echoed through the void, rattling in his head, though with the creeping shadow of death overcoming him, he could not decipher the words.

A hand reached toward his face, blocking the light. Blocking . . . everything. At the touch of those fingers, heat shot through him.

Vorn arched his spine in shock. Then dropped into nothingness.

He blinked . . . and a jolt wove through him.

"Sire, easy—you're injured!" Azyant grunted.

Feeling not an ounce of pain, Vorn sat up. He no longer even felt tired or haggard. He drew up a leg and tried to gather his wits . . . only to see . . . "Waves," he breathed.

Hovering a solid meter off the ground, Aliria was shouting something to the people who had gone strangely still. Paralyzed. Literally paralyzed. Unmoving. Their gazes on her, though it seemed they were frozen in the midst of killing one another.

"Those who set their blades against Vaanvorn Thundred this day do also set their blades against the Ancient. And as a Lady of Basilikas, I will answer that threat." She alighted next to—

"Waves," he muttered again, seeing two more Ladies on either side of her.

Each Lady was appealing in her own way, one with auburn hair, another with arms that warned she was well familiar with the blade she wielded. Another whose stance betrayed she was ready for any engagement . . . All with violet eyes that seemed to punish darkness for existing. It was impossible to tell age. Rank he guessed by the epaulets of their armor, but he could not decipher the escalation.

Around them were strewn the bodies of countless Irukandji. Not one remained alive in the throng. They had been purged by the fury of the Ladies.

Radiant and fierce, Aliria looked around at the immobilized civilians, then at her Sisters. "This day, we have saved your king from this senseless violence." She shifted and extended a hand to him, the people still unmoving, save for their eyes. "But now is the time for you to turn your rage and thirst for freedom against your true enemy—the blue-marked raiders. More will come. War looms on the horizon, and the Irukandji, who lost their humanity in depravity long ago, will be the first wave. They have stolen into your city and streets, murdered those you love. They are your enemy, though they are not the last enemy. That comes later. For now, turn away from your rebellion and toward a man of noble character who is even on this battleground, literally giving his blood to protect his people—you! So rise up, Jherako! Rise up and join your king!"

Vorn struggled upright, though he was not entirely sure he had gained his feet on his own power, and went to her side.

"He knows your pains—he has seen your grief, your poverty, your sorrow.

In his short time on the throne, he has set his hand to rectifying wrongs, purging corruption." She smoothed a hand in the air toward the people, the glamour falling away and the people returning to themselves. A clatter of swords falling where they had been stayed. But the fury of the battle faded as attention swung as one to the Ladies. And then to him.

"Speak to them, share your heart," she said.

He started, realizing he had heard those words in his head. Not with his ears.

"Vorn, speak to your people. Assure them of your dedication to them."

This was what he had wished for. Time to speak with them. He turned from Aliria, grateful, and held up a hand. "What a sight—" He faltered when his voice echoed as if he were shouting in a cave. He glanced at her, and she nodded for him to continue. "What a sight we are today. Friends raging at friends." Vorn motioned to his bloodied undervest. "Staining our clothes with the blood of our neighbors." He scanned the line of Faa'Cris, a little— no, a lot— disbelieving. "The Ladies have shown up to save us from ourselves. We should be ashamed to set our blades against one another." He stroked his beard, feeling dirt and stickiness even there. "Jherako was once a powerful nation, greater than Kalonica or any other realm on this planet. We have fallen. Fallen so far."

He swallowed and set a hand over his heart. "A moment ago, our vizier tried to take my heart for what he viewed as weakness." He tightened his jaw, looking to Aliria who—he cared not how she argued—was resplendent. Stunning. Terrifying. "You named me the Errant for going against the norm. For eliminating the corruption from this government. I tell you—I do not act from weakness. Nor from cowardice. As you have heard, too, we are warned by this Lady"—he extended a palm toward Aliria—"that a terrible time and enemy are coming. I will not stand idly by. We must strengthen ourselves, this realm, and prepare our children for the future. The first step I take in that preparation is to ask this Lady to be my queen-wife."

An uproar assailed the air.

Surprise sprang into her features as she swung toward him, face alight. Question dancing in those seaborne eyes—a fitting mark of Jherako's future queen. Then a coy smile slid into her glorious visage. "You did not ask," she chastised.

Vorn pivoted to her, went to a knee, and proffered his sword. "Lady, I *beg* you to be my queen. To guide me with your wisdom. To commend me toward honor and strength. To seek the counsel of you, the Ladies, and the Ancient. This day, I swear to you that my sword is yours. Would you so honor me?"

Still arrayed in her ethereal form, Aliria swung those wings with a deliberate flourish as she faced him. "I accept your offer, Vaanvorn Thundred." She took the sword, then used it to tap each of his shoulders. "Among the Ladies of Basilikas, you are deemed honorable." With a flick of her wrist, she popped his sword back at him. "Vorn, I deem you . . . worthy."

Vorn caught the hilt, then stood in awe as she lowered her span, crossed her arms, and inclined her head to him. He recalled her telling him that very first time they'd met that he was not worthy, that she would *never* give him herself or an heir. In this moment—this powerful, humbling moment—he understood how much this cost her. How deeply she had been affected and affected him. In awe, he watched the other Faa'Cris repeat the crossed-arms gesture, their wings lowering in a cascading effect that left him speechless.

Aliria rose and smiled at him. "How is your heart, Vaanvorn Thundred?" Her voice had a mocking tone—no, a memory. There was a memory attached to it of that time outside the barn.

He stepped in, took her hands. "It is yours, my Lady." He set his mouth to hers in a light kiss that received the vocal applause of the hundreds gathered. "And your heart?"

"King Vaanvorn, it is yours."

ACKNOWLEDGEMENTS

When I settle in to write a story, I first sketch out the meat of the story by turning off my internal editor and just letting the story happen—events, characters, arcs—and I'm very intentional about the structure, word choices, and character placement, because ultimately, I want y'all to love the story. Then I do a quick pass of the story with edits and deepening and layering. Before it goes any further, I enlist my Gatekeepers: amazing, very particular, and experienced readers who let me know what they think of the story, its characters, and their arcs. And this is my special acknowledgement of my trusted heroes—Narelle Mollet and Kimberly Gradeless. You've read all my books but you are honest with me in what works and doesn't. I'm so grateful for you two! Also, a special thanks to Katie Donovan and Mikal Dawn who read early versions and gave me feedback. I am so grateful for all of you!

A gazillion thanks to Steve Laube for letting this story happen—it wasn't part of the original plan, but it worked well as an "extra" for the series. Thank you to the Enclave staff who work tirelessly to bring our books to life and delivered into your hands! Thank you to the Oasis Media family for all your heart/soul poured into forging a market for Enclave's type of fiction. You are a beautiful blessing! Thank you!!

The biggest 100,000 thank yous to my incomparable editor, Reagen Reed. I've learned so very much from you about world building and deepening character development within and in collusion with the worlds. When I turned this story in, I had a nagging sense there was something 'missing,' that I couldn't decipher no matter the rewrites, the edits, the prayers, and the desperate tears. However, I was able to surrender it to the process, because I knew it would be in your more-than-capable hands. That with over a decade of experience under your belt, you would help me find the problem and fix it. Not only did you do that, but helped me make this story *great*. The cherry on top was that you loved LADY and said that, of my heroes, Vorn may be your favorite. WOW! Thank you, Reagen. You are a beautiful godsend.

ABOUT THE AUTHOR

Ronie Kendig is a best-selling, award-winning author of over thirty-five novels, divided between speculative fiction and paramilitary suspense. After a nearly ten-year stint on the East Coast, she and her husband readily gave up big-city life and returned to their beloved Texas. They now survive on Sonic runs, barbecue, and peach cobbler, which they share—sometimes—with Benning the Stealth Golden and A Andromeda the MWD Washout.

THE DROSERAN SAGA

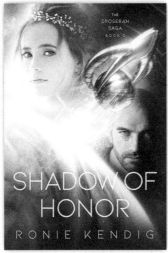

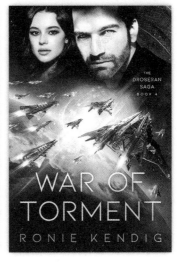

THE ABIASSA'S FIRE TRILOGY

Available Now!

Embers

Accelerant

Fierian